Dear Reader,

A funny thing happened on the way to the delivery room isn't how most women talk about the miracle of life, but the phrase perfectly fits Cheryl Anne Porter's story *Drive-By Daddy*, Harlequin Duets #21. Yes, the hero really does deliver a baby by the side of the road…but leaving mother and child behind is more difficult than he expected. Then Patricia Knoll weaves a charming tale of the eccentrics and matchmakers in a small town and the intrepid girl reporter who is trying to get herself out of Hicksville in *Calamity Jo*.

In Harlequin Duets #22 Liz Ireland returns with *The Love Police*. Sure, police officer Bill Wagner is a hunk of burning love, but that doesn't mean he has the right to interfere in Trish Peterson's love life—or does he? Then, fans of Colleen Collins will enjoy the return of Raven from *Right Chest, Wrong Name* (Love & Laughter #26). He's changed his rough and rugged image slightly…but magazine editor Liney Reed wants to pull out the *animal* in him to sell her magazine. Only problem is she finds herself far too attracted to the *primal* man he really is.

Treat yourself to a good time with Harlequin Duets.

Sincerely,

Malle Vallik

Malle Vallik
Senior Editor

"Not even your choice for a husband?"

The Love Police

"You were Mr. Heartthrob in school," Tricia accused.

"Was I?"

Bill's deep voice unnerved her.

He lifted a hand to touch her hair. "Was I your heartthrob, Tricia Parker?"

Her pulse raced and something caught in her throat. "Peterson..." she gasped out. "It's Peterson now."

His hand fluttered down to rest on her hip. "A rose by any other name would smell as sweet..."

Shakespeare. Dear heaven, she was lost!

She sighed and melted into him as he coaxed a fire in her she'd long considered doused. In unison they tilted against the wall behind them, needing it for support as bodies became an awkward tangle of intertwined legs and arms.

Teenagers, she thought. *We're behaving like teenagers.*

And then she really *was* lost....

For more, turn to page 9

Rough and Rugged

"I'm not getting raw," Raven said. "End of story."

"You won't be totally raw. I mean naked. You'll have on your…your underwear." When he didn't respond, Liney added, "That is, if you're wearing any."

He leaned down. "I'm wearing underwear," he said roughly. "But considering how snugly they fit, I might as well not be, if you get my drift."

Liney cleared her throat. "You could, uh, use a blanket. That way no one will see your…"

"What?"

"Underwear," she said quickly.

Raven's scowl smoothed out a little, then he began unbuttoning his fly. Each button made a popping sound as it was opened.

"Don't you want a blanket?" Liney asked.

"No." *Pop. Pop.*

She wanted to say something—to be the appropriate, in control vice-president. But when she opened her mouth, all that came out was a raspy sound, like air leaking from a tire.

For more, turn to page 197

HARLEQUIN DUETS

ISBN 0-373-44088-X

THE LOVE POLICE
Copyright © 2000 by Elizabeth Bass

ROUGH AND RUGGED
Copyright © 2000 by Colleen Collins

LIZ IRELAND

The Love Police

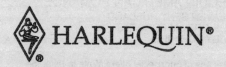

HARLEQUIN®

TORONTO • NEW YORK • LONDON
AMSTERDAM • PARIS • SYDNEY • HAMBURG
STOCKHOLM • ATHENS • TOKYO • MILAN • MADRID
PRAGUE • WARSAW • BUDAPEST • AUCKLAND

Dear Reader,

The idea of leaving a place and returning later in triumph has always appealed to me, though unfortunately, I've never been able to pull off such a coup myself. This is the joy of fiction.

Nevertheless, while I grew up in a Texas town not too far from fictional Bee Lake, and might have been a tad on the chubby side, this story is entirely pulled from imagination except for one detail: in Dallas, in the nineteen-fifties, there was actually a Love Bandit stalking Lover's Lane, and my own father was there (doing what, you might ask—me too!) the night of his capture. Some stuff you just can't make up.

Liz Ireland

Books by Liz Ireland

HARLEQUIN DUETS
5—THE BEST MAN SWITCH

HARLEQUIN LOVE & LAUGHTER
59—THE HIJACKED BRIDE

HARLEQUIN AMERICAN ROMANCE
639—HEAVEN-SENT HUSBAND
683—THE GROOM FORGETS
767—BABY FOR HIRE

Don't miss any of our special offers. Write to us at the following address for information on our newest releases.

Harlequin Reader Service
U.S.: 3010 Walden Ave., P.O. Box 1325, Buffalo, NY 14269
Canadian: P.O. Box 609, Fort Erie, Ont. L2A 5X3

1

"WHY DOES A WOMAN marrying Mel Gibson's dentist want a homemade wedding dress?" Sylvie Wagner inspected her old friend Tricia Peterson with the practiced eye of a professional seamstress, her thin fuchsia-covered lips clamped over several straight pins. "If I were marrying the Prince Charming of the novocaine set, I'd hotfoot it over to Vera Wang or Escada."

Tricia pirouetted in her nearly finished wedding gown. It was downright gorgeous, done in tailored, simple lines, the most beautiful garment she'd ever put on her back. The eggshell-colored silk was textured and rich, and the cascades of beading Sylvie had painstakingly worked into the material made it look fit for a princess. The neckline plunged fairly low, and the bodice fit snugly on her newly thinned torso, making her feel practically svelte.

The last time she had tried on one of Sylvie's creations, she'd been a porky Madonna wannabe in high school, and the results had been less than successful—through no fault of Sylvie's. In those days, Tricia had been Pudgy Pat Parker, the class chubbette, the town joke, and even in Sylvie's cool outfit she'd resembled a Madonna-Roseanne hybrid. Since then, forty pounds had been painstakingly shed so that even her own discriminating eye sized herself up as *almost* slender.

There were other less dramatic changes as well, such as hair dyed to a lustrous auburn color she suspected rarely appeared in nature. And of course, she had a different name. She'd switched from Pat to Tricia as soon as she'd hightailed it out of Bee Lake, Louisiana, at age eighteen. The change in her last name she owed to a first marriage that was over one week after she'd changed her name on her driver's license.

But though over thirteen years she had remade herself from Pat Parker to Tricia Peterson, from the proverbial ugly duckling into an only slightly flawed swan, she had to give most of the credit for her appearance today to Sylvie's dress.

"I always said that you would be the only one to design my wedding dress."

Sylvie grumbled. "People are apt to make all sorts of stupid promises when they're in high school."

"I'd rather have a Sylvie Wagner than all the Vera Wangs in the world."

A bark of laughter erupted from Sylvie's pin-clinching lips. "You slay me."

Honestly, Tricia didn't know how the creator of such an elegant, romantic dress could be so tough and cynical. What she'd said was the truth. She and Sylvie might not have seen so much of each other in the years since Tricia had moved from their small hometown to Baton Rouge, but she'd never grown apart from her funny, talented best friend who had stood staunchly beside her during the years of junior high and high school.

Heaven knows she'd needed a friend even after she'd left Bee Lake. During her early twenties Tricia had survived one disastrous marriage and had floated from job to job. Finally she'd discovered she had a head for business and had opened her own book store and café, which providentially coincided with the coffee boom. A little financial success—and Sylvie's encouragement—had given her the confidence finally to slink into a strip mall diet center one afternoon and the fortitude to eat like a malnourished rodent for two years running.

Then, to celebrate the purchase of her first size-eight dress ever, she'd splurged on a sun-filled vacation in Cancun, where she planted her slimmed down, but still achingly self-conscious, butt on a beach towel for all of ten minutes before attracting the eye of one Manson Toler, Beverly Hills dentist. Manson smiled his Hollywood grin at her and told her she was the most attractive sight he'd seen yet in Mexico, and before you could say "former fat girl," Tricia was whisked away on a whirlwind romance.

Now she was engaged to a wonderful man. She was making a triumphant return to throw a cautiously lavish wedding in the town that had labeled her a loser from kindergarten on—itself a dream come true. And she would soon be starting a new life in Beverly Hills! Life was pretty darn close to perfect.

The sound of clumping coming from Sylvie's living room brought her back to earth with a thud. Moments later, Tricia's twelve-year-old son leaned against the door frame, his oversized adolescent feet encased in a pair of limegreen-and-black in-line skates. He looked Tricia over from head to toe with a visible cringe. "Are you actually going to wear *that* in front of *people?*"

The question failed to ruffle Tricia, except perhaps for Sylvie's sake. Her son was at the stage where everything she wore or said embarrassed him. "Tom, didn't I tell you not to wear skates inside?"

"I'm not hurting anything."

"Tom…" Tricia sent him a gaze that was meant to be stern and withering, but Tom merely rolled his eyes. His clothes were typical adolescent style—baggy jeans and an oversized baseball jersey. His short brown hair stood out from his head in tufts, as if he'd just stepped out of bed. It always looked that way. Though Tricia itched to Aqua Net it into place, she knew that if she came within combing distance of that head, she would be taking her life in her hands.

"What if I went outside?" he asked. "Couldn't I keep them on then?"

"Of course, but—"

Before she could warn him against skating across the linoleum, he zoomed across it and hit the kitchen door flying. Tricia doubted that Tom had actually walked anywhere since, in a moment of maternal weakness, she'd caved in and bought him those skates for his last birthday.

She turned to her friend apologetically. "I'm sorry, Sylvie—it's the wedding he objects to, not the dress." She stared hard at where he'd crossed the kitchen. "I hope he didn't scratch up your floor."

Sylvie laughed. "He didn't—and I wouldn't worry so much if I were you. Kids are always stubborn at that age. And as for the skating everywhere, Tom's just like Casey."

"Bill's girl?"

Even an indirect reference to Sylvie's brother caused Tricia's ears to perk up. Bill Wagner had been Tricia's dream man all through school—though of course he hadn't known it. While the only sport she had been involved in was being the butt of jokes in P.E. class, he'd been captain of the Bee Lake High Killer Bees football team. She'd been Pudgy Pat; he'd been the school hunk.

Though Tricia hadn't even caught a glimpse of him now for more than twelve years, Sylvie talked about him all the time, and she knew he had a daughter just about Tom's age.

"They're both at that hostile stage." Sylvie's breath caught. "You know, you really ought to call Bill while you're in town!"

Her heart froze in dread. In her mind, Bill was still the golden boy, the football hero, the dreamboat hunk all the girls had the hots for. "I couldn't."

Tricia knew that Sylvie had always harbored the crazy notion that her best friend and her brother were a perfect match.

When Sylvia invariably asked, "Why not," Tricia invariably searched for an answer that wouldn't force her to reveal the sniveling insecure coward who still lurked beneath her new and improved exterior. From her diet meetings she learned that some women were motivated by a desire to go back to their hometowns in a blaze of glory and flaunt themselves in front of the men who had snubbed them, which sounded great, in theory. But deep inside, Tricia couldn't help but fear just one glance at Bill would cause her fat cells to expand, her pores to fill up and her hair to start sticking out like Tom's.

"Because I'm getting married."

"Does that mean you can't talk to men anymore?"

She shot her friend a quelling look. "You can stop trying to sell your brother to me, Sylvie. I'm a practically married woman."

Sylvie heaved a sigh. "Oh, all right. I guess I can't blame you for preferring the dentist to the stars over a small-town cop."

"Manson Toler is successful and wealthy, but it's more than just those qualities that attracted me to him. He's a wonderfully courteous, fine man."

Ever since their first candlelight dinner in Cancun, Manson had made her feel like something special, wining and dining her like she'd always seen in the movies. And she supposed it was an added plus to be swept off her feet by a man who didn't know that the only date she could get to the junior prom was her geeky cousin Mort.

"Courteous and fine aren't exactly the key characteristics of a dream lover," Sylvie drawled. "But then, I can't imagine anyone having a dream lover named Manson. Especially in *California*."

Tricia pursed her lips. "It's a family name." She'd had to explain her intended's unfortunate name more than once, especially to her mother, who couldn't even seem to remember it. "You must know that I wouldn't sell my bookstore and uproot my entire life this way for just anybody."

"So just what is so great about the illustrious Dr. Toler?"

Tricia knew what her friend wanted—juicy details. But Tricia wasn't used to spilling details of her love life, mainly because she'd never had many love-life details to spill. "For your information, Manson is very romantic. Well, as romantic as I'm likely to find in this lifetime. I'm thirty-two, not fourteen."

"Oh, I see—you're over the hill so it's time to marry a dentist."

"A dentist who can tango," she retorted with pride. "And if that's your charming way of saying that I'm mature now and willing to look at a man's character instead of what kind of car he drives, then yes, you're right."

"Okay, okay," Sylvie said, apparently resigned to the fact that her curiosity would not be assuaged. She studied the drape of the wedding gown's hem before slanting an inquisitive glance back up at Tricia. "What kind of car does he drive?"

"A Lexus, fully loaded."

"I guess *loaded* is the key word here."

Tricia punched her playfully on the shoulder. "Wait till you meet him, Sylvie. You'll wish you were walking down the aisle with him."

Sylvie moaned mournfully. "I won't be able to walk down the aisle with anybody while I'm living in Bee Lake. Not with my brother."

As far as Tricia could tell, Bill Wagner had one flaw—he was a cop with a special flair for policing his sister's romances. Poor Sylvie hadn't had a relationship in years that her brother hadn't managed to shoot enough holes into to make it sink faster than the *Titanic*.

"Maybe you should try starting up a romance with someone from out of town again."

Sylvie dismissed that idea. "Even if I went to Bora Bora, Bill would find a way to bust things up."

"You have to admit, he's saved you from some sticky situations. Remember that last guy, that what's-his-name?"

"Ted was a hunk," Sylvie said, defending her latest romance-gone-rotten.

Tricia gave her friend a level stare. "He was a *married* hunk."

"Okay, so nobody's perfect," Sylvie muttered, a rare blush rising to her cheeks.

"He probably never would have fessed up about the wife and kiddies if Bill hadn't checked him out."

Her friend sighed. "I suppose not."

For the first time in years, Tricia took a really close

look at Sylvie and was shocked at what she saw. A streak of gray in her dark blond hair. A hint of crow's feet beginning to scratch at the corners of her bright blue eyes. Bony shoulders slumping over her sewing box.

All their lives, Sylvie had been the wild one, the carefree one, the one who wore weird clothes of her own making when other girls just wanted to look like everyone else. But now she looked a little weary, and who could blame her? For seventeen years she had been scampering on that hamster wheel of dating and never quite found Mr. Right.

"Why don't you get out of here, Sylvie?" Tricia asked suddenly. "You could make a lot more money in Baton Rouge. And if I rented you my house..."

Her friend looked at her skeptically. "You're selling that house, remember?"

"I had planned to, but maybe renting it would be even better. Or you could buy it."

"I don't know anybody in Baton Rouge," Sylvie said. "And don't say you could introduce me to people, because you won't even be there, Miss Beverly Hills."

"Then why don't you come to California and open a business there?"

Sylvie barked out a laugh. "Right. All I have to do is hang a shingle next to Versace."

"Who knows? It could happen." Tricia lifted her skirt and twirled. "This dress is something that Grace Kelly would have been proud to wear. Or Audrey Hepburn."

Sylvie smirked. "Or a third-rate actress about to belt out 'Don't Cry for Me, Argentina,' in a dinner theater in Munsie."

Tricia refused to be put off by Sylvie's relentless

cynicism. "If you can make me look this good, believe me, that's talent."

Sylvie shook her head. "I'd invest Manson's millions in Weight Watchers if I were you, not in Maison Sylvie."

Tricia huffed in frustration. "I'm trying to save you, and you won't even get in the stupid lifeboat!"

"Don't worry about me. I'm an expert dog paddler."

Now that her life was practically perfect, Tricia possessed the zeal of a missionary when it came to people turning their lives around. It seemed impossible that *she* had managed to break out of her rut and find Mr. Wonderful while Sylvie—beautiful, funny, stylish Sylvie—languished in Bee Lake, single. She would give anything to see her friend happy.

Sylvie leaned back on her elbows and smiled up at her. "It's not so bad here, Trish. Even if I could leave, I don't know if I would. Really. That brother of mine and I are codependents now. He rescues me from bad relationships, and I've kept him from being unhappy and lonely since his divorce."

Bill was unhappy? Lonely? "But I thought he and his wife had been miserable."

Sylvie nodded. "They were. You know—two teenage sweethearts who marry and a decade later realize they have nothing in common but a fading high school scrapbook. Bill was happy to get custody of Casey after Andrea walked out on him. But now it's been two years and I can tell he's lonesome."

Bill Wagner. Lonely. Unbelievable! Tricia was about to ask for a rundown of Bill's dating history since his divorce—just out of idle curiosity—when the sound of wheeled boots clamoring up the steps brought their conversation to a screeching halt.

"Hey, Mom! Weren't you supposed to be at Grandma's at eleven?"

Tricia darted a glance at her watch and sucked in her breath. It was five past eleven already. "Oh, no!" Her gaze met Sylvie's in alarm. "Mother's going to have her shutterbug friend Irene there. She wanted me to sit for some pictures."

Sylvie nodded. "Just take the dress for the day."

"But I've got to run!"

"So jump in the car and go. What can happen to that dress during a ten-block drive?"

Tricia began to breathe a little easier. "I'll be back by this evening." She snatched up the bag that held the clothes she'd worn over and paused on her way out to clasp her hand appreciatively on her friend's shoulder. "Thanks again for everything, Sylvie."

Sylvie pursed her lips in the closest thing she had to a smile. "Hey, you know I wish you the best of luck in this marriage, Trish. And who knows? With you marrying Dr. Toler, I just might run into Mel in his dentist office waiting room someday and be swept right off my fallen arches."

TOM SLUMPED AGAINST the passenger seat window, moping as only a twelve-year-old could. He seemed paralyzed by the thought that they would have a car wreck and he would be discovered riding in a car with a mother who was wearing a wedding dress.

"Would you like to go to the movies tonight?" Tricia asked him, testing the conversational waters.

"There's only one theater in town, and it's showing *Dumbo*."

Tricia remembered it had been one of her favorites as a kid. "Oh! I wouldn't mind seeing that again."

Tom shot her a you've-got-to-be-kidding stare.

"All right, so Bee Lake is a little poky—but just think, in a few weeks we'll be living in California. That's the land of movies!"

Her upbeat spin was met with a ragged sigh.

"I bet Mr. Boring would love to sit through *Dumbo*. Twice."

"*Manson* likes new films," she said. "Remember? When he visited Baton Rouge we went to see a Jackie Chan movie, and you both enjoyed that." *She* had been bored to tears, but that was another matter....

He squirmed unhappily for a moment as they came to a stop sign. "Mom, couldn't we just go on like before, like, the two of us doing our own thing?" He sent her a plaintive look. "What do you need to get married for?"

She frowned and reached over to hold his hand, which he only very reluctantly allowed her to do. "I love you more than anything, Tom, but don't you understand? I met Manson. Since he lives in California and we live in Louisiana, it would be difficult to keep up a relationship if we weren't married. Besides, some kids would die to live in California."

"Yeah, but *they* wouldn't be dying of boredom."

Tricia stepped on the gas and turned onto Sycamore Street, where her mother still lived. True, Manson wasn't the best with kids, but she could hardly fault him for that. He'd never been around them much before. He and Tom just didn't know how to communicate yet, but that would fix itself. In time. She hoped.

She stopped the car at the curb in front of her mother's frame house and turned to her son. "Everything will work out, Tom. Just think of the things you'll be able to have now."

"Like what?"

"Well…like any kind of lessons you want, maybe camp in the summer, good schools.…"

Tom's mouth dropped open in horror. "Jeez, Mom. You don't mean that now you'll finally have some serious money, you're going to start throwing it away on *some school!*"

He got out of the car and began to roll away from her. Perplexed as always by the yawning gap between her own views and her son's, Tricia, too, opened her car door and stepped out. She slammed the door, hiked up her wedding dress, and was just about to dash into her mother's house when she saw that Tom was already skidding around the corner of the block on his skates.

"Tom!" she cried out. "Be careful!"

She tilted her head, listening, and thought she might have heard a faint "Okay!" hollered back at her from that bright flying streak that was her son, right before he disappeared onto the next street. Then again, he might have yelled "No way!", another favorite retort of his.

She heard Johnny Cash thumping out of her mother's house and took a breath to prepare herself. "Folsum Prison Blues" was one of her mom's favorites. Peggy Parker might be one of Bee Lake's most beloved citizens, but as a mother she could be a trial. Especially growing up as achingly self-conscious as Tricia was, having a mother who drove your school bus and wore neon-colored polyester pantsuits, sported a bouffant jet-black hairdo and wore enough makeup to single-handedly keep Max Factor in business hadn't always been easy. Over the past decade, her one fashion concession had been trading in her pantsuits for sporty jogging suits. Now retired, she concentrated on bridge, canasta and, for this week, wedding plans. In that order.

Tricia took a step and then stopped—not because she meant to but because she couldn't go any further. She was caught on something. She twisted to glance behind her and groaned in dismay. She'd slammed the back of her dress in the car door. Now she was going to have a big grease stain on her dress—Sylvie would love that!

With a sigh, she tugged at the front door handle to free herself. Then she tugged again. It was locked. She was always careful about locking her doors as soon as she stepped out of the car. Unfortunately, she remembered as she rooted through her big suede purse, she wasn't always equally careful about taking the keys out of the ignition first. She peered inside the window to see the keys dangling on the other side of the steering wheel, taunting her.

Terrific!

Breathe, she reminded herself. As key-in-the-car catastrophes went, this one wasn't too terrible—except for her beautiful dress! Luckily, she was in a perfect position to call on someone who had thirty-two years of practice getting her out of jams.

Mommy.

"Mom!" she bellowed toward the windows of her mother's white-painted wood-frame house. She listened to the faint echo of the word and realized the edgy hysteria in her cry wasn't too far off from Tom's when he yelled at her for any of a gazillion reasons. The tone was probably one of those things that got passed down from generation to generation, like pointy chins and big feet.

She inhaled and let loose another lusty wail.

"Mom!" Then she cupped her hands around mouth and did it again.

God, that felt good.

Or at least it did until she realized the only voice answering her belonged to Johnny Cash. They had something in common now. He was still stuck in Folsum Prison; she was still stuck to her Toyota. "Mom?"

Not a curtain fluttered. Tricia let out a huff of exasperation. Time for Plan B.

"Tom!" she yelled. The humid air swallowed her voice. "Tom?"

No answer. He had probably reached the other side of town by now.

She rubbed her temples, where a slow pounding was beginning to build. What next? She could wait for her mom and Irene to come back out of the house, but then again, once they got started those two ladies could deplete Venezuela's supply of coffee beans before calling it quits. And waiting for Tom wasn't practical, either. Besides, it might be better if her son didn't witness his prime authority figure looking *this* foolish.

There was only one alternative left, as far as she could figure. She reached down, glad that her trapped dressed at least allowed her that much mobility, scooped up some loose pebbles from the road and began chucking the little rocks at her mother's windows. After a half dozen direct hits, there was still no visible movement inside the house.

Tricia groaned in frustration. Her arm was still extended in throw position when she saw a black-and-white sedan pull onto her mother's block. A cop.

He screeched up in front of her and parked on the tree-lined street. The patrol car's window rolled down, and a cop wearing reflective sunglasses peered back at her. "What are you, a delinquent bride?"

"No, I'm a *stuck* bride!"

The officer got out of his car, slowly, and took off the glasses, revealing a devastating set of blue eyes. Very familiar blue eyes—the very eyes that still, after all these years, made intermittent surprise appearances in Tricia's dreams. Bill Wagner!

And wouldn't you know it, he was more heart-stoppingly handsome than ever. While the years sometimes put a little paunch on some men, Bill still looked as muscled and buff as when he quarterbacked for the Bee Lake Killer Bees. And here *she* was with her rear end slammed in a car door. What a moment for a reunion!

2

TRICIA DREW UP her shoulders and summoned all the dignity she could muster.

As he sauntered closer, it became even more apparent that the years had been good to Bill. It seemed impossible, but he was even better looking than she remembered. Beneath the brim of his policeman's hat, intelligent blue eyes, a strong jaw and a nose that, unless Tricia misremembered, had been broken at least once, all combined in a face that looked not only handsome but now full of character. The short-sleeved uniform shirt he wore stretched over broad shoulders and displayed his arms that were mostly corded muscle. She gazed at his wide chest, then shook her head, forcing herself to look Bill in the eye.

The smirk had deepened. "Are you having a, uh, problem, ma'am?" He peered around her rear, considering her dilemma with unguarded interest.

Usually Tricia didn't relish being called a ma'am, but the way Bill said the word, in a soft, honeyed drawl, almost made it sound like a compliment. Or perhaps it only seemed that way because his gaze had snagged appreciatively on her exposed leg.

"I'd be real grateful if you could help me out, Bill."

The smirk disappeared, and his blue eyes widened in surprise.

So. He hadn't recognized her.

Tricia grinned. The last decade hadn't been half bad

to her, either, she suddenly recalled. "You don't remember me?"

His eyes lit with vague recognition, and he held up
a finger. "Sure I do. You're..." He shook his head.

"Do you want a hint?"

"No." His forehead creased in concentration. "You
look so familiar...."

Tricia laughed. "Try this: you blew up at me one
time when Sylvie and I gussied up your golden re-
triever Crunchy's fur with a curling iron."

His mouth dropped open.

"And I'm standing in front of my mother's house."

He swung his gaze toward the modest white house,
then back to Tricia, in disbelief. "You're...?"

"That's right."

Recognition, then amazement, registered on his
handsome features as he looked her up and down. "I
can't believe *you're*..."

At some point, Tricia went from feeling smug back
to feeling uncomfortable again. A little surprise was
pleasing—slack-jawed amazement was carrying things
a little too far. She half-expected him to poke her newly
firmed-up flesh and scream, "My God, it's Pudgy
Pat!"

Blessedly, he didn't. Instead, he—finally—exclaimed, "Pat, it's good to see you!"

"Tricia," she corrected, feeling a flutter in her stomach as she basked in Bill's openly admiring gaze. She'd
waited thirty-two years to have those eyes twinkle at
her in just such a hungry male way. She wasn't going
to let herself be shortchanged. "It's Tricia Peterson
now."

He scratched his chin. "Yeah, I guess Sylvie told
me...."

"I just came from Sylvie's. Got my daily allowance of cynicism."

He grinned. "She still talks about you all the time. She said that you—" He held up his hands and brought them close together, making a reducing motion. "But she never said you—" His words cut off abruptly, but Tricia could just imagine what choice descriptor was rushing through his head. *That you were no longer shaped like a large marine mammal...*

They stood awkwardly for a moment, nodding and smiling at each other.

"Sylvie made my dress," she said in an attempt to cut through the uncomfortable silence. "Isn't it beautiful?"

"It sure is. It's..."

Tricia saw him trying to keep from guffawing at her and laughed herself. "It's stuck in a car door!" she moaned. "What am I going to do?"

"It's an interesting situation...one I haven't come across before." He threw another admiring glance at her exposed leg.

An unexpected flush of warmth washed over her, and she felt the urge to cover herself. Being caught like a butterfly pinned to a board made the dress tug against her every curve and the long skirt ride up her legs, revealing the sneakers she had slipped on for the drive home. Her eggshell-dyed pumps were also locked in the car.

She cleared her throat. "I called for my mother but I think she's inside talking."

He nodded. "She and Irene have Johnny Cash cranked up. Happens all the time."

Sometimes Tricia forgot that in small towns everyone knew everything about everyone. And Bill, being a cop, would know more than most. "So…do you think you could help me out here?"

He paused, considering the matter, which gave her a precious moment to ogle him some more. He'd been twenty-two and newly married the last time she'd even caught a glimpse of him. Twelve years later, he had a rougher quality to him. Time had etched its handiwork in the lines in his face, taken the boyish chipmunk look out of his cheeks, and hardened the muscles that now probably rarely hefted a football. She liked the changes.

A lazy smile pulled across his full lips, making her suspect that he knew she had been eyeing his bod. "So…Sylvie tells me you're getting married."

He wasn't going to answer her question, apparently. "That's the plan."

"Hmm." He studied her. "So you're really going through with it?"

"With what?"

"Getting married."

Tricia bit back a laugh. "What do you think I'm dressed for? A Maypole dance?"

"Just because you have a dress doesn't mean you have to get married."

"The dress has nothing to do with it. If I don't get unstuck before next week—which is beginning to look like a distinct possibility—I'll be married attached to this car."

His gaze hovered too long on her curves for her peace of mind. He nodded toward her feet. "You should keep the tennies. Good effect."

Tricia pursed her lips impatiently, but it wasn't just Bill who was frustrating her. Her reaction to the man made her uncomfortable. An engaged woman wasn't supposed to go weak in the knees just because another man looked at her twice. Especially a man who was being rather unhelpful. "I'm so glad my outfit meets with your approval."

He folded his arms across his chest. "You know, Sylvie has some reservations about your bridegroom."

"Then it's lucky she's not marrying him."

He lifted a hand. "Now don't get all excited. She's just worried about you running off to California and marrying a man named Manson."

Tricia rolled her eyes. "Oh, for heaven's sake—it's a *family name!* Manson Toler is a dentist and he wouldn't harm a fly. I bet his novocaine shots don't even hurt."

"Have you had this guy checked out?" he asked.

"Of course not," she said, not even bothering to hide her exasperation now. She felt more trapped than ever—and what's more, she was starting to understand a little of Sylvie's anguish over her meddlesome older brother. "He's a highly respected man, and very well known in his community."

"What community is that?"

"Beverly Hills."

Bill didn't look overly impressed. He just rubbed his clean-shaven jaw and muttered, "Interesting."

"May we please stop focusing on my fiancé and attempt to unstick me from my car?"

His baby blues widened innocently. "Hit a nerve?"

Tricia's lips twitched into a wry smile. "Oh, no. I'm sure you think brides like to hear their intendeds' characters impugned by people they haven't spoken to since Boy George topped the charts."

"Actually, I meant it as a compliment."

"Oh?" She had to hear this!

"Sure." He took a few steps forward and leaned against the car with her as if he had all the time in the world. And who knows? Maybe he did. Bee Lake wasn't exactly the crime capital of the world. "See, when Sylvie told me about you and your wedding, I wasn't paying that much attention. In one ear and out the other, you know?" His gaze cut a quick glance over to her, and seemed to linger ever-so-shortly on her breasts. "But now that I've seen you again, I tend to agree with Sylvie. I don't know if you should marry that guy."

His words, so unexpected, stunned her. In fact, she wasn't sure she'd heard him correctly. "What?"

"You deserve better."

Of all the outrageous... "You don't even know me!"

He looked offended. "I've known you since you were ten."

Ignored her since she was ten was more like it! Just thinking about all the years she had trotted after him caused indignation to swell in her. She'd subsisted a whole month once on nothing but Figurines and Tab hoping to lose enough weight to catch his eye, to no avail. "Bill, you barely spoke to me all those years. You wouldn't have known I existed if I weren't Sylvie's friend."

"Believe me, you've got my attention now."

His husky sexy voice affected her more than she cared to admit. Tricia stared into his blue eyes and felt her mouth hang open far enough to catch flies. This was absurd! Bill was actually flirting with her—or maybe his reflex to block Sylvie's romances extended to friends of Sylvie's as well. She couldn't begin to fathom how she should respond to him. With outrage? With laughter?

But in the back of her mind, a little voice asked, *Is he really lonely?*

"Listen, Bill," she said, finally mustering up a properly indignant tone. "You're way off base here. I'm practically a married woman now. And just so you don't lose any sleep over poor misguided me, I've got several good reasons for marrying Manson, the foremost of which is because I care very deeply for him."

He shook his head mournfully. "Then it's even worse than Sylvie intimated."

She needed to have a long talk with Sylvie tonight, Tricia thought, steaming. "You don't think a woman should care about the man she's going to marry?"

He crossed his arms, mirroring her rigid stance. "I think it should go a little beyond *caring*."

"And who are you, some kind of marriage guru?"

"No, just the voice of experience."

Bitter experience, apparently. But who hadn't had a taste of that? Her first husband had bolted after less than a year, which was one reason she had waited so long to pick a mate the second time around. "Well I'm sorry things didn't work out for you." She was unable to keep the haughty edge out of her tone. "But I can assure you that Manson and I are going to forge a bond to last a lifetime."

"Forge away. I was only trying to help."

"Speaking of help...?" She nodded toward her rear end.

"Oh, yes." He peered curiously at the car door slammed on her dress. "You've still got a little quandary to deal with."

As much as she hated to admit it, the way Bill drawled the word *quandary* in his soft Louisiana accent sent a little thrill down her spine. "If you could just call a locksmith, I would appreciate it very much," she suggested, tamping down the illicit shiver.

"Locksmith? Heck, I can get you out myself."

But how much more lecturing would she have to endure before she was freed? Suddenly, Sylvie's stories of boyfriends being punched out, told off or interrogated, not to mention ticketed for not signaling, came back to her. No wonder Sylvie had such a difficult time nailing down a love life, with Bulldog Drummond here for a brother!

Bill strode back to his patrol car, leaving her to fume and lust in peace. Somehow Sylvie had given Bill the idea that Manson was boring, which was just plain wrong. Manson had plenty of interests. For instance, he was the only person she knew who finished the crossword puzzle in the newspaper every morning, never fail. That certainly indicated a wide breadth of knowledge. And he just loved those nature shows on PBS. She'd seen a million of them in the past few months, everything from water beetles to wildebeests.

Manson was wonderful. Why couldn't people understand that and be happy for her?

"Here we go." Bill strolled back to her car with a wire coat hanger in his hand.

A coat hanger? "That's not very professional looking."

"It usually works though."

Once Bill finally set about his task, Tricia couldn't help watching him. For one thing, he was only inches away. For another, his good looks were very easy on the eye.

Manson, she instructed herself. *Think about Manson...*

Manson Toler was heaven-sent, as far as she was concerned. The best thing to come along since low-fat potato chips. Not only did he do all the right romantic things but he was also an honest, wonderful man. And he had resources at his disposal that could make a real difference in Tom's future.

Okay, so maybe he didn't quite match up to Bill in the looks department. So what? He was tall and dapper, and besides, everyone said that bald men were sexy. By that yardstick, Manson was only a few years away from being irresistible.

"Got it!" Bill said triumphantly.

The words jolted Tricia out of her thoughts. Bill took off his hat—revealing a thick head of short-cropped golden hair. Shiny. The kind that made her itch to run her hands through it. She could just reach out...

He squinted at her. "Something wrong?"

"No, no," she said, swallowing.

"Well then, let's try this out." He pulled on the door handle and smiled when he heard the satisfying click of the door opening. *"Voilà!"*

Tricia immediately stepped away from Bill and did a damage check on her skirt.

"Just a little oil stain," Bill observed. "Sylvie should be able to do something about that."

She groaned. Even Sylvie probably couldn't work such a miracle. The thing was a huge brownish black circle right dead center of her rear end.

"Maybe it's an omen," Bill said, a mischievous glint in his eye.

"What's that supposed to mean?"

"About your wedding...it's beginning with a dark stain."

"That's preposterous! I don't believe in superstition. I'm a completely rational woman, and Manson Toler is the man I want to settle down with."

He smiled knowingly. "Your mind might have told you to settle down, but I think your eye is still roving."

"What gives you that idea?"

He sauntered forward with a big grin. "The way you were looking at me just now."

Tricia's face flamed. "I was not!" A patent lie. She'd been practically licking her chops. "W-well, if I was, it was only because I was stuck! Where else could I look?"

He shrugged and gestured to the green foliage all around them. "It's a pretty day. Why not take in the scenery?"

Because she'd been too busy taking in the sexy policeman's good looks. But she had been *thinking* about Manson, she reminded herself.

Thinking about his ever-widening bald spot.

"This is absurd," she said, gathering her skirt as she backed away from Bill. "I'm a grown woman. I certainly don't have to answer to anyone concerning my choice of groom!"

"No, just to yourself." He smiled. "And to him, of course. You'll have to say 'I do' to him."

A frustrated cry escaped her throat. "Sylvie is right about you and your meddling. You have to be the most exasperating big-brother type I've ever met!"

He bent in a mock bow. "And you, Tricia Parker, are the most beautiful woman I've ever had the pleasure to save from a locked Toyota."

The unexpected compliment knocked the wind out of her sails. "Thanks," she said, sounding woefully ungrateful. "And my last name's Peterson now."

He laughed.

"What's so funny?"

"I was just remembering. You always were a little on the defensive side."

"I'm not being defensive! I have nothing to defend!"

"Not even your choice for a husband?"

"No! You're just saying that because Sylvie's put the idea into your head that I should marry... Well, at least someone more like..." She let her sentence dangle unfinished between them.

He beamed. "Someone more like *me?*"

She crossed her arms, willing away the seductive vision of Bill decked out in tux, waiting for her at the end of an aisle. "Manson Toler is everything I want in a man," she declared, "and next Saturday, the day we're married, will be the happiest damned day of my life!"

She spun away and stomped up the steps of her mother's porch, scoffing. Dark stain, indeed! Next Saturday, she was going to be a married woman again, and this time around she was going into the arrangement older and wiser and marrying the perfect man. Everything would work out perfectly, barring some unforeseen cataclysm.

But what on earth could possibly happen to prevent her from becoming Mrs. Manson Toler?

BY THE TIME BILL pulled his car into his garage that evening, his daughter had acquired a new best friend: Tom Peterson, the son of Tricia, alias Pat Parker, a.k.a. the bride in distress.

Over their dinner of chili dogs, Casey wasn't the only one listening in rapt interest as Tom bemoaned his mother's imminent nuptials. Bill, for all his knowing that he'd probably made a damned fool of himself this afternoon flirting with a woman who had one foot in the honeymoon suite, couldn't quite manage to appear as disinterested as he wanted to. Even Geneva, his housekeeper, who usually rushed home after serving dinner to watch *Wheel of Fortune* in the comfort of her own living room, tarried this evening to hear the tale

of the newly slenderized former Bee Lake resident who
had flown off on a one-week vacation to Cancun and
had come back engaged to a rich Beverly Hills dentist.

"It's like something out of a soap opera. And the
wedding's going to be *right here*," she said excitedly.
"I bet that'll be something!"

Tricia's son frowned. Geneva had missed the slant
of his story entirely. Tom saw the coming wedding as
high tragedy. "But the guy she's marrying is a total
dork!"

Casey, not surprisingly, was in sync with Tom. Bill's
daughter was blond, blue-eyed, petite—and a hopeless
tomboy. And, having just been blessed with the gift of
braces, she had a special animosity against all dental
practitioners, which gave her an emotional stake in the
drama of Tom's mother's wedding. She tossed back
her blond braid and fastened her sympathetic gaze on
her new friend. "What a drag! I think you ought to
convince your mom not to marry him. You've got a
whole week."

"Casey..." Bill warned, in that fatherly tone that
shocked him every time it came out of his mouth—
never more than tonight, though, when he chastised his
daughter for suggesting Tom do the very thing he himself had been attempting this afternoon.

Pat Parker! He was still stunned at the change in her.
Back in school, she had been shy and a little defensive,
undoubtedly because she had been heftier than was
fashionable. He remembered the nickname from junior
high. Pudgy Pat. Mean kids' stuff. He'd probably
called her that himself. But mostly what impressed him
about her at the time was her standoffish manner. The
few times he'd been alone with her, she wouldn't speak
to him. And of course, he'd been an arrogant jock,
accustomed to girls doing their bubbly best to impress

him. Pat's silent treatment had done a number on his confidence.

But today she had unnerved him in a whole different way—she was like an entirely different person! She *was* an entirely different person. *Tricia.* And now that she was finally talking to him, he realized that all those years ago her silence had been masking a quick, wry wit. Not to mention that those extra pounds had been hiding a body that would pretty much cause any man driving by to throw on the brakes. It had been a long, long time since a woman had affected him that way, but as Bill had stared at those legs, those curves, and into those honey brown eyes, he felt his hormones rejuvenate at least ten years.

All that nonsense Sylvie had been whispering in his ear for the past couple of years—most of which he'd ignored—came rushing back to him. Sylvie thought Bill and Tricia would make a perfect pair, an idea he'd always considered laughable.

He wasn't laughing now.

"The worst part of it is, I think she's marrying Manson the dork on account of me," Tom moaned.

"Now why would she do that?" Geneva asked skeptically. Her elbows were propped up on the tablecloth, her coffee untouched since she had become absorbed in the story.

"'Cause I heard her telling my grandma that Manson would be a *positive role model* for me." His eyes rolled heavenward. "The only role model he could possibly be is for the world's biggest dweeb."

Bill chuckled. "He can't be that bad." Then, envisioning Tricia throwing herself away on someone unworthy, he frowned. "Can he?"

"Yeah," Casey said excitedly, "what's he like?"

"Well for one thing, he's almost *forty*." The emphasis on that numerical milestone made it sound as though the man had one foot firmly in the Home for Aged Dentists. "And he's stupid. He snorts when he laughs. And to top it all off, he's just weird looking. He's practically bald, and he's tall and skinny with a little pot belly. He looks kind of like Big Bird, plucked."

Casey shrieked with laughter. "How awful! Your mom is sacrificing herself just like Loretta Young did in that movie my dad and I were watching the other night."

Tom frowned. "Loretta who?"

"Young," Casey explained. "Only in that movie the woman sacrifices everything for her daughter by marrying a really boring guy." She shook her head grimly. "You don't even want to know how that story turned out...."

Tom nearly leaped out of his chair. "How? What happened?"

Bill bit back a laugh. When Casey had graduated from strictly Nickelodeon fare, he'd started watching old movie channels with her at night as a way of avoiding embarrassing *Melrose Place* and racy TV-movie-of-the-week situations. He hadn't ever given a hoot about black-and-white oldies before, except as something to surf by on the way to ESPN. But now he liked them almost as much as Casey. Especially the funny ones. But Casey the tomboy was perverse enough to prefer the melodramatic films with Joan Crawford and Barbara Stanwyck and Loretta Young. Lord knows there were enough of those to keep her away from R-rated movies on HBO for the next decade.

"The point is," Casey told Tom, her voice growing in intensity, "you've got to *do* something. You can't

let your mother marry this man! How could you live
with yourself, knowing what she'd sacrificed for you?''

Tom was flummoxed. "What am I supposed to do?
I already told her I think the guy's a geek.''

"You've got to think of something better than that,"
Casey told him.

Torn no doubt between real-life drama and the lure
of Pat Sajak, Geneva forced herself up from the table,
shaking her head. "With only a little over a week, I
don't know what you two think you're going to accomplish. Sounds to me like the woman's already made up
her mind.''

Tom sighed. "Maybe Manson won't show up for the
wedding.''

Bill listened to it all, feeling almost as glum as Tom.
But why should he be worrying about any of this? He
barely knew the woman; he didn't give two hoots who
she married. And yet he couldn't keep his imagination
from harkening back to those long legs of hers, and
her smile, and her apparent embarrassment when he'd
caught her staring at him as if it were Christmas and
he were a sweet, sticky candy cane.

Geneva said good night to them all, but Bill barely
heard her leave. His mind was miles away.

What *would* Big Bird look like, plucked?

"I know!" Casey yelled, bringing both Bill and Tom
out of their stupors. "What you need to do is change
your mother's mind.''

Tom frowned. "How?''

"By convincing her to marry somebody else!''

Bill immediately felt guilty, as if he'd put this idea
into his daughter's head. Which was ridiculous, naturally. He had no interest in who Pat Parker—correction,
Tricia Peterson—married. The matter was just a tidbit
of local gossip. After all he'd been through to extricate

himself from his own marital fiasco, he certainly didn't want to get involved in someone else's.

And from what Tricia had told him today, he was sure it would be a fiasco. Poor kid.

"Somebody else?" Tom asked.

"Somebody better," Casey clarified.

"That could be anybody!"

"Well, start with somebody who's handsome, more exciting," Casey suggested. "Someone really neat, like Cary Grant or Gary Cooper or Ray Milland."

"Ray Who?"

"Or at least someone with hair," Casey said.

Unconsciously, Bill combed his fingers through his own thick locks. His daughter was getting way out of line here. He should really say something.

Tom sighed. "Geneva's right. The wedding's in a week. How am I gonna find somebody that fast?"

Bill wondered whether anyone would consider marrying a poor cop with alimony payments rather than marrying a rich dentist....

And then he gave himself a swift mental slap. *Not your business, buddy boy.*

A frown tugged at Casey's lips. "It might be hard, especially considering your hair requirement. That cancels out a whole lot of men."

Tom shook his head. "It's hopeless."

Suddenly, Casey shot up out of her chair, electrified by her own brilliance. "Dad!" she yelled.

Bill jumped. He stared at her, afraid for a moment that she was going to suggest that he try to woo Tricia away from her intended. Maybe because that's what he'd been thinking himself. Thinking and rejecting, he corrected.

But as usual, his daughter's mind was galloping way

ahead of him. "You knew Tom's mom way back in the old days, didn't you, Dad?"

He laughed. "Yes, I distinctly remember her being in the gymnasium on the day they demonstrated that new invention, the wheel."

Casey sent Tom a long-suffering look before turning back to him. "I only meant, you must know somebody his mom liked. Right?"

Bill sat back, thinking. The trouble was, Tricia and he hadn't run in the same circles. He'd mostly thought of her as his kid sister's friend. As he struggled now to come up with a vision of her walking in the high school hallways with somebody, or sitting at a football game next to some boy, his mind came up a blank. Except... "I do remember she went to the junior prom once with a guy named Mort. He's a vice-president down at the bank now."

"Bank is good," Casey said approvingly. "Is he married?"

Bill shook his head. "Divorced." But he doubted Mort was going to trump Manson in the charisma department.

Fortunately, he didn't have to burst Casey's bubble—Tom did the job for him.

"Not my cousin Mort!" He slapped his forehead in despair. "He's a dweeb, too. And on top of that, he's my mom's cousin! She can't marry her cousin."

"Ashley and Melanie got married, and they were cousins," Casey informed him sagely.

"*Who?*"

"Besides, maybe this Mort isn't as bad as you remember," Casey went on. "I think we should go to the bank tomorrow and check him out. Would that be okay, Dad?"

"If Geneva and Tom's mother agree." He felt duty-bound, however, to give the marriage-meddling duo a warning. "You two shouldn't get your hopes set on this. Tom's mother might have reasons for marrying this Manson character that you can't imagine. You can't always stop people from making what you consider mistakes."

Although, in his private, strictly non-parental opinion, it was usually worth a shot.

Two splotches of red appeared in Casey's cheeks, and Tom shifted uncomfortably. "We just wanted to take a look at the guy," Casey said in their defense.

"Yeah," Tom piped in. "Maybe Mort won't even be interested in my mom."

Not interested? Ha! He couldn't imagine a red-blooded man on the planet who wouldn't be interested.

Bill put the thought aside and nodded. "Just as long as you two don't let your hopes outrace your reason."

There. He'd done the Ward Cleaver bit.

Now he hoped like hell those two would figure out a way to stop that wedding!

3

"I WANT TO BE a policeman when I grow up."

Tricia's fork clattered noisily against her plate. It was as if the word *policeman* had somehow bounced from her head to her son's, then out of his mouth. But how could that be? She looked guiltily from Tom to her mother, trying to detect whether either knew that she had been thinking about Bill Wagner all through breakfast.

Through breakfast? Who was she kidding? She'd been daydreaming about the man ever since yesterday at eleven o'clock!

"Are you all right, Tricia?" Her mother stared at her through round, startled eyes. But then, the way her mother slapped on eye shadow and mascara, she always had a startled look about her. "Your face is bright pink, honey!"

Trying to steady her nerves, Tricia dabbed at her lips with her napkin. "Last year you wanted to be a hockey player," she reminded Tom.

"Yeah, but last night when Mr. Wagner brought me home, we rode in his patrol car." He was bouncing up and down in his chair at the memory. "He showed me the radar gun and how the car's flashing lights worked and everything. I wanted him to turn on the sirens, but he wouldn't."

Peggy's jet-black eyebrows arched dramatically. "Why not?"

Tom frowned. "He said it would be like disturbing the peace."

"Fuddy-duddy!" Peggy exclaimed, looking at Tricia as if for confirmation that this was party pooper behavior. Beneath that bouffant jet-black hairdo worked the mind of a juvenile delinquent.

"Maybe we should be grateful he didn't give Tom a lesson on breaking into locked cars."

The statement wasn't lost on Tom. "Can he do that? Cool!"

Peggy waved a hand dismissively. "Picking locks is nothing."

"Mother!" No wonder it was so hard to raise a level-headed kid, with everyone undercutting her best efforts all the time. MTV and grandmothers. "Being a policeman is dangerous."

Her mother nodded and sent Tom a stern, warning glance. "Especially in Bee Lake. We're a regular hotbed of crime. Did you know we've had a series of robberies lately?"

Tricia had thought her mother was joking. "Really?"

"It's terrible! A man has been attacking couples— sometimes while they're in secluded areas. Lovers' lanes. They're calling him the love bandit." She cackled. "I guess his strategy is to catch his victims with their pants down."

"It doesn't sound like such a big deal to me," Tom muttered. "I bet Casey's dad could take on a stupid love bandit any day."

Tricia didn't want to think anymore about policemen, especially not about Bill Wagner, so she got up from the table and announced her plans for the morning. "I've got to do something about my dress," she told her mother. "What do you think would get that oil stain out?"

"The dry cleaners."

Tricia laughed. Her mother wasn't the type to spout tried-and-true home remedies when modern conveniences would serve just as well. Unfortunately, the dry cleaners seemed to be her only choice, since she was still too embarrassed to call Sylvie for advice. That would entail fessing up to having been so thoughtless as to slam her magnificent creation in a greasy car door. She would also have to tell Sylvie that she'd had a run-in with Bill, which was sure to throw Sylvie's match-making imagination into overdrive.

Tom stood up. "Mom, can I go over to Casey's?"

She shot him a look. "Are you sure you wouldn't be wearing out your welcome?"

"Officer Wagner said it would be okay."

Officer Wagner. Bill. It seemed all conversational outlets led back to that one fiendishly handsome, blue-eyed man. "All right, but call us this time when you're ready to come home, and we'll pick you up."

"Okay!" In a flash, he was darting out the door.

"Wait—don't you want me to drive you over?"

"No thanks, it's not far."

Tricia attempted to hold back the twinge of disappointment, but the effort was akin to beating out a forest fire with a whisk broom.

Peggy chuckled. "Were you hoping to drop by the Wagner residence to get a gander at Bill looking daisy fresh in the morning?"

"Of course not!"

Her mother eyed her knowingly. "I see—your thoughts are always with Mason."

"Manson," Tricia corrected her. She frowned and began to gather up her purse and her poor wedding dress. She hugged it to her and reminded herself how lucky she was. Life had never been this good, and it was all because of Manson. "Do you need anything from downtown, Mom?"

"No thanks. Don't dawdle. We've got a million things to do, not the least of which is to try to talk sense into Julie Tuttle."

"The organist? What's the matter?"

"She insists that hymns are too old fashioned. Refuses to play anything but Carpenters songs."

That was peculiar. "The Carpenters aren't old fashioned?"

"Says it's more romantic." Peggy leaned toward and spoke in her most confidential tone. "Well that's poor Julie for you—girl's been caught in a time warp since 1974, and of course you know why."

Tricia shrugged. "Watergate?"

"No—it was the year she didn't make drum majorette, poor thing. I think that really traumatized her."

Tricia laughed. "Oh, mom. I'd hate to hear what people are speculating made your time warp stop in 1960."

Peggy made a face and fluffed her bouffant do. "I was just stating a fact. But be that as it may, I know you don't want to be marching down the aisle to 'Rainy Days and Mondays.'"

"Okay, I'll be home as soon as I can."

Tricia left the house and drove downtown, dreading the next day. Her mother insisted on throwing her a bridal shower, but unlike most showers, at this one the bride was expected to do most of the work herself, including cleaning and baking. Tricia could hardly balk, however, since her mother had insisted on springing for caterers during the reception.

In fact, she couldn't criticize anything her mother

did. When Tricia had married Tom's father, she didn't want to have the ceremony in Bee Lake, so they'd eloped. Peggy had howled at being deprived of the opportunity to send her daughter off with a big shindig. But in retrospect, it had been just as well. The marriage hadn't even lasted till Tricia's junior year in college, when Roy Peterson, who had first caught Tricia's eye by being a romantic musician type, had run off to Amsterdam to join a rock band. Till heavy metal do us part. The news of his son's birth hadn't lured Roy back to the States any more effectively than his marriage vows had kept him there.

As she rounded the corner by the dry cleaners, lost in thought, she caught a glance of two preteen streaks skating into the bank across the street. Tom and Casey?

She kept staring behind her, wondering what business her son could have at the bank, until she plowed right into someone. She jumped back, startled—and was shocked to find herself staring straight into Bill Wagner's blue eyes.

He doffed his police cap and smiled broadly at her. "Just the lady I was hoping to run into."

She hugged Sylvie's dress to her like protective armor. "Was the collision all you thought it would be?"

His chuckle was a deep rumbly sound that gave her goosebumps even though it was already a steamy summer morning. "I wanted to apologize in case I might have seemed a bit overbearing yesterday."

"Oh, that's all right," she replied. "I was the one who probably seemed rude. I never thanked you for coming to my rescue."

"Haven't you heard? Rescuing damsels is what public defenders are for." He grinned, and it felt as though her heart swelled in her chest. "I also met your son last night."

"I know. Becoming a cop is all Tom talked about at breakfast this morning."

"He's a nice boy," Bill said.

"Nice." She frowned. "You are talking about a boy named Tom Peterson, aren't you?"

"My daughter Casey's quite taken with him, in her tomboyish way. Of course, now she's very concerned with Tom's worries."

"What worries?"

"Oh, you know...the wedding."

She could just imagine her son at the Wagner house last night, pouring out his heartache over being forced to relocate to Beverly Hills.

"Tom doesn't seem to care for your husband-to-be."

Tricia's shrug was in direct opposition to the anxiety she felt. "Tom's like all kids. He hates change."

"I guess that's so." Bill leaned against the wall of the dry cleaners, as if settling in for the long haul. "Still...what he said got me thinking." Those sparkling blue eyes zeroed in on her. "According to Tom you met this Manson in Cancun two months ago...."

Tricia pursed her lips. "That's correct, officer."

"And since then, you two have visited each other four times."

"That's also correct," she said, feeling increasingly uneasy about where this line of inquiry was taking them. "But I don't suppose that Tom happened to mention that one of those times was for an entire week, and that Manson and I talk on the telephone and e-mail all the time."

"E-mail!" Bill pushed away from the wall and put his hands on his hips. "Good grief! What can you learn about a guy through e-mail!"

She mirrored his stubborn stance. "Enough to know that he's the man I want to marry."

One blond eyebrow arched up. "And you don't think you're being a little too hasty?"

She sent a glance up to the heavens for patience. "I'm thirty-two years old, for goodness sakes. I'm capable of knowing whether or not Manson Toler is the man for me, which, for your information, he most definitely is."

Bill stepped back, shaking his head. "Sylvie always said you were headstrong."

"And she always told me that you were a meddling worrywart pain in the butt!"

She halfway expected him to sock her in the nose or give her a citation for insulting an officer. Instead, he surprised her again. He grinned. "Did she really?"

Tricia laughed in spite of herself. "Well…I added the bit about being a pain in the butt."

"Okay, okay," he said, striking a conciliatory tone. "Maybe I was worrying for nothing."

She willed herself to calm down. How could she stay mad at a guy who looked like Brad Pitt in a cop uniform? Even if he was gestapo chief of romance. "Listen, it's nice of you to be concerned, but I'm really not your problem. And Manson is perfectly nice. You can meet him at the wedding and see for yourself."

"When is he coming down?"

"Next Thursday, a couple of nights before the wedding. We figured it would be nice to have at least one romantic night together before all the marriage hoopla began."

Bill nodded, though his lips thinned as though he'd just swallowed something sour. Maybe he'd been hoping that if he cornered her on Main Street in front of the dry cleaners, she would blurt out that she secretly suspected Manson of being a tax fraud or an ax murderer or a closet Spice Girls fanatic.

But why did he care? That's what she couldn't figure out. Maybe he didn't really. His protectiveness could simply be a sort of big-brother knee-jerk reaction—*see happy couple, bust them up.* He'd done it often enough to Sylvie.

"Still, it sounds as if you don't know many details about his life," Bill said.

"Details!" Tricia scoffed. "Doesn't anyone have an ounce of romance in their souls anymore?" Or maybe they just didn't know the heartbreak of growing up four sizes larger than every other female. If they did, they wouldn't have wondered why Tricia would run off with the only thing in pants who'd looked her way in college. Or that she would have been equally swept away twelve years later, when, lying on a beach in her first bikini ever, a handsome man told her that she was drop-dead gorgeous.

"Don't you have an ounce of caution?"

She glared at Bill's face—his sexy, gorgeous face— and felt a single heavy raindrop splat down on her parade. "If I don't make it back from my honeymoon in Maui, I give you permission to head up the investigation."

"That's not funny."

"It would be if you knew my fiancé," she told him. "Now if you'll excuse me, I have a busy day ahead and I need to get this dress to the dry cleaners."

He donned his cap again and reluctantly stepped aside. "Didn't you tell Sylvie about the stain?"

She grimaced. "Not yet."

"Don't worry. My lips are sealed."

Naturally, she had to verify. Her gaze went immediately down to investigate the fullness of those lips of his and the easy way they spread over his even white teeth when he grinned. As he was doing just now.

Horrified, she looked into Bill's blue eyes and saw that she had been caught ogling him again. With a huff of dismay, she skulked past him and quickly escaped into Dub's Dry Cleaners. The place was steaming hot, which was convenient to hide her red-faced embarrassment, though she wondered how Dub and company stood working there with only a single hurricane fan to circulate the heavy air.

"Hey, there!" Dub greeted her. Then, when his old hawkish gaze honed in on her, he nearly fell backward. "Why, if it isn't little Pat Parker! Why, just *look* at you, or what there is left of you!"

"Hi, Dub." Tricia smiled. "Actually, it's Tricia Peterson now."

"I remember when you was knee-high to a doodlebug." And probably he remembered that she'd also been shaped much like a doodlebug. The elderly man, who had been taking care of delicate fabrics in Bee Lake since time immemorial, shuffled over to the counter to take the wedding dress from her. "Say, I heard you was gettin' hitched again."

"Yes, the wedding's next Saturday. Do you think you could take care of this stain for me?"

"Ethel Greenblatt said you all was planning a big wingding."

"Yes, next Saturday. This stain—"

"Ethel said you's marrying a foreigner or some kind."

"He's from California."

He shook his spiky gray head mournfully. "Oh, well. Guess it can't be helped."

"What about this stain, Dub?" she asked, steering him back to business. "It's grease, I think." As if she didn't know. "Like car grease maybe."

He eyed the stain for a moment. "Huh." Then he

studied it some more. "My, my." Finally, he looked back up at her. "Dress'll be ready tomorrow."

"Do you think you can get the stain out?"

"Doubt it," he said. "But it'll be ready tomorrow."

"Well what if you can't get it out?" she asked, beginning to feel panicky. "Is there anybody who *could* get it out?"

"Oh, sure."

She nearly sagged against the counter in relief. "Who?"

"God." Dub gave her a full denture grin, and his chest heaved with silent chuckles.

All the way home, when she should have been worrying about the dress and all the things she had to do before tomorrow, her thoughts kept returning to Bill. What was he doing in Bee Lake, still single after all these years? What was the matter with women in this town? Was their something in the water that caused female immunity to sexy single cops?

As she walked into the house, she found the living room a shambles. Couch cushions were pulled out, every drawer was thrown open, magazines were scattered all over creation.

"What happened?" Tricia was terrified the house had been robbed.

"I lost it!" a muffled voice exclaimed. Her mother was on her knees at the other end of the room, rifling through a drawer filled with bridge cards, old TV guides and stray rubber bands.

"What?"

"The picture of you and Maynard that we were going to put out for the guests tomorrow."

"Manson, Mom. His name is Manson."

Her mother had insisted that since no one in town knew Manson, they needed to at least put a picture of him out on display. Tricia had brought one home especially for that purpose—a posed portrait of herself and her fiancé that they had taken last month in California. They had just been inspecting it last night, in this very room. Even her mother, who usually went for the more rough-hewn types, agreed that Manson was very distinguished.

Another ten minutes of searching didn't turn up the photo. "Lord only knows what's happened to it!"

Tricia laughed. "It's no big deal. I'm sure it'll surface eventually."

Her mother tilted her head and sent her an ominous look. "Unless Tom got a hold of it…"

"Oh, Mom," Tricia scoffed, "what would Tom want a picture of Manson for?"

Her mother grinned slyly. "A dart board?"

"PAT PARKER! Well, well!" Mort Finley squinted at the photo Tom and Casey showed him. The picture used to have Manson in it, too, but with a pair of nail scissors he'd found in the bathroom Tom had carefully excised him. So where his mother had her hand lying on Manson's shoulder, it was now lying on air. It looked a little funky, but Mort didn't seem to notice. "My, my, my! She looks a lot different than she used to."

"She lost some weight," Tom said.

"I'll say!"

Tom wanted to punch him. No wonder his mom worried about her weight so much when people like Mort—not much to look at himself—made such a big deal of it. As far as Tom was concerned, people like Mort making fun of his mom was the reason he had to eat Lean Cuisine instead of hot dogs.

He and Casey exchanged glares over the man's head. Maybe this hadn't been such a good idea.

"She's a real looker!"

That quickly, Tom and Casey's glares turned to rapturous smiles.

"My mom still talks about you all the time," Tom lied, "and how much fun you two had at the junior prom."

Mort drew back in shock, so that his chin almost disappeared into his turkey wattle neck. Unfortunately, Uncle Mort hadn't improved any since the last time Tom had seen him. But maybe even having a Mort-type guy interested in her would prove to his mom that there were other men in the world besides Manson Toler.

This plan had to work, it had to. Tom just couldn't stand the idea of moving to California, where he didn't know *anybody!* And even if he did know some people, how could he be sure they would like him? Even Manson didn't like him, and he was supposed to. Why would the rest of the people in the state be any friendlier?

Mort cleared his throat. "I always got the impression that maybe she hadn't enjoyed herself too much at the prom...."

Tom swallowed anxiously. "Why?"

"'Cause she broke out in hives and made me take her home at eight-fifteen."

"Oh." Over Mort's head, Casey and Tom exchanged despairing looks again. "Then I don't suppose you'd want to come over to my Grandma's house tomorrow? She's having a little get-together in my mom's honor."

Mort's forehead wrinkled. "You mean the wedding shower?"

"Oh…" Tom laughed nervously, then gulped. "You heard about the wedding?" He felt like kicking himself. He should have figured that everyone in Bee Lake would know about the wedding already!

Casey, unfazed by this disturbing new turn of events, tossed her blond braid and said coolly, "Oh, the wedding's off now."

That got Mort's attention. Tom's, too! What was she talking about?

"It is?" Mort asked.

"It—it was a last minute thing," Tom sputtered.

"Very sad," Casey agreed.

"But now Grandma's decided that since they'd planned the shower, they might as well celebrate my mother's *not* getting married." Boy, that sounded lame!

"And reintroduce her to the single men of Bee Lake," Casey told Mort. "Only the best ones, though."

"Mom sent me over to invite you," Tom said, trying not to think about all the trouble he was digging himself into.

Mort puffed up as much as his narrow desk chair in the New Accounts cubicle at First Bee Lake Bank would allow. He straightened his tie and said graciously, "I'd be very pleased to attend. What time?"

"Noon," Tom told him. "Are you gonna go?"

Mort almost giggled. "I'll brush off my best suit tonight."

Casey grinned, but Tom shuddered.

"If Uncle Mort's all that's standing between my mom and matrimony," he said once they'd clumped out of the bank, "I'm toast."

Casey fanned herself with his mom's picture, unconcerned. In fact, she almost looked encouraged. "We can do more."

"More what?" he asked. "Damage? How's Mom gonna react when Uncle Mort tells her what we said?"

His new friend—who was extremely intelligent for a girl, he'd decided—crossed her arms and rocked back thoughtfully on her skate wheels. "The question is, how is your mom going to react when every single man in Bee Lake arrives at her door."

"Huh?"

She waved the picture. "I say we take this picture, copy it, and make a flyer inviting everybody. We can leave it in all the guy places. You know...at the fire station, the Chamber of Commerce, Art's pool hall...."

Tom was nearly overwhelmed. "That's so boss!"

Surely, surely, if they sent a million men her way— or even as many as they could scrounge up in Bee Lake—his mom would realize she could marry someone else. After all, she'd fallen for Manson fast enough, and women were so fickle. In sixth grade, girls broke up with some guy in homeroom, and by lunch period they were going with somebody else.

How different could grown-up girls be?

4

"NOW THAT'S STRANGE!" Peggy slowly hung up the receiver to the kitchen wall phone and sent Tricia a puzzled glance. "That was Doug Winburn, the high school junior varsity coach. He wanted to know if he needed to bring anything for the party."

Tricia leaned back in her chair—an old habit she always seemed to revert to when at her mother's house and when her son wasn't around—and craned her neck to check the cookies in the oven. Ostensibly, she was making sand tarts. Mostly, though, she was sitting around being nervous about her upcoming walk down the aisle—and hoping her mother would remember when to rescue the sand tarts. "Is his wife coming to the shower?"

Peggy's jet-black brows knit together. "Last I heard, Doug was still single."

"Maybe he's dating somebody who's attending."

"That would explain it," Peggy said, going about checking on the cookies the old-fashioned way by actually crossing the room to look in on them. Halfway to the oven, she stopped and turned, a long-tipped red fingernail tapping her lips. "No...I seem to remember Jane Ellen from bridge club telling me that Doug just broke up with that Turner girl. You know, the one with crooked teeth who made such a spectacle of herself the time she was elected Queen Bee for the Bee Lake Pride Parade?"

"Not really."

"Lord, Pattie, how could you forget? The girl got loaded and toppled right off her hive float!"

Tricia could barely recall the incident, though she didn't doubt her mother's tack-sharp memory for one instant. She only wondered why her mother could remember something that happened ten years ago when she couldn't even nail down the name of the man her daughter was going to marry in seven days.

Seven days! Her stomach fluttered. How was she ever going to make it through the next week without dropping dead from a panic attack?

She stood, trying to focus on something else. "Maybe Doug What's-His-Face got back together with Whosit Turner, or maybe he found somebody completely new."

Peggy looked doubtful and a little indignant. "If he did, nobody at bridge club told *me* about it." She brought out the sand tarts and pointed to a sheet lined with neat rows of tiny quiche hors d'oeuvres. "Those go in next."

Tricia dutifully threw the little cheese tarts in the oven, and returned to leaning back in her chair. Anxiety consumed her. If only her fiancé weren't half a continent away. Was Manson having second thoughts?

Not that *she* was. She was just nervous. After all, half of Bee Lake would be at the ceremony, and Sylvie had mentioned asking Bill to escort her. Tricia had never reckoned the possibility of getting married in front of Bill, the heartthrob of her youth.

"Now I wonder *who* among our guests could be having a fling with the football coach...." Peggy tapped her foot impatiently. "I hate not knowing things!"

A knock at the door almost caused Tricia to tip over backward.

"Good heavens!" Peggy exclaimed, patting her on the shoulder as she went to answer the door. "You're as nervous as a cat! How are you going to stay calm when Millard gets here?"

Tricia opened her mouth to make the necessary correction, but at that moment Peggy flung the door wide and Bill stepped inside.

She shot to her feet. In the intimacy of her mother's little kitchen, Bill seemed almost larger than life. While Manson was tall and lean, Bill was just a little under six feet, and muscled all over. Especially his arms and chest. She imagined how different it would be being inside those arms instead of in Manson's....

Not that she had any reason to be comparing Bill to Manson.

She forced a smile. "Hi. Did you bring Casey?" Maybe she and Tom were going to pal around together today. Give them something to do during the shower.

Although, now that she thought about it, she hadn't seen Tom in over an hour.

"Actually, I came to talk to you," Bill said.

There was an awkward silence as all the warmth fled from Tricia's extremities to her face.

"Well!" Peggy beamed a smile at her daughter. "I'll just run along into the other room."

"You don't have to go, do you, Mom?" Tricia reached out to stop her, but of course her mother was too spry to be caught.

"There are flower arrangements to attend to in the living room. Just make sure the hors d'oeuvres don't burn, Pattie."

In a second, she was gone, and Tricia gazed after the flapping kitchen door uncomfortably. She didn't want to be left alone with Bill. When she turned back to him, she let out a nervous chuckle. "My mom, folks. She still doesn't trust me with a lit oven."

"She still calls you Pattie."

Tricia shrugged. "I guess it's hard to change your image with someone who's known you since diaper-changing days."

His white teeth flashed at her. "The old you-can't-go-home-again conundrum."

"You can, as long as you remember your Prozac."

Bill laughed, then looked around the kitchen at the sheets of baked goods piled up on every available surface. He took off his hat and ran a hand nervously through his short, thick hair, something Tricia itched to do herself. "I guess you all are busy. Maybe I shouldn't have come over this morning."

She shrugged. "No big deal."

"That's not what I've heard," Bill replied quickly. "In fact, I was half-offended that I didn't get an invite."

That was weird. What man in his right mind wanted to be invited to a wedding shower? She chuckled nervously, trying to imagine Bill playing the safety pin game or bride bingo. "It's just going to be an intimate little affair."

He stared at her, and she silently questioned if he was wondering, as she was, whether her choice of the words "intimate little affair" could be considered a Freudian slip. "I mean, I imagine there will be a lot of no-shows."

"I'd expect quite a turnout."

She still couldn't wrap her mind around a guy taking so much interest in what would surely be a humdrum wedding shower. But who knows? "Well…let's hope so."

"But I didn't come here to talk about your party,"

he went on, looking distinctly more businesslike. "I suppose you guessed that already."

"I was beginning to wonder." He coughed, covering a laugh, and she looked at him anxiously. "Is something wrong?"

He shifted his weight from one leg to another, then slapped his cap against his thigh. His thigh, she noticed, was as muscled up as his arms were. Was it leftover football-star muscle or did the man work out? Or, for that matter, were some men just muscly? When it came right down to it, what she didn't know about men and their red corpuscles could fill an encyclopedia.

He cleared his throat, and, flushed, she dragged her gaze up from his lower half.

"Um, what I came to tell you about was your fiancé...Dr. Toler."

She gasped, and her fingertips jerked automatically up to her cheeks. She hadn't watched a newscast since coming to Bee Lake—anything might have happened! Was there an earthquake in L.A.? A three-million-car pileup on some highway? A gunman in a post office? "My God, what's happened?"

Bill's expression turned ominously grim. "I don't mean to alarm you, Tricia, but the fact of the matter is, your fiancé's racked up a hell of a lot of parking tickets."

Slowly, her fingertips melted down the hollows of her cheeks and fell limply back to her sides. As her body went noodly with relief, indignation built up steam inside of her. "*Parking tickets?* You came here and nearly scared me to death because Manson has a couple of parking tickets?"

"Ten. And a speeding violation as well." The information was delivered in a humorless crime-doesn't-pay *Dragnet* tone.

"Good grief!" she shrieked. "The man lives in L.A.! It's the land of moving violations!" She sagged against the counter, absently popping a sand tart into her mouth. "I thought something terrible had happened."

He tilted his head. "And this doesn't worry you?"

She studied his earnest expression and nearly howled with laughter. *"Traffic tickets?"* she asked in disbelief. "No!"

His lips thinned. "Well, actually, there's something else I didn't tell you."

Oh, God, here it comes. The parking tickets were probably just a warm-up. She held her breath, wondering what crime Manson was guilty of. Tricia suddenly saw herself on *Oprah*, tearfully revealing the secrets her fiancé had hidden from her. From the dire expression on Bill's face—his expression practically oozed pity for her—it was certain to be something involving severed heads. "What is it?"

"A couple of months back, a Manson Toler of Starcrest Drive in Beverly Hills failed to report for jury duty."

Tricia blinked. What…he…*jury duty?* She couldn't help it. She cracked up.

Bill frowned as he watched her lean against the counter, her shoulders rocking with laughter. "I don't see what's so humorous."

"My God, Bill," Tricia said, wiping a tear from her eye, "you had me convinced Manson really was some kind of lunatic!"

"I don't think a citizen skipping out on his civic responsibilities is something to be laughed at."

She straightened. "No, of course not," she said soberly, then giggled. "Has he ever been caught jaywalking?"

Bill crossed his arms. "Not according to my source at the L.A.P.D."

Tricia shook her head, attempting to will away her hysteria. When she finally did, she remembered to be angry with this virtual stranger who'd gone snooping into her love life. "Did it ever occur to you to ask me if Manson had a criminal record?"

"I tried yesterday," he said defensively, "but you didn't seem to take the matter seriously. And I must say, you're shrugging it all off rather lightly now, too."

"Parking tickets!"

"Leaving traffic tickets unpaid, not to mention skipping out on jury duty, shows a marked disregard for civic responsibility. Is that the kind of role model you want for your child?"

"Oh, honestly," she muttered. "I'm sure there's a good reason why Manson didn't go to jury duty. Maybe he forgot. Maybe his car broke down."

"Or was impounded for unpaid tickets," Bill sniped.

"Why are you spying on my fiancé?"

"I was just concerned for you, that's all. You seemed to know so little about this man."

"Good grief, Bill, when you asked me if I knew anything about him, I thought you meant other things, like how good a sport he is when he loses at cards or whether he snores..."

A dark blond eyebrow sprang up in curiosity. "You don't know whether he snores?"

She blushed. Weren't people supposed to stop blushing at thirty? "Well...no. I don't."

He watched her closely, causing her cheeks to burn that much more intensely. No doubt he was speculating about how many times she had slept with Manson. Thank heavens there was nowhere he could investigate that! Although perhaps if he knew that she and Manson had decided to have a real old-fashioned honeymoon, he would have a little more respect for the man.

"I thought you might want to know something more about him," Bill told her, "and wouldn't know the way to go about finding out."

She groaned in frustration. "What are you, the love police? Aren't women who know you able to make foolish marital decisions for themselves, just like the rest of the female population?"

Her sarcasm whizzed right over his good-looking head. "Why would you want to make a foolish decision?"

She tossed up her hands in resignation. "Uncle!"

"Then you're not at all concerned about what kind of influence this man will be on an impressionable young child?"

"I assume you're referring to Tom." *Impressionable young child* brought to mind an apple-cheeked cherubic youngster, not her little hellion on wheels. "Well, let's put it this way. I was equally alarmed yesterday morning when he announced his intention to become Jack Webb, Jr."

"Okay, okay," Bill said, relenting. "I'm sorry if I overstepped my bounds. I was just worried about you."

At those last words, a knot unexpectedly hitched in her throat. Worried? About her? It seemed so long since anyone, especially a man, had been looking after her. Suddenly, she felt guilty for being so brusk with him, so sarcastic. He'd been pushy, sure—but pushy on her behalf, at least.

"I'm sorry if I sounded rude," she said, looking up into his blue eyes. When they were focused on her, it was hard to look anywhere else. She swallowed, then gestured toward the kitchen table. "Would you like to sit down? Have a sand tart?"

His lips pulled into a wry grin. "No, I think I've done enough damage here today."

"Oh, but—"

"Besides," he said, patting her lightly on the arm, "I've got to get back on patrol."

Those little pats seemed to send little bolts of lightning straight to her central nervous system. And she was already on edge. She stepped back slightly. "Oh." She didn't know why she felt so disappointed.

"Well…" he drawled, not moving, "I guess I'll be moseying along.…"

She nodded, realizing she'd been standing there as tongue-tied with him as she'd been at fourteen. "Feel free to drop by later for some coffee if you like. There might be a couple of people here you know."

"A couple?" he asked, putting his cap back on his head. He laughed. "I'll say!"

With another chuckle, he walked out the door and disappeared down the wisteria-trellised walkway. Tricia frowned thoughtfully as she shut the door behind him. Funny the way he kept laughing about the wedding shower. Maybe he really had been hoping for more than a halfhearted invitation.

She shrugged, sank down into her kitchen chair and munched absently on another still-warm sand tart. Her arm tingled in the exact place he'd patted it; she rubbed the spot gingerly. Why was Bill so interested in her upcoming marriage? Was it because she was Sylvie's best friend…or because he liked her?

The back door rattled and Tricia jumped up, half expecting Bill to saunter through again. But in the next moment, her son rolled into the kitchen, followed by Casey. They were both weighed down with plastic grocery bags. In their knee pads, helmets and nearly identical baggy clothes, they looked like shrunken hockey players back from a shopping expedition.

She began to poke through the bags as soon as they deposited them on the counter and table. The contents she found might have been her dream menu in days of yore—multi-liter plastic vats of real soda, five kinds of chips and dip, cheddar puffs and crackers, cookies, pecan sandies, those nasty sugar wafers she loved so much, miniature powdered doughnuts and cheese, cheese, cheese. Just the sight of so many fat grams lumped together made her newly sleek thighs quiver in anticipation.

"What is all this?"

Tom looked nervously at Casey, then back to her. "Some stuff for the party."

Some? "Tom, it looks as if you've just spent a year's allowance on junk food!" And this from a kid who guarded his allowance money so carefully that he usually made her cough up for Icee's and candy bars, claiming that since he needed them for sustenance they fell under the realm of parental responsibility.

"We weren't sure what to get," Casey replied when Tom merely looked sheepish. "*I* suggested the cheese and crackers, since adults seem to be big on cheese."

A herd of wild Weight Watchers escapees couldn't even make a dent in all this stuff. "Guys, this is wonderfully thoughtful of you, it really is, but I feel terrible that you spent so much time and money. We're just having a few women over and we have plenty of food."

They blinked at her, and she began digging through the bags for the register receipt. When she found it, she almost fainted. "Seventy-two dollars!"

"Brie cheese is very expensive," Casey informed her.

"Where did you two get that much money?"

"We both chipped in."

Tricia shook her head, closing the bags; she knotted the one with the sugar wafers, just so she wouldn't accidentally rip into them. For a moment, she even had to blink back tears—not because of this gloriously disgusting junk food she couldn't eat, but because of Tom, bless his heart. Could this be a milestone for them, a sign that he was letting go of his bitterness over her new marriage, an offering of acceptance of Manson? After all, the wedding shower represented the coming of the big event he'd done nothing but dread since he'd heard about it, and here he was actually pitching in and helping her prepare. Putting aside his own feelings for her happiness.

Her little boy was becoming a man.

She put her hands on his shoulders. "Tom, I'll never forget this."

His face turned beet red and something like a strangled gurgle erupted from his throat. But of course he was embarrassed about her showing affection in front of Casey. Boys were like that.

"Don't worry," she told Tom and Casey, "I'm sure the store will take back all the food and we can get your money refunded."

"Uh, Mom, if I were you I might want to wait till *after* the party to take the food back."

"Why?"

Casey tapped her on the arm and nodded toward the oven warily. "You might need those Cheetos, Mrs. Peterson."

Smoke was seeping out from the oven doors. In a panic, Tricia ran over to rescue what were certainly charred, shriveled quiches and was engulfed by a billowing black cloud. She jumped back, coughing, just as the fire alarm started bleeping piercingly.

Peggy flew threw the swinging doors. "Oh dear!" she exclaimed, flapping her arms. "Please don't burn all the food—we're going to need it!"

"You sure will...."

Tom and Casey exchanged glances and sneaked out of the kitchen under cover of darkness.

5

PEGGY PARKER COULD sure throw one hell of a party.

It wasn't so much the food or the music or the people, Bill realized, so much as the exuberant atmosphere spilling out of that little house on Sycamore. The little living room crammed with people laughing, dancing and stuffing their faces was so raucous that he wondered whether he might be the only person in town just shy of a lamp shade on his head. But then, it was hard to be slaphappy when the woman he'd dreamed about all last night was dancing with Larry Gringold by the light of day. Larry Gringold, who owned the pharmacy. What the heck was he doing here?

Bill would have been jealous, but it seemed every man in town intended to have a dance with the bride-to-be. Dwayne Sullivan, manager of Sullivan's Stop-n-Shop. Out in the middle of the day! Gary Limpett, a fireman. Had Bee Lake closed its doors for this occasion? Bill scanned the room and counted practically every bachelor in town, all playing hooky from whatever job they were supposed to be doing. One of the guys had the foresight to bring beer to the party, and just like that, the wedding shower had morphed into a strange kind of bachelorette party.

The women were here, too—town matrons, young wives, even Bill's second-grade schoolteacher—all looking slightly dazed yet pleased that single men of every stripe had crashed their wedding shower. They were handing out plates of cheese straws and sand tarts as quickly as the guys could gulp them down, and when those ran out, potato chips followed.

And in the middle of it all was Tricia. Bill still felt a jolt of surprise every time he took in her new look, but he was slowly getting used to it. She was sheathed in a sleeveless pale yellow pencil dress that ended mid-thigh on her long shapely legs, and her feet were encased in matching yellow pumps. The sedate silk scarf that was supposed to accessorize the sedate little outfit had gone askew, however, ruining the sweet impression she apparently intended to make; the knot had worked its way to the back of her neck and the scarf fluttered crazily around her shoulders as she tossed her head while doing a reasonable twist to Chubby Checker.

Her partner was another matter. Larry's version of the twist was a little more unpredictable, and no wonder. He had been a basketball star back in his school days, but his six-foot-seven lanky frame didn't serve so well for boogying down in a small living room, and the overall impression wasn't helped by the fact that he was wearing a suit his mother must have bought him for graduation 1979. Twisting one way, Larry's tan polyester hip jutted sharply out, nearly felling Myrtle Simpson to his right. Twisting the other way, the knobby knees topping off his flared pant legs first nearly took down Tricia, only to pop back in place as his other hip jerked to the left. Other dancers—including Tricia—gave him wide berth, some stopping to stare, which Larry took both as a compliment and a reason to really cut loose. He grabbed Tricia's hand and began to bob his carrot-topped head in an astounding Egyptian strut back and forth in front of her, then at the end of the song swung into a last hip-grinding finale.

In the moment it took for the turntable on Peggy's ancient hi-fi to change LP's, Bill positioned himself. The slightly saccharine tones of Johnny Mathis sang out "Misty." Tricia looked hesitant to risk a slow dance with Larry, who now wiped his sweaty brow as he caught his breath. His orange hair was plastered to his scalp. Like a good sport Tricia stepped into place just as Bill reached up and tapped Larry on the shoulder.

"Mind if I cut in?"

After his amazing performance, Bill would have thought the man would want a rest. Larry opened his mouth to speak, but before he could protest the interruption, Tricia smoothly stepped into Bill's arms. "Of course he doesn't care—Larry's the nicest guy in town. Always has been."

The words brought a broad grin to Larry's face—which remained as he retreated to a chip bowl.

Bill grinned as he looked into Tricia's eyes. If you'd asked him two days ago, he would have guessed that she had garden variety brown eyes, but now he saw they were honey brown with intriguing flecks of green. This close he could see her skin was dusted with freckles and that her cheeks had color in them that wasn't applied with makeup. She also had a body that was thin, soft and surprisingly firm, homage he supposed to the same rigorous exercise plan that had helped her lose weight.

They stood apart, just dancing for a moment, before either of them spoke.

"Thanks for the rescue."

Bill sent her a nod. "It's all part of my job description, remember? Not to mention, if Larry's bump-and-grind twist got any more out of control, it might have amounted to a civil disturbance.''

Tricia laughed. No sound had ever seemed so good to him.

"What amazes me," Bill said, "is that you convinced Peggy to play anything else but Johnny Cash."

She rolled her eyes. "Johnny was the first hour. When someone suggested dancing I told Mom we simply had to break out something else. I don't think she's bought a record since 1972."

"That's not so unfortunate."

Her eyes widened in mock astonishment. "What? Bill Wagner, a musical reactionary?" She sent him a knowing grin. "As I recall from sneaking into your room with Sylvie in the old days, you had quite a selection of fabulous eighties music. Flock of Seagulls, Men Without Hats, Duran Duran?"

Bill winced.

"And don't tell me you parted with your Supertramp collection."

He laughed in surrender. "I've still got all those records, somewhere."

"They'll make nice artifacts for Casey to dig out of the attic someday."

"Along with my Betamax tapes and old typewriter, other relics she probably won't understand."

Tricia smiled. "Ah, the good old days. It's a relief that they're over, isn't it?"

He shrugged. "I dunno. Those pre-nose ring days seem kind of innocent to me now."

"I'm relieved Tom hasn't discovered body piercing and tattoos yet. That will probably be next year's crisis."

Bill could relate. "It's the rap music that gets to me. So annoying! How can they stand it?"

"Because they know it annoys us."

"Kids these days!" Bill joked.

Tricia laughed again. "Grousing about tattoos while we shuffle along to Johnny Mathis—we'll be the life of the old-folks home someday."

"You will be if you keep up your dancing skills. You looked very good doing that twist. Very sexy."

The natural color in her cheeks heightened as she stared up at him, and he became achingly aware of their hands clasped together, her hand on his shoulder, his arm at her waist. Their breathing seemed in perfect sync, and he felt their bodies moving infinitesimally closer. A stab of desire to haul her up against him so that they could simply sway together for the duration of this wonderful old song was nearly unbearable. Usually he was a little uncomfortable slow dancing, but today he barely noticed. All his attention was focused on Tricia.

Electricity crackled between them, and for a few moments Bill couldn't say if they were still shuffling their feet or whether they were standing stock still in the middle of the room, in front of everyone. His mind was frozen, his gaze fixed on those brown eyes of hers that were so much more than just brown, and her lips, pink and ever-so-slightly parted. He wanted to kiss her. His whole body was taut with the tension it took to keep him from bending down and sampling her lips. Did she want him to? He hadn't kissed a woman since his wife, and now he was standing in front of half the town, aching with desire for a woman he barely knew. And yet a woman he'd known most of his life.

A woman who was about to be married to someone else.

The realization was a splash of ice water in his face, bringing him out of his Tricia-induced trance. He looked around the room, amazed. They were still moving, he noted with relief. No one was gaping at them. His blind moment of lust had gone unnoticed.

Except maybe by Tricia, who looked distinctly uncomfortable.

"Thanks for the compliment," she said after the moment had passed. "I guess I just needed the right partner."

He pictured Larry's wacky, near-dangerous moves and felt a chuckle rumble out of his chest. "It's lucky you got out of that twist in one piece."

"Believe me, he's not even the wildest dancer here." She looked across the room to identify another Arthur Murray candidate and seemed stunned for a moment at the dense gathering around her, as if she hadn't quite realized the number of people stuffed into Peggy's house. The dancing area between the TV and the coffee table was packed, but guests also bunched around the door, the couch, the old piano, and spilled into the hallway toward the kitchen. "How did all these people get here?"

That wasn't hard to answer. "Automobile. There's not a place to park on Sycamore."

"But why?" She gestured with their clasped hands all around the room. "How did Larry or any of these guys know to come here? One minute we were drinking iced tea and the next minute men with six-packs started pouring through the front door." She glanced up at him, a quizzical grin tugging at her lips. "For that matter, what are *you* doing here?"

"I was invited."

She blinked up at him in confusion. "Mom didn't tell me."

"Oh, I'd be very surprised if your mother had anything to do with this."

Tricia's lips were still screwed up in confusion. "But then who did?"

Johnny Mathis switched songs, and while he crooned about Sunny getting blue, Bill stepped back and pulled the piece of paper he'd retrieved from the firehouse out of his back pocket. He unfolded the flyer and handed the evidence over to Tricia, who read it with raw amazement.

Calling all single dudes!
Come one, come all to a party for Tricia Peterson
(she used to be Pat Parker but she's lost weight—
a lot!)
At 2106 Sycamore 3:00 Saturday.
Mega food and other refreshmints! Come meet
Tricia!
Be their or be square!

Her face grew paler the further she read, and slowly, her free hand lifted to lips parted in horror. Bill mentally reviewed first aid for fainting spells.

"Oh, Lord! How can I face everyone?"

He laughed. "You already have. Don't worry about that. These guys are just glad for a chance to party."

She glanced around as if to verify that, as a matter of fact, no permanent harm was done. People weren't looking at her as if she were an idiot. Her dignity was as intact as Larry's, at least.

In the next moment she looked at him, eyes flashing. "Tell me, officer, how long has it been since Bee Lake had a case of infanticide?"

"Don't send Tom to the gallows just yet. I don't think he's the only one to blame."

"Who else?"

"Casey. I'm afraid this flyer is my daughter's hand-iwork, right down to the bad spelling."

"But the picture…"

There was no way Casey could have procured this picture of Tricia. Bizarre as it was, Bill couldn't figure out where anyone could have gotten it. "What are you doing in that photo?" he blurted out of curiosity. "Are you gesturing at something? It's so strange that your hand is just dangling in midair."

She groaned. "Like Vanna White on her way to turn a letter. That's because my arm was supposed to be around someone!"

"Who?"

"Manson! I wondered why the picture had disap-peared—if I had known who had it I might have been more worried."

"I guess our children are in cahoots," Bill told her.

"But why on earth would Tom do this?"

"Maybe he wanted you to meet some eligible men…maybe to let you know that it wasn't too late to change your mind."

Her jaw dropped. "Oh, no. I thought he was trying to come to terms with everything—and now this stunt!"

"Don't take it too hard. To me this stunt seems com-pletely logical and, frankly, very astute coming from a twelve-year-old's perspective. You might even say you could be proud of your son."

"I beg your pardon?" She did an exaggerated dou-ble take as she folded the flyer back into its tiny square. "Would you care to explain that?"

Bill hesitated, realizing he might have piped up un-wisely. "I'm not sure you want to hear it."

She folded arms. "Oh yes I would!"

"Well, it's just that I think he sees through what you're doing."

She eyeballed him with the relish of a cat about to pounce on a mouse. "And what's that?"

"Possibly, making the biggest mistake of your life."

There, he'd said it. Now he just had to wait for her anger to explode like Vesuvius redux.

The eruption wasn't long in coming. "This is outrageous!" she exclaimed in something between a whisper and a shriek. When several people turned to stare at their argument, she simmered down enough to inquire in a bristly voice, "Did you make a special trip out here just to pass on that bit of wisdom?"

He shook his head. "Maybe Tom and Casey figured if you met some other men, you'd realize that you didn't need to fall for the first smooth operator to come your way."

Tricia resorted to the old counting to three trick that he sometimes did when he pulled over a particularly bullheaded driver. "Manson is not a smooth operator. He's not a crook. He's not anything!"

"You don't make him sound very appealing."

She groaned in frustration. "Don't you understand? I'm not Sylvie. My romance isn't your problem!"

She spun on her heel and beelined it for a bowl of potato chips. Bill itched to follow her, but when he saw Tricia and Sylvie putting their heads together and glaring his way, he changed his mind and went in search of something to drink besides cheap beer or soda. Snaking his way through the familiar hoard, he came to only one conclusion.

She wasn't in love with Manson. She couldn't be.

He ducked into the kitchen, which was blessedly empty, grabbed a plastic cup from a plastic bag on the counter and went to the tap. As he downed the cool water, his mind methodically sifted through all the things Tricia had told him about her husband-to-be. Fine and upstanding. Perfectly charming. Law-abiding—he discounted that one. And finally, *he's not anything.*

When faced with slander against her fiancé, what woman in love wouldn't come out and say, "Back off—I love the guy!"

Or something like that.

The kitchen doors swung open, and his sister stood there, hands on her slender hips, glaring at him. "Back off, Bill!"

Bill smiled. "Hi to you, too. Did Tricia send you in here?"

Sylvie shook her head and crossed to a stray plate of miniature powdered doughnuts, the kind Casey could eat by the bagful. Why would Tricia have those around?

"No, and you should be glad. She's a hair's breadth away from snapping." Sylvie popped a little doughnut in her mouth. "Honestly, are you trying to bust up her engagement?"

He lifted his shoulders, evading that question. He would leave the obvious busting up maneuvers to Casey and Tom. In fact, it was a shame he would have to ground Casey for a few days after this incident and cause his dynamic duo to lose precious time from such a worthy endeavor. "I thought you didn't want Tricia to marry this guy, either," he pointed out.

Sylvie grunted through a mouthful of doughnut. "This guy? Take a look at *this guy!*" She held out a photograph for him to inspect. It was the other half of the photo in the flyer; Bill could tell immediately because there was an outline of Tricia lopped out.

Gritting his teeth, he tried to eye the man impartially

but he felt a sharp sting of dislike for Tricia's fiancé, who was no great shakes as far as he was concerned. First of all, he was obviously too old for Tricia; also, he had a sharply receding hairline, a dark tan that screamed desperate male vanity, and an outfit Bill wouldn't be caught dead in. It was just a suit, but the coat was a weird shade of blue, his vest underneath was pastel with little geometric designs all over it, and his tie was some garish thing that would get any red-blooded man hooted out of Bee Lake.

"Isn't he gorgeous?"

At first, Bill thought his sister was kidding. But she had that shine in her eyes he'd seen so often before when she talked about some creature she was smitten with. Great. He'd always thought Sylvie would take his side in this. Now it was two against three. But two of his three were about to be grounded.

He shrugged. "I suppose. Sort of a suave Mel Cooley."

Sylvie punched him.

"Ouch! Okay, he looks all right for a man who ducks his parking tickets."

Sylvie tsked him and stared down at the picture. "He's a dreamboat. Look what a snappy dresser he is!"

Bill rolled his eyes. "Give me a break."

"Hey, that's important. You might get a date every once in a while, too, if you traded in your jeans and polo shirt look when you're not in uniform. You look like an escapee from 1989."

"Better than looking like a suntanned fop."

One of Sylvie's dark blond eyebrows arched sharply. "What's gotten into you?"

"What's gotten into you?" Bill shot back, a little

more heatedly than he'd intended. "I thought you wanted to play matchmaker."

"I did. For years I did." Sylvie appeared to struggle with this incongruity. "But Bill, have you seen Tricia?" She practically had tears in her eyes, and Sylvie was usually about as sentimental as a tin can. "She's happy, for God's sake. I've never seen her so happy. She's so bubbly, and dancing with every guy who asks, and so optimistic about her future."

"That's because there are all these people around," Bill pointed out. "All women get giddy during parties."

"You obviously didn't see her on prom night," Sylvie pointed out. "But, of course, hardly anyone did. She was only there twenty minutes."

"Teenagers go through bad patches."

"Tricia's first thirty years was a bad patch. But now she looks good, she feels good, and part of that has to be Manson." When Bill opened his mouth to object, she talked him down. "I'll admit I was skeptical to begin with, but now that I've seen Manson and talked to him—"

"Talked to him? When?"

"On the phone just a little while ago. Tricia was dancing with you, and Peggy was busy, so I took the call."

"What did he say?"

Sylvie shrugged. "Oh, you know, polite chitchat. Small talk. Heard-a-lot-about-you kind of things. He has a surprisingly sensual voice for a dentist."

Bill sighed in disgust. Traitor!

Sylvie chuckled to herself. "Also, he thought it was funny that I went to my high school graduation without any underwear."

"*What?*"

"Wipe that protective scowl off your lips. It was fourteen years ago. Ancient history."

"And how did he find out about this no-underwear incident?"

"Tricia told him." Sylvie put a hand on his arm. "You see, they must know so much about each other. They're intimate. He's her Lancelot, her lifeboat out of the choppy seas of singledom. As her best and oldest friend, I'm begging you. Cool your jets."

Fine thing when a guy couldn't even count on his sister to take his side. Bill stood there, his hands clutching into fists and then releasing, and tried to see the situation logically. Or at least through Sylvie's point of view. The wedding was in a week. Tricia was in love.

Was *he* in love?

He laughed to himself, letting a little of the bottled-up tension inside him fall away. He did tend to over-react sometimes, didn't he? Of course he was smitten with Tricia. She'd taken him by surprise. But Sylvie was one hundred percent correct. He didn't know the setup, and since he wasn't in love with her himself, it wouldn't be fair to simply blunder into Tricia's life, busting up a hope she had for happiness.

Tiny hope that it was.

He glanced down at Manson's perfect teeth and George Hamilton suntan and sighed. "Okay. I'll back off."

Sylvie gave him a sisterly pat. "Good cop. Have a doughnut."

He frowned down at the plate of powdered sugar and processed flour and scowled. "No policeman would be that desperate."

"YOU MEAN SHE'S still letting you skate around town?"

Tom nodded. "Yeah."

"And you're not grounded?"

"Nah. She'd only do that for something stupid, like if I flunked a class maybe."

Casey couldn't believe her ears. Here she was, practically a prisoner in her own home. Her dad had grounded her for a whole day—and it was a miracle it hadn't been more. She'd expected a week at least. But even so, for a whole day she couldn't watch television, couldn't play video games, couldn't even skate down her own driveway—and here was Tom wheeling around town when he'd done the exact same thing she'd done. It was so unfair!

"Your mom must be completely cool."

Tom screwed up his face. "Are you nuts?"

"I'm serious. I'll bet she's never heard of tough love." Not like her dad. She sank down on the leather couch in a sulk. "You should try having a cop for a dad."

"That'd be righteous."

"That's all you know." She smacked a piece of gum and thought what it would be like to have a mom. A real mom, not the absentee kind she had, who'd dumped her two years ago to run off to New Orleans with a race-car driver who Casey had dubbed Grease-ball Boyd. Casey had been to visit her a few times but she hadn't enjoyed herself in the tiny apartment her mom shared with the strange guy she couldn't help but resent. Greaseball Boyd wasn't as good-looking as her dad. He wasn't as friendly as her dad. Once Casey had asked her mom what she saw in him, and her mom had said adventure. Boyd had been her ticket out of Bee Lake. But couldn't she have just bought a ticket at the bus station and saved them both the trouble of having to listen to some guy belch in front of the television?

Tom frowned. "I can tell Mom's real mad at me, but she's afraid if she punishes me I'll hate skanky Manson even more. As if that was possible!"

Casey felt so bad for Tom. He probably disliked Manson as much as she disliked Boyd. Only at least her mother had just up and left one day, and it was all over quickly. Poor Tom was tied to the railroad tracks, with nothing to do but watch the stepfather train barreling down on him. "I'm sorry our plan backfired, Tom. Especially now that I know your mom is so nice."

"Huh?"

"She didn't ground you," Casey reminded him. "And even though I could tell she was mad at me, she gave me the powdered doughnuts to take home, plus all the money I'd chipped in for the food."

"She was just afraid if she didn't give the doughnuts back she'd eat them herself."

"Still." Casey shrugged. How could you make a kid understand how lucky he was? "Your mom leaves you alone. My dad watches me like a hawk. He tries not to let me know, but it's hard not to figure out you're being watched when a police cruiser follows you home from school every day."

Tom laughed. "He does that?"

"Yeah, he stays about a block behind so I won't notice."

"It would be cool to have a dad who was a cop instead of..."

He didn't finish. Poor Tom. She wished she could loan him her father for a while. He was strict but he really wasn't so bad, she supposed.

"I know how you feel. I wish I had a mom like yours. At least your mom didn't set her sights on Greaseball Boyd. My dad's been so lonely."

They stared at each other in shared misery. His mom, about to marry a geek. Her lonely dad...

Slowly, both of them straightened. And blinked. His mom? Her dad?

If they'd been cartoons, lightbulbs would be shining over their heads. Casey felt her lips pull into a huge smile, and she jumped up in excitement.

"Omigod! That's it!"

Tom shook his head worriedly. "I don't know..."

"Come on! It would be so cool! You said you didn't want your mom to marry Manson, right?"

"Yeah, but—"

"And you said my dad was cool, right?"

"Sure."

"So what's the problem?"

"Our last plan didn't work out so well."

"Haven't you ever heard of try, try again?"

"Haven't you been grounded for long enough?"

Casey laughed. "We got it all wrong last time. None of those guys were right for your mom. But Dad would be. He's really good-looking—even Aunt Sylvie says so, and she hardly ever admits anything nice about anybody out loud." Tom's reluctance was written all over his face. "You could live right here, near your grandma, and we could hang out together. Changing schools wouldn't be so bad, because you'd already know somebody. Wouldn't that be better than going to school in Los Angeles? There are gangs there, even in seventh grade. You could be viciously attacked while you were just standing at your locker or eating lime Jell-O in the cafeteria. You wouldn't want that, would you?"

Tom's face registered the full horror of her green-Jell-O-and-torture scenario. He was swayed, she could tell.

"And wouldn't having your mom marry my dad be better than having her marry a geeky dentist?"

Slowly he nodded. "Definitely."

She felt a rush of excitement. "Yes! This is gonna be so cool!"

"But how is it going to work?" Tom asked. "I mean, it's not like your dad and my mom are best buddies or anything."

Casey pursed her lips. "No, but Bee Lake is real small. It's pretty likely they could bump into each other...with a little help. Get it?"

Tom grinned in understanding. "Got it."

6

"BLAME TOM if you want to," Peggy said. "Personally, I had a good time."

She was sweeping up the last traces of crumbs from the living room and humming "Misty" under her breath. Every time Tricia heard the song, she felt tense and fluttery, as if Bill were still holding her, still looking at her. She had the strangest urge to call him and rehash the party. He'd stayed until it was almost over, even danced a few more times, though not with her.

But, of course, calling him would be silly. His attitude toward her engagement was so infuriating! Why should she want to talk to a man who only exasperated her? Also, Sylvie had promised her that she would persuade Bill to lay off. She didn't want to do anything that might have Deputy Dawg swooping down on her again.

Her mother's high, warbly version of "Misty" rose in intensity, setting her nerves on edge. She had to stop thinking about Bill. "Mom, could you please *not* play Misty for me?"

Peggy leaned on her broom, eyeing her closely. "What are you so wound up about?"

"Nothing."

"Yes, you are, I can tell. You've been sitting on that couch in that slouchy T-shirt you say passes as a nightgown for a half hour now, doing nothing but staring into space and snapping at anyone who says boo. It's like you're sixteen again—not a moment in time I care to relive.''

"Me neither."

Her mother shook her head. "Well if you won't tell me what's wrong, I wish you'd get some nicer nighties so at least you'd look better when you bit my head off."

Tricia winced. It *was* as if she were sixteen again.

"Do you wear that T-shirt when you're with Mason?"

"Manson."

"Of course it's no skin off my nose if you spend your honeymoon looking like Archie Bunker. But I've never yet heard of a man who was turned on by a woman in a tatty T-shirt and old underwear."

"For your information, I bought some very nice things for Jamaica."

"Good. You've been so long finding a man, I'd hate to see you lose this one for lack of a decent negligee."

"Please keep your voice down, Mom. I want Tom and Manson to get along, but Tom is resentful of him. I try not to mention the honeymoon too much."

"Well, maybe you should consider that when you dress. You certainly don't want Tom to be without a father because you have no fashion sense."

Spoken by the woman in the nylon orange workout suit!

"You didn't seem so worried about my not having a father, if I recall correctly."

Her own father had run out on them when she was six. Peggy had worked as a school bus driver and at other jobs to make ends meet, but most of their lives had been touch and go. Growing up, Tricia had yearned for a man to come into their lives and make her feel as if she was part of a real family like everybody else's, or at least like the ones on television, which seemed to be where all the normal people lived anyway. But though Peggy had a few men friends, she was fiercely independent. Tricia sometimes thought that was why she herself had married Roy so early, mistake that it was. She'd wanted *someone* to get married.

Her mother shrugged. "Well, I suppose you know what you're doing with this wedding." She cackled. "I only wish I did! Did I tell you the caterers want to dye the deviled eggs? Say it'll look summery. I think it will just look peculiar!"

At least they agreed on something.

"And the battle with Julie Tuttle rages on." She sighed. "Honestly, Pattie, between your oily dress and our Karen Carpenter-loving organist and blue deviled eggs, I sometimes wonder if this wedding will ever come off."

"Me, too."

Peggy looked startled. "Oh, dear—you're having second thoughts!"

Tricia stiffened. "No, I'm not."

"Really? Well, thank heavens for that! After all the work we've done, I'd hate to see you bug out."

Tricia laughed. A little too forcibly. "How silly!"

Jet-black brows rose ominously. "It's happened before. It ain't over till the fat lady sings, you know."

"Why is it everything always boils down to weight?"

Peggy barked out a laugh. "Okay, so it's not over till the thin lady says 'I do.'" She squinted. "You *are* going to say 'I do,' aren't you?"

"Of course. I'm completely in love with Manson."

Peggy nodded. "Good. That's a load off my mind. I thought from the simpering way you kept looking at

Bill Wagner today that you might still have a little crush on him.''

Tricia froze. Had she been that obvious? Who else had noticed?

Had Bill?

Peggy leaned back and picked up the TV remote. She zapped on Letterman.

Tricia felt queasy inside during the opening monologue. Lame jokes about the president weren't going to stop her thinking about Bill. Nothing would, she feared.

Until Tom came out of his room, screaming at the top of his lungs and barreling down on them like a runaway locomotive.

''Prowler! Everybody hide! The house is being broken into!''

He dove over the couch back, landing between Peggy and Tricia with one last shriek.

Tricia's heart stopped. ''What makes you think—''

''I saw him!'' Tom's chest heaved as he attempted to catch his breath. ''Outside my window!''

Peggy hopped up and scurried to the phone.

''I already called 911,'' Tom said. ''They're on their way!''

Her mother then veered toward a window, panicking Tricia. ''Don't, Mom, they might see you.''

''Good. Do I want a prowler to think the house is empty?''

''But what if he has a gun?''

Tom bounced up and down excitedly. ''He does have a gun—I saw it!''

Tricia gasped. Gun-wielding goons, here in Bee Lake? ''Are you sure?'' she asked Tom. Of course, *she* wasn't going to go near those windows to find out.

"Yeah, and he was wearing one of those whatcha-macallits—"

"A ski mask?" Tricia asked.

"Yeah!"

"Here comes the police car," Peggy announced as she peeked through the curtain.

"Did they send Officer Wagner?" Tom asked.

Peggy squinted into the window pane. As usual, she was calm in a crunch. "No...just Joe and that young Clark fellow. You remember him, Pattie—he's very good-looking. Married, of course."

Lannie Clark. Tricia groaned, the nerve factor grinding up another notch.

Her mother laughed and clasped her hands together. "Oh, I remember. He used to call you Bacon Butt in school. You couldn't stand him!" She kept chuckling as Tricia tried to hotfoot it out of the room.

But her mother threw open the door on the first official sounding knock, sending Tricia diving behind the couch.

"Hello, Mrs. Parker. We had a report of an intruder," said a voice that was sheer blast from her past.

"That was from my grandson." Peggy presented Tom. "He's my daughter's boy. You remember Tricia." She gestured toward the couch, behind which Tricia was half squatting, praying the man who had once been one of her most vocal taunters would not be able to see her butt now, bacon-like or not.

"Sure, I..." Blue eyes stared glassily at her. He *was* good-looking, Tricia thought, which just proved that there was no justice to be had in this world. When the former odious seventh grader recognized her, he almost dropped his hat. *"Pat?"*

"She's not Pat anymore," Peggy said in a stage

whisper. "She started calling herself Tricia years ago. Isn't that odd?"

Lannie just kept gaping at Tricia.

She tweedled her fingers in a wave. "Hi," she said, then she looked pointedly over at her mother. "Mom, maybe you and Tom should show the gentlemen where he saw the intruder. Remember him?"

Peggy nodded. "Of course!" She shuffled the men and Tom out the door, but Tricia could still hear her telling the men, "You'll have to excuse my daughter. She was moping around in her panties when the crisis hit."

Tricia buried her head in her hands. Same hometown, same mom, same humiliation. Was a wedding really worth it?

Ten minutes later, the incident was over. "The intruder must have seen Tom call the police and been scared away," her mother guessed.

"I swear I saw him," Tom insisted for the twentieth time.

"We believe you," Tricia assured him. "You did the right thing."

"I bet Officer Wagner would have got here sooner. Don't you, Mom?"

At the mention of Bill, she felt her stomach clench. For fifteen minutes, she'd actually forgotten him, but now his image came rushing back to her and was sure to be there as she tossed and turned on her pillow. "I'm surprised he didn't pop up."

"He would have caught the guy!"

"Isn't it funny how all conversation leads back to Bill?" Peggy asked.

Tricia threw a warning glance over at her mom. "I think after all this excitement we all need to go to bed."

Back in her old room, however, there was no hope of sleep. Tricia's heart was still racing from the intruder episode—or was her tension leftover from the party? She was also worried about her oil-stained dress. She would have to fess up to Sylvie tomorrow. But she just couldn't get a moment of shut-eye. Her mind relentlessly jumped from the intruder to Bill to her wedding dress...then to Bill again.

How was she going to explain the oil stain to Sylvie?

What was that noise outside her window? She wondered whether she should call Lannie back.

Bill's blue eyes were better looking than Lannie's blue eyes. Why was that?

Would that stain put a screeching halt to her friendship with Sylvie?

She should have checked the locks again.

She should have told Sylvie in the first place.

She shouldn't have danced with Bill.

She shot up in bed. She *had* heard a noise!

She jumped out of bed, shoved her feet into the sneakers she'd worn that evening, and tiptoed toward her window, heart beating like a wild animal's. Someone was out in the yard, she was sure of it. Someone had peeped into her window!

A shadow moved in the darkness, and she jumped back. Hunkering down, she raced toward the living room and the nearest phone, but stopped short of picking up the receiver. Two false alarms in one night might make them think something screwy was going on here. She turned, searched for a weapon and grabbed the fireplace poker. Its heaviness was reassuring, as was its pointy tip.

Stealthily, so as not to wake her mother and Tom or tip the intruder off to her presence, she opened the front door and sneaked out without a sound. She hoped. As she crept around the house, however, she began to worry. What if the person she'd seen had circled the house and was now *behind* her? Terrified by the prospect of being jumped from the rear, she flattened herself against the house's cedar siding and shuffled crabwise toward her bedroom window.

It was probably nothing, she thought, clenching her poker as she circled tightly around the camellia bush by her window. Probably just a coon or a possum. Or even just a cat. Silly to get all riled up over nothing but a—

Her right shoulder smashed against something firm but definitely human. Tricia let out a cry that was half battle cry, half Curly whoop straight from The Three Stooges. She whirled, arms noodly with fear yet poised to do battle with her fireplace implement. Adrenaline coursed through her body, and though her eyes couldn't focus in the darkness, she took a mighty swing. The poker missed its human target and thunked against the house.

"Hey!" a voice hissed. "Watch it with that thing!"

Tricia squinted into the darkness, trying to see the face behind the familiar voice of the intruder.

The blinding bulb of a flashlight shone in her eyes. "It's me, Tricia."

The light blinked off, and Tricia sagged against the wall in relief. "Bill! Thank heavens!"

He pulled the poker out of her hands and lectured sternly, "You could put a person's eye out with this."

"That was the idea!" She was still waiting for her heartbeat to calm down, but when she finally was able to focus on Bill's blue eyes glinting in the darkness, that ornery muscle kept galloping along. "What are you doing here?"

"I was driving in my cruiser on the highway with the radio on and I heard you had an intruder."

Because it was dark, they were whispering. "I thought you were the prowler!" And come to think of it, he did happen to be prowling underneath her bedroom window. "Why didn't you knock on the front door?"

"The lights were out. I deduced you'd all gone to bed."

Tricia grunted. "Bee Lake's own Sherlock Holmes."

"I wanted to make sure the intruder didn't come back."

"Well he w. 't now if he has any sense. This camellia bush is already overpopulated."

Bill's deep chuckle rumbled toward her through the dark. It was strange to be standing here with him in shadow, the thick, fragrant night air swirling around them on a barely-there breeze. She couldn't see much more than his silhouette, except his eyes...the outline of his jaw...the glint of his teeth as he smiled at her. Pinpricks of awareness shimmied down her spine, making her stand up taller and inch away from him a little.

He, in turn, inched toward her. "I would have figured you for the call-the-police-first type."

"Well, now you know. I'm the chase-them-with-the-poker type."

"Brave," he said, a label that would have made her flutter with pride if she hadn't suspected he was kidding.

"Maybe when you grow up running the gauntlet of fat jokes every morning even before you get through the schoolhouse door, it steels your nerves a little."

Bill let out a rueful laugh but said nothing for a moment. For some reason, Tricia felt the anxious need to fill the silence. Especially since he was so close to her she could almost hear him breathing. She felt antsy. "Of course, you probably wouldn't know anything about that."

"What?"

"About being tortured at school. You were Mr. Heartthrob."

"Was I?"

His deep voice unnerved her. It didn't help that at that moment she remembered she was still in just her T-shirt and sneakers. Why hadn't she slipped on some shorts?

He lifted a hand to touch her hair, which seemed like the first time he'd touched her not just in a friendly way, or accidentally. There was nothing accidental about the sexy gleam in his eyes, either. Any nerve ending that had possibly slept through the past hour sprang to life now. He intended to kiss her, sooner or later.

God help her, she hoped it was sooner.

"Was I your heartthrob, Tricia Parker?"

Her pulse raced, and a great jittery gob clogged her throat, choking her voice. "Peterson..." she gasped out. "It's Peterson now."

His hand fluttered down to rest on her hip. "'A rose by any other name would smell as sweet...'"

Shakespeare. Dear heaven, she was lost!

She didn't even wait for him to take the initiative. She'd waited for him to do that for thirty-two years and it had gotten her absolutely nowhere. Older and more foolish now, she simply hurled herself at him in the darkness, attaching herself to him, her lips seeking his like a cruise missile after its target. She'd anticipated this moment for so long yet she wasn't half prepared for the explosive power of it.

Bill didn't disappoint. His lips were warm and firm, yet giving—just perfect. He expertly slanted his head, allowing her to explore this fount of perfection. Their tongues touched, danced. In those glorious moments, Tricia was unhooked from reason. Bill was all there was. Bill, and his lips, and the firmness of his body as she glommed on to his shoulders, then his neck. She ran her fingers through his short, thick hair—God how she'd always wanted to do that! She reveled luxuriously in the thatch of short soft bristles like Ivana Trump might savor a new mink, her hands gliding over the strands, then combing back through them reverently.

And that was just his hair. What she could feel of the rest of him promised a whole new world to explore. His chest pressed into hers, and she remembered the fleeting surreptitious glances she'd managed to catch of it in high school, when he was Bee Lake lifeguard or coming off the football field. Was it still muscled and smoothed, abs washboard tight? If what she felt through the thin cotton of his shirt was any indication, the answer was affirmative. His legs, as they tangled with hers, felt strong and sturdy, which was good, since her knees were so weak they never could have held her up on their own.

And then there were his lips. They alone could provide years of exploration. His mouth was warm and giving, the center of her concentration, which is why she groaned in displeasure when he pulled away from her. Sensing her disappointment, he kissed her again, then, pulling her hips more tightly to him, rained kisses down her chin and neck.

Her concentration flew south, where his hands were just discovering what his eyes had apparently missed. Namely, that she had no pants on. His hands massaged her thighs and skimmed the hem of her T-shirt, then traced the elastic barrier of her panties. She sighed and melted into him as he coaxed a fire in her she'd long considered doused; she in turn clawed at his shirt, pulling it from his pants, running her hands beneath it to feel the smooth warmth of his skin. It was like a relief to have skin against skin, and yet it wasn't enough, not nearly enough for either of them. In unison they tilted against the wall behind them, needing it for support as bodies became an awkward tangle of intertwined legs and arms.

Teenagers, she thought. They were behaving like teenagers making out in the back seat, driving themselves to the point of no return. Home plate. And just minutes before they'd never kissed, had only flirted. She began gasping for breath, for reason. Warning lights went off in her head, red and white strobing lights... They seemed so real!

"Uh-oh."

When Bill followed this remark with a muttered curse, her eyes blinked open, then squinted against the red light blaring through the darkness. Its source was the top of a police car. A car door slammed, and footsteps crunched toward them.

"Okay, hands up!!!"

The voice of Lannie Clark, coming back to haunt her again!

Quickly, Bill untangled them. Lights from surrounding houses winked on. Curtains pulled back in curiosity. Behind them, the window opened just as Lannie's flashlight beam spotlighted Bill shoving his shirttail in and Tricia snapping her panties into place.

"Oh my God!" Lannie yelled in surprise, his exclamation accompanied by a sharp bark of a laugh from behind them.

Tricia twisted to glare at her mother, whose head poked out the window.

Lannie began backing off, though he apparently didn't have the presence of mind to turn off his flashlight. "Sorry, Bill."

"No problem," Bill snapped irritably.

It was the first time she'd ever heard him speak sharply to anyone. But, given the circumstances, a man could be excused for being a little on edge.

Lannie cleared his throat, and stammered, "See, we had another call...."

"Oh! That was me," Peggy explained. "I heard a noise. I had no idea..." She laughed.

"Mother!"

Bill let out a ragged breath. "You can cut the light, Lannie."

"Oh! Sure!" The world went blessedly dark again. "Sorry."

Though Tricia doubted any amount of darkness could hide her humiliation now. She was glowing with it. Could things get any worse?

In the next moment, Tom's head popped out next to Peggy's, and his young eyes bulged when he took in the scene. "Gee, Mom! What were you and Officer Wagner doing out there?"

"I SHOULD HAVE KNOWN this wedding was doomed!"

Tricia tried to calm her mother as they pulled into the church parking lot. "It's not doomed. I've told you. Last night was nothing. I was just going out to investigate the noise I'd heard and I ran into Bill, and he grabbed me, and one thing led to another..." Tricia's voice trailed off weakly.

Her mother parked her boat of a Buick in the lot, which was empty except for a Frank's Flowers van. "Darling, if you're not sure, maybe we shouldn't be planning the flower arrangements today."

"Of course I'm sure," Tricia said as they got out of the car. "It was just an innocent little kiss."

"Well, there's one consolation. If the ceremony doesn't come off, we'll at least be spared hearing 'Close to You' on an organ."

"I'm getting married Saturday," Tricia insisted as they traipsed toward the church. "End of story."

Peggy shook her head. She was wearing her best nylon jogging suit—hot pink—for the task ahead. "All right. You won't hear me say another word. But if something goes wrong, I hope you have a plan for those ten dozen pastel-dyed deviled eggs."

"Mother, if something goes wrong, I'll probably eat them all myself."

They walked on in silence for a few moments until Peggy let out a chuckling sigh. "Oh, well, I suppose you have one less thing to worry about at least. I don't guess Lannie'll be calling you Bacon Butt anymore."

Tricia pursed her lips. "I don't have anything to worry about anyway, except what kind of flowers we're going to decorate the church and reception hall with."

"And what you're going to say to Sylvie about that dress."

The reminder of that chore was like a punch to the gut. "Oh, yeah."

"And what you're going to say to Bill the next time you see him."

Double punch! "I'm not going to see him." Her voice bristled with resolve.

But her mother didn't look convinced. "How are you going to manage that? Bee Lake isn't Baton Rouge, you know. You're bound to bump into each other."

"I don't see why."

"Dear heart, he's Sylvie's brother."

She shrugged. "Even if I do see him, there's no reason I should get all out of joint about it. He's just a friend."

"Whatever you say, Pattie."

Tricia set her mouth in a grim line and tried to get her thoughts in order. "Let's just concentrate on flowers, Mom." And forget about Bill and their moonlight camellia bush tussle.

They entered the church, a small window-filled building that brought back a flood of memories. Mostly of sitting in itchy dresses, waiting for the sermon to end so she could go home, read the funnies and have a big breakfast. But she'd always loved the neat rows of simple oak pews leading up to the elaborate altar backed by a stained-glass window of Jesus's baptism. Back then she'd always thought the depiction made Jesus and John the Baptist look like long-haired seventies rock stars, but now the resemblance eluded her. It was simply a beautiful piece of stained glass, and the space around her stirred much more reverent feelings in her.

"You'll have to say 'I do' to him."

A shiver went through her as Bill's words came back unbidden. What was the matter with her today? She loved Manson. He was the best thing that had ever happened to her. She'd known Bill Wagner for thirty-two years, and he'd never said two words to her until three days ago, whereas Manson had been smitten at first sight. Manson was intelligent and handsome and successful....

Not that Bill wasn't. And there was definitely something admirable about a man who stayed in his hometown, serving his community, and was satisfied with his life. It showed a well-adjustedness that Tricia feared she could only aspire to. Bill was also undeniably intelligent. Salutatorian of his class. Sylvie said he did well in college, too. And as for looks—

"Tricia!"

Tricia popped back to consciousness to find her mother and Frank's wife, Trudy, staring impatiently at her. How many times had they called her name?

"Good grief! Where were you?"

Tricia feared her blush would give her away.

Trudy giggled and nudged Peggy. "Maybe the bride was thinking about that long walk down the aisle toward her number one man."

Peggy coughed to cover a laugh, slanting Tricia a knowing glance. "Whoever that might be."

Trudy chuckled. "Now where shall we start? Rose clusters at the end of the pews? Daylilies?"

Tricia tried to concentrate. "That sounds fine."

The florist blinked. "Well which—roses or lilies?"

"How about camellias?" Peggy piped in with a broad wink toward Tricia that perky Trudy missed completely.

"What a terrific idea, Peggy! Camellias!"

"Roses," Tricia contradicted.

Her decisive tone took a little of the perk out of Trudy. "What color?"

"Pink." Tricia was in no mood to shilly-shally,

which probably was the reason she let Trudy talk her into another terrific idea.

"I think a really neat thing is when two sprays spelling out the bride and groom's names are put at the front of the church. That way the guests can remember which is the bride side, and which is the groom side."

Peggy laughed. "And what their names are."

"That, too!" Trudy said, effusing such enthusiasm that she wore Tricia down.

A fire truck's siren wailed down the street, coming closer. Trudy's brow puckered worriedly. "Oh, dear. I hope someone's house isn't on fire."

"Sounds like it's coming this way."

They ran to the front of the church. Sure enough, the town's big red fire engine was pulling up in front of them, followed by two police cars. Tricia's heart did a worrisome trip, and for an absurd moment she was held in suspense. Would he be there or wouldn't he?

Bill got out of the first cruiser as the firemen went running up the church steps. So much for avoiding the man! Her lips pulled into a smile, then were forced into a passive expression, then pulled into another grin as his blue eyes glinted at her. Her cheeks flooded with warmth, and suddenly her stomach felt as if she were in a runaway elevator.

Lon Hanson, the fire chief, spoke to Peggy. "Where's the fire?"

Peggy, Trudy, and Tricia exchanged puzzled glances, then gazed back at the man in confusion.

"I don't have a clue," Peggy said.

"We had a report of a fire in this church." He looked at them all. "Someone saw smoke?"

Tricia caught Bill staring at her. Their gazes met and held.

"There's no fire here," Peggy said.

Maybe not, there but there was something simmering in Bill's eyes. They burned into hers until Tricia thought she might melt into the sidewalk. With effort, she forced herself to focus on Lon, who was scratching his chin.

"I wonder who called in."

"Some kind of nut, probably," Peggy said.

Lon sighed. "Probably so..." He turned, waved off his troup and returned to his fire engine.

"Imagine!" Peggy exclaimed after the fire truck and one of the police cruisers had left, leaving only Bill standing below them. "I guess there are practical-joking nuts everywhere now. Even in Bee Lake!"

While Trudy and Peggy tsked over their rising crime problem, Bill cleared his throat to catch Tricia's attention. As if he'd ever lost it. He beckoned her over, then moved toward the privacy of a clump of azaleas.

Reluctantly, Tricia followed after him, stopping him short of his goal. "One more trip into the bushes with you would ruin my reputation forever."

He grinned, sending her heart on a wild roller coaster ride. "Sorry. I didn't mean to put your virtue in jeopardy."

She arched a brow skeptically. "Is there something you wanted to say to me?"

He'd already apologized last night, albeit in a very backhanded way. *"I'm sorry I can't say I'm sorry that happened,"* he'd said after the neighborhood had turned out its lights again and gone to sleep. *"That's a first kiss I'll never forget."*

Which made it sound as if there would be others. And there certainly wouldn't be, if she could help it. She reminded herself of the necessity of refraining from kissing him as he scratched his jaw thoughtfully. His strong, perfect jaw. A sharp ache pierced her.

"I wanted to talk to you about these incidents," he said.

Tricia sighed. "I know, I know. We just need to avoid each other, Bill."

"What?"

She rushed on. "If we keep meeting up spontaneously on the street and in bushes, it's just going to be the same thing all over again. Maybe it's just bridal nerves, or maybe I'm just reliving a childhood crush for some odd reason...."

Bill looked uncomfortable. "Tricia, I—"

"Please don't apologize again. It's silly. We're adults, we can control ourselves. Believe me, I've vowed never to kiss you again, or even think about it, which will be harder but I'm sure I can manage."

His lips turned down in a frown. "I admire your resolve."

She squared her shoulders. "Good."

"But that wasn't what I wanted to talk to you about."

"It wasn't?" Fire burned in her cheeks.

He shook his head, grinning.

"Then for heaven's sake, why didn't you stop me!"

"Because I was too interested in what you were saying. Not that I agree one bit, mind you."

Her jaw clenched. "Will you get on with whatever it is you were going to tell me? Mom's been staring at us nervously now for five minutes."

"Okay." He nodded curtly, and a little frown pulled at his lips. His cop face. "I think I might know who's responsible for these incidents...meaning these calls to the fire and police stations."

Oh. *Those* incidents. Tricia felt like an idiot. "Who?"

Bill hesitated. "You might not like this...."

Tom! Tricia jumped to the most logical conclusion. *He's going to say they traced the calls to Mom's house.* She felt a stab of disappointment in anticipation of his words. "All right, go ahead. Who's the culprit?"

"Manson Toler."

7

TRICIA LAUGHED, which was Bill's first indication that she wasn't taking this problem seriously.

"Manson?" She held a hand to her lips.

"This isn't a laughing matter."

"No, of course not," Tricia retorted. "It's obvious I'm dealing with a lunatic."

"At least you're beginning to see reason."

"You, Bill! You're the lunatic!" she exclaimed. "You'd have to be crazy to think that Manson would ever think of pulling these silly stunts—and from all the way in California? Why would he do that? You've got the wrong man."

He shook his head. "Pardon me, but I think you have."

When it came to men, most women, like his sister, refused to listen to reason, but he'd expected better from Tricia. Well, he hated to burst her bubble, but... "I've got some information about your fiancé that might make you change your mind about Dr. Toler. Things he probably hasn't told you."

She crossed her arms, eyes flashing. "Did you dig up some more traffic violations? Maybe a ticket for forgetting to signal—I heard you used that against one of Sylvie's love interests to great effect."

Bill stiffened reflexively, a little embarrassed by that reminder. He should have known Sylvie would blab about that incident. "That man was a very unsavory character—and he did forget to signal. On a left-hand turn, too. Very dangerous.''

She let out a long breath and looked up at him, head shaking. ''All right, let's have it. What has Manson done that's so terrible.''

''I assure you, it has nothing to do with traffic tickets. This information is of a personal nature.''

Her eyes narrowed, which made him wonder whether she wasn't a little more curious—and doubtful—than she wanted to appear. ''I'm listening.''

''Well, for one thing, your Manson has been married before. Twice.''

Tricia paled.

''One of the times was to a woman of questionable character,'' Bill went on. ''She did time for robbery.''

She was silent for a moment, though her mouth hung open in apparent astonishment. ''Who told you this stuff?''

''A reliable source.''

''Who?''

Bill wasn't certain Tricia was going to like this, but he couldn't lie. ''Well, I've got a friend who's a detective in L.A. He's as honest as the day is long.''

''I'll bet!''

''I can see you're a little surprised.''

''Only by your nerve.''

''Then you knew about the wives?''

''Of course I knew! Do you think I wouldn't have asked if he'd ever been married? Do you think he wouldn't have told me? And since when in this Liz Taylor age has being divorced twice been a sin?''

''It's not, although it does mean he's a two-time loser at the marriage game.''

Her sharp chin jutted upward. ''Well maybe he'll be third time lucky.''

"What about the wife in jail?"

"Your Sam Spade out in L.A. only got half the story," Tricia informed him. "She was arrested for shoplifting a miniskirt when she was seventeen. Her parents left her in the clink overnight to teach her a lesson. I would think you of all people would approve of that method."

"Oh."

Bill felt a little silly now. He'd overreacted again. What was it about Tricia that made him commit these blunders? Chasing a woman, kissing her in bushes...that wasn't his style. All his life he'd been levelheaded when it came to women. When his wife had run off with another man he'd taken it on the chin and let her go, salvaging what he could of his life and going on from there. He'd been on a perfectly even keel until three days ago, when he'd seen Tricia pinned to her car.

"I'm sorry," he confessed. "You're right. I jumped to conclusions."

His apology seemed to beat a lot of the fire out of her. She bridled like a fighter who'd just knocked out his opponent with the first punch of the first round. "That's okay. I suppose you meant well."

"No, I didn't."

She looked up at him. "You did it maliciously?"

"I meant to bust you and Manson, I'm ashamed to say." He felt humbled by the admission. "I'm afraid Sylvie's characterization of me as the wrecker of romances is true. But only when I care about the person involved."

She looked into his eyes and desire hitched in his chest. "I'd like us to be friends, Bill. Will that ever be possible?"

Friends.

He stubbed his toe in the dirt, knowing the bitterness of the second-place finisher receiving the consolation prize. Friendship would be his year's supply of Rice-A-Roni. "Of course," he agreed. "Let's see...you've already got Sylvie and Mr. Wonderful. What kind of friend are you lacking?"

"I don't know...." Her eyes looked off dreamily. "I guess just somebody else to laugh with. The kind of pal you used to have pre-parental responsibility. Remember?"

"Barely." Besides he'd thought Manson would fulfill that role.

"The days of wine and roses—before I was concerned with things like baseball practice and PTA meetings." Tricia laughed. "Oh, well. I'm only here for five more days, and they're jam-packed. Please don't think you have to keep me company, Bill, because you don't."

"Because you don't want us to kiss again," he guessed.

Blotches of pink colored her face. "I just don't want you to feel obligated."

"To kiss you?" He smiled. "I wouldn't. I might feel compelled to, though."

"I meant to entertain me."

"But kissing is the best entertainment I know."

She huffed in exasperation. "You see? It's impossible, *You're* impossible!"

She turned on her heel and marched off toward Peggy. As she retreated, part of him longed to trot after her like a stray puppy, tireless in its need for affection. But Tricia had said affection was the one thing she didn't want from him, and Bill didn't want to push his luck.

Not just yet.

"THAT BROTHER OF YOURS! Honestly, Sylvie, he's half J. Edgar Hoover and half Pepe Le Pew."

As usual, Sylvie held a bundle of straight pins in her lips, so Tricia couldn't tell whether or not she was frowning at her brother's misdeeds. Frankly, she seemed more absorbed in the dilemma of the dress stain than the drama of Bill and Tricia. And Manson, Tricia reminded herself. She couldn't forget the most important player in this drama.

"So I take it my brother's approach isn't working?"

"Of course not! How could it? I'm practically a married woman."

The door between the living room and the kitchen where they were sitting rattled, making Tricia and Sylvie tense lest Tom and Casey burst through in a rush of wheeled energy. But nothing happened. In fact, Tricia could swear she heard whispering voices just on the other side of the door.

Sylvie looked at the door suspiciously, then shrugged. "Probably just a kid's football hitting the door or something. So what did you tell Bill?"

Tricia nodded. "That I'm going to marry Manson and that's that."

Sylvie cast her an ominous gaze. "As the saying goes, it ain't over till it's over."

Tricia buried her head in her hands. "Oh no, not you, too. Mother was saying the same thing—intimating that I was stuck on Bill and would ruin all her plans by not showing up to my own wedding, which is ridiculous. I just don't understand Bill. You told him to lay off, didn't you?"

Sylvie nodded.

"Then what's his problem? I was picking out flowers at the church today—his and hers altar sprays, for heaven's sake. Could it be any more obvious that I *want* to get married in five days? And even if I didn't, Bill doesn't strike me as a particularly fast worker, either. Not unless his *Dragnet* routine appeals to some women.''

"I don't know...." Sylvie grinned. "I find his persistence a little charming."

Tricia's mouth dropped open in astonishment. "*You?* You, who've had untold number of romances wrecked by this man?"

Sylvie shrugged. "That's different. In my case, he sends my men packing, and I'm left with nothing but a brother to go have pizza with. I don't know if I'd mind being wooed by both a handsome L.A. type *and* a hunky cop. That's a win-win situation."

"Except Manson is the only serious wooer in this situation. That brother of yours hasn't exactly been performing a hearts-and-flowers routine."

"C'mon," Sylvie said. "Aren't you just a little bit tempted?"

Tricia frowned at her friend's insistently inquisitive tone, one that she hadn't heard since their truth-or-dare days. And just as in those days, she felt compelled to tell the truth. "Okay—tempted, maybe. I suppose anyone would be. But..."

"But you're in love with Manson." Sylvie sounded almost disappointed. Maybe she thought being in love with one's fiancé was too unimaginative and humdrum.

"It's not just that," Tricia explained. "It's also a matter of style. Bill's been pestering me like a pesky flea, whereas Manson swept me off my feet."

For once in her life, Sylvie dropped her cynical shell and looked wistful. "He did?"

"In Cancun, it was romance with all the trimmings—flowers, candlelight dinners, walks on the beach. I was overwhelmed. I'd never had a big romantic love affair before. And since then, he's been the perfect gentleman, always calling, always picking up the check—believe me, after living with skinflint rock-'n'-roll Roy, that was new to me, too.''

''Sounds as if you're in love with romance.''

''What's the matter with appreciating a little show-manship? At least with Manson, I know it won't just be lust, then boredom. He'll work hard to keep the romance alive.''

''*He* will?'' Sylvie asked.

Tricia frowned. ''Well, of course, I won't have to work at it. I care for him deeply.''

''Uh-huh.''

''Oh, now don't you get started. You're just rooting for your brother—it's nepotism, pure and simple. But excuse me for preferring the hearts-and-flowers approach over the sneaking-through-the-bushes-and-scare-you-half-to-death approach. I'm just funny that way.''

''Okay. Enough said. The good-looking rich guy wins. What's new?''

Tricia slanted a pleased glance at her. ''You really think he's good-looking?'' Sylvie's standards for male beauty were usually much more rigorous than her own, maybe because Sylvie was beautiful enough herself to be choosy. But Tricia had never heard her cite Manson's type as desirable.

''His face has personality, and he dresses well. That little paunch in his tummy is sort of endearing, I think. And when I talked to him on the phone, he made me laugh.''

Tricia smiled. ''He has a good sense of humor—unpredictable, too. He likes Hong Kong action movies and Woody Allen. He'll watch nature shows and *The*

Simpsons. He reads dental periodicals and British mysteries.''

''Hmm.'' Sylvie looked deep in thought, which made Tricia wonder if she hadn't given her a very good description of Manson. Although she'd always thought Sylvie was a big British mystery enthusiast herself. At least, that's what she always picked up at the bookstore when she came to Baton Rouge.

''I know you'd like him.''

Sylvie took the pins out of her mouth and grinned. ''You don't have to sell him to me. The sweep-me-off-my-feet whirlwind approach would be my choice, too.''

''DAD, HAVE YOU EVER swept a woman off her feet?''

Bill choked on his hamburger. One minute he and Casey had been sitting in the restaurant in comfortable silence—which really meant that he had been day-dreaming again about Tricia—then out popped this question. He gulped down some water, tried to regain his composure and put on his best concerned-father expression. ''Why do you ask?''

She shrugged her thin shoulders and tossed her braid. ''Mrs. Peterson was talking about it today.''

Tricia? Bill leaned back a little, fussing with a tomato that had dislodged from his burger, and tried not to appear as interested as he was. ''What did she say, exactly?''

Casey leaned forward conspiratorially. ''Well, she and Aunt Sylvie were talking. Aunt Sylvie asked her why on earth she would marry a geek like Manson Toler—you know, the dentist guy—and Mrs. Peterson said that he had swept her off her feet. She said how he had taken her to dinner a lot, and given her flowers, and said they'd walked on the beach a bunch. I guess that's what she meant by sweeping her off her feet, but it doesn't sound very unusual to me, except of course the part about being on the beach. That probably makes a big difference." She frowned. "Is that how *you* would sweep a person off their feet, Dad?"

Bill cleared his throat to cover a laugh. "I'm a little rusty on the exact procedure, but it's something like that."

Casey tilted her head, clearly not satisfied. "Oh, and there was another thing. He paid for dinner. She said that was a switch." Casey pinned her gaze on him expectantly. "You would pay for dinner, wouldn't you?"

He chuckled. "Unless I'm out with an eavesdropper. Hope you brought some cash."

Casey crossed her arms and leaned back in the booth. "I can't help it if I just happen to be in the next room when Aunt Sylvie and Tom's mother are talking real loud."

"Of course not."

"Besides, now I can tell Tom for sure that his mom's a liar."

"Why?"

"Because his mom said that you didn't know how to sweep a woman off her feet."

He'd been on the verge of giving Casey a lecture on privacy, but now all his *Father Knows Best* impulses flew out the window. "They were talking about me? What did they say?"

"Well, they were talking about your technique with women...."

"And?"

Casey pursed her lips. "Do you watch *Dragnet* a lot, Dad?"

He laughed in spite of himself. "I get the picture."

"But she was wrong, wasn't she? You're at least as good as some geeky dentist."

It pained him to be reasonable on this issue. "Well…it depends. Don't forget that we've never met this geek—er, this dentist. He might be a very nice man."

"Tom doesn't think so."

"Well, Dr. Toler will be here in five days, and then we'll be able to see for ourselves, won't we?" *Five days…* Bill gnashed a bite out of his burger, which might have been made of cardboard for all the attention he was paying to it. He couldn't help it. He oozed misery. Regret sat in his heart like an open wound. He'd known Tricia all his life, practically. She was Sylvie's best friend—they talked all the time, and Sylvie went to visit in Baton Rouge every few months if not more. All the time, Tricia had been there. And where had he been?

Staring right through her, apparently. It shamed him to realize it. He'd never considered himself a bully, one of those kids who would taunt her with names like Pudgy Pat and Pork Rind. But maybe he'd been something worse—the peanut gallery the bullies played to, one of the kids who laughed and said nothing. And then, when he was older, Pat was barely a blip on his radar. When he thought of her at all it was as a chubby, slightly odd friend of his sister who would come over to the house and stare at him wordlessly. He'd always wondered why Sylvie hung around with her, but it never occurred to him to talk to her and find out for himself, even though Sylvie said often—as recently as sixth months ago, he remembered now—that he and she would have a lot in common. He'd laughed it off, carrying with him as he did the memory of Pudgy Pat.

He wasn't laughing now. Now he was slumped in a

diner booth with his daughter, five days away from
losing someone he'd never given a second glance until
three days ago. For the first time since Andrea had left
him, he felt loneliness deep in his bones.

"Dad?"

He glanced up. Casey was staring at him expectantly. "I'm sorry. What were you saying, Case?"

"Well, I was just saying that, to me, it didn't sound
like this Manson guy was offering that much. Just obvious stuff, and like maybe she wasn't used to it, and
that's why she's going to marry him. Tom says when
she and the geek are together, they don't talk that
much. That doesn't sound like true love to me. Does
it to you?"

"No." Poor Casey. She had no way of knowing she
was pouring salt on his wound. Upending a whole
shaker of the white stuff, actually. "But what you have
to understand, Case, is that we're only seeing half—"

"And if she was in love with him," Casey burst out,
interrupting his sentence, "why would she have told
Aunt Sylvie that she was tempted by you?"

Whatever he was going to say was zapped from his
mind like a fly hitting a bug light. His mouth was still
open to speak, but for the life of him he couldn't form
a word. Tempted? Did she say that? Really?

Casey obviously felt the need to fill the conversational void while his thoughts sprang from hope to cau-
tious optimism to flat-out exhilaration. "I think she
said that because she's not really in love with the dentist. Not true love, I mean." She let out a dramatic sigh.
"It's just like that Barbara Stanwyck movie we were
watching the other day, where Barbara gets jilted by
the good-looking guy and marries the dull boring guy
just cause he's convenient. That was so sad."

"Yes, it was."

"I just think it would be a crime for Tom's mom to marry that guy and never know true love. Don't you, Dad?"

"Yes, I do."

And what was his business, if not fighting crime?

PEGGY PARKER BUSTLED through her kitchen, batting Tricia's hand before it could pick up another luscious, powdered sugar-drenched lemon square. "Stop it! If you keep this up, my canasta group will starve and you'll never fit into your wedding dress."

The canasta group would never starve with the amount of sandwiches, Jell-O molds, desserts and dips piled on Peggy's counters. Even in her heyday, Tricia couldn't have tucked away that many calories. The dress was another issue. "There might not be a dress for me to fit into anyway."

"Well just in case there is, stop eating like Jabba the Hut."

Tricia sighed.

"And stop sighing. Don't you have anything to do tonight?"

"Not really."

Tom was with Casey. Her mother had a living room full of cardsharps disguised as little old ladies. Sylvie said she had something to do tonight—probably another date. In short, the whole world, with the exception of Tricia, was off having fun.

Peggy planted her hands on her hips and gave Tricia a disapproving frown she hadn't seen since the long summers of childhood when she'd whine to her mother about being bored. "Good heavens! I thought we were past this stage. *Find* something to do. Come play canasta."

Tricia smiled. "No thanks. I brought a book. I'll just go to my room and read."

"Have you called Madison yet?"

Manson had phoned twice while she was over at Sylvie's, but Tricia hadn't returned the calls. Somehow, she couldn't think of anything to say to him right now, and if she did speak to him, she was afraid something in her voice would give away the fact that she was having prewedding jitters. Which is surely all this really amounted to. There was no sense panicking Manson with any of her nonsense. "I think I'll call him back tomorrow."

"Suit yourself," Peggy said, picking up the pitcher of tea. But the look she shot her as she went back to her guests intimated that she thought Tricia's behavior was mighty peculiar.

Maybe it was. Wasn't it the groom who was supposed to be nervous? Wasn't Manson the one who should be getting cold feet at the idea of hurling himself into wedded domesticity with a woman he'd met on a beach and had really only seen a handful of times? Wasn't he the one who should be looking back with nostalgia, almost longing, upon his years of singlehood, which up until this moment had seemed miserable, frustrating and lonely? Wasn't he supposed to be worrying about spending the next forty or fifty years with a person who might have all sorts of annoying habits that would drive him absolutely wild in a matter of a few weeks, but once he discovered them it would be too late, too late, too late…?

Tricia's pulse raced. She was light-headed, and her skin felt clammy too. But feverish. Maybe she was having a heart attack. Should she call her mother? 911?

Reaching for the nearest first-aid treatment, she popped a forbidden lemon square in her mouth and waited for it to work its therapeutic magic on her. She chewed slowly, savoring the tart-sweet flavor, not even caring about the dusting of powdered sugar that sprinkled onto her T-shirt. For a blissful moment, nothing bothered her. She didn't care about the wedding. In fact, maybe if she didn't fit into her wedding dress, that would be a perfect excuse to call the whole thing off....

She swallowed and immediately felt disgusted with herself. What a horrible thought! Poor Manson—what would he do if he could read her mind? He'd dump her, that's what. And then where would she be? Her house was on the market, and she had signed the papers turning over her bookstore to her assistant, Marie. Her belongings were packed and ready to be shipped to California during her honeymoon. Everything was set, right down to her and Tom's medical records, which had been transferred to Manson's physician in Los Angeles.

Why would she even consider calling off her wedding? Why? Three days ago she was the luckiest, happiest woman in the world. What on earth was wrong with her?

A rap against the glass pane on the kitchen door nearly toppled her off the stool she was perched on. She went to the door and discovered Bill on the other side of it. Bill, in jeans, polished boots and a tweedy jacket and tie, looking very sexy. As usual. But tonight he appeared freshly scrubbed, shaved and combed, and the air around him was thick with the smell of piney soap. Tricia leaned against the doorjamb, propping herself up against the knee-weakening effect the man had on her.

He grinned and held out a bouquet of summer flowers obviously fresh-picked from his garden. They were wrapped in a paper towel decorated with blue ducks and tied around the stems with a rubber band. "Surprise."

Tricia laughed and took the flowers with pleasure, examining the pretty jumble of larkspurs, daisies and freesia. "Thanks."

When she looked back up at him, Bill's smile had dimmed a bit. "Did I catch you at a bad time? Were you cooking?"

Her black T-shirt made the perfect backdrop for the powdered sugar she'd just dribbled on herself. Tricia groaned. "Not cooking, consuming. Would you like something?" She beckoned him into the kitchen with its eye-popping display of food.

Bill hesitated. "Actually, I was sort of wondering if you might like to run out for a bite."

Tricia's heart lifted, but her mouth stammered out incoherent excuses. "Oh, I couldn't, you see, because...I—I don't know—"

"My treat," Bill said. "As a peace offering. I spoke to Sylvie, and she said that you'd seemed a little upset with me. I'd hate to leave it at that."

"Oh, but—"

"She's taking care of the kids."

So. That was the "something" Sylvie had to do tonight—what a trickster! But Tricia couldn't deny that she was restless. Even going out and resisting the temptation of Bill would be preferable to sitting in the kitchen alone with her nutty, reckless thoughts.

"Give me a minute to change?"

Bill nodded. "While you're gone, I'll just sample a few of Peggy's goodies. She'd probably be offended if I didn't."

Tricia chortled at his rationalization and dashed through the living room to her bedroom, where she rifled through her closet for something to wear. Unfortunately, most of what she'd brought were jeans, khaki slacks and T-shirts galore. But Bill was dressed up. The only nice things she'd packed, she'd intended for her honeymoon.

Biting her lip, she made a snap decision and snatched a little red dress made of slinky rayon with a flip skirt. She snipped the store tags off the sleeve and slipped it on before she could think of the implications of raiding her trousseau to go out with Bill. It was just a dress, after all. And maybe it was wise to wear it before the honeymoon. She wouldn't want to get to Jamaica only to discover one of her outfits was uncomfortable. She jammed her feet into a pair of sandals, ran a brush through her hair and made a quick stop at the bathroom to brush her teeth. Then she streaked across the living room so fast she hoped she was only a red blur to Peggy's eye.

"Be back later!" she sang out as she shot through the door to the kitchen. Then, not wanting to stop her forward trajectory, she grabbed Bill by the elbow and yanked him toward the back door. "Let's get out of here before my mom starts asking questions!"

Bill chuckled. "She might tell us to be back by ten."

An old Chevy convertible was parked at the curb. Tricia stopped, amazed.

"Did you think I would pick you up in a police cruiser?"

"No, but...isn't this the same clunker you got your senior year?" She imagined them having to propel it along with their feet, Flintstones-style.

Bill went rigid, prepared to defend the honor of his car. "It runs like a Porsche."

Tricia felt a lot more relaxed once they were finally ensconced in a quiet corner booth at Mazie's, a pretty good dive a couple of miles out on the highway leading to town. It felt good to be out of the house, and what was the harm? Manson wouldn't want her to be sitting at home bored. He wasn't. In fact, he and his L.A. buddies would be getting together this week for a bachelor party.

"I'm glad you came by." When he sent her a pleased smile that made her think he might have misinterpreted her remark, she clarified, "I was going a little buggy in that house. Too much thinking about wedding things. The wedding is always on my mind."

She wouldn't want him to think her decision to come out with him meant she was having second thoughts.

He tilted his head and sent her an understanding grin. "Weddings are quite a production. Did you get married in Bee Lake the last time?"

Sometimes she forgot that Bill had been married before, but of course he had. He'd married young, like her. And he'd been run out on, like her. And both of them had been left with the responsibility of raising a child on their own. It made her feel a kinship toward him.

"No, I didn't." She shrugged ruefully and confessed, "At the time I was terrified that if I got married here, in front of my mom's friends, Roy would leave me waiting at the altar. It seems silly now, but back then I was sure I would be humiliated in front of the whole town."

Bill didn't make fun of her odd mix of superstition and paranoia. "Andrea and I did the whole church bit with all the trimmings. The marriage wasn't any more successful than yours, though."

"It lasted longer."

"Maybe we had quantity, but not quality. When Andrea and I married, we'd barely dated anyone else. Everyone, ourselves included, just assumed the ex-jock

and the ex-homecoming queen belonged together. The
next ten years were like a slow realization that things
could have been different, until one day Andrea decided to shake everything up by running out on us.''

"Roy and I only limped along for a few months, and
then he did his Houdini routine and hasn't reappeared
since, except to send Tom a birthday card when he
remembers.''

"His loss.''

The two simple words were incredibly uplifting. Tricia took a sip of wine and basked in the gratification
of understanding company. Not to mention the company of the best-looking man she'd ever been in public
with. "I can't imagine a woman leaving you," she
blurted out before she could stop herself.

Bill laughed. "Thanks.''

"No, I mean it. You're so incredibly self-confident
and normal.''

His face scrunched in skepticism. "You should ask
Casey about that—although I suppose kids always
think their parents are weird.''

"That's because if they knew it was really the other
way around, their fragile psyches couldn't take it.''

Bill laughed. "But really, you make me sound disgusting. As if I'm perfect. I'm not.''

"I didn't say you were perfect," Tricia corrected.
"For instance, you've got this habit of trying to bust
up perfectly good relationships....''

He sputtered in protest, but she cut him off. "*All* of
Sylvie's boyfriends couldn't be that bad.''

"Couldn't they? Did she tell you about the one who
had three kids by two different women and had child
support in arrears?''

Tricia laughed. Only a professional would say *in arrears*. "I think she described him as the cool one.''

"And the man who was married?" Bill asked.

"A hunk."

"And the one who wanted to marry her for a green card?"

"Her exotic Latin lover." Tricia chuckled. "Okay, so maybe she's not the best judge of character. But she'll never learn if you don't let her make her own mistakes. Look at you and me—our first marriages were unwise. And we learned. And now…"

Her voice puttered out, and she realized she didn't have the fortitude to pitch her upcoming nuptials with her usual optimistic spin. Bill glanced away, taking a long silent swig of his iced tea. The muscles in his neck flexed as he swallowed—or maybe they were twitching from the effort of restraining himself from saying something disparaging about Manson. Tricia shifted uncomfortably, accidentally knocking her bare leg against the rough denim of Bill's. They tensed. Brown eyes met blue. Her leg retreated back to the proper side. The silence was grueling.

Bill put down his tea. "I just can't stand to see someone I love make a mistake."

She looked at him, wanting to ask him questions she knew she wouldn't like his answers to. *Did he mean he loved her, or was he still just thinking about Sylvie?*

Bill paid for the meal and they walked outside into the fresh night air. Tricia looked at her watch in dismay.

Bill glanced at her. "Is the night still young?"

"Yes, and my house will still be full of canasta players."

"Then let's kill some time. How long has it been since you've hit the hot spots of Bee Lake?"

"*Hot* spots? A vice squad would go out of business in this town."

"You'd be surprised."

Tricia laughed as she got into the front seat of the Chevy. There was something nostalgic about the way the backs of her legs stuck to the vinyl seat covers. "Mom said her neighborhood watch disbanded out of boredom."

"We've got problems, same as anywhere else."

"Oh, right...that thief in the area. What's he called?"

"The love bandit."

Even their most hardened criminal sounded like a joke. "Where to first?" she asked. "What's the big ticket in Bee Lake these days?"

"How long has it been since you played putt-putt?"

There was only one answer to that. "Not long enough."

But she had a good time, mostly because Bill looked so funny swinging his way through the Peter Pan-land putt-putt course. He took his game very seriously, it seemed.

"You're supposed to let me win, you know," she told him as he hit one off the gangplank. "I'm the guest."

He levelled a cutthroat gaze on her, looking as determined as the cartoon Captain Hook he was aiming for. "This is no game for sissies, Trish."

Trish? She almost protested the diminutive, then stopped herself. She had to admit, she kind of liked it, just as she liked the familiar, easy way Bill talked to her when he wasn't in his love-cop mode.

After exhausting themselves on the putt-putt course, they went for frozen yogurt. After yogurt, to a pool hall off the highway where she roundly stomped Bill at a game of eight ball. Once he'd tasted defeat, Bill suggested something less competitive, so they drove down to the lake that gave the town its name.

They parked near the sandy beach where during the day kids played, teenagers sunbathed and adults were known to occasionally play hooky. And, she noted, it appeared to be a prime parking spot for teens—there was already another car parked a hundred feet away, and the passengers weren't visible. She and Bill stared at the vehicle, trying not to imagine what was no doubt going on in there.

Tricia cleared her throat. "You were a lifeguard here for three summers, weren't you?"

"Best summers of my life," Bill said.

Not hers. With the lure of Bill, Tricia would hang out at the lake as often as possible, even though she wasn't a particularly good swimmer and her fair skin tended to burn and peel. "I went through a lot of sunburn ointment in those days."

He tilted a glance at her. The wind ruffled his hair, making him look amazingly like the boy who'd had her heart in the palm of his hands all those years ago. "You were always so quiet."

"I was shy."

"And now?" His eyes probed her face...for what?

"Now I know that it's more important to feel good about your accomplishments than the way you look. I wasted years being cowed by other people's prejudices."

"If people didn't notice before they were just idiots. You're beautiful."

He just blurted it out, and now the statement hung awkwardly between them. Part of her wanted to flee, to avoid any response at all, yet another part of her wanted to scoot across the bench seat and throw her arms around him. She compromised by putting her hand over his.

"Thank you," she said. "That was a wonderful thing to say."

His blue eyes registered frustration. "But I mean it. I—" He let out a breath of exasperation, then muttered. "Oh, the heck with it."

Tricia thought perhaps he was going to turn the key in the ignition and peel out of the parking area. Instead, she found herself pulled into Bill's arms.

His lips descended on hers, and a fury of emotions coursed through her. The first was surprise. Her instinct was to fight the strong arms holding her like a protective band, but his warm lips talked her out of it. Desire pounded through her. And relief—like being able to finally scratch an itch that had been bothering her for days. For years.

It was so tempting to take up where they had left off in the camellia bush, but Bill's kiss was gentler this time. Slower. She slid her hands up the fabric of his shirt across his chest, to his shoulders, which felt strong, sturdy and warm beneath the cool cotton. He was sensual in a way she'd never known. Rugged. All man.

He lifted her to him so that she was almost on his lap, and the feeling of him pressing into her was almost excruciatingly powerful. She was overwhelmed with need, yet they couldn't, they just couldn't....

A gruff voice broke through her sensual fog.

"Okay, lover boy—party's over!"

8

IT WASN'T THE VOICE of any cop Bill knew.

Bill twisted toward the voice, but in doing so wrenched Tricia against the steering wheel. The horn blared.

"Quiet!" their assailant hissed at them. "And face forward, lover boy!"

But Bill didn't even have to look to know that the man was a Caucasian of medium height, wore black jeans, a black T-shirt and a red ski mask. Or that his weapon of choice to intimidate his targets was a .38 with a four-inch barrel. The love bandit!

"Give me your wallet—and lady, you hand over your purse."

To get to his wallet, Bill had to dislodge Tricia from her current position, which she did herself when she dove toward her purse to give it to the man as quickly as possible. "Here," she said, reaching inside what seemed more like an airline carry-on than a handbag. She upended the thing, tumping a surprising array of stuff onto the seat between herself and Bill, then she tossed the empty suede shell at the bandit. "Here! It'll look great with your outfit!"

Bill winced. She had obviously never been taught how to handle a holdup situation.

"The wallet!" the man said in an exasperated, almost whiny voice. "And while you're at it, take off those rings."

"My engagement ring?" Tricia asked, balking.

Did she not notice the gun pointed at her, or what?

"Give them to him, Trish."

She shot Bill an exasperated glare. "Do you know how much Manson paid for this ring? It's a pure, blue three-carat stone!"

Oh, right. *That* would make the bandit not want it.

"Lady!"

"For God's sake, hand it over, Trish."

Indignant, Trish tugged the ring off her finger and gave it to the thug, but not without a glare Bill could feel even without looking at her.

"I haven't forgotten you, lover boy. Fork over your wallet."

"Okay, okay."

Bill lifted up as if to reach into his back pocket, and as the love bandit took a split second to drop Tricia's ring into her purse, which was draped rather daintily from his arm, Bill turned and with all his might brought his hand against the man's wrist. The gun went flying and Bill sprang into action, using the car's door to knock the man in the legs. He jumped out of the driver's seat and tackled the guy, who turned out to be stronger than he looked. They rolled twice in the dirt before Bill could throw a punch—but when he did he discovered the love bandit must know more about making love than making war. A second hit practically knocked him unconscious.

It also seemed to light up the whole lake.

"What the hell?"

The headlights of five cars honed in on them, including the car that had been parked a hundred yards away. Moments later, the sound of Sheriff MacCready boomed out at them over a megaphone. "This is the police. Bring yourself to a standing position with your hands up.''

Bill rolled his eyes. Of all the times for a sting operation!

"Bill...?" Trish's voice quavered.

"It's okay, Trish, we've got him."

Practically every man in the Bee Lake force gathered around for the capture of the love bandit. One of them was Lannie Clark, who had come from the other parked car. "I couldn't believe it when I saw your car pull up, Bill. I thought this was your night off."

Bill frowned. Behind him, the sheriff himself was reading the love bandit his Miranda rights. "Yeah, well..."

"I couldn't imagine how you found out about the sting," Lannie continued excitedly. "We only planned it tonight when we had a tip-off from two kids outside a bar. We tried to get you but you were out."

"Yeah, I was."

"Lucky thing you found out in time. You really got him good!"

"Yeah, lucky," Bill mumbled, going along with this fiction, as if he and Trish hadn't been making out in the front seat of a car for any other reason besides civic duty.

"I guess—" Lannie frowned. "Hey, are you hurt? Your mouth's bleeding."

Reflexively, Bill brought the back of his hand up to his mouth. He had a feeling the redness Lannie detected wasn't blood. The love bandit hadn't thrown a single punch.

Lannie's eyes bulged in his head as Tricia came running up, her hair mussed, her slinky dress wrinkled. One thin strap drooped off her shoulder, and she didn't bother to put it to rights. Her lipstick was smudged, and she was mad as hell.

"Why didn't you tell me there was a sting going on?" she raged. "Were you trying to get me killed?"

"It's all right now," he said.

"Did you know about this?" she persisted.

"Well…" He tried not to look over at Lannie. "Not exactly, no."

A few feet away, Lannie snickered.

"Thank heavens it's all over!" Tricia said, sagging against him. She looked shaky and more vulnerable now than she'd seemed when there was a gun in her face. "I thought we were goners!"

"Yeah, I could tell you were real nervous." He put his arm around her. Lannie or no Lannie, she looked as if she could use some propping up. "Is that why you threw your purse at the guy?"

She laughed. "I was just so shocked. I mean one minute we were—" She stopped short, glancing at Lannie and all the others who had gathered to listen to her side of the story.

"Mind if I get a picture?"

Before Bill or Tricia could answer, a bulb flashed, then another and another. Bill raised his hand against the glare—but Dane Hewitt from the *Bee Lake Gazette* had already gotten all he needed. "What do you know!" Dane exclaimed in surprise. "It's Pat Parker, isn't it?"

The smile Tricia sent the journalist was lopsided at best. "Actually, it's Tricia Pe—"

"Sure!" Dane said, interrupting. "Remember me? Dane, Dane Hewitt. We were in photography class together. Gosh you look a lot different!"

"I dyed my hair."

Bill laughed, but Dane didn't seem to catch on. "Still a shutterbug?"

Tricia blinked at his rapid-fire questioning. "Not really."

"Say—this'll make a great front-page spread." He lifted his hands as if blocking out the headline. "Hometown Girl Returns—Helps Capture Love Bandit. What do you think?"

"It was really the police who did all the capturing," Tricia said. "There's no reason to mention my part in any of this."

"Modest hometown gal Pat Parker! Human interest—this'll be great!" He turned to catch up with the sheriff, who was leading the man in black away, but shouted back at them. "You'll get your picture in the paper—I promise!"

She turned and looked at Bill doubtfully. "Surely a little crime story won't be featured very prominently...maybe buried in the second section somewhere?"

"Oh, sure," Bill quipped. "I doubt the capture of the town's most notorious criminal in a decade rates front-page coverage."

Tricia groaned.

A half hour later, as he pulled up to her mother's house, Bill could tell that his efforts this evening had failed to sweep Tricia off her feet. About the only comforting thing to come from their lakeside incident was the interesting fact that although Tricia had recovered her engagement ring, she had so far been content to let it remain safely tucked away in her purse, not on her finger.

She turned to him with a whimsical smile. "Thanks for a lovely evening, Bill. I can't remember the last time I've been treated to a night of crime fighting. It was very stimulating.''

He grinned. "It was till the bandit showed up.''

Her smile melted into a scolding expression. "We shouldn't have done that, you know.''

"Why not?'' he asked innocently.

"For one thing, whenever we kiss the police tend to show up. The second our lips touch it's like dialing 911.''

"It's only happened twice.''

"A third time might summon the National Guard. I think we'd better keep it platonic.''

"No good-night kiss? Not even a friendly peck on the cheek?''

She shook her head, then extended her hand. "Friends, Bill.''

He sighed in defeat. "All right, if you insist.'' He took her hand in his, then turned it palm up. Slowly, he brought the hand up to his lips and whispered the words against the soft flesh of her palm. Tricia stiffened, and he thought he could detect a little shiver run up her body. He never knew such a simple, hokey Galahad gesture could be so sensual.

When he looked up at her again, her lips were parted softly, almost as if they had kissed. Her hair blew gently around her face, making her look young, vulnerable and achingly desirable. It took every iota of willpower he possessed not to drag her up against him caveman-style and kiss her again, National Guard be damned.

Gritting his teeth, he released her hand and watched it drop bonelessly to her side. "Friends,'' he agreed.

She remained zombielike beside him.

He reached across and opened the car door for her. "Night, Trish.''

She blinked. "Good night, Bill." She shook her head, turned and wobbled toward her front door on her sexy sandals. But then, maybe the shoes had nothing to do with it. Looking at her hips swaying toward the front porch, he felt pretty wobbly himself.

"GOOD LORD IN HEAVEN! What have you done now?"

Tricia's eyes blinked open. Her mother's words were not a particularly soothing wake-up call, but for disturbing morning eye-openers, nothing beat the front page of the paper, which her mother was holding up three inches from her face.

Hometown Gal Bags Bandit! the headline shouted. And just beneath the words, Tricia and Bill, caught pop-eyed in the flashbulb's glare, were gaping out at any Bee Lake resident who could pay thirty cents for the local weekly rag. They looked guiltier than the love bandit did in his tiny picture below the fold, and no wonder. Bill and Tricia, their mouths still smudged with lipstick, had their arms looped around each other. Her head was resting on his chest. The strap of her sexy little dress was falling off her shoulder, which in the photograph just made her look half-naked.

Tricia lifted a hand to her lips as she stared forlornly at the picture. "Oh…my…God."

"You didn't tell me you were at Bee Lake with Bill last night!"

Tricia had been up till almost two o'clock the night before trying to convince her mom that there was nothing going on between herself and Bill—nothing, at least, that was going to in any way affect Saturday's wedding plans.

And now this!

"I didn't think it was important," she said.

Her mother gaped at her, aghast. "Not important?

The fact that you were necking with Bill Wagner and got caught by the love bandit?''

It was getting caught by the photographer that was the real thorn in her side. Tricia folded the paper so she wasn't staring at herself and Bill. "It was a sting operation. Didn't you read the story?''

"I read it twice," her mother said. "Not to mention, I read between the lines. And so will everyone else in Bee Lake. Myrtle Simpson's already called to ask if she should bring her gift by or if the wedding's been cancelled."

Tricia straightened up. "Of course it hasn't been cancelled! For heaven's sake, it was just a coincidence. That photo looks very incriminating, but I assure you, Bill and I are just friends."

"You mean after your lakeside adventure he didn't give you a good-night kiss?''

She managed to lift her chin and put her mother's fears to rest. "We shook hands."

Never mind the fact that the handshake was more sexy than most of the kisses she'd received from Manson—and had a more devastating effect on her. She shivered just remembering the frisson of desire that snaked up her spine as her lips ever-so-lightly brushed her palm. And that memory prompted her to recall the wild moments she'd spent wedged between Bill's lap and Bill's steering wheel, moments before the law and the local paparazzi caught up with them. She knew she was blushing furiously, so she pretended to be very interested in a discount tire ad in the back of the paper.

"You know, we have to go talk to Pastor Temple today," Peggy reminded her.

She nodded furiously. "I'll be ready. Don't we have plenty of time?''

"It's not the time I'm worried about, it's your inclination."

Tricia laughed. "Don't be silly, Mom." She pushed her hair off her shoulders and shrugged nonchalantly. "I'm very eager to talk to Pastor Temple. I need to let him know when to stop the ceremony to let Sylvie read a poem."

Peggy's jaw dropped. "Sylvie? *A poem?*"

This was a little embarrassing. "Yes, well, originally Manson wanted to read it, but I thought that was a little corny so I was going to wait and hope that he forgot about it. But I showed it to Sylvie, and she actually liked it and volunteered."

"What is it? Robert Frost or something?"

If only! Tricia tried but failed to mentally block out the verse that rhymed *Tricia* with *kiss ya.* "No, it's one hundred percent Manson Toler."

Her mother's mouth scrunched in distaste. "Well, I suppose it will go down better than if Manson read it himself." She sighed and looked at Tricia closely. "Are you sure you want to go through with this thing?"

It pained her to hear her long-hoped-for and carefully planned ceremony reduced to "a thing." "Of course," Tricia said. "Don't worry so much, Mom. Everything will be fine."

"Good. Because Myra Tomlinson says the bridal cake's been made up."

Tricia frowned. "Already?" It was still days before the wedding. "Won't it go stale?"

"The layers are sitting in the deep freeze in her garage."

Tricia pictured her lovely white wedding cake resting next to sides of beef and an ice-encrusted carton of old ice cream. "That's comforting."

"Well, it's good to know something's done."

Her mother left her sitting in bed with the paper, which she tried to avoid looking at. But, of course, she had to. Gazing into Bill's eyes in newsprint was the next best thing to real-life gazing. Plus she didn't have to feel self-conscious about ogling him at her leisure, remembering how those same eyes had sizzled at her just before their kiss. The whole night seemed like a dream to her...and this was the cold reality of dawn.

What was she going to do about this paper? What would everyone say?

What would *Manson* say when he saw her publicly entwined with the best-looking cop on the Bee Lake police force?

Maybe she could buy up all the papers and hide them!

She frowned. She was almost positive that was something Lucy and Ethel had attempted on an *I Love Lucy* episode. It hadn't worked for them, and given her luck this week, she wouldn't have much success, either. So what was she going to do?

"Don't worry—I've bought up practically every copy in town."

Tricia looked up, stunned. Bill Wagner was standing in the doorway of her room holding two large steaming cups. "What are you doing here?" she said, lifting the covers up a little higher on her chest. She was suddenly achingly aware of being garbed in nothing but her T-shirt and a pair of flannel boxers.

He stepped into the room. "I came to pick you up."

"Pick me up?"

"To go to the dump," he explained.

She laughed. "That's the most untempting come-on I've ever heard."

He grinned back at her and handed her one of the

cups. She had half a mind to refuse, but the aroma of the coffee wafting toward her was too seductive. Plus, she needed something to help her tangle with Bill this early in the morning; though in a pair of faded, tight-fitting jeans and a striped T-shirt that hugged his chest just like she would have liked to, the man himself qualified as a potent morning stimulant.

He sank down onto the bed next to her, something she wasn't at all sure she was happy about. But she had to hand it to him, she was now wide awake.

She tilted her head. "Who let you in?"

"Tom."

She should have known—men always stuck together!

"Did you read the article?" he asked.

"Not exactly." She was too embarrassed to admit she'd just been looking at his picture. Drooling over it, actually.

"The Love Bandit was a Bee Lake graduate. A local. Seems he was trying to steal enough money to save up for an engagement ring for his sweetie."

"A love bandit in more ways than one."

Bill nodded. "Which is just another example, I suppose, of the crazy things people will do when they want desperately to get married."

His eyes pierced her and she squirmed uncomfortably. "I think you'd better go, Bill. Ever since last night I've had to assure Mom that she won't be left with a churchful of people and no wedding party on Saturday."

"But I can't leave without you," he argued. "Don't you want to be there when the newspapers are officially hurled into the oblivion of the Bee Lake landfill?"

She laughed. "I thought that was a gag. You *really* bought up all the papers in town."

He smiled proudly. "All the ones I could find. Some got delivered, naturally...."

She folded her arms over her chest, biting back a chuckle. "And what was your inspiration for this hare-brained scheme?" Of course, she didn't have to mention it was the same scheme she'd come up with.

"I Love Lucy."

She cracked up. "I don't think it will work, Bill."

"Well, it's worth a shot."

"At any rate," she explained, "I have to go see Pastor Temple later this morning. About the wedding ceremony."

He didn't respond. Instead, he seemed preoccupied by her room. He gazed at the bookshelves lined with her old schoolbooks and yellowed paperback copies of Beverly Cleary stories she couldn't bring herself to part with. The curtains at her window were the same yellow as the bedspread, only checked, and the eclectic mix of furniture—the iron bedstead, the mahogany dresser and an old plant pedestal holding up a television set—showcased her mother's expertise at rummage sales.

"Is this the way it looked when you were a girl?"

She smiled nostalgically. "Minus the Andy Gibb posters. Mom finally threw those out a few years back."

He nodded with approval—though whether from the decor or Peggy's decision to ditch Andy Gibb she wasn't quite certain at first. "Pretty good digs."

She'd been lucky. "One of the compensations for being an only child—I always had plenty of room to myself."

"And you never had to share the remote," Bill observed. He scooted back next to her and flipped on the TV set. To her surprise, he bypassed all the morning shows and sports channels and stopped at the classic movie station. *"Bringing Up Baby* is on."

She sat up a little straighter, amazed by the way he was immediately absorbed by the movie. But then so was she, even though she'd already seen it about a hundred times. She had half a mind to tell him that he couldn't just waltz into her bedroom at the crack of dawn and start watching television. But there were worse ways to wake up in the morning, she decided, than by a handsome guy bringing you coffee and watching an old movie with you.

"This is my favorite scene," he said.

Hers, too. The back of Katherine Hepburn's dress had just ripped clear off in the middle of a nightclub— a fact that only Cary Grant has noticed. When she finally figures out what has happened, she orders Cary Grant to get behind her, and the two of them march in quick lockstep out of the room.

Bill roared with laughter, nearly spilling his coffee.

As if beckoned by the sound of television, Tom wandered in and seemed not the least bit surprised to see Bill and Tricia in bed together. "What's so funny?"

He looked at the screen, registered black and white, and rolled his eyes. "Old movies are so dumb!" He spun on his heel and made a quick exit.

Tricia blinked. If it had been Manson and they had been watching TV together, Tom would have whined and fussed and tried to change the channel until Manson became exasperated and left. Why was his attitude toward Bill so different? It couldn't be just a matter of preferring a cop over a dentist. She looked at Bill and tried to puzzle it through, but when she studied his chiseled profile, she decided it wasn't much of a mystery. Bill was just the type of man any kid would be proud to have at parent-teacher day. He was a local ex–football hero, a cop, the quintessential normal guy. There was nothing stuffy or nerdy about the way he looked, and he really seemed to be able to relate to children.

Being childless himself, Manson tended to view Tom either as he might a foreigner, with different language and customs, or as a complicated machine that might explode if he pushed the wrong button. Plus, the way he spoke to him sometimes—in the loud, ferociously pleasant tones a stewardess might use to address a toddler—made Tom cringe and Tricia worry that things might never be ironed out. There would definitely be bumpy roads ahead. Whereas with Bill...

She ducked her head and took a bracing swig of coffee, ashamed of her traitorous thoughts. It wasn't a fair comparison. Bill had Casey, so naturally he would get along with children, especially kids Tom's age.

She tried to focus on the movie again, but her mother rapped on the door and walked in. "Tom said Bill—"

Peggy saw Bill sitting cozily next Tricia in the bed and stopped midsentence, her mouth still hanging open.

Tricia looked up guiltily, knowing there was going to be more explaining to do. She tried to strike a careless expression, as if she were completely nonchalant about being caught in bed with Bill. "We're just watching a movie." She hated the defensive way the sentence came out, so she tacked on an invitation. "Care to join us?"

Peggy looked from Bill to Tricia, from Tricia to Bill, and shook her head resolutely. "I don't think so. You haven't forgotten Pastor Temple, have you?"

As a matter of fact... Tricia cringed. "Of course not!"

"Good. And Bill, it's a good thing you dropped by, since I was going to call you."

He looked up with interest. "Anything wrong?"

"Goodness, no! But you know, Malcolm is coming day after tomorrow."

Tricia froze with dread. Surely her mother wasn't going to give Bill a lecture about necking with her daughter at Bee Lake! She barely could find her voice as she turned to Bill to translate. "She means Manson."

Bill nodded, though his lips turned down and he pressed the mute button on the TV. "What did you want me to do?"

Lay off my daughter, she half expected her mom to say. But instead, Peggy grinned and asked, "Will you loan me Casey? I thought it would be nice if after Pattie's fiancé arrived we could give the couple a little private time before the wedding. So after the rehearsal, I thought I'd arrange a monster-movie night."

Tricia guffawed into her cup. "You mean you wanted an excuse to watch *Anaconda* again." Peggy loved scary movies.

But even so, her scary movie night was the perfect way to hint to Bill that he needed to remember that she had a fiancé who would soon be here.

He looked ruefully at Tricia. "After all the work I do trying to instill wholesome tastes."

Tricia smirked. "My mother's a corrupter of youth when it comes to movies. If it doesn't scare the pants off you or have Elvis in it, she doesn't see the point of watching."

He laughed, then turned back to Peggy. "Can I come, too?"

"Of course! It'll be a triple feature. I've got my own copy of *Godzilla.*"

"Good, it's a date." He got up to leave, shooting a

glance back at Tricia. "I suppose the most appropriate genre for Tricia's wedding eve would be horror."

He ducked out of the room before the pillow Tricia chucked at him could hit its target.

BILL'S EFFORTS to rid the town of the *Bee Lake Gazette* weren't entirely successful.

"What's going on between you and my brother?" Sylvie demanded to know when she came by that afternoon. "In the last installment of this saga, you hated him."

"I never said I hated him," Tricia corrected.

"You compared him to an obnoxious cartoon skunk and a flea. Imagine my surprise when I saw you plastered all over the morning papers half-dressed with Officer Le Pew. I almost choked on my breakfast!"

"It was nothing."

"Last night he came by my house and asked me to babysit the kids while he, quote, 'went out with Trish.' *Trish?* You've gotten to the endearment stage and haven't told me?"

"We just went out to dinner and stuff last night."

Sylvie jumped on her paltry evasion. "What's 'stuff'? Making out by the lake like teenagers?"

Tricia shrugged helplessly. "I didn't know that's where kids made out."

Sylvie's eyes bulged with disbelief. "Come on—everybody did."

"If you'll recall, I was the wallflower of Bee Lake High. A one-date wonder, and desperate as I was, I wasn't about to endure any groping from Mort the Wart."

"I guess you're making up for lost time now."

"Nothing is really going on. Just a harmless flirtation. We watched a movie together." She didn't mention they watched it at eight-thirty in the morning, in bed. "*Bringing Up Baby*. Just silly stuff."

Sylvie wrinkled her nose. "You might have picked a better film."

"I like the classics."

Sylvie preferred those noisy action pictures with explosions, car chases and villains that were pure evil. Tricia wished she could fly her in the next time Tom and Manson wanted her to sit through a Jackie Chan movie.

Sylvie sighed. "Well anyway, it's all very depressing."

"Why?" Tricia might have called the Bill situation confusing, ill-timed or even a little ethically dicey, but she wouldn't call it depressing.

"Because you're being swept off your feet by two guys, while I've never been swept off my feet by even one!"

"You've had all sorts of romances."

Sylvie tossed up her hands in frustration. "But the minute I'm about to be swept, Bill swoops in and scares my broom away. And if I don't have a broom, how am I ever going to get a groom?"

"I can see your problem."

"I can't believe you're taking Manson for granted like this," Sylvie said hotly. "What if he finds out about your goings-on with Bill?"

Tricia felt her heart freeze. "There's nothing going on for him to find out about. Not really. That item in the newspaper was just a freak incident."

Her friend's lips pursed skeptically. "You're kissing one man and you're going to marry another guy in four days?"

"Bill and I have agreed to be friends. Pals."

"Pals. Like Romeo and Juliet were pals, it sounds

like." Sylvie stopped to consider. "Say...maybe now's the time I should make my move."

"What move?"

"My move on a man! While Bill is otherwise engaged." A gleeful grin broke out across her face. "He hasn't been this preoccupied with anything since Casey got her first tooth."

Tricia laughed, trying to imagine Bill with a little baby. He probably was one of those worried, fawning daddies she used to see at the park when she'd take Tom. The kind of man who spotted his kid on the monkey bars at all times, who wiped down the swings with disinfectant before his precious baby could sit in them, who always regaled the other parents with examples of why his child was the brightest, the most coordinated, the all-round most fascinating.

"It's no joke," Sylvie said. "I'm a desperate woman. And the trouble is, I'm even running out of men for Bill to get bent out of shape about. I might actually have to waste this precious opportunity for lack of an inappropriate love object."

Trish looked down at her friend and felt real sympathy for her. Maybe they needed to change the subject. "So what have you decided to do about the dress?

Sylvie brought out a sketch she'd carried in with her. "Here. I'm going to cut a panel out of the back and replace it."

Tricia frowned at the makeshift drawing, which made it look as if she was going to have a banana-shaped appendage attached to her rear.

"It's just a quick sketch," Sylvie said, noting her hesitation. "It'll look great, I swear. Plus you'll have a little kick train."

"Isn't this sort of drastic?" She hated to see a huge

hunk ripped out of the dress. "Couldn't we just put a patch over the stain?"

Sylvie levelled a withering stare on her. "Oh, sure, what would you like—a little yellow smiley? A Keep On Truckin' logo?"

"Okay, okay, I bow to your superior fashion wisdom."

"Good," Sylvie said, tossing the sketch aside. Then she released a melodramatic sigh.

So much for diverting her attention.

"I wish *I* were getting married Saturday!"

"The right guy will come along, Sylvie. I'm sure of it. He might even be slightly appropriate."

Sylvie shuddered in distaste. "What fun would that be?"

"DAD, HAVE YOU EVER thought about getting married again?"

Bill slammed on the brakes—and they were nowhere near a stop sign. *"What?"*

Casey didn't have to repeat herself, though. He was amazed. Never in all the time since Andrea had left had his daughter whispered a word about his remarrying.

"No, I haven't," he answered her honestly, swerving over to the curb so the impatient honking drivers behind them could go about their business, undeterred by his family drama. "I wouldn't have thought you'd like that."

"Don't you think I'm getting to an age when I could benefit from a maternal influence?"

"I don't know...."

"Everyone says I'm a tomboy."

"Well, lots of girls are."

"Not popular ones."

"There's more to life than being popular, you know."

She scowled at him disbelievingly. "Like what?"

"Well, like making good grades and being kind to people...." He wished he could think of some reason that didn't make him sound like Parson Weems.

"Well, if I can't be popular, it would be nice to have a brother or sister so I could be sure that someone would want to talk to me." She eyed him seriously. "Couldn't you at least manage that?"

Bill gulped, astounded. "Well, I don't know. That's a tall order. It's not just something you do on a whim."

"Oh, I know. They showed us a film at school."

He squirmed uncomfortably.

"You're supposed to get married first," Casey explained to him.

"Well, yes, but there's more to it than that. There's a lot of time involved. Why, if I had a kid now, I'd be an old man by the time he or she went to college. Let's see, I'm thirty-four, and if you add eighteen..." He paused to calculate.

"Fifty-two, Dad. That's not so old." She shrugged. "Sean Connery is almost seventy, and I bet plenty of women would jump at the chance to make a baby with him."

Bill frowned. Maybe he ought to wean Casey away from her movie fanaticism a bit. "I wouldn't know about that."

"Aunt Sylvie said she would."

Naturally! Probably the next thing he knew he'd be rescuing his sister from some May-December fiasco. "I'm not James Bond, Casey. Just a cop."

She let out a long sigh of disappointment as he pulled the car back onto the road, but, thankfully, she let the subject of marriage and more babies drop.

Unfortunately, the subject was still lodged firmly in Bill's head. And not because he was appalled that Casey should mention it. In fact, he was relieved. He *wanted* to get married, he discovered to his dismay as he mulled the idea over in his head. He was a marrying man, and always had been. Was it any coincidence that he'd taken his first trip down the altar at age twenty-two? Or that when Andrea had run out on him he'd felt like a complete washout? Not to mention, everything had seemed a little out of kilter since then. He missed the company of a woman.

And as for Casey wanting a little brother or sister...well, it didn't necessarily have to be a baby. An older sibling might be better for her—say, a scrappy boy who could beat up anybody who made fun of his sister for being a tomboy.

He tried to hide his look of frustration from Casey. He didn't want her to think he was actually considering the matter of marriage, even if he was.

Because how could he get married again when the only woman he wanted was about to go to the altar with someone else?

9

"MANSON CALLED while you were out," Peggy announced to Tricia as she walked through the front door. She grinned proudly. "See? I got it right this time! I told him to try you over at Sylvie's."

Tricia felt herself torn between disappointment and irritation. Sometimes it seemed Manson was calling every five minutes. "I must've just missed him."

"He wanted to remind you what time he was coming in tomorrow so that you wouldn't forget to pick him up at the airport. I told him it wasn't likely you'd forget your groom." She shot Tricia a worried glance. "Would you?"

Tricia chuckled listlessly and let out one of Tom's expressions. "As if."

She hurried to her room, where she flopped on the bed and stared at the pink princess phone. She was suddenly assaulted with an outrageous idea she never would have considered a week ago: bugging out. It would be so easy to cancel everything, she thought. Manson was a thousand miles away, and there was no reason why they would have to see each other again. It would be the easiest thing in the world....

Except what would she be left with, besides a cake in the deep freeze? A cop who's flirted with her a few times? Bill hadn't made any declarations of undying love. Bill hadn't even given her any indication that he wanted to marry again, and why should he? His wife just ran out on him two years ago. It had taken Tricia at least five years after Roy had deserted her before she even wanted to look at another man. And it had taken another five years after that to find a man who wanted to look at her. And that man was Manson.

For a moment, she harkened back to that sunny beach in Cancun. She'd been lying on one of those cheap aluminum loungers, sipping a daiquiri, when suddenly, there he was, staring at her with unalloyed interest in those dark eyes. Her heart tripped a little now just thinking about it. For months Manson had meant everything to her. She had daydreamed about him, had shortchanged the time she spent at her beloved store and had risked the wrath of Tom in her pursuit of him. The moment he'd asked her to marry him had been the supreme moment of her life, topping even the day she'd hauled all her fat clothes to Goodwill. Manson was her man.

Bill didn't fit into this picture. He had simply flattered her by letting her think she had turned his head, and now she was getting carried away because she had scant experience with men anyway and had a hard time telling a smoothie from the genuine article. She would be a fool to let her plans to legalize a solid and true relationship be affected by his flirtation. After all, the man had a track record of busting up romances willynilly. Once her engagement was over he'd probably move on to the next happy couple.

She picked up the phone.

But her hand stopped halfway to her ear. What if Manson detected something in her voice? What if he heard a telltale quaver and jumped to the wrong conclusion? She wasn't good at covering up—not that she actually had anything to cover up. A kiss? What was that? She could count the number of men she'd kissed on one hand. Could Manson say the same? She drew up a little indignantly at the very idea of him criticizing her, even if it was only in her imagination.

But, of course, she couldn't call him if she felt irritated. What would that accomplish? He might think she was being touchy because she was having second thoughts.

But she wasn't having second thoughts!

Resolute, she punched in Manson's number and waited.

And waited.

His answering service picked up, announcing that he couldn't take her call because he was on another line. Tricia sighed with relief. When the beep sounded, she burst forth with the perkiest can't-wait-till-the-big-day message a bride-to-be had ever left on a groom's answering machine, then hung up quickly, very satisfied with the reasonable, mature way she was handling herself.

"I WISH SYLVIE were here! Did she say where she was going?"

"No, but she certainly seemed in a hurry."

Tricia had been run ragged with errands, everything from the drugstore for suntan lotion to a final okay on the flowers to taking Tom and Casey out to the movies. After dropping the kids off at the theater, she'd returned home to discover Sylvie had come and gone. She'd dropped the dress by for Tricia to try on to see if the panel in the back worked.

In her nearly finished wedding gown, Tricia twisted to examine her friend's handiwork.

"Well," her mother drawled, "I guess it's better than looking like you had a run-in with the Exxon Valdez."

Tricia twirled in front of the mirror, enjoying the way the train flipped behind her. Sylvie had just tacked down the back panel, in case Tricia decided she didn't like it. But if she hadn't liked it, what on earth would she have done?

"I think it looks good," Tricia declared as the doorbell rang. She glanced quizzically at Peggy. "Were you expecting company?"

As if she had to ask! It seemed her mother always had a stream of people ebbing and flowing through her home these days.

"Oh! That's bridge club. I told them to come by for coffee today. Everyone's been curious about your dress since I told them about the oil stain on your rear," Peggy said, as she jogged through the living room—probably the only time she'd actually jogged in one of her workout suits. "Come out and show them, honey."

Tricia rolled her eyes, feeling childish as she stomped into the living room and was greeted by reverential oohs and ahhs of five of her mother's most boisterous friends. "I'll get the coffee," Peggy said, leaving Tricia to get pawed over by women inspecting Sylvie's beadwork, the dress's drape and the choice of fabric.

"So soft!" Irene cried. "But don't those beads make it heavy, darlin'?"

Brownies appeared on the table, as well as a two-liter bottle of diet soda. Seconds later, Johnny Cash was blaring through the house singing "A Boy Named Sue," and the party was in full swing.

Tricia stood numb in the middle of it all, not quite believing how fast the atmosphere could change. The doorbell rang again, and at Peggy's insistence—she was wrestling with the last stubborn cubes lodged in a metal ice tray—Tricia went to see who it was.

As soon as she saw Bill standing there in his blue uniform, understandably gawking at her outfit, she tugged him over the threshold with relief. She'd dreaded meeting him again, but now that they were face-to-face, she attached herself to him like a drowning woman who'd just been thrown a buoy. "Thank God you're here!"

He laughed. "I was about to say the same thing to you. I got off on my lunch hour, went home, and Casey was gone."

"She's at the movies with Tom."

"That's what Geneva told me. Then I went over to Sylvie's and she was gone, too."

"That one's harder to explain. I can't find her either."

"She probably had to run an errand," Bill said absently. He was giving her a long up-and-down stare that was causing her to feel very nervous. Heat pooled inside her, making her cheeks burn. He couldn't seem to take his eyes off her dress.

"Don't act so surprised, you've seen it before," she told him, recalling the day she'd been stuck to her car like a butterfly pinned to a board.

His eyes suddenly looked inexpressibly sad. "But that was before I knew the person in it."

Tricia felt her heart wrench, and she gulped to catch a breath. "It still feels a little unreal to me. Like I'm dressed up for Halloween."

He grinned. "Miss Havisham from *Great Expectations*. All you need is some tears and a few cobwebs."

"I don't think Sylvie would approve."

"It's your dress. Why the dickens should she care?"

Tricia groaned. "A punning policeman! Just for that, I'm going to feed you to the sharks." She grabbed him by the arm, turned him around and announced to the hoard around the table, "Hey, everybody, look who's here!" Then she gave a shove that propelled him toward the swarm.

The ladies le' out oohs and ahhs similar to their reaction to her dress, and they flocked around him like flies on molasses.

"Come have a brownie, Bill."

"You sit down and tell us all about that bandit fellow you caught."

"Are you on duty? Do you have time for a rubber of bridge?"

He sent Tricia a long-suffering glance, then answered all the questions put to him good-naturedly, to the delight of the women. With his breezy ways and all-American good looks, he was just the type of man women would naturally like to mother.

Then she amended the thought. *Some* women would like to mother him. To her, Bill put in mind a completely different relationship. Pirate king to her shipwrecked damsel, for instance. Viking warrior to Saxon maid.

Or, given the bickering nature of their relationship, maybe Fred to Ethel.

"I was just telling Margery that Tricia isn't going to be able to dance in that getup of hers," Libby Walton told Bill.

As if he would care.

But he pretended to. Hand to chin, he sized up the dress's train, then took his own sweet time giving the rest of her the once-over, taking extra moments when he reached her breasts, which were pushed up unnaturally by some suffocating infernal contraption—a kind of girdle for her chest her mother had insisted she wear. By the time his gaze reached her lips, Tricia was sure she was pink all over.

"I think she could," Bill declared, "depending on what kind of dance it was. I couldn't see her doing a jitterbug, say, or the mashed potato."

Mashed potato? "I'm not going to be in a Twiggy movie, I'm just getting married."

"A waltz!" Irene exclaimed out of the blue. "Peg, you got a waltz handy?"

"Johnny doesn't do many of those...."

"Oh, for heaven's sake, not Johnny Cash." The two women fussed over Peggy's record collection until Irene pulled out what she exclaimed would be just the thing. "Miss Patti Page!"

The sad, soothing strains of the "The Tennessee Waltz" started, and Irene glanced between Bill and Tricia, gesturing with outstretched hands for them to get together. "Go on you two, try it out."

Murmurs of encouragement followed.

Tricia looked into Bill's searing blue eyes and froze in place. "Oh, but I..."

"C'mon, Pattie," her mother yelled over the music, "you need to give that dress a trial run while you've got a man around."

Bill stood and tweaked a bow toward Tricia. "May I have the honor?"

She hesitated.

"For Pete's sake, hurry before Patti Page sings herself hoarse," her mother called out.

Put that way, Tricia couldn't help laughing. She stepped into Bill's outstretched arms and glided around the room to the waltz. Like the old song said, he was easy to dance with. He held her close and guided her so expertly his last name might have been Astaire or Kelly. She had to resist the temptation to shut her eyes and sway around the room dreaming that she was in an art deco ballroom.

But somehow, the running commentary from the brownie table made her ballroom scenario seem doubly unrealistic. No one seemed to notice that though she was standing in Bill's arms she couldn't look into Bill's eyes, or that she was practically quivering with lust.

"See, the train's fine. She's not stepping on it."

Irene eyed them critically. "Turn her around quick, Bill, and let's see what happens."

Tricia laughed. "I'll bet Ginger Rogers never put up with this kind of indignity."

"Ginger never danced in sneakers, either," her mother observed.

Tricia had forgotten she was wearing them, and now the whole room hooted at her blue sneakers as the doorbell rang.

"Gonna wear those on the big day, Tricia hon?" someone called out to her.

She and Bill angled around Peggy as she crossed to the door. "At least they're not high-tops," her mother said.

More laughter ensued, and in the raucous spirit of things, Bill twirled them around elaborately then ended in a deep dip. Tricia whooped in surprise as he grinned down at her.

But no one else was laughing. In fact, the room had fallen eerily silent, except for Patti Page. And no wonder. When Tricia craned her neck to the side, she saw Manson standing in the doorway next to Sylvie.

Manson. The airport. Dear heaven! "Omigod! I forgot!"

Bill tipped them both back up to standing.

Oddly, the next thought in Tricia's mind was that Manson looked incredible—and incredibly out of place. He wore a tweed jacket and bright blue shirt, matched with a flowery tie. After a few days in Bee

Lake, she could see now why Bill had criticized him. The look was definitely not rural Louisiana.

Then, slowly, she caught on to the slight irritation in his expression as he forced a smile. "Apparently."

She felt like a toad. How could she have forgotten? How could she have been carousing with Bill and her mother's friends, leaving Sylvie to pick up her fiancé? How?

The air in the room was tense, and Tricia couldn't help feeling that most everyone was looking at her with highly deserved disapproval.

Stepping out of Bill's embrace, Tricia prepared to rescue the situation by recovering her composure, sweeping to the door with aplomb and introducing her fiancé to the bridge gang, who would naturally make a big fuss over him. But the moment she took a step, a clean, crisp *rip* sounded from the general direction of her behind, and she felt a telltale draft over her hind quarters. Frozen with dread, Tricia reached around, only to discover that the back panel of her dress was gone.

"Don't worry," Bill whispered, "it only ripped to your knees."

Her knees?

"Tricia?" her mother asked, "are you all right?"

Tricia's hand went to her mouth to cover her open-mouthed expression of horror. Thank God Patti Page was still cranked up and crooning, or the whole room might know that she was standing in front of them with her panties exposed.

"Tricia?" Sylvie asked, echoing her mother. "Is something wrong?"

Tricia shook her head. "No, I'm just so…sorry!" She looked over at Manson, who was gazing at her quizzically.

"Is it really Wednesday?" Bill asked, as if reading the back of her underwear.

She shot him a dirty look and whispered to him through the corner of her mouth. "For heaven's sake, get me out of here!"

She could feel Bill's broad smile behind her. "If you'll excuse us, Trish and I were practicing a new dance step—the Cary Grant strut."

He grabbed her hips and bumped up against her with a suggestive *oomph,* then propelled them forward in quick lockstep toward Tricia's bedroom à la *Bringing Up Baby.*

"I'll be right ₋ack, Manson!" she called as they disappeared through the door.

She slammed it behind them, then turned to stare at Bill, stunned. "I can't believe this!"

"What, that Manson showed up?"

"No, that I almost exposed half the town to my panties!"

His lips quirked.

"My fiancé probably thinks I'm crazy."

He shook his head, smiling. "Don't sell yourself short. The whole room probably thinks you're crazy."

"This is serious!"

Bill sobered, grinned, then fought to force his lips into a serious scowl. He finally surrendered the battle and exploded in laughter.

Tricia put her hands on her hips and frowned at him as he doubled over with mirth, then felt her own lips twisting into a grin. "It's not funny," she insisted.

But a stubborn titter rose in her throat. Attempting to suppress it only made things worse. The more she tried to stop laughing, the more the guffaws and hoots poured out of her. She gripped her side, then glanced over to see Bill laughing so hard he had to wipe a tear away. He was crying!

Together they fell back onto the bed in hopeless, uncontrollable giggles. Tricia released a moan. She'd never laughed this hard—her stomach ached, her jaw ached, and something else was wrong. "I think I'm about to pop my breast girdle!"

Bill sent her a puzzled look, then they both roared with laughter.

Sylvie opened the door and marched into the room, glaring at them disapprovingly. "*What* is so funny?"

Her commandant tone only cracked them up more. Neither could answer her without risking a fresh wave of hysteria.

Sylvie tsked at them uncharacteristically. "You two are behaving worse than Casey and Tom! Bill, what are you even doing here?"

He tried, he really did. "Stepping on Trish's dress," he managed, then burst into laughter again.

Sylvie turned her attention to Tricia. "How could you forget to pick Manson up? I came by earlier, and your mom said you were taking the kids to the movies!"

Tricia swallowed a chuckle and wiped away tears. "I was."

"But I come back here with your fiancé and you're dancing with my brother! As if that isn't bad enough, the two of you start acting like loons. Manson is confused, to say the least, though I must say he recovered the situation out there admirably. He's already charmed all your mother's friends."

Tricia tried, and failed, not to look at Bill. They cringed with suppressed laughter, then Bill pushed himself off the bed. "I'm sorry, Sylvie, I didn't know Manson was about to show up."

Tricia straightened. "And I just plain forgot, and then Mom had all these friends over and Bill was there...and my dress ripped. What could we do?"

That caught Sylvie's attention. "Your dress ripped?" She looked as if she felt responsible for the catastrophe.

"Well, it wasn't sewn down completely, so I guess when Bill stepped on it..." She winced.

Bill looked at her. It was all over.

The two of them dissolved into helpless mirth once again, leaving Sylvie standing over them, clucking. "All right. I guess I can go out and explain this to Manson as delicately as possible." She glared at her brother as he tried to get himself under control once again. "But it might help, Bill, if you beat a hasty retreat. I saw jealousy in those brown eyes when he saw you two together."

Tricia straightened up, feeling strangely indignant that Manson would be jealous of such a ridiculous incident. "Bill was only helping. For Pete's sake, we're all adults."

Of course, an adult shouldn't forget to pick someone up from the airport....

Sylvie leveled a skeptical look on her and Bill. "I suppose so, even though no one could tell it from looking at you."

Chastised, Tricia and Bill looked at each other soberly. Then they giggled. Then they fell back again, cackling.

Tossing up her hands, Sylvie left the room in exasperation.

"I NEVER KNEW what a character your mother was," Manson said, chuckling as he picked at a thick french fry.

"I thought I'd told you all about her." Hadn't he listened to all the stories she'd told him?

"I guess you did," Manson agreed, then looked back down at his food.

She hadn't meant to sound argumentative, but maybe she had. Somehow ever since Manson arrived in Bee Lake, they had experienced a critical breakdown of communication.

She glanced down at the hamburger she'd ordered and felt her appetite slip away from her completely. She hadn't eaten all day. Usually she munched ceaselessly when nervous, but today she couldn't force down a bite. Tom, on the other hand, was consuming everything in sight, chewing relentlessly but saying little.

They were seated in one of Mazie's huge curving corner booths that made her feel as if she were miles from the people she was eating with. It didn't help the flow of conversation any to have to shout across a huge round table over the noise in the crowded restaurant.

"How's the burger, Tom?" Manson asked in his loud stewardess tone.

Tom shrugged and mumbled back at him. "'kay."

At her son's unresponsiveness, Manson looked pointedly at Tricia, who felt her already shaky confidence slip another notch. She'd so wanted these two to love each other as much as she loved them both, but watching the tension reignite between them, that vain hope began to fade. What was worse, her mind couldn't help assigning blame. Why couldn't Tom sit up and act halfway human? Why couldn't Manson lay off Tom, not push him?

Why did she think this was ever going to work?

Manson suddenly grinned. "Say, here's your friend Bill!" The table's collective gaze turned to where Bill,

Sylvie and Casey stood at the front of the restaurant, eyeing the full tables in dismay.

Tom perked up. "Cool!" He waved an arm at them and cupped his free hand over his mouth. "Hey, Casey!" He shouted in his best full-throttle yell, so that the entire restaurant was now looking toward the trio in the doorway.

To Tricia's surprise, Manson beckoned them over insistently, and when they hesitated, he got up and herded them over himself. "Tricia," he said when they all came back to the booth, "please assure these people that there's room here for all of us."

Casey had already hopped in the booth and helped herself to a cellophane wrapped cracker; only Bill and Sylvie hesitated. "Of course," Tricia said, relieved at least to see Manson animated. She scooted over, and Sylvie waited for Bill to sit next to Tricia. Then Sylvie slipped into the booth, followed by Manson, who had a friendly grin for Tricia's best friend. It pleased her to see them getting along so well.

"There!" Manson exclaimed happily. "This is cozy, isn't it?"

"You can say that again," Bill joked. "Any cozier and we'd be stacked on top of each other."

"Like Lego," Sylvie said.

Manson snorted with laughter, causing Casey and Tom to exchange significant glances. What exactly it signified, Tricia couldn't say.

She tried not to look over at Bill, but curiosity got the best of her. They hadn't seen each other since their bout of hysteria; but they were completely sober now.

"Where's Peggy?" Bill asked.

"Oh, she had some things to do."

"Peggy's busy fixing the house up for horror night," Manson said. "I think she's making green popcorn."

"Eeeeeww!" Casey exclaimed, wrinkling her nose. "That's gross."

"I think that's the point," Bill told her.

Manson grinned. "I think it sounds neat. I like a good horror movie myself, so I talked Tricia into joining the fun. It's going to be a triple-feature sleepover type of thing."

Tricia smiled. "Ever since coming to Bee Lake, Manson has expressed more enthusiasm for watching *Godzilla* than he has for our wedding."

She tried, but failed, to avoid looking Bill in the eye. He appeared rather grim suddenly. Why? Was he remembering, as she was, when they'd come to Mazie's the night they caught the love bandit?

"So...you two are getting married tomorrow," Sylvie said, eyeing Manson and smiling. "Pardon me for saying so, but you don't look it. The soon-to-be bride and groom eating burgers? Is this an L.A. custom?"

Manson grinned. "Unorthodox, but tasty. Besides, my brother was bushed from the long plane ride from Seattle, and my parents aren't coming in till tomorrow morning, so it was better to give everyone a rest before the big day."

Sylvie looked doubtful. "Shouldn't we take your brother something to eat?"

"He said he ate on the plane."

"Plane food's no good," Sylvie insisted, flicking a glance over at Tricia. "Maybe you should take him the burger that Tricia's not eating. What's the matter, Tricia?" she teased. "Nerves?"

Tricia grinned sickly in response. Was it nerves when everything you put in your mouth tasted like Styrofoam? Or was it cold, clammy fear?

Or cold, clammy feet?

She glanced over at Bill, who wasn't eating anything, either, or saying anything. In fact, he looked the way she felt, which wasn't good. The packed room was beginning to crowd in on her, the many voices fusing into one dizzying cacophony. She took a deep breath and tried to shake the wooziness from her bones, but the added oxygen only seemed to make her a little more lightheaded.

"I think…" She began pushing herself to the closest end of the booth. "I think I need some air."

A path immediately cleared for her, which was good, because at about that moment the room started whirling. She sensed the rest of her booth jumping up to help but was concentrating too hard on getting to her feet to know this for a fact. She took one step, listed, reeled, then felt herself fall backward as the world went black.

10

SOMEWHERE AROUND the middle of *Anaconda*, Tricia began to wonder whether she might be losing her mind. In thirteen hours she was going to be married, and she just couldn't keep her mind on that damn snake, no matter how many people it devoured.

She and Manson were sitting on the couch with a bowl of green popcorn between them. Casey and Tom were lying on their stomachs in front of the television—mere inches in front of the television—with a bowl of popcorn between them. Peggy was in her favorite chair, avidly watching the movie, and Bill and Sylvie were positioned on either side of the couch, with Bill nearest Tricia.

It wasn't just her wedding that had her preoccupied. It was Bill. She looked over at him, noting how his eyes glazed over as he watched the horror unfolding on the twenty-seven-inch screen. What was he thinking about? Tomorrow?

He glanced at her and caught her in the act of watching him. Their gazes met and held. There was something woebegone about his expression—and then he looked at Manson. Then back to the screen.

She couldn't stand it anymore. Tricia stood and took the half-full popcorn bowl to the kitchen as an ostensible reason for her to be getting up in the middle of the movie.

Peggy scrambled after her, her face pinched with worry. "Is something the matter, Pattie?"

"No, Mom. Go back to the movie. I think that snake has already digested his last human and might be ready for another meal."

Her mother laughed. "This is what I call a great movie."

"It's a shame Elvis couldn't be in it. Maybe he could sing 'Love Me Tender' to that reptile and give it a whole new attitude."

Her mother's black brows knit together. "Are you *sure* you're feeling okay? You're probably still a little woozy from that fainting spell you had."

"That sandwich you gave me when I got home made me feel a lot better."

Peggy nodded. "I always say, bologna works miracles. They should manufacture it in pill form."

Tricia laughed halfheartedly and looked at the back door with sudden longing. "You know, I might take a little walk."

Peggy nodded, throwing an anxious glance back to the living room. "You do that, hon. I need to get back to my movie."

Tricia went outside and made it ten feet down the walkway before she heard the door opening behind her. She half expected to see her mother come running out bearing a sweater or more bologna. But when she turned, she saw Bill strolling toward her. Much better than a cold cut. Her heart pounded a little more insistently in her chest, and her cheeks heated with a tingly warmth. The effect that man had on her was sinful.

But not as sinful as the thoughts going through her mind. Like how great he looked. How completely sexy and kissable. God, she wanted him. The realization hit her like a two-by-four. She wanted Bill Wagner and always had, and maybe always would. And the way his blue eyes were glinting at her made her fear he was most likely thinking the same thing.

"Are you okay?" he asked as he approached her.

"Just needed some air," she said, using as casual a tone as she could muster when her pulse was pounding in her ears and every nerve ending was marshaled at full attention.

"Maybe you should have something to eat."

She laughed. "You sound like Mom. Don't worry. I ate half a vat of popcorn in there."

"Popcorn's nothing."

"It's green popcorn. That's almost like a vegetable."

He frowned and looked into her eyes with heartbreaking seriousness. He buried his hands in his jeans pockets, and the wind ruffled his short hair. He was amazing.

"Actually, I'm glad you came out here," he said, his voice gravelly and low. "I was hoping for a chance to talk to you." He swallowed. "Alone."

She tore her gaze away from the burning blue of his eyes and glanced guiltily back at the house. Why couldn't it have been Manson who had followed her? Talking with Bill was just going to stir up all sorts of trouble and complicate matters further, because the minute she opened her mouth, she was liable to blurt out all sorts of inappropriate things…like how much she suddenly regretted the fact that it was Manson she was marrying tomorrow, and not Bill. Or the fact that if Bill so much as kissed her, she didn't know whether she would be responsible for her actions.

Go back inside right now, her conscience instructed her sternly. *Don't listen to Bill. He's only going to tempt you more.*

But her voice said, "There's a bench just down the way, by the bus stop."

They walked toward it in tense silence, occasionally darting longing looks at each other. This was it, then. He was going to make a desperate last-ditch plea for her not to marry Manson. Maybe he would even beg. What would she do? What *could* she do? She was practically salivating in lust for the man right beside her while the man she was going to marry was just a hundred yards away, completely absorbed in a movie about a snake with a mammoth aggression-control problem.

They sat down. She could only pray he couldn't hear her heart thumping, couldn't read the raw desire she felt sure was stamped all over her.

He turned to her, his lips quirking up in a rueful smile. "Lady, I owe you one whopper apology."

She tilted her head, unsure where this was leading. "Apology for what?"

He laughed. "For everything! For being so obtuse. For not believing you when you said Manson was a hell of a guy."

This was Bill talking? About Manson?

Her mouth popped open, but she could think of no reply.

"I understand now why you thought I was so wrongheaded to investigate Manson like I did. No wonder you thought I was a lunatic." He shook his head with regret and mused down at his boots. "The man is as good as gold."

As good as gold? *Bill* was saying Manson was as good as gold? Of course Manson was a terrific person...but she never expected to hear that from Bill, tonight of all nights!

For some perverse reason, Tricia felt like defending

Bill's actions now. "But you couldn't have known that before you met him. I was flattered."

His eyes rounded in surprise. "You wanted to kill me!"

She flushed. "Well, yes…maybe I did. But now I see that what you were doing was out of the goodness of your heart. Those background checks you ran on him were wonderful gestures."

She'd almost said *of love.* Were they?

He looked doubtful. "I was a knucklehead. You told me all along he was an on-the-level type guy, and I can see that now. Just looking at him you can tell he's as honest as a preacher."

"Well." Tricia bristled. This wasn't going quite how she expected. "I never did find out why he didn't show up for jury duty.…"

"You know what? I can even see why you all think he's handsome," he said, albeit a little resentfully. "Sylvie always told me she thought bald men were sexy. I thought she was nuts. All I could think about was Telly Savalas—you know, *Kojak.* Some ultracool guy who said 'baby' a lot. But I saw the way women were looking at Manson tonight. Like he was a sex god or something. Even Silvie."

Manson? *Sex god?*

She looked at Bill's hair, thick and blond, and bit her lower lip in something like agony. Sexy? Bill was devastating. He hadn't changed clothes since her fainting spell at the other restaurant and was still wearing his faded, fit-to-perfection blue jeans with a polo shirt. They weren't expensive clothes, but Bill had the type of body that didn't require money to show it off, although picturing the man in Armani was practically enough to make her swoon again. The full-throttle hormone rush she got every time she looked into his eyes was embarrassing.

"You know what I like best about Manson?"

Apparently the lovefest wasn't over yet.

"No, what?" Tricia asked in lieu of screaming.

"He's just an ordinary guy. You'd never guess he spends his days looking at the tonsils of the rich and famous."

"I guess one bicuspid's pretty much like the next," Tricia said. "Whether it's Mel Gibson's or not really doesn't matter."

"But the man never name-drops like so many other people would. He doesn't mention what neighborhood he lives in or what kind of expensive car he drives...."

Bill sighed.

"Maybe *you* should marry Manson," she bit out.

Bill tossed back his head and laughed. "I just thought you might feel better if I finally congratulated you on your choice of groom."

So why was she loving her fiancé less—and Bill more—the more Bill flattered him?

"But what about Tom?" Bill had always seemed so concerned about him before.

"Oh, I wouldn't waste too much energy in that direction. No kid likes a stepparent at first. Everything will be okay."

That's what she'd always thought. That her relationship with Manson would work out okay. But now she realized she wanted so much more than okay. She wanted laughter and love and heart-pounding passion.

She wanted Bill.

And now *he* was pushing her toward Manson!

There was a lump the size of France in her throat, and she gulped down air to try to get rid of it. But it was no use. Tears didn't come easily to her, but when they threatened, there was no stopping them. "I think..." She squeezed her eyes closed to hold back moisture and prayed she could get up and go back inside before making a complete idiot of herself. "I think I need to go back in."

"You're not going to faint again, are you?" Bill asked, looking worriedly at her. "Trish?" He reached out a hand to cover hers.

At the electricity sparked by his touch, she bolted off the bench and ran for the house but was stopped when Bill caught her arm. She whirled back toward him, nearly slamming against his chest.

"What's wrong?" he asked. "I thought you would be glad that I apologized for misjudging Manson. He's a great guy."

Of course Bill felt obligated to own up when he was wrong. That was the honorable thing to do, and he wasn't one to shirk responsibility. That was part of the reason she loved him.

Oh, God. There it was. She loved him.

Fresh tears coursed down her cheeks faster than she could frantically wipe them away in a futile attempt to regain composure.

Bill stared at her, his expression a blend of sympathy and utter confusion. "Was it something I said?"

"Yes!" she said, finally reclaiming her voice, though she had to gulp for air.

"But I was just talking about Manson...."

"I know! You can't seem to stop talking about him!"

"And that upset you?"

"It's not what I expected, that's all."

Bill looked even more puzzled. "But I thought I owed you an apology—for all the things I'd done and said about him. I thought that would make you feel better.''

''Why?''

''Because…'' He seemed to search the stars for the correct answer, or at least one that wouldn't set her off again. But the answer wasn't there, and his head tilted back toward her in curiosity. ''What did you expect?''

Now came the true humiliation, but she deserved it. She straightened her shoulders. ''I thought…I thought you wanted to speak to me because you didn't want me to get married. To Manson.'' She burned under his steady blue gaze, knowing she had said too much, yet unable to stop herself from confessing more. ''I thought you were going to make a last-ditch effort to get me to call off my wedding.''

Bill said nothing. He just stared at her. But then, he didn't really need to say anything to answer all the recriminating questions bouncing around inside her head. *Did she really think he was low-down enough to steal a woman away the night before her wedding? That he would go out on a limb like that, committing to a woman he barely knew? Did she really think a man who hadn't paid her the slightest attention for her entire teenage and adult life would suddenly fall in love with her in one short week?*

Bill stammered. ''I couldn't…I…''

''Please don't explain,'' Tricia interrupted. ''I understand now. You just wanted to make things square between us. It was foolish of me, not to mention insanely egotistical, to think that a man like you would…I mean…''

He grabbed her by the shoulders. ''Will you stop babbling that self-defeating nonsense and listen?'' he asked, his voice gruff and urgent. ''When I said I couldn't, I only meant that I couldn't beg you not to marry Manson because I knew you wouldn't want me to. I was trying to make peace with the situation, when really I wanted to—''

He cut off his sentence, leaving Tricia clutching at possibilities, and her heart racing. ''You wanted to…?''

''Yes!'' Both his arms held her firmly against him, and their faces were inches apart. ''God, yes, I wanted to!'' he exclaimed, then bent down to capture her lips.

She threw her arms around him in a rush of joy and relief and longing. He never did say what he'd wanted to do, but he didn't have to. Whatever it was, she was all for it.

She clung to him for all she was worth, reveling in the wonderful feeling of being in his arms, of having his lips against hers, when just moments before she'd feared the closest she would ever get to him again was a handshake. Or, if she was lucky, a hug.

This was much, much nicer. She sighed, wanting to get closer to him, *needing* to feel the hard muscles beneath his clothes nuzzled up against her. She snaked one of her legs through his, causing a groan to issue from her lips.

A car whizzed by, honking its horn.

The two of them sprang apart, practically panting.

''What are we doing?'' Tricia said on a whisper. ''Out here in the open…right on the street…''

''You're right,'' Bill said, looking as if he were on the brink of launching into his good-loser routine again. Then he took her hand and began tugging her down the sidewalk away from her mother's house. ''Come on.''

''Where are we going?''

''Someplace where we can be alone. Just for a little while.''

That sounded dangerous. And unavoidable. Especially when "someplace" turned out to be his place.

"What about Casey?" She'd hoped the quick ride over in Bill's convertible would blow some sense into her, but if anything, the closer they came to their destination, the more she wanted to be there. Now she felt as though she were halfheartedly grasping at straws, not even wanting to be saved.

"They've still got *Godzilla* and *Species* to go, and your mother said she could sleep over."

"I should be back before the second feature," she said.

They stepped inside the door, and Tricia only had a moment to take in a flash of comfortable leather furniture and an entertainment center before being swept off her feet—literally. Bill scooped her up in his arms as if she were light as a feather, then strode across the room.

"Where are we going?"

His chuckle reverberated through her body. "I was heading for the bedroom...unless you have a more imaginative locale in mind?"

She blushed. "Not really."

To tell the truth, there wasn't anything in her mind at all. She felt as if she were working on pure instinct, like an animal—all selfish desire and barely restrained civility. But when Bill pushed through the bedroom door and tipped her back down to her feet again, there was no question of restraint or civility. She snaked her arms around his neck and kissed him full on the lips.

Bill pulled her up against him until they were as close as two dressed bodies could be. And then there was no holding back. They kissed, caressed and tasted each other until the rest of the world was blotted out and there was just the two of them. Clothes started to get in the way, so they shed them, item by item. The barrette holding her ponytail was unsnapped, her hair freed of its confines. He combed his fingers through it. "I love your hair. I love the color of it."

His husky whisper was almost her undoing. "It's dyed."

He waggled his brows sexily. "My regards to Clairol."

Her shirt was tossed aside next, then his. The glorious feeling of skin against skin made her shiver with sensation. He kissed his way down her neck, across her shoulders, down her chest until he reached one breast and began laving it with his tongue. She feared she might pass out again. He teased the nipple thoroughly until it was a tight, aching bud...then he started to work on its partner. It was pure, wonderful agony.

She hooked her leg between his, twining around him so that she could feel his very obvious desire for her. Heat puddled inside her at her most-intimate core, making her need for him more urgent, completely unstoppable. Grinning, she reached down, unbuttoned his jeans, then worked the zipper down slowly over his swollen manhood. He closed his eyes and let out a hissing sound through his gritted teeth.

"Trish...wait..."

"I've been waiting since I was fourteen," she whispered.

"Then maybe we should take it slow."

She sent him a sexy smile. "Too slow and we'll overshoot the double feature." She reached inside his pants and began to massage him slowly. "We wouldn't want that, would we?"

He shook his head and gave her a searing kiss. "Let's send out for more movies."

They touched and tasted until they were almost to

the brink, then pulled back and started over again. It was a maddening and irresistibly sensual exercise the likes of which she'd never known before. Finally her jeans sagged around her ankles and were kicked away, and then, as if losing her pants somehow were connected to their joint equilibrium, they fell back on the bed in a tangle of arms and legs.

Tricia's throat felt tight with longing. She'd dreamed of this moment for so long. When she was a teenager, she'd imagined them together a million times.... First, Bill would take her in his arms, whisper how much he cared for her and how he had always loved her from afar. Then, with a dramatic quaver in his voice, he would confess he wanted to make mad love to her as well as his desire to marry her and take care of her always. Then, as if by magic, she would appear in some sleek sexy bit of lingerie, he in silky boxers she'd seen in catalogs yet could never imagine Bee Lake men actually wearing beneath their old faded Wrangler jeans. They would kiss—magic! lightning! music!—and the mingled scent of Brut and Jontue would signal the beginning of a long, leisurely night of lovemaking, just as she'd seen on the silver screen performed by such greats as Meryl Streep and Robert Redford.

Which just showed what a numbskull she'd been.

The reality was that they were both too primed with desire to say a word beyond low moans, a few heartfelt grunts and whispered words of passion. The scent of the evening was popcorn, and the lingerie wasn't up to snuff, fantasy-wise. She'd dressed sensibly—so the bra Bill unhooked and the panties he peeled off of her were old beige things she'd probably picked up on sale at Target. The boxers of her imagination were in reality very practical briefs. And their lovemaking was anything but slow and movie-star tasteful.

But occasionally, she thought just before she was swept away in a swirl of desire, reality was a lot better than imagination....

11

BILL'S DAY BEGAN with a crash and a muttered curse.

The muttering he assumed came from Trish—after the crash, which sounded suspiciously like the bashing of some tender body part against a door, although he couldn't say for sure. Both of these were followed by another sound—something being dropped?—a little further away. Then there was a quick scurrying down the hall, or maybe it was in the next room. This had to be either Trish or Bee Lake's klutziest burglar.

He squinted against the sunlight streaming through the venetian blinds and glanced over at the alarm clock. Five till ten!

The double feature was definitely over by now.

He swung out of bed, stepped into his jeans and hurried out to investigate what sort of state Trish was in. Her clothes, which last night had been puddled around the bed, had now disappeared, he noted as he left the room. She wasn't in the bathroom, either. Frowning, he followed the noises through the living room toward the kitchen, where he heard the sound of the microwave in use.

Trish was reheating old coffee and nipping nervously at her finger. When she saw him standing in the doorway, she jumped. "You scared me!"

She looked frantic. Her hair was still smashed on one side where she had slept on it, and she had sheet lines on her freshly scrubbed cheeks. One strap of her tank top dangled off her shoulder; she was only wearing one tennis shoe. And her bewitching brown eyes were as round and big as tractor tires.

In short, she was simply gorgeous. "That's some good morning after the night we had."

The only answer he received was a blush. She spun on her heel, stared at the microwave as if willing it to go faster—since Mr. Coffee wasn't even fast enough for her this morning—and drummed the fingers of her free hand against the blue countertop.

When she glanced back, he grinned. "In a hurry?"

She whirled back toward him, then nearly bumped her head on the oven vent when the microwave beeper sounded off behind her. Only once she'd extracted her coffee and administered some caffeine for her jitters could she speak. "Do you have any idea what time it is?"

He looked at his watch. "Ten. I guess we overslept a little."

His understatement made her quake, and a shrill, high-pitched bleat erupted from her lips. "Overslept? We over-everthinged!"

"I'll say." He grinned, mentally picturing just a few of the sexual gymnastics they'd engaged in during the long exhausting, exhilarating night.

"We were just supposed to be over here for a *little while!* You promised to get me back before *Godzilla!*"

"I'm afraid I dozed off. After…you know…I was drained. Of energy."

Her skin went from pale green to fiery red in nothing flat. "What am I going to do?" she asked, near tears. "My wedding's in an hour, and I haven't even been home yet! What will I say to Mom?"

There was another question he was even more interested in. "What will you say to Manson?"

If the term "racked with guilt" had a face, it would be hers. "What *can* I say? The last time any of them saw us, we were headed out for some fresh air!"

She was in a bind, all right. Fearing she might have a heart attack in his kitchen, he tried to jolly her out of her panic a little. "We could say that movie of theirs sent us out on an all-night snake-killing mission."

She sent him a withering glare. "This is no joke. We were last sighted kissing on the sidewalk right under a streetlight on Sycamore Street. What if *that* got back to Manson?"

Her question threw him for a loop. So what if Manson found out they'd been kissing? Surely he was going to figure that out sooner or later. When she told him the wedding was off, and why, he would probably guess he and Trish hadn't spent last night answering 911 calls.

Unless…

Blanching, he gazed back at Trish, who was still in a swivet, biting her lower lip and pacing in front of the refrigerator. She muttered something, took a slug of coffee, then shook her head, apparently discarding whatever idea she'd just had.

He cleared his throat and tried to broach the subject gingerly. "Are you, uh, worried about how Manson might react?"

"Don't you think he's going to wonder what I've been doing all this time?" When he didn't answer, she dropped her coffee cup in the sink. "I can't stand here talking, Bill. I've got to go."

All the air gushed out of him at once, leaving him feeling like a limp deflated balloon the morning after a raucous New Year's bash. He couldn't believe it. Last night they'd had the most glorious sex he'd ever experienced in his life, with the woman he wanted *in* his life, and she was worried about getting to the church on time. To marry somebody else!

"Pardon me, but have I missed something here?"

She blinked at him. "What?"

"Trish, last night was incredible."

She looked frozen, like a deer in front of headlights. "And?"

"And I thought..." His words trailed off. She seemed so unresponsive, he couldn't think of a thing more to say.

He ran a hand through his hair, trying to figure it all out. Wasn't *she* the one who'd initiated their lovemaking last night, telling him she was disappointed that he hadn't come to talk her out of her wedding? Hadn't he been the reticent one, trying to take the high road, to play the good loser? Of course, once the dam had burst, he'd been as responsible for their actions as she was, but initially, he'd been ready to grit his teeth and allow her to ride off into the sunset with the nice-guy dentist. He'd been looking heartbreak in the eyes, and not flinching.

Then she'd beckoned him with those tearful brown eyes and had told him she *wanted* him to try to bust up her engagement, and he was a goner.

Growing a little angry, he stumped over to the coffeepot and poured himself a cup of yesterday's coffee. He didn't bother to heat it. After all, the lady was in a hurry.

"Bill?"

He looked into her honey-colored eyes and experienced disappointment and irritation in equal measure. The urge to strangle her was almost as powerful as the urge to pull her into his arms and kiss her like there was no tomorrow.

Or better yet, no today.

She tilted her head. "Aren't you going to say anything?"

He tried his damnedest to appear nonchalant. *As if!* Did she think this was a common occurrence—sleep with a woman and then have her run off to Jamaica on her honeymoon with someone else the very next day? He hadn't been with a woman since Andrea left him. Two years he'd waited, just to make sure he found the right person. He thought he'd found her.

Didn't she realize that?

The blank, impatient stare she sent him indicated she didn't. Or if she did, she didn't care. It was hard to believe the woman he'd held in his arms last night could be so callous, but the evidence was piling up.

"Well then." She lifted her chin a notch, as if the pointless phrase gave them closure.

The breath gushed out of him again and he felt disappointment in every pore of his body. He'd never dreamed this would happen. "Well."

"Can you drive me home? I really need to get going."

To get ready. For the wedding. He remembered how beautiful and sexy she'd looked in her wedding gown and began to feel ill. He couldn't stop himself from blurting out, "Can you really marry Manson now, Tricia?"

She jerked in response to his question, spilling coffee down her red tank top. She jumped back to get a paper towel and wiped at the stain. "I—"

She gazed up at him, maddeningly silent. What was she waiting for? For him to give her his blessing?

He certainly wasn't going to do that, though he supposed he did owe her a ride home. He turned on his heel and heard her traipse after him, hopping on one foot as she slipped on her other shoe. She was in so much of a hurry to get to Manson that she couldn't sit down and get dressed properly, he thought bitterly. And yet he couldn't forget that if he felt as if he'd just been kicked in the gut, he had only himself to blame. He'd known all along that she was determined to rush down the aisle—from day one, she'd done nothing but insist she couldn't wait to be Mrs. Manson Toler.

The drive to Peggy's house was spent in morose silence. Bill itched just to throw on the brakes and beg, plead and grovel until she said she wouldn't marry that guy. He wanted to take her in his arms and show her again what she couldn't possibly find in the arms of another man. Chemistry like theirs just didn't come along every day. She had to know that.

Part of him hoped that Manson had found out about them kissing. Or that he would never forgive her for staying out all night. In fact, maybe Manson, in a fit of jealous pique, had already caught the first plane back to Los Angeles....

Then again, Manson didn't strike him as the type to become overemotional about anything, except maybe people not flossing.

He pulled up to her mother's house and turned to Tricia, praying he didn't look as grim and resentful as he felt. "Good luck." He practically bit the words out.

She eyed him carefully, as if he might detonate. "So...will I see you later?"

Did she actually think he was going to appear at her wedding? This was the limit! "No."

"I'm sorry, Bill. About everything. I thought..."

The sentence dangled for a moment, then she shook her head, got out of the car and ran up the walkway to her mother's house.

TRICIA PRAYED she wouldn't have to see her mother. But when she ran through the house, all was silence. In her room, she found a note on her bed.

Pattie: I've gone to the church to check on the caterers. Please be there by 10:30. Also, Manson called.

Manson had called here? Had he said anything about last night? And where was Tom? People certainly didn't seem to be very communicative today!

She dropped down onto her bed, brooding. Scenes from the night before raced through her mind. Bill, kissing her all over; Bill, nuzzling her in sleep; Bill, waking her up at three in the morning to make slow, sumptuous, incredibly satisfying love. Just the memories made her burn with yearning all over again.

Why hadn't he just said three simple words? One "I love you" would have made everything crystal clear in her mind. Even a hint that he wanted her in his life on a permanent basis would have had her on the phone to Manson like a shot. Hell, even a semipermanent basis. But how much time in her life had she spent loving Bill and not having him love her back? She didn't want more of that. Not when she had...

Manson! What was she going to say to him?

Screwing up the courage, she picked up the phone and dialed his hotel room. No one answered. Probably because he was already at the church. It was 10:25 a.m. What was she going to do?

Don't think, she ordered herself. She could make important life decisions on the way to the church. Right now she just needed to get dressed!

Blotting Bill and Manson and lovemaking and vow-reciting out of her head, she battled her way into a pair of too-small pantyhose and struggled with that piece of armor calling itself a brassiere. By the time she was finished with her underwear, she was already sweating buckets, despite the fact that she'd caked on enough deodorant to keep a small country from perspiring.

She tossed the dress over her head and fastened the buttons, nearly dislocating her shoulder in the process of getting the high ones in the back. Next she slapped on makeup at the speed of light, though her hands shook as they applied lipstick and rouge, and nearly poked an eye out with the mascara wand. Her hair she did up simply in a loose bun, jamming in a million pins to make sure it stayed in place underneath the veil. Finally, she shoved her feet into her dyed-to-match eggshell pumps and dashed over to look at herself in the full-length mirror.

She gasped at the result. Every time she looked at her reflection, she still half expected to see her old, forty-pounds-heavier self. But now as she gawked at herself she realized she looked like a bride out of a magazine, just as she'd always dreamed. Her heart picked up. Maybe the decision she had to make wasn't so terribly traumatic after all. A little of her old enthusiasm returned. She was coming back to her hometown in triumph; dazzling the natives with her thin body and gorgeous, rich fiancé had been a dream of hers for years. And now it was happening, and she felt...

Terrible.

Despite her armor-plated breasts, she sagged in resignation. It was no use. There was nothing triumphant about marrying one man just because he was the first to ask when there was a man five minutes away who she was eating her heart out for.

Manson *was* as good as gold, better than she deserved...but he'd caught her on the rebound, just as she was recovering her self-esteem. He'd swept her off the beach in Cancun and told her all the things she'd always dreamed of hearing. Their times together had been a fantasy-come-true; newly thin woman has dream man fawn over her, offer her everlasting love and a huge house in Beverly Hills. She wouldn't be surprised if Mr. Roarke and Tattoo had been on that beach in Cancun, too.

But just because she appreciated what Manson had done for her didn't mean she loved him. And if she didn't, she couldn't marry him. Bill was the only man she wanted to marry.

That Bill had never mentioned marriage to her—or love or anything but the great sex they'd had—was something she would have to deal with later.

She looked at the clock on the bureau and felt her heart pound with dread. Fifteen minutes. That was all the time she had left.

She didn't know if she could face weaseling out of her wedding alone. She picked up the phone and called Sylvie's, but no one answered. She and the kids were probably already at the church. *Everybody* was already at the church, including the florist, the organist, the caterers...

Her poor mom! All the work she'd gone through. All the worrying she'd done.

Not to mention, Tricia's bookstore was sold, her house was on the market, her worldly goods were in the hands of movers.

A lump formed in her stomach, but there was nothing to do for it but go. She rushed out the door and jumped in her Toyota, then pushed the pedal to the metal, half expecting flashing lights to appear behind her, and half hoping it would be Bill. Miraculously she screeched up to the church parking lot without a mishap—which was probably the only thing about this morning that was trouble-free.

With only five minutes to spare, the parking lot was packed. Every person her mother invited had apparently shown up. An organ version of "We've Only Just Begun" wafted out of the church, making Tricia's stomach do a sickening flip.

She rushed up the steps and skidded to a stop in the church's vestibule. Peeking at the crowd, she saw her mother seated next to Irene, talking. In her robin's egg blue mother-of-the-bride dress, Tricia almost didn't recognize her.

Manson, naturally, was not at the altar waiting for her yet. He was probably in the vestry hall, along with two hundred pastel-dyed deviled eggs and the thawed wedding cake. The side of the church designated as the groom's by the carnations spelling out Manson's name was distressingly empty. It appeared none of Manson's friends or relatives had made it. Only a few townspeople had chosen to sit on that side, maybe to make the groom feel welcome or perhaps just out of a sense of balance.

She cleared her throat loudly enough for half the congregation to swivel in their pews to gape at her. Catching Iris's eye, Tricia gestured frantically toward her mother until someone yelled out, "Hey, Peggy—Pat's here!"

Her mother's eyes widened and she jumped up and bustled toward her in a flurry of blue. There was not a person in the church who wasn't watching her little drama now.

"Where have you been?"

"It's a long story, Mom."

"Well thank goodness one of you decided to show up!"

"Manson isn't here *at all?*" If Manson wasn't here, how was she going to call off her wedding? "Has anyone heard from him?"

"No one," Peggy said. "I was hoping he'd called you."

Tricia clutched at her stomach and tried to move out of the view of a hundred curious faces. "Do you think…?"

She didn't finish. She didn't have to.

"I don't know what to think!" Peggy exclaimed. "Everyone's behaving so peculiarly. Where's Tom? He was supposed to usher. Where's Sylvie? I thought she was going to read that silly poem. Everybody's here but the wedding party—except you, of course." One look at the green pallor of her daughter's face made her amend her statement. "And you look as though you might not be with us much longer."

Feeling as if her wobbly legs might not hold her up much longer, Tricia leaned against the wall for support. *Left waiting at the altar.* It was her old nightmare—only now it was a reality. She'd meant to return to her hometown in a blaze of glory, but instead she'd created a big flop. Pudgy Pat strikes again!

How had something that had seemed so right a mere week ago turned into such a mess?

Her mother looked out the front door. "Thank heavens!" Peggy shouted, loud enough for the whole town to hear. "Here come Tom and Casey."

The two youngsters, dressed up in their Sunday best except for their ever-present in-line skates, clattered up the church steps and zoomed right up to Tricia, who grasped Tom both for support and to keep him from rolling right past her.

"Where's Sylvie?" she asked them.

The two kids, panting from exercise, looked up and

shook their heads in unison. "We don't know—when we got over to her house, she wasn't there," Tom said. "We went back to Grandma's house, but you'd already left. All we found was this note in the mailbox, addressed to you!"

From Manson, no doubt. Her Dear Jane letter.

With trembling hands, Tricia took the plain white envelope from her son and opened it. When she saw the familiar handwriting, however, she gasped in surprise.

Dear Trish,

By the time you read this note, Manson and I will be on our way to Maui. I'm so sorry. Believe me, I wouldn't be doing this if I wasn't cockeyed crazy about the guy, and if you and Bill hadn't conveniently disappeared during the movie last night (where were you guys?) I might never have discovered that your Mr. Right was actually mine. You were wrong about Manson, Trish—he's more than wonderful and courteous. He's adorable and loveable and the greatest lover this side of Sean Connery.

Manson? Tricia wondered with growing amazement.

I owe you, friend. For once my brother wasn't able to sabotage my romance—mostly because he was so preoccupied with you. Bill loves you, Trish. He's just too much of a gentleman to steal you from another man. As your (hopefully still) best friend, I command you to marry him!

If you still feel like speaking to me after this all shakes down, and I pray you will, I hope you'll come visit us (and your furniture) in Beverly Hills. I bet we'll have lots to catch up on!

All my love, Sylvie

PS—Manson says to keep the tickets to Jamaica. Isn't he sweet?

Peggy jumped up and down with inquisitiveness. "For heaven's sake, what does it say?"

She handed the note to her mother. "Sylvie's getting married."

Amazingly, Tricia wasn't trembling anymore. Her legs weren't wobbling. And truly, all she could feel was relief—maybe getting left at the altar wasn't the worst thing that could happen. In fact, maybe Manson and Sylvie's elopement was the best outcome she could have hoped for.

"I always said I'd give anything to see Sylvie happy. I guess one almost cast-off fiancé is a bargain."

Peggy looked up at her with concern. If Tricia expected one of those tearful Hallmark card mother-daughter moments, she was in for a shock. "What on earth are we going to do with all those deviled eggs?"

Tricia laughed. Her mother always was one for looking at the practical problems in life. "Maybe we should hand one to each guest on the way out."

When she looked up from the note, Peggy's eyes widened. Tricia followed her gaze and saw Bill standing in the doorway, silhouetted by sunlight. She sucked in her breath. He was in his police uniform and he looked absolutely dazzling.

He rushed to her. "Sylvie just called from the airport and told me the news."

Tricia nodded. "She sent me a note." She plucked it out of her mother's hands and folded it up tightly. She didn't want Bill to see what his sister had written. She didn't know whether Bill really loved her or not;

it could just be Sylvie's wishful thinking. In any case, one dumping per day was quite enough, thank you.

"If I'd known, I'd have..." His teeth practically gnashed.

She tilted her head, grinning wryly. Still the love police. "You'd have what? Sent a fleet of patrol cars after them? Locked Manson in the slammer?"

His expression turned to astonishment. "What?"

She folded her arms over her chest. "I know you. If you'd caught Manson running off with your sister, you'd probably have marched him up the aisle by force and made him marry me."

Impulsively, Bill took her hands in his. "Are you nuts? If I'd known there was even a whiff of romance between those two, I'd have bought the tickets to Maui myself!"

Her mouth flopped open in disbelief moments before her lips pulled up in a joyous smile. "No kidding?"

"Believe me, Trish, I'd have toasted their love affair with champagne and a marching band!"

Tricia's heart skipped crazily. "But you never seemed to want Sylvie to get married."

"Not to one of her jerks," Bill admitted. "But that's the beauty of this—I've already checked Manson out thoroughly. And you know as well as I do that the man is as good as gold."

She laughed. "Yes, he is, even though his elopement has left me with a churchful of guests, a reception hall full of food, and a rather embarrassing announcement that needs to be made before the organist runs out of Carpenters songs."

Although, given Julie Tuttle's extensive Carpenters repertoire, she wondered if that were possible.

Peggy touched her arm. "Don't worry, Pattie. I'll

take care of everything." She frowned. "Though I'm not sure what exactly I'll tell everyone...."

Bill stopped her. "Why don't you tell them to sit tight."

Startled, Tricia looked up into eyes of heartbreaking blue and felt as though she might burst with the hope that leaped up in her.

He gazed at her in all seriousness. "That is, unless you've decided you don't want to get married at all."

"Not *want* to?" She'd probably wanted nothing else from the moment of their first encounter a week earlier. "What do you think I'm dressed for, a Maypole dance?"

He pulled her into his arms and poised his lips just over hers. "Pat-Tricia Parker Peterson, would you mind changing your name just one more time, to mine?"

"Not in the slightest!" she cried joyfully. "Oh, Bill, I love you!"

He finally brushed his lips against hers. "I love you, Trish."

They kissed, taking their time to revel in this moment when all the confusion was finally cleared and they could just savor the joy of being with each other. No guilt. No mixed emotions. Just pure happiness.

Five minutes later, Tricia was marching down the aisle, as planned, toward a completely unplanned-for groom. She'd always heard that weddings inevitably produced a few surprises, but even she couldn't have imagined this.

Only two people in the whole church weren't completely astonished by the last-minute turn of events. Grinning in triumph, Tom and Casey sat in the pew directly in front of the Manson carnations no one had thought to take down. When the groom finally kissed the bride, they looked away, not in embarrassment, but because this was their moment.

Their eyes met.

"Cool," Tom said.

Casey's face broke out into a full-braces grin as Julie Tuttle broke into a rousing rendition of "Top of the World."

"Totally cool," she agreed.

COLLEEN COLLINS

Rough and Rugged

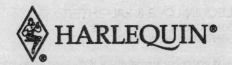

HARLEQUIN®

TORONTO • NEW YORK • LONDON
AMSTERDAM • PARIS • SYDNEY • HAMBURG
STOCKHOLM • ATHENS • TOKYO • MILAN • MADRID
PRAGUE • WARSAW • BUDAPEST • AUCKLAND

Dear Reader,

In my first book, *Right Chest, Wrong Name,* I introduced
Raven Doyle, a fellow who wore ripped T-shirts over
his refrigerator-size chest, sported a sinister Fu Manchu
moustache and wore a garish red, yellow and blue
iguana tattoo on his oversized biceps. Despite his
rough appearance, Raven was a good-hearted man,
who collected recipes from women's magazines and
yearned for true love. When some of you asked what
happened to Raven, I knew his story was far from
over....

Now Raven's back—but he no longer wears ripped
T-shirts and his upper lip is clean-shaven (he still
sports the tattoo). And although he thinks he's driven
his Harley cross-country to find a new life, he doesn't
realize he's about to find a new love.

I hope you enjoy this book. I love to hear from
readers—you can write to me at P.O. Box 12159,
Denver, CO 80212.

Best wishes,

Colleen Collins

Books by Colleen Collins

HARLEQUIN DUETS
10—MARRIED AFTER BREAKFAST

HARLEQUIN LOVE & LAUGHTER
26—RIGHT CHEST, WRONG NAME
54—RIGHT CHAPEL, WRONG COUPLE

1

"I NEED A MAN NOW. Not tomorrow afternoon. Not the day after. *Now!*"

On that crisp imperative, Caroline "Liney" Reed reached into her purse, tapped open a box, and plucked out a cigarette. Squeezing it between her index and middle fingers, she held it high in the air, twiddling it like a mini-baton, as she listened to the New York agent prattle on the other end of the cell phone. Liney picked out key phrases, ignoring the rest of the verbal static.

"No," she interrupted, snapping the cigarette in two on the one-syllable word. "The model you flew out does *not* match the description I requested. I asked for John Wayne. You sent me Lord Byron. That's like asking for meat and getting soufflé." She tossed the broken cigarette onto the hot asphalt, squished it for good measure with the toe of her tan leather pump, then looked longingly at the squashed, shredded mess. Damn. If only she hadn't stopped smoking last week. At this moment, she'd hawk her BMW for a single nicotine puff.

Pivoting sharply, the phone pressed against her ear, Liney continued speaking as she paced across the parking lot. "*Cooking Fantasies* is on a tight schedule— we need to complete this photo shoot by Friday. Not Saturday. *Friday.* I've tucked Lord Byron into a taxi—

he's on his way to the Cheyenne airport to catch a return New York flight as we speak. Meanwhile, I need a *man*—a rugged, dirt-in-his-laugh-lines John Wayne man—by daybreak tomorrow, Tuesday, or your agency name is crud.''

Swiveling, she strode back several feet, the tap-tap of her heels in counterpoint to the agent's hyperpitched promises of John Wayne arriving by morning. Despite Liney's temper nearly matching the August asphalt-melting Wyoming heat, she knew better than to offer any more ultimatums. If this modeling agent could fly in a John Wayne tonight, then the shoot still had a good chance to be completed by Friday and Liney would meet her schedule. And right now, that goal was all that mattered in her nicotine-free world.

"Great," she said into the receiver. "Call as soon you get Mr. Rugged on a plane. My cell phone will be on—all night." With a brisk goodbye, Liney punched a button, severed the connection, and shoved the phone into her purse. After blowing out an exasperated breath, she said to the world in general, "Why do I have to handle everything?"

"Need me to get somethin'?" A weathered cowboy, dressed in faded jeans and wearing boots that looked as though he'd walked in them for most of his life, straightened from leaning against the side of a dusty red pickup.

"No, Gomer. I'm just venting." Tucking a stray hair back into her French twist, Liney wondered what were the odds of anyone else on the planet finding a gofer named Gomer. But within an hour of their arrival this morning from L.A., that's exactly what her crew had done. Her crew were currently outside Cheyenne, in the midst of stunted grass and sagebrush, dismantling the camera and props for the "A Rugged Man Cooks" shoot. And all because a print agent in New York didn't know the difference between rugged and ruffled.

Gomer navigated a toothpick from one side of his mouth to the other. "Think you'll find what you need?"

Liney squinted at the old guy. Shave off thirty years, stick him in gym for a week, and Gomer might have fit the bill. Opening her eyes, she fought the urge to sigh. Or snap another cigarette. "Maybe. The agency swears they'll have an 'appropriate' man for me by tomorrow morning."

"Do they have John Waynes in New York?" He quirked a white, bushy eyebrow.

She and Gomer had only spent the last nine hours together, since eight o'clock this morning, but Liney noticed that he had a way of asking questions that zeroed in with painstaking accuracy. This time it felt more pain*ful* than painstaking, however. If New York didn't have a John Wayne clone for this magazine shoot, she might as well kiss off her career at Harriman Enterprises. A career that was all of one month old. A career that none of the other vice presidents at the L.A. corporate offices wanted her to have because they thought she, at twenty-seven, was too young, too "green" to be hired as Vice President of Print Communications. Her first proving ground was to revamp *Cooking Fundamentals*, a magazine that was rapidly losing readership.

Liney tackled the challenge with the zeal that had earned her "Most Likely to Succeed" in high school. Wanting to appeal to women readers, who comprised eighty percent of the subscribers, Liney decided to light a fire under their imaginations rather than their stoves.

First, she renamed the magazine *Cooking Fantasies*. Second, she brainstormed the premiere editorial piece to be "A Rugged Man Cooks"—with sexy photos of a hunky, megamasculine man cooking in the Wild West. Third, Liney announced that she would personally oversee this production from start to finish. She knew vice presidents didn't get down and roll in the corporate day-to-day dirt, but this was Liney's make-it or lose-it opportunity. She not only had to succeed, but *excel* to prove herself to the top brass.

Which wouldn't have been such a roll-in-the-dirt project if Dirk Harriman, out of the blue, hadn't uprooted from L.A. and transplanted himself to a diner on the outskirts of Cheyenne, Wyoming. Dirk Harriman's presence in the corporate hallways and meetings had been a constant reminder to the other V.P.s that she had a strong supporter. Without him, she felt she was swimming, naked, with sharks. Therefore, she insisted the shoot be in Cheyenne because she also secretly hoped to convince the CEO to return to his senses *and* L.A.

Coming out of her reverie, she realized the old cowboy's eyebrow hadn't settled back down. It remained cocked, waiting for her response. "Do they have John Waynes in New York?" she repeated. When he nodded, she answered, "They better have, Gomer, or I'll be forced to dress you up and put a frying pan in your hand."

He guffawed. Lifting the battered Stetson from his head, he swiped at his brow with the back of his arm. "Me, your John Wayne model. Better take them pictures from a long ways off or smear a gob of Vaseline on the lens 'cause I'm about as John Wayne as a Jersey is a bull." He waved his hat toward the Blue Moon

Diner. "This dry heat has me parched. Goin' inside, get some iced tea. Suggest you do the same before you melt like a pretty ice cream cone in this summer broiler." He slipped his hat back on before strolling toward the front door of the diner.

Pretty ice cream cone. Liney smiled. That was the nicest compliment any man, or anyone for that matter, had given her in a long time. In the Harriman Enterprise offices she'd already caught wind of the nickname whispered behind her back. "Dragon Lady." If they knew she'd been called a sweet, icy confection, they'd have disagreed—well, maybe except for the "icy" part.

Liney twisted her single-drop pearl earring. "Dragon Lady" hurt. She knew she was trying too hard, pushing others to meet high expectations, but didn't they know her efforts were for the company? Late at night, when she'd get home from the office, she consoled herself by thinking such nicknames were part of the price of being successful. And focused. And a woman. After all, did they ever call a male manager a "Dragon Gentleman"? No, men were allowed to be tough and goal-oriented. Heaven forbid a woman had those same traits! Still, after hearing it whispered one too many times, she had decided to quit smoking. Maybe if she wasn't seen inhaling and blowing out smoke, "Dragon Lady" would eventually go away.

A distant rumbling interrupted her thoughts. Turning toward the dirt road that led from the highway to the diner, she spotted a moving dust cloud. It rapidly approached, the dirt mushrooming behind a massive black-and-chrome beast. Shards of yellow-gold sunlight glinted off its metal. As the beast came closer, the rumbling intensified, filling the world with a prolonged, steady roar that made Liney feel as though a self-contained hurricane was headed her way.

In the midst of the thunder and metal sat a man, his black mane of hair whipping in the wind as though some internal force was about to be unleashed. His large, muscular body leaned back, riding the beast with an unassuming confidence that sent a trickle of sweat down Liney's back. Brawny arms gripped the raised handles. On one bicep was a colorful tattoo, although just exactly what she couldn't yet tell. It looked bold and flagrant, as though he didn't give a damn what the world thought. As he pulled into the Blue Moon Diner lot, Liney didn't know whether to run or stand her ground. She did the latter only because her legs refused to budge.

The engine growled like a tethered lion as the rider slowly cruised in a semicircle, checking out the diner. Watching him intently, she fumbled again in her purse for the cigarettes. As she touched the hard edge of the box, she spied the taut outline of thigh muscle through his jean-encased legs. A man that size—how did he shop? She'd helped numerous guy-pals cultivate their sense of power dressing. In her sleep, she could match the perfect herringbone tie with the correct dress shirt. But this man before her? One probably took him to a garment factory, stripped him naked, then swathed him in yards of coarse, rough-edged fabric. How else did he find clothes to fit?

As images of endless swathing swept through Liney's mind, she wished she hadn't worn silk. Without looking down, she knew her sheath dress was clinging uncivilly to her sweaty chest. She tried to hunch a little, but the darn dress remained glued to her torso.

When he eased to a stop and dropped his foot onto

the asphalt, she dropped her gaze. The boot was black, like the machine—and roughened, like the man. When the engine finally halted, Liney thought her heart had as well.

He swung one leg over the machine and stood. He was tall. Over six feet. After stretching his tree-sized arms, he shook his head, like an animal shaking off water. A white T-shirt stretched across a tightly muscled abdomen. Across it were the words, Go Within or Go Without.

Trying not to think how long she'd gone without, Liney heaved in a ragged breath. As she attempted to quell the shaking of her thighs by tightening her knees, she realized she didn't need any rugged John Waynes winging in from New York. Mr. Beyond Rugged—the rawest, wildest, beastliest specimen of manhood this side of New York—stood before her like a gift from Corporate Headquarters in the Sky. He was *exactly* what she needed. A recipe of all the untamed manlymen she'd ever imagined…a teaspoon of bad-boy Bruce Willis; a sprinkle of the dark, somber John Travolta; a cup of George Clooney.

Women would not only try the recipes, they'd probably lick the magazine pages. Sales would escalate. Liney's career would be intact. *Goodbye Dragon Lady, hello victorious Vice President.*

The recipe walked toward her as he removed his leather gloves. His coal-black eyes traveled down her outfit and then back up to her face. "You okay?" he asked. Maybe she had to wrap him in yards of rough-edged fabric, but his voice was the opposite. Deep. Velvet-edged.

This close, she smelled the arousing scent of sweat and aftershave that rose from his heated skin. She slowly closed, then opened her eyes. Good. He was real, not a heat-induced mirage. "Yes, I'm okay," she said, her voice barely above a croak. "And you're perfect."

He hesitated, obviously a bit baffled by her response. As he stuck the leather gloves in the back pocket of his jeans, he murmured, "I asked because of those..." His gaze again lowered.

She followed his line of vision. In her left hand were four crushed cigarettes, mangled into a pile of white paper and tobacco. "I must have..." *crushed them during my swathing fantasy* "...accidentally squeezed them." She quickly brushed the mess from her hands, coughing a little to distract him.

He gave her a concerned look. "How many do you smoke at once?"

Defensively, she rolled back her shoulders...and immediately regretted the action. If he hadn't seen the dress stuck to her sweat-covered chest before, he sure did now. "I don't smoke," she said quickly, crossing her arms under her breasts. "I just carry them for...for good luck." She hadn't the vaguest what she meant by that comment, but rather than admit that, she kept her face expressionless as though she knew exactly what she was talking about. It worked with co-workers. Maybe it also worked with beastly, rugged men.

"Well, those good-luck charms will shorten your life. Former smoker myself, so I know the battle." Before she could respond that she was only snapping, not smoking, he motioned toward the diner and asked, "You know Belle, the owner?"

Not personally, but Liney and the rest of Harriman Enterprises had heard how Dirk had fallen in love—

and married—a showgirl named Belle O'Leary who owned a diner in Cheyenne, Wyoming.

"Belle and Dirk are out to dinner." She knew because Gomer had driven her all the way back to the Blue Moon Diner so she could talk to Dirk about the Lord Byron fiasco. That's when Liney found out Belle and Dirk were out, *again,* on one of their ongoing we're-just-married-and-can't-get-enough-of-each-other dates. Liney had never seen two people so enamored of each other. They made lovebirds look like platonic pals. She was beginning to think Dirk had lost not only his business sense, but his personal sense.

A shadow crossed the man's face. "I've been driving three days to see Belle…guess I can wait another hour or so."

As he headed back to his bike, Liney followed. She had to start convincing him to be her rugged man. "Why don't we go inside and get some…iced tea?" she asked, stealing Gomer's line.

He looked over his shoulder—that bulged like the distant Rockies—and raised one black eyebrow. "Tea?"

She shrugged, trying to ignore how the thick black tendrils of his hair curled over the neckline of his T-shirt. Tried not to imagine how more of that thick, black hair probably carpeted his back, his chest. "Sure," she said hoarsely. "Tea." Actually, she'd kill for a double latte but it didn't appear they made them at the Blue Moon Diner. Earlier, Liney had managed two sips of its black coffee, but stopped before it put hair on *her* chest.

Reaching his cycle, the man opened a fringed, black leather pouch attached to the rear fender and pulled out a wallet. Without turning around, he said, "Tea's okay. But is that what you really want?"

What was it with men today? Just as Gomer had zeroed in on an issue, so had this man. Some defiant urge to not be bested surfaced. Before she could stop the words, they glibly rolled off her tongue. "If you don't want to join me for iced tea, all you have to do is say 'no,' not second-guess my intentions as though I'm some kind of needy child who's skirting the issue."

He stopped midmotion and stood stock-still…except for one neck muscle that ticked spasmodically. Unfolding to his full height, he slowly turned around. It was like watching a mountain revolve. By the time he'd completed a half turn, her nose was level with "or Go Without."

How ironic that she'd spent three precious days last year at that workshop "The Manager Within" so she could learn efficient ways to persuade and enthuse others. Staring at the words mere inches from her face— she realized she could write her own seminar, "The Manager Without," as that's exactly what she'd be doing if she didn't curb her tongue. Her fingers fidgeted as she fought the urge to snap another cig.

Raven stared down at the top of the woman's head. Her auburn hair was arranged in one of those fancy tight buns, the way his ex-fiancée, Charlotte, had styled her hair. And so far this woman, just like Char, seemed to have zero respect for a man after he'd dismounted from a long, grueling chopper ride. But unlike how he dealt with Char, whose mission in life was to change him, he was going to speak up because *nobody,* especially no tight-bunned, designer-labeled female, was going to try to change him again.

He loomed over her, which made her bend backwards to see his face. In the measured diction pounded into him by Char's vocal coach, he said, "In the last three days, I've ridden several thousand miles from L.A. I blasted through a downpour that nearly drowned me, ate blacktop when my bike hit an oil patch, and nearly kissed the back of a semi that jackknifed on a hairpin turn...and after all that, you cop a 'tude because I question why you, a total stranger, are inviting me to *tea?*" He lowered his voice to a dusty growl. "Whatever you really want, lady, you must want it pretty damn bad."

A rush of pink stained her cheeks. Those eyes, like two drops of melting chocolate, looked so beseeching. So...needy. Maybe that needy child comment wasn't too far off. But if she'd had to skirt issues growing up, she'd since learned to confront them head-on with the charm of a diesel engine.

After licking her lips, she whispered haltingly, "I-I have a business proposition."

He looked over at the diner with its bright stripes of blue and white. At the big moon face on top, circled in the neon words "Blue Moon Diner." At the signs in the window advertising everything from chicken-fried steak to biscuits and gravy. Then he looked back down at the neatly coiffed woman with pearl earrings. Thanks to Charlotte's retail name-dropping, he guessed the dress to be Molinari. And those Gucci shoes he could recognize in the dark because he'd once had to find a similar pair of Char's during a power outage.

Pearls. Molinari. Gucci. What in the hell was a high-class dame doing outside a diner in Cheyenne, Wyoming, propositioning him with a business deal? He was beat. It was hot. Wanting to cut this encounter short, he scowled at her with a look he knew terrified grown men. Surprisingly, those chocolate-drop eyes didn't even blink. Obviously she wasn't afraid of his theatrics—if she even noticed them. He had the impression she was skilled at penetrating top-layer issues and boring into the core problem. If she were a tool, she'd be one hell of a drill.

Then it hit him. *Business. Proposition.* He recalled Charlotte and her girlfriends gossiping about the recently arrested Beverly Hills Madam, who had made more money plying her trade than the city's best plastic surgeons. He looked at the woman in front of him with her saucer eyes and rosebud lips. This obstinate, classy number, a call girl? Maybe he was an L.A. kinda guy, but he had difficulty buying the notion of a Blue Moon Madam. In his mind, he heard a quote from one of the self-help tapes he'd been listening to while on the road. "You attract what you fear." If that's the case, he was in some kind of fear-induced Charlotte flashback, although she would never have propositioned him, *especially* in front of an establishment that served chicken-fried steak.

This woman confronted issues head-on, so he'd do the same. But he'd let her down easy. Times must be tough in Cheyenne if women of the night were working remote diners in the heat of the day. "My apologies," he said in a civilized tone that would have made his vocal coach weep with joy. "But I'm not interested in…sex."

She raised her heart-shaped face a notch. Those brown eyes narrowed until all he saw were two pinched slits fringed with lashes. "I beg your pardon," she said, her voice rising higher than her bun. "I'm a woman of business, not a woman of pleasure."

He believed *that*, no matter how she meant it.

She released an indignant breath—until this moment, a skill he thought only Charlotte had perfected. After blinking rapidly, the woman-of-no-pleasure seemed to rethink the situation because he could once again see her pupils. "Let's start over," she said evenly. "My name is Caroline Reed. But everyone calls me Liney. I'm the Vice-President of Print Communications for Harriman Enterprises. My proposition is legitimate and strictly business. For the next few days, I'd like to hire you, not the other way around—" she smiled tightly "—to be the star of my magazine project. I think you're the kind of man who'd appeal to women's..." Her gaze wandered as she obviously appraised him. After drawing in a ragged breath, she said, "Let's not go there again. It's too hot and we've had enough misunderstandings already. May I invite you inside for a glass of iced tea to discuss this properly?"

As she motioned toward the diner, he saw how her silk dress clung in sweaty patches to her slim frame. Cool, collected call girls didn't get so worked up propositioning one lonely biker. Plus, after her vehement denial, he bought the bit about her being a veep...who did *everything* properly. What she didn't understand, however, was he'd traveled thousands of miles to escape being subjected to the whims and ploys of a cultured, *proper* woman who thought Raven was her project. To please Charlotte, he'd taken classes, such as ballroom dancing, in order to change himself into the man she wanted him to be. After their relationship had crashed and burned, he realized the only person you can change is yourself.

Wanting to improve his life, he'd spent the last three days' ride listening to tapes on following your dreams and nurturing your soul. Time and again, he heard that at each moment, we're recreating ourselves anew. So, at thirty-five, he decided to do just that—create a new Raven. Not a new man from the outside, which is what Char had tried to do, but a new man from the inside. A man who cared for his soul. He envisioned opening his own bike repair shop, but instead of the typical hangout with greasy grub and bikini posters, he'd have health food and inspirational books. He'd not only fix people's cycles—the external—he'd help adjust their spirits—the internal. Of course, to fulfill this dream, he knew he'd have to find a job once he hit Cheyenne. But he never thought his first job offer would be...

"The *what* of your magazine project?" he repeated, eyeing her suspiciously.

"I want you to be the star."

"Why?"

"Because you're..." She probably just meant to flick off a bead of sweat from her hairline, but her index finger slid into that bun-do and got stuck. She tugged, smiled nervously, then tugged again. Her finger flew out so fast, he almost ducked. As though nothing odd had just transpired, she repeated, "Because you're the...the perfect rugged man."

Shades of Char. She, who also wanted him to be her big bad boy...until the urge went out of style. "I'm no actor—"

"Model," Liney corrected.

"Don't—doesn't matter. I'm recreating myself, but not into some 'rugged' man for a magazine ad, pushing things people didn't even know they wanted."

With a purposeful glint in her eye, she extended her hand. "I didn't catch your name."

He felt like saying, "I didn't throw it," but he'd

learned the hard way that intentional rudeness could hurt, bad. Especially when you were sincerely reaching out. In this case, Liney was literally doing just that— reaching out. He accepted her hand. Clasping her small and delicate fingers, he suddenly felt oversized and clumsy. Like a bear touching a fawn. He gently shook, careful not to snap anything. "Raven. Raven Doyle."

For a long moment, they just stood there, holding hands. The warmth of her skin penetrated his, seeped through the muscle, down to the bone. As his stomach did a funny clench, he felt a movement of surprise in her fingers. Did she feel what he felt?

With a nervous laugh, she slid her hand from his grip. "Raven, the magazine isn't selling anything, except cooking."

"Cooking?" She was all business again. The clench had probably been a hunger pain. "I like anything to do with the kitchen," he admitted.

Obviously sensing her edge, she eagerly explained, "And that's exactly what this is about. Cooking in the great kitchen of the outdoors. I'm overseeing a shoot for a magazine called *Cooking Fantasies,* which used to be called *Cooking Fundamentals*—"

"*Cooking Fundamentals.*" He nodded. "Good read, but a bit old-fashioned. Char and I—well, *I* tried one of its recipes. A stuffed, braised lamb shoulder."

She glanced at his shoulders before meeting his gaze again. "So you know it?" She beamed. He liked how her face lit up when she smiled. All the tenseness disappeared, leaving her much softer looking. She dipped her head toward the Blue Moon. "Let's go inside and talk. You'll like hearing how the magazine's coming of age, away from its stodgy, old-fashionedness...." She turned and began walking toward the diner.

Raven stood for a moment, watching her. If he wasn't mistaken, she was still twittering about the magazine as though he was within earshot. The drill again, oblivious to everything else as she bored to the core of the topic. Charlotte never got excited about anything unless it had to do with gaining or losing weight. But Liney obviously had a passion for something other than body fat.

Was it his imagination, or did he detect vanilla? He inhaled fully, realizing it was her perfume that still lingered in the air. *Vanilla.* He almost groaned. A kitchen aroma mingled with a woman's scent—for Raven, a combination more combustible than fire and oil. Still breathing deeply, he watched her slim figure sashay away in that silk number. She had a purposeful way of walking, as though she always knew where she was going. He envied that, especially now in his life when he was starting over from scratch.

Starting over from scratch. He needed to stay focused on his goals and not be sidetracked by a pretty face with a spicy rack. In the last few weeks, he'd sworn off women a hundred times. Yet even as he counted to one hundred and *one,* he began walking, following her toward the diner. I'm going inside to discuss a job, he justified to himself. *After all, if I want to open my own bike-and-book shop, I need to start making money.*

As he muttered other good reasons he was following Ms. Vanilla, his gaze skimmed down her back and over a compact rear that undulated gently beneath the silk dress like two slow-moving pistons. As a warm breeze gusted past, he saw the hem ripple flirtatiously against the back of her firm calves.

He swore off women for the hundred and second time, wondering how high he'd be counting over the next few days.

"SIGN ON THE DOTTED LINE and you'll be my rugged man." Liney stilled, then blinked rapidly. "I mean, *Cooking Fantasies'* rugged man." With a great show of professionalism, she laid the legal document on the white-and-gold flecked Formica counter and pointed to where Raven had to sign his name.

Gripping the ballpoint pen, Raven swiveled slightly on his stool. He tuned out the background noises of clattering plates and chattering diners and focused on his thoughts. *It makes sense to sign.* During the last hour, Liney had enthusiastically explained the new look of the magazine and the importance of the premiere editorial, "A Rugged Man Cooks." Except for himself, he'd never seen anyone get so worked up over a cooking magazine. That alone enticed him. But if he were totally honest, the money cinched it. Four days' work and he'd have a down payment on a small shop, his bike-and-book shop dream.

"Is there a problem?" asked Liney, leaning in.

A middle-aged waitress, little pink packets of sweetener safety-pinned to her blouse, stopped on the other side of the counter. "You'all usin' the ketchup?"

When Liney shook her head "no," the waitress grabbed the bottle in front of them and scurried off.

Returning her attention to Raven, Liney said, "The faxed copy looked legible when I took it off Dirk's machine in the back.'' Now that Dirk lived at the diner, a back room had been turned into his office. She hunkered over the legal form, scrutinizing its readability.

Raven fought the urge to lick the air and taste that tantalizing vanilla scent. *That* was his problem. She might be sweetly accommodating right now, but she was also a vice president who was all business and part drill. And he was signing on for her pet project. *You attract what you fear.* Had he traveled eleven hundred miles just to end up in another controlling relationship with a Char clone? *That* thought was enough to make him leap from his blue vinyl-covered stool, tear out of the front door, and mount his chopper for another blacktop-eating thousand miles.

But he was tired of running. He hadn't bought this T-shirt for nothing. Go Within or Go Without. Taking a calming breath, he closed his eyes and went within, trying to hear that voice of intuition that the ''Hearty Man'' tape called ''heart intelligence.'' Breathing out, he focused on the fact this ''rugged man'' gig was for only four days. That was a big thumbs-up. Especially considering if he'd married Char, he would have signed away his rights for a hell of a lot longer—like a lifetime. Besides, he'd just done a grueling ride in three days—he could certainly be a ''rugged man'' for four.

Opening his eyes, he bent over the paper and signed his name. Beside him, he heard Liney on her cell phone, telling someone to ''cancel John Wayne.''

After he finished, Liney dropped the phone back into her purse as she pressed closer. ''Look at your handwriting,'' she exclaimed, admiring it as though it were a rare art object. ''So bold, so masculine, so unreadable!''

Resentment roared through his veins. Was she going

the Char route? For her, he'd changed almost everything—how he spoke, how he dressed, even how he chewed food—but no way in hell was he going to change the way he wrote! That was like changing his being left-handed to right-handed....

Oblivious to his internal combustion, Liney pursed her rosebud lips in a small smile of satisfaction. "That fits in with everything else that makes you the perfect rugged man. That scrawl, that—" Looking back down at his signature, she took such a deep breath, her small breasts strained against her silk dress. "—that masculine slash of ink would make Zorro jealous."

Okay, he'd forgive the "unreadable" comment.

Liney folded the signed paper with the precision of a brain surgeon and stuck it into her purse. "Excellent! We're in business." She brushed a curl off her face and looked at the round chrome clock on the back wall. "Six o'clock, dinnertime." As she looked at him with those big chocolate-brown eyes, that wayward curl tumbled back over her forehead, giving her a rumpled, just-out-of-bed look. "Hungry?"

His stomach did that clenching thing again. He grasped the edge of the cool counter, wishing it would temper the rush of carnal heat that blasted through him. He was worn down from the cross-country ride, that was all. And face it, he was so damn lonely after what he'd been through, even a drill with breasts looked good.

"Hungry?" she repeated a little more softly.

"Hundred and three." He bit the inside of his cheek. When would he learn to go within instead of spouting without?

"What?"

"Yes. I'm hungry," he mumbled. He hadn't eaten

since that tofu taco somewhere outside Salt Lake City. Grabbing two of the menus from a silver-pronged holder, he handed one to Liney.

"My treat," she said, opening hers.

"I'll pay." He maybe had a twenty tucked in his wallet, but money was the lesser issue. Just because he'd signed away his name didn't mean he gave away every last ounce of his self. If Liney took care of everything, made every decision, he might as well have learned nothing from his experience with Char.

"Nonsense, Raven. It's on the corporate expense account." As she read, she made a series of disapproving clucking sounds followed by a release of exasperated breath. "Is there anything on here that isn't all fat? Looking at this, you'd think one of the four food groups is *lard.*"

He knew Liney had passions for things other than body fat, but the outburst resurrected memories of every meal he'd ever shared with his former fiancée. Char claimed she didn't have a head for numbers, but take her to a restaurant and she could count fat grams like a math savant.

Another disapproving grunt came from behind the other menu. "They smother half the items in gravy! Do you realize how much fat—"

"Why don't you suck on some lemons?" he interrupted in a grumbling aside. "They have zero fat content." He pretended to be absorbed in reading his menu, but knew damn well she was glaring at him with unholy fat fury.

"Suck on a—"

"You ready to order?" asked a cheerful young girl with curly chestnut-brown hair. She held a pencil and a pad, totally unaware she was in the middle of a serious fat-gram war.

"That Chicken Surprise looks tasty," piped up Raven. "What's in it?"

The girl scratched her chin with the eraser end of the pencil. "Chicken, bell peppers, corn, carrots, some other veggies, all over rice."

"Hardly any fat—I'll take it." Raven folded his menu and stuck it in the holder. He knew he'd dug a hole with that comment, but it was too good to resist. After months of tiptoeing around Charlotte's whims and peeves, it felt great to speak his mind. Like breathing lungfuls of fresh air after being locked in a stuffy room.

The girl scribbled on her pad. Glancing up at a flushed, tight-lipped Liney, she asked, "And you?"

Liney tapped a finger against her menu. "Let me see...I'll have a side of...do you have fresh fruit?"

"Yes," the girl said, "it's canned."

Liney pressed her neatly shaped eyebrows together in what Raven guessed to be a moment of uncanny food reflection. "Fresh isn't canned...." she said under her breath, in a tone that made canned sound like a second cousin of road kill. "I'll have a small glass of apple juice. A side of toast, dry. A side of...what are 'greens'?"

"Collards. With butter. They're great!" the girl enthused.

Liney shuddered, a reaction that started as a slight shake of her shoulders and traveled to a quivering curl at the top of her bun-do. If he were in L.A., he might have mistaken that quiver for an oncoming earthquake. "Skip the greens. I'll have a side salad. No dressing. Just some lemon—" She shot a look at Raven, who cocked a knowing eyebrow in return. "—lemon wedges on the side, please." Liney then folded her menu and slid it into its holder.

After the waitress left, Liney and Raven sat in an awkward silence. Finally, carefully enunciating each word, she said, "Just because I try to avoid fat in my diet, you don't need to suggest I'm a sourpuss."

Raven did a double take. "I never said you were a sour—"

"You told me I could go suck lemons," she said, her voice breaking on "mons." She cleared her throat. "Same thing."

Maybe she was a big vice president, but he bet inside she was still that needy little girl. He'd spoken his mind, all right, but forgotten, as his Hearty Man tape lectured, to speak from his heart. He reached over and laid a hand on hers. It was like covering a flower with a mountain as his huge, tanned fingers engulfed her small, pale ones—as fragile, no doubt, as the rest of her. He recalled another line from one of his tapes. *Communicate as you go, don't wait 'til you blow.* He and Liney would be working closely together over the new few days—he needed to bridge their misunderstanding now.

"I'm sorry," he said, meaning it down to the tip of his leather boots. "I shouldn't have made that lemon comment. Guess the fat talk got to me." He'd skip further explanation about Char, the Fat-Gram Savant.

Liney glanced at him with moistened eyes. "Thank you." Lifting her chin a notch, she added, "I'm really not a sourpuss, you know." She touched the corner of her eye as though extracting a pesky eyelash, but Raven had already seen the surfacing tear she pushed back. "If...if you were to pick a nickname for me, what would it be?'' she asked with exaggerated non-chalance.

Strange question. But he also saw that she was upset and trying valiantly to act otherwise. He wondered how often she'd been in boardrooms in one of her power suits, acting as though she didn't have a single jumping hormone for fear the men would dismiss her as a weak female. Thanks to his best pal Lizzie, he'd learned to be sensitive to how women were sometimes treated. The least he could do was show Liney he wasn't that kind of man.

"Let's see," he said, playing the game. He looked at her erect posture, an impressive feat considering she had been sitting on a stool, with no back, for the last hour. The thought "Little General" came to mind, but he didn't need to listen to his inner voice to know *that* name would go over like a ton of lemons. He skimmed over her soft cream dress, past her alabaster skin—Al? Nah—and up to her auburn hair swept into that twisty-bun number.

"Bunny?" he suggested

"Do I look like a *rabbit?*"

He glanced at her lips. "Rosebud, then."

"Rosebud?" She pinned him with a look. "Not that sled from the old Orson Welles movie—"

"No," he murmured thickly, "a rosebud for your petal-soft, pink-tinged lips." *Petal soft? Pink-tinged?* He reared back, aware he'd been leaning dangerously close to Rosebud. So close, in another moment he'd have had the opportunity to decide for himself if those luscious lips were petal soft. Put it in reverse, buddy. Backpedal, backpedal. *One hundred and four.* "I mean, lips are like petals." He let his gaze wander around the diner, unable to face those brown eyes brimming with gratitude. "Which, uh, means they're usually soft—"

"I understand," she interrupted, her voice warm with appreciation. "I'd take that nickname any day over…" With a small shrug, her voice trailed off.

Just as they'd held hands in silence outside, they now sat quietly, his hand still covering hers. Her face was visibly relaxed. When she let go of her worries, she looked younger, even glowed a little as though some hidden self—a sparkling, effervescent twin— came to the forefront. He had the strange wish he could spend the rest of his days making her laugh, helping her let go of the things that didn't really matter. As soon as that thought hit, he mentally clamped down on it. *Backpedal, buddy. You're holding hands with your boss. Which is about the same as holding hands with Char and you know where that got you. What that made you. You became a…*

"Chicken Surprise?" The young waitress, juggling one large plate and numerous side dishes, looked questioningly at the two of them.

"That's me," mumbled Raven. In the clatter of allocated plates, glasses, and silverware, he eased his hand from Liney's, who didn't seem to notice as she swept into the all-consuming activity of positioning side orders like a general positioning troops.

Liney, placing the plate of lemon wedges to the right of the salad, sneaked a peak at Raven, who was muttering under his breath. If she wasn't mistaken, it sounded like…numbers? "Don't tell me you're counting fat grams," she teased.

He flashed her a dark look. "No," he growled.

So much for their moment of camaraderie—if that's what that handholding moment was. Men. Go figure.

She picked up a piece of toast and examined it. It didn't appear to be soaked in butter, but you never knew in places like this. Laying it back down on the plate, she blotted at it with her paper napkin, then held it up to the light to check for any telltale greasy spots.

"What were you before this magazine gig? A food inspector?"

She lowered her napkin. "No," she said crisply, "I was the senior director of marketing at Cirrus."

"Oil company?"

She paused, fighting the urge to snap a cig. "You don't have to watch me, you know. You can mind your own business, eat your Chicken Revelation—"

"Surprise—"

"Whatever, and act as though I'm not here." She sliced a look at his T-shirt. "Maybe go within so I can eat without your judgments." Making a great show of ignoring him, she neatly bit off a corner of toast, pleased it was indeed dry, but not wanting to show even one twitch of antifat satisfaction to Mr. Watchdog sitting next to her.

They ate in silence for several long minutes, interrupted by sizzling and clanging sounds whenever the swinging door to the kitchen rocked open. Staring at her salad, Liney couldn't stand not knowing what Raven was doing. Was he watching her every move? Ignoring her? She hated herself for even wondering…it was as if she'd regressed to junior high, where she spent her entire eighth grade year fretting if Eddie Walton, the student body president and pubescent stud of the universe, was ever going to glance at her, the second-period hall monitor and pubescent nerdette of the schoolyard.

After playing with her salad, moving bits of it this

way and that, she spared a glance from her all-important lettuce-rearranging to check out Raven.

Elbows on the counter, slowly chewing his food, he met her gaze with such a cool you-don't-throw-me-babe look, she almost dropped her fork. Then he winked at her. A saucy, slow wink that burned away any lingering memories of Eddie Walton. Her mouth went slack before she had the wherewithal to turn her head back to her city of side orders.

The gall of that man! First to tease her, then to rag at her, then to *wink*. Just because he'd signed on as the Rugged Man didn't mean she had to take guff from him. Furious, she stabbed at her salad, stacking chunks of lettuce into a green shish kebob on her fork before propelling the wad into her mouth. Immediately, she regretted the action. She could barely touch her lips together, much less chew.

"Liney, time for me to scoot," interrupted a craggy male voice.

She looked over at Gomer, trying desperately to keep her mouth closed.

His bushy white eyebrows pressed together. "You all right, honey?"

She nodded, her eyes watering. Flaring her nostrils, she eased in a slow stream of oxygen before she suffocated. But there was no way she'd admit to her foolishness. Not in front of Watchdog.

"Gotta be careful with hot food," Gomer warned. "Don't want to burn that pretty little tongue of yours."

Raven snorted something just out of earshot.

With a supreme effort, she chewed and swallowed the mini-head of lettuce. After a little cough, she said hoarsely, "I'll go with you, Gomer. I need a ride back to the shoot.'' Because of the two-hour commute from Cheyenne, she and her crew were staying on location.

Looking down at her assortment of food-filled plates, he placed a caring hand on her arm. ''Whoa there. Little thing like you needs to eat or these Wyoming winds will blow you away. Wish I could wait, but I gotta leave now so I can get to the store before it closes. Promised your people I'd pick up some supplies for tomorrow. Can you get another ride?''

''I'll take her.'' Raven reached over Liney to extend his hand to the older gentleman. ''Raven.''

''Gomer.''

As they shook hands in a male-bonding ritual as old as time, Liney fought the urge to place her hand on top and chant, ''Three potato, four!'' Maybe her immature reaction was because she felt as though the two men had just sealed her fate, just as the vice presidents back in L.A. would love to do. Or maybe it was being in the middle of cowboy country where a man was a man and a woman was a side dish.

Speaking of which, she pushed away the nearest plate as a signal she was leaving with Gomer, despite the fact he was already heading toward the door. No way was the Winking Wonder calling the shots. She swiveled and started to slide off the stool when her body lurched, as though jerked back by a mini-bungee rope. Her legs continued to slide toward the floor while her dress remained stationary.

As in a bad dream, she stood, facing the entire diner, showing a lot more than her attitude. At a nearby table, a family stopped eating and stared at her openmouthed. It flashed through her mind to never order fried okra. On the other side of the room, a little boy pointed at her and yelled, ''Look at that lady with no clothes!''

In delay mode, she finally emitted a hysterical shriek. Or meant to. When she opened her mouth, all that came out was a high-frequency squeak. With a rush of adrenaline, her motor skills returned. As she flailed for balance with one hand, she frantically grasped behind her and felt where the edge of her hem had become soul mates with one of the brass rivets that tacked the vinyl to the seat.

Gomer, thinking she was waving goodbye, grinned and waved back as he exited out the front door.

In one smooth movement, Raven eased off his seat and positioned himself in front of her. His massive size successfully blocked out the rest of the room. Hell, he could block out the sun if he stood just right. Grateful for his sheer bulk, Liney stopped her thrashing and remained stock-still.

"I'm such a klutz. My dress is caught," she said between clenched teeth.

"I noticed. The dress part, I mean."

Probably not all he noticed. Liney quickly glanced down, mortified to see that her pink-flowered underwear with the eyelet trim could be clearly seen through her taupe-colored tummy-paneled panty hose.

She jerked her head back up. "Don't look down," she commanded.

"I won't. Again. Looked over 'cause I thought I heard a distant train screeching to a stop…then realized it was you." He slipped his arms around her as he felt for the errant rivet. "Hold on to me," he instructed.

She hesitated, then realized if she didn't, he'd release her hem and she'd sink in a silky, flower-pantied heap to the floor. Not wanting to put on more of a show than she already had, she inched her arms around him. Or as far as they would go, which was probably somewhere before the "Go" and after the "Without." Raven's brawny chest brushed and rubbed against hers, causing her skin to prickle pleasurably. Panting shallowly, she told herself it was due to the hysteria and not Raven's wa..n, masculine bulk enveloping her.

"You okay?" he inquired, his lips pressed against her ear.

Whorls of heated breath remained after he spoke, tormenting a sensitive patch of skin right below her earlobe. Afraid she'd squeak again if she opened her mouth, she opted to nod. *Breathe in. Stop panting.* Just as she'd done with the lettuce adventure, she slowly eased in a stream of air. Her senses filled with the scent of musky aftershave. Within her, a small flame sparked to life, igniting places that hadn't felt sensation in a long, long time....

"There," he murmured as he tugged down her dress. "You're free."

For a moment, she didn't know if that was a good or bad thing. Testing her voice, she whispered, "Thank you."

"You're welcome." After a pause, he added, "You can let go now."

She realized her fingers were digging into his sides, like a cat clinging desperately to a tree limb. Or in her case, like a woman-who'd-gone-without-too-long clinging desperately to a man she'd like within. Pulling her hands loose, she prayed she didn't leave sweaty imprints.

Raven stepped back as she stood. After quickly running her fingers down the sides of her dress, she reassured herself she was again decent. Lowering her voice so only he could hear, she confided, "I'm shaking so badly I can't walk." If this kept up, she'd have to crawl out of here on all fours, which would increase the stories the Cheyenne-ites would tell of her ad infinitum.

"You don't have to go anywhere just yet, so let's finish dinner." Taking her by the elbow, he helped her back onto her stool. "After we're through, I'll give you a ride."

As though she needed that promise. Underneath the counter, she gripped her knees to stop them from shaking harder.

"JUST SWING YOUR LEG OVER," instructed an impatient Raven, "and sit." It was early evening in the Blue Moon Diner parking lot. The sun was still bright, it was still hot, and Raven was still coaxing Liney to mount the back saddle on his bike.

"I can't *swing* that high," she protested testily, "unless I lift my dress and I *refuse* to do that again. Look at them." With a nudge of her head, she indicated the square windows that dotted the outside of the diner. Faces could be seen in each pane, chewing while checking out Liney. "Don't people in the Wild West watch TV? Surely they'd find those shows far more interesting than me."

"Maybe you're their first taste of dinner theater."

"Then I wish I was 'Bye Bye, Birdie' 'cause I'd sure like to fly out of here." She heaved a sigh. "Go on without me. I'll take a taxi." She lifted the cell phone from her purse.

Raven clenched his fists in aggravation. They'd had this discussion three times in the last two minutes. "It's getting late. We're a good ten, fifteen miles from town and the taxi won't get here for at least thirty minutes. Anyway, as I've told you before, I won't leave you alone." Although he should. He was beginning to understand why she wore that bun—probably to disguise the helmet she wore underneath.

She held the phone midair, a subtle threat that she'd still do what she wanted.

He raked a hand through his hair. Logic wasn't working. Appeals weren't working. Time to resort to the old Raven, the guy who acted before thinking, the guy the new Raven swore he'd never be again—but as his "Life Rules" tape counseled, rules were made to be broken if for the right reasons. Without waiting another beat, he hunched over, scooped one arm underneath her compact behind, and tossed her over his shoulder caveman style.

"Are you crazy?" she huffed, prying at his arm with her free hand.

Hugging the front of her thighs to his chest, he felt her helmet-head hang somewhere over his shoulder. Good. Maybe more blood would rush to her brain cells and she'd realize she'd left him no other choice. He headed toward the bike.

"Put me down, you—you cretin!" When she kicked a little, he put one hand around both slim ankles and held them firmly in place. She muttered a curse that surprised—and impressed—him. Even Charlotte, after missing a Neiman Marcus shoe sale, had never put together such an imaginative string of words.

Two giant steps and they reached the bike. Slipping his hands to her small midriff, he lifted her effortlessly over the back saddle. Centering her over the leather seat, he commanded, "Open your legs."

Her mouth opened wide, but nothing else. "I can't believe—!"

"Okay, I'll open them...."

With a dramatic roll of her eyes, she scissored them open. He gently lowered her onto the seat. Blowing a curl out of her eyes, she glared at him. "If I didn't want to flash the entire diner by swinging my leg back off, I'd throttle you."

He whipped his gloves out of his back pocket. "They've already seen what you have to flash, so what's stopping you?"

Stumped, or stunned—he couldn't tell which—she blinked rapidly enough to generate her own breeze. He wondered if people ever talked back to Miz Vice President—from her reaction, he'd say no. He mounted the driver's seat and started the engine, which growled menacingly. Leaning back, he said over his shoulder, "Is this your first Hog?"

He detected vanilla, which meant she had leaned closer to talk. "My first what?"

"Hog." He smacked the side of the leather seat to indicate his meaning. "Harley. Motorcycle ride. Is this your first?"

She paused. "Yes." In his rearview mirror, he saw her slip the phone back into her purse. In her own heel-digging way, she was accepting this ride, her first. He wondered what else she hadn't experienced in life and, surprisingly, the thought saddened him. Gently, he said, "Just lean back, Rosebud, and enjoy the ride. Trust me, you're safe."

The waitress had told them there was a motel a few minutes down the highway. Although they'd both be staying on location for the shoot, he and Liney had discussed that it made sense she stay this first night at the motel and have Raven pick her up in the morning. With a two-hour ride to the location, he didn't want to chance their getting lost at night in the middle of the wild frontier. Besides, Raven needed to touch base with Belle, who hadn't yet returned to the diner. She had promised him a room in the back, which gave him a place to crash and regroup before his "Rugged Man" adventure.

As he and Liney rode to the motel, the passing scenery was a mix of the new and the old—apartment complexes rising between farmhouses. Inhaling the sage-tinged air, Raven thought how the landscape reflected his own journey. He'd started out in Tinsel Town, the new, and now he was in Cow Town, the old. And ironically, all because of a cookbook.

Almost a month ago, when he'd heard through the grapevine that Belle had been willed a diner but didn't know which end of the spatula to grip, he'd taken it upon himself to send her one of his favorite cookbooks. A few weeks later, she called to thank him and discovered he was no longer living in Bel Air with his socialite fiancée, but crashing in Hollywood on the floor of his best pal Lizzie's tattoo parlor. Hearing how Raven's fiancée had not only dumped him, but crushed his heart and spirit, Belle insisted he hop on his Harley—the only item he still owned—and hightail it to Cheyenne, Wyoming. She said her husband had gone through a similar L.A.-to-Cheyenne self-journey and he'd be great to talk to. Needing desperately to get out of L.A., Raven hightailed it from his highbrow heartache.

A motel appeared on the left, an L-shaped single-story structure shaded by a cluster of cottonwood trees. Above the office was a gargantuan spur with the words "Silver Spur" outlined in white neon. Raven pulled into the parking lot, stopped, and dismounted the bike. When he held out his hand to help Liney, she just stared at it, then proceeded to slither out of her seat, a combination of bends and folds that a contortionist would have applauded. Hell, Raven almost did, as he'd never seen a woman go to so much trouble just to avoid swinging one leg.

Primly patting down her dress, Liney then paraded past him to the motel office without so much as a good-bye.

If she'd been gracious he would have informed her that thanks to the windy cycle ride, her bun had erupted, giving her a Bride of Frankenstein look. How-ever, he couldn't begrudge her self-righteous rage. Even *he* knew he shouldn't have gone the "cretin" route, hoisting her over his shoulder without her per-mission...and he'd apologize as soon as she came back out.

He waited, hoping the desk clerk liked Frankenstein movies.

When Liney stepped back outside, a look of surprise crossed her face when she spied him. Immediately, she tightened her features. Striding purposefully past him, a key jangling in her hand, she said dismissively, "You can go now."

He followed her, something he'd done a zillion times with Charlotte, and swore he'd *never* do again with *any* woman, even if she were on fire and he was carrying a bucket of water. Well, so much for rules. Infusing his words with diction and earnestness, he said, "I'm sorry I picked you up like that, but I wanted to get you on the bike."

She halted so abruptly, he nearly ran into her. With-out turning around, she said tersely, "I'm *not* a cave-woman. You can discuss issues with me, not manhan-dle me to get your way."

He didn't like that he'd resorted to that old Raven behavior either—but rather than explain how hard he was trying to be the new Raven, he simply apologized. "You're right. I was wrong. I'm sorry."

She gave her shoulders a small shrug, as though releasing the resentment lodged there. Then she pivoted slowly to face him. "Thank you." He was starting to know those chocolate-brown eyes. Within them, he saw a flicker of gratefulness that the two of them were okay again.

She gestured to a nearby forest-green door with a metal number 2 nailed to it. "That's my room." She began speaking rapidly, as though reciting a mental check list. "I'll purchase some toothpaste, et cetera, from the lobby gift shop. Afterwards, I need to phone Dirk, go over some business. Please pick me up at four tomorrow morning."

"Four?" He needed some rest after three days on the road, not a nap before another strenuous two-hour ride, after which he was supposed to play model. "That's not a time, that's a sentence."

She raised her chin a notch. "The shoot is scheduled to start at sunup. If we leave at four, we won't be there until six."

"Will the world stop if we leave at five?"

She stared at him, hard. He stared back. He knew she was drilling to the core, but he gave her his best no-way-in-hell attitude to work through first. Neither flinched for a long, solid minute.

One well-shaped eyebrow arched. "Four-thirty, then. Not five. Four-thirty. Or we're both out of jobs."

She was good. Real good. "I understand why you're a veep—uh, vice president." He nodded. "Okay. Four-thirty."

She offered a small smile, murmured some kind of "good night," then headed purposefully into the room marked 2. He'd barely reached his bike when he heard a distant train screeching to a halt. He stopped. That was no train, that was...

"Why didn't you tell me my hair looks like a fricking beehive!" Liney stood outside her room, her eyes wide with horror, her hands pressed to the sides of the hair as though through sheer will she could compress the mass back into its former shape.

From somewhere nearby, a bird twittered as though enjoying his predicament. Raven scuffed one boot against the asphalt, wanting to phrase his response just right. At a time like this, a woman needed compassion, understanding.

And a man needed life insurance.

"Because," he said, wishing one of the lines from any of his tapes would materialize in his brain. Unfortunately, his mind was a vast blank canvas. He was on his own. "Because it doesn't look like a beehive. It...it looks like the Bride of Frankenstein."

3

BRIDE OF FRANKENSTEIN. Cruising down the highway at four-twenty the following morning, Raven wished the roar of the Harley would drown the memory of his open-mouth-insert-boot comment from the night before. After his verbal bun-blunder, Liney looked more like "The Wrath of Khan" than the Bride of Frankenstein. Her sound effects escalated from distant-train sounds, too. She'd emitted a primal shriek, similar to a bald eagle's mating call he'd once heard on an animal documentary.

After the eagle impersonation, she stuttered something about her looking *far* better than Madeleine What's-Her-Name in that Mel Brooks remake. Then Liney stomped back into her room and slammed shut the door. Too hard. It flung back open and whacked her in the rear. After unleashing a string of colorful door epithets, she closed it with a resounding thwack.

But that was yesterday. And today was today...very, very early today. Still half-asleep, Raven squinted against the chilly rush of air as he barreled down the highway past farmhouses, silos, and apartment buildings. He was more accustomed to falling into bed at four-twenty in the morning, not being showered, dressed, and reporting to work. The only positive aspect of this predawn maneuver was that nine hours had passed since the Bride of Frankenstein fiasco...and maybe, the Hair Gods willing, Liney was rested and ready to put the bun disaster behind her.

Raven pulled into the Silver Spur parking lot, eased to a stop outside room number 2 and sat, letting the engine idle in a low growl. Light illuminated the horse-and-cowboy theme curtains, so he knew Liney was up. He had to hand it to her—when she said early, she did early. Unlike Charlotte, to whom early meant the crack of noon.

The door opened. Through a slant of yellow light, Liney stood in the same silk dress she'd worn yesterday. Being backlighted, her face was in shadow, so he couldn't decipher her mood. But he could see that her auburn hair was pulled back from her face in some kind of spirally son-of-bun do.

"Could you please turn off the engine," she said, the temperature of her voice nearly matching the nip in the air. "People are trying to sleep."

As any decent human being should be doing at this hour, Raven thought. His New Day Resolution was to watch what he said, so he refrained from opening his mouth and cut the engine. The only sounds that broke the silence were birds twittering in a nearby cottonwood and the drone of faraway traffic along the highway.

"I'll get my purse." She disappeared for a moment, then returned, flicked off the light in the room, shut the door, and headed toward the bike. The sun was teasing its way over the horizon, gradually lifting the dark shades of night. In the shadowy daybreak, Raven saw Liney's mood had lifted as well, and he thanked the powers that be she no longer mentally resided in Bad Hair Bride-ville.

Skipping any salutations, Liney launched into directions. "Take the highway back past the Blue Moon." She pointed toward the road he'd just been on, holding her arm straighter than a drag pipe. "Then turn right on…"

He'd already gotten the same directions from Belle, who'd gotten them from Gomer last night after he'd called to check on Liney. As she rattled on, Raven didn't interrupt, as the old Raven would have done, to tell her he already knew every fork and turn. Instead, he focused on his breathing and simply nodded. When she finished, he reached into his fringed saddle bag and pulled out a neatly folded bundle of clothes. "Take off your dress and put these on." He paused. "Please."

She stared at his offering. "What are those?"

"Jeans and a sweatshirt. With Belle's compliments."

"Why is Belle giving me clothes?"

"Because I told her you didn't have anything to wear besides that…" he was going to write those "Hearty Man" tape people and suggest they add a section on talking to women about fashion "…that creamy chic-y silky number." He mentally congratulated himself on assembling that sentence without stumbling, once. He might recognize the designer, but he'd never been on the spot to do a fashion show voice-over.

Liney crossed her arms under her breasts. "I can't arrive at the shoot wearing jeans and a sweatshirt." She said "jeans" and "sweatshirt" in the same tone formerly reserved for canned fruit.

Raven dared to venture where few men had gone before. He was going to tell a strong-willed, designer-conscious woman what to wear. Worse, to insist she dress down from silk to denim, which for her must be like switching from Gucci to Kmart. Or dry toast to biscuits and gravy.

"Let's cut to the chase," he said authoritatively. "It's cold out. And it's gonna—going to be a long ride. If you insist on wearing that dress, it will billow in your face. If no cops pull us over for indecent exposure…" he paused, knowing that would get to her "…you'll be swiping at your flapping hem, probably lose your balance and fall off the bike. If that happens, I'll be forced to stop and maybe call an ambulance. At the very least we'll miss the first day of the shoot." He was on a roll. Might as well wrap up this speech with one of Vice President Liney's conversation-stopper lines. "And," he concluded in his best voice of doom, "we'll both be out of jobs."

In the silence that followed, Raven swore he could hear Liney's mind working. Tick tick tick. Checking points on a mental pro-con list. After glancing at her watch, she plucked the clothes from his hands. Obviously, the pro side had the most check marks. "Because I knew I'd only be here one night, I prechecked out yesterday evening—" her free hand flitted to her head as though to precheck her bun as well "—so I left the keys in the room. I can't go back to change." She shifted from one foot to another. "Please turn your head."

"Sun's not up yet—I can barely see."

Although, this close, he definitely saw the defiant thrust of her chin. "I like my privacy—"

"I'm turning my head." She acted like one of his kid sisters—needing privacy even though nobody was looking. Why was it girls—women—always seemed to think men were desperate to catch a peek of flesh?

Didn't they realize that some guys liked a woman's soul as much, if not more, than her skin?

Behind him he heard swishing, stomping, and zipping...and several muttered comments that the jeans were so tight she couldn't breathe. "All right," she finally announced, "I'm ready to swing my leg."

It was a miracle—she could speak although she couldn't breathe. Fighting the urge to grin, he swiveled in his seat, ready to offer instructions for mounting the bike.

But when he saw her, his throat clogged like a blocked intake port.

She had moved several feet away so that the Silver Spur sign provided a hazy neon backdrop for her silhouette. In place of the chic silky dress, which was draped over one arm, were the body-hugging sweatshirt and body-molding jeans. Okay, he liked a woman's soul. But damn, he would have to be blind to not see that Liney's slender frame had more curves than a mountain road.

She stood at an angle, which displayed the upward turn of her pert breasts. Below, her body tapered to a slim waist. His fingers twitched involuntarily as he recalled gripping that waist before he lifted her onto the bike yesterday. She'd felt sensuously sleek and warm, hardly what he expected from such an uptight, cool veep.

And those jeans. Too tight? Just right, he'd say. They hugged her like a jealous lover. Clung to her compact bottom and embraced a pair of legs that traveled half the length of her body. He hadn't brought riding shoes—hadn't thought to ask Belle if she had any spare boots lying around—so Liney still wore her Gucci pumps, which made evident the seductive tilt of her pelvis. She was more than a Rosebud. She was a woman in full flower.

"You going to show me how to swing?" Liney asked, striding toward him.

He nearly toppled off his bike. One hundred and...what the hell was he up to? Six? This called for several numbers. *Hundred and six and seven.* He gave his head a shake, hoping it might jolt back into place the *loose*—and he did mean loose—pieces of his imagination that had split from the new I-don't-need-a-woman Raven.

Later, he wasn't sure exactly what happened. He recalled rising slightly and leaning forward so he could direct Liney on how best to mount the bike. But he'd barely opened his mouth to speak when he heard a whizzing whoosh, followed by a resounding *smack.*

"Raven?"

A lush, vaguely familiar voice broke through the blackness. With great effort, he opened his eyes. Against the gray-blue sky, the green leaves of a cottonwood undulated gently in a breeze. Along the periphery of this leafy scene, two faces peered intently into his. He closed his eyes again, relishing the whiff of vanilla....

"Raven! Wake up!" An escalating series of sniffs culminated in a grief-stricken moan. "Raven, ohmyGod, Raven! I killed my Rugged Man! I need a cigarette!" Something snapped.

His eyelid seemed to rise magically before he realized someone was gently prying it open. He rolled his eye, trying to focus on one of the hovering faces.

"He ain't dead," said a gravelly male voice. "Just kissed the wrong side of your slipper, that's all."

Kissed? Slipper?

The gravelly voice continued, "Gotta pack o' ice for his noggin. We keep it handy in the motel office in case one of our customers parties too hard...or gets kicked too hard." Raven swore he heard a raspy chuckle as something cold pressed again his left temple. "Here's a coupla aspirin, son."

Raven managed to focus on a liver-spotted hand holding two white pills. He accepted the offering, washing them down with a proffered glass of water. "Thanks, man. Whoever you are."

"Pete. Silver Spur motel manager."

Returning the glass to Pete, who squatted next to him, Raven looked down at the cracked asphalt. "I'm lying on the road?"

"Motel parking lot," the female voice corrected. Smooth fingers gently stroked his jaw, chin. "Oh, I'm so sorry. I accidentally..." The words dissolved into more tear-garbled sounds. He hadn't heard this much sniffling and snuffling since he'd taken his kid sisters and their friends to see *Sleepless in Seattle*.

Raven raised his gaze from the asphalt to two watery chocolate drops. It took him a moment to realize they were eyes—and whose—although why he was lying on the ground and she was sitting still baffled him. He closed his eyes, forcing the fragmented pieces of recent memory into a complete picture. Ungodly predawn ride. Sun-of-bun do. Slim, killer body.

He opened his eyes and zeroed in on her woeful brown ones. "Liney?"

"You recognize me!"

He frowned. "Why not? You haven't changed your—" The eagle documentary flashed through his mind. Only a man with a serious death wish would say the word "hair" at a time like this. His stomach flinched. Is that what'd happened? He'd forgotten his New Day Resolution and blurted something about a Frankenstein french twist to which Liney had violently reacted? Jeez. Some women really got into their bad-hair days.

But she didn't look miffed. Far from it. Her button nose was red from crying. He backtracked the mascara-smudged trail of a tear up her cheek to those big, sad eyes. "I accidentally kicked you when I swung my leg," she confessed shakily, then shrugged as though unable to fathom what exactly had happened, either. "I thought the jeans were too tight. Thought they'd constrict my ability to swing properly, so I put more oomph into my kick so I could clear the bike…" She thumped a fist against her chest in a mea culpa motion. "…and I accidentally kicked you in the side of the head." Her guilt-laden voice rose so high, Raven winced. "It must have been those kick-boxing lessons I took last year.…"

He blocked out the rest of her words. So that was the *whoosh* and *smack*. And to think last night he'd encouraged her to swing her leg. He made a note to never ask her to relax and kick back. Or if he did, to make sure he was in the next county.

Pressing her fist against her heart, Liney released a worried breath. Raven was awake and speaking. And better yet, recognizing people…well, recognizing her because he'd only met Pete a few moments ago. Relief flooded her veins, warming her after the bone-chilling accident. Thanks to the ice pack, the bump on his head should be minimal, although it was under his hair so the camera wouldn't catch it anyway. Her Rugged Man—well, *Cooking Fantasies'* Rugged Man—was back in top-model shape. Wasn't he?

"Can you focus?" she asked. What if he couldn't? She moved her head to the side. His gaze followed. Good. She leaned close, checking that he wasn't cross-eyed or anything. Those coal-black eyes stared back at her, and not at each other. Excellent. Although, worse case scenario, they could always position him so his eyes wouldn't both be seen at the same time....

"What're you doing?" he asked gruffly.

She reared back. "Just checking...that you can focus."

"I can focus better when someone isn't two centimeters from my face," he confirmed. "Trust me, I've been on the dark side of hurt before." Raven held the ice pack to the side of his head as he moved to a sitting position.

"Anything else you need?" Pete asked. "Coffee?"

"No thanks," Raven answered, "Had a few cups at Belle's."

After a brisk nod, Pete stood. "Then I'm gonna hit the sack—try to catch a few more z's before we open. Looks as though this crisis is resolved." Rubbing his eyes, he ambled toward the motel. Without looking back, he said, "Leave the ice pack outside the office door."

Liney watched the older man's exiting form, grateful he'd responded so quickly to her frantic pressing of the night bell several—five, ten?—minutes ago. She didn't remember exactly what she'd said, but Pete must have heard the words "kick" and "killed" because despite his years, he'd beaten her to the downfallen Raven.

Downfallen. She'd never been able to successfully saw a branch off a tree, yet with one blow she'd felled this redwood of a man. Turning back to Raven, she whispered, "I'm *really* sorry."

He glanced at her leather pumps. "Good thing you don't wear bowling shoes. Or bowl. You'd be lethal with a twenty-pound ball in your hands."

"Lethal—?" She started to defend herself, but stopped when a teasing smile creased his features. He seemed to know—and like—the surprise effect he had on her because his eyes twinkled mischievously. Just a few minutes ago, she'd been crying over him, thinking she'd killed him. After remorsefully spilling her guts, something Liney Reed never did—in public, anyway— he was poking fun at her. Just like yesterday in the diner when, after their fat fight, he'd winked at her. The gall of the man!

"You look a little…steamed." Raven offered her the ice pack.

Obviously he could focus. Too well. Her mouth twitched as she ached to come up with a suitable retort, but couldn't conjure a single steamed word in her defense. She didn't like how she felt around him. Emotional one moment, off-guard the next. Being out of control—of herself or others—was not her style.

He thought he had her pegged, just like the employees back at Harriman Enterprises. Well, she'd show him she could lighten up, take a joke. Forcing a smile on her face, she said awkwardly, "Good thing I don't wear spike heels. I'd be lethal with a volleyball in my hands."

"Volleyball?" He quirked one black eyebrow.

"Spike. Volleyball." When he stared back at her as though she'd just landed from another planet, she explained, "I—I was making a joke."

After a beat, he said, "Oh-h-h," then pressed the ice pack back to his head.

Her heart shrank a little. This is exactly how she felt

at work—uncomfortable when it came to small talk. Maybe she ran the show, but she never felt like part of the team. *When in doubt, resort to the business at hand.* "I'll call us a taxi," she said matter-of-factly, swearing internally that she'd never make another joke as long as she lived. Or longer. She reached for her phone, which she'd managed to wedge into the back pocket of these spray-on jeans.

Raven's hand clamped around her wrist, stopping her midaction.

"I don't leave my bike," he said in a low, this-isn't-up-for-discussion tone.

She met his determined gaze. "It will be secure here at the motel—"

"Either I ride it or I stay with it. And baby, like it or not, I'm *riding.*" He released his hold and rose to his feet.

His muscular, larger-than-life body took forever to unfold—it was like watching a mythological god rise from the earth to touch the heavens. Liney's head bent back so far, her bun touched her upper back. Her gaze wandered up over bulging thighs and skimmed quickly over a snug pocket of denim between his hips. Up, over the broad expanse of his chest to the strong jaw and full, curved lips. Her visual journey ended at his mane of thick, black hair that was still wild and unkempt from his earlier ride. Or maybe it was always unruly, like the man.

At that last thought, her heart increased its tempo from regular thudding to merciless pounding. She opened her mouth slightly so she could pant, unnoticed.

His gaze slid downward. In a rumbling tone, like thunder from a mountain top, he asked, "Liney, what time is it?"

Would he ever call her "baby" again? Maybe it had been a momentary slip of the tongue—and from here on out, he'd view her as the uptight, overly efficient vice president. Struggling to her feet, she flashed on one of the fairy tales she'd read as a child. *Jack and the Beanstalk*. If only she could climb Raven, as Jack had the stalk, she might enter a magical kingdom where she'd be a princess and not a Dragon Lady. She flipped her wrist, still feeling the warm imprint of Raven's grip. "Nearly five."

"We can make it by seven *and* both keep our jobs." He cut her a glance. "If you can the worries."

"Can the—?"

"If you stop worrying," he translated. "Stop obsessing about calling taxis or my eyes focusing or anything else but our getting on the bike and on the road."

After being knocked out, he was ready to mount that chrome-and-metal beast and ride? He was rougher than Bruce Willis. Tougher than John Travolta. More macho and hot than George Clooney. If her insides weren't rocking with awe, she'd be appalled at Raven's brash, cocky "can the worries" attitude. Or at least, she'd pretend to be.

Besides, way deep down, she knew he'd pegged her this time. If they gave degrees in worrying, she'd have a Ph.D. But it had gotten her where she was. Besides, if he'd grown up having to be three-fourths adult, one-fourth child, he might have a tendency to worry, too.

For the next few minutes, Raven did some stretches and deep breathing while Liney canned her worries and folded her clothes, glad to be occupied with some activity other than eyeballing her model as though she'd never been within five feet of a male before. She was carefully placing her dress and purse in the saddle bag when Raven's voice boomed behind her.

"I'm back to a hundred horsepower," he announced. "I'll deposit this ice pack, then we can hit the highway. Swing your leg over Macavity while I'm gone."

She turned to see him strolling toward the motel office with that loose-hipped, I-own-the-road walk. That man healed faster than Aimee McPherson.

"Macavity?"

He half turned, never breaking his pace. Gesturing toward the Harley, he said, "The bike."

Macavity. She stared at the massive black beast. Maybe Raven's father was a dentist? She faced the bike as though it were a formidable enemy. She'd been a flop in her kick-boxing class, something she avoided telling anyone because Liney Reed never failed. Besides, failing the class was due to her ingrained klutziness—she'd always been more mental than physical. In school, she'd been an A student until it came to anything remotely athletic. To this day, she was the only student at Montecito Elementary School to receive an F+ from Mrs. Acheson, the formidable girls' physical education teacher. But even with practice, Liney had never learned to throw a ball straight.

Raven had a point about her being lethal with a bowling ball. Fortunately, she didn't have to throw balls as a vice president. Just words. And attitude.

She inched closer to the back fender and eyed the leather passenger seat, her goal. There was no head in her path this time, so swinging and landing her behind on the seat shouldn't be overly difficult. She hoped. Now that she'd discovered her kicking strength, however, she had to be careful not to swing her leg and propel her entire body over the bike. Klutzy was bad enough. Flying through the air would be mortifying.

She stole a glance in Raven's direction. He was still strolling across the parking lot toward the motel office. Excellent. She had the opportunity to swing and fail a few times without observation. The only redeeming value to this exercise was she'd never have to mount this mechanical beast again. For the rest of the shoot, she'd be riding with Gomer in the pickup.

She pivoted, aligning her left thigh so it was parallel to the machine.

One.

Two.

On three, she swung her leg in a wide arc, clearing the rider's seat. With a thump, her rear end landed solidly on the passenger seat. Success! Dumbfounded, she sat, amazed she'd pulled this off on the first try. If only Mrs. Acheson could see her now. Forget Mrs. Acheson—if only Raven had caught this amazing feat. She looked over expectantly. He was hunched over, leaving the ice pack outside the office door.

Darn. He missed it. Surprisingly, the thought triggered an old hurt that she hadn't remembered in a long time. An eleven-year-old Liney, waiting up past bedtime to show her father a watercolor she'd painted at school. He'd been late, as usual, because of the overtime he put in at the local refinery. Trudging through the front door, smelling faintly of petrol, he barely glanced at her painting, instead asking if she'd finished her homework. Even now, she could still hear the weariness in his voice, see the dull exhaustion in his eyes. "You don't get anywhere in this world unless you do your homework," he'd said, washing his hands at the kitchen sink. "Winners make A's. Losers paint pictures."

He hadn't meant to be cruel, just realistic. With an extended family to support, and a new job after a long layoff, he'd wanted to help her better understand the world. Wanted to toughen her up. But even with that adult understanding, the child Liney had gone to bed, clutching her picture, thinking, "He missed it."

"You did it!"

She looked up from her reverie. Raven towered over her, a half smile pulling at the corner of those full lips. "You did it," he repeated, his voice warm with pride. "You swung and landed, like a true Harley Babe." He turned up his smile. "Sorry. Like a true Harley Woman."

Her insides tingled with happiness—more at Raven's acknowledgment than her "swing success." Right now, he could call her a Harley Babe, a Woman Babe—if he wanted, a Babe Ruth Babe! It didn't matter. More important were his words of congratulations. She bet Mrs. Acheson's ears were burning at this very moment—her F+ student had just swung a mean leg and landed on target. But as all these thoughts tumbled through Liney's mind, she just sat, unable to do anything but grin at Raven. Like an eleven-year-old kid who'd stayed up for a pat on the head.

"What're you grinning at?" he asked, tugging on his leather gloves.

"I…I liked being congratulated." She almost added liking being called a Babe, too, but she suddenly felt silly. Worse, vulnerable. Her simple confession undoubtedly said more about her than a ten-page bio. She wished she could snatch the words back out of the air, pretend she'd never said them.

"Hey, you deserved it." He hadn't caught the niche in her armor, which said as much about him as her confession had about her. The man didn't jump on people's frailties. "I missed the first kick—" he winked "—so to speak. Even sorrier I missed the second."

As he mounted the bike and started the engine, Liney leaned against her backrest and stared up at the golden drop of sun in the sky. It blazed bright, but she felt brighter. Happier. *He's sorry he missed it.* She could almost imagine the ache of many years ago climbing into the clouds and disappearing....

4

"READY TO ROAR, BABY?"

"Sure," Liney said, her voice catching on the single word. She looked down from the golden sun to the silvered mirror that angled off the motorcycle handlebar. In the reflection, Raven's dark eyes snared hers with a roguish glint.

"I was talking to Macavity," he explained, his voice barely topping the growl of the engine. "But I'm glad you're ready, too." He winked.

She quickly looked down, hoping he didn't catch the heat flooding her face. *Guess he calls everyone Baby, including Macavity.* She wondered if Raven was one of those guys who loves his car—or in this case, his cycle—as much as he loves his woman.

His woman. Was there one in Raven's life? A wave of disappointment washed through her, which surprised her. She didn't care if he had a woman…or a dozen of them. Did she?

As though I need to think about that. Her cheeks were no doubt a lovely fuchsia after answering to "Baby." If she started dwelling on Raven's sex life, her entire face would flame crimson, which he'd probably see reflected in that little tattletale mirror.

She squeezed shut her eyes. *Think work. Think deadline.*

She opened her eyes and stared at the back of his

black T-shirt, which stretched mercilessly over an expanse of bulging muscles that could rival the Laramie Mountains topography.

Think stud.

Get your mind off the T-shirt. She dropped her gaze to his rump, snugly fitted into a pair of well-washed blue jeans. If the T-shirt was bad, those jeans were evil. A quarter-sized threadbare spot, positioned at the top of his back pocket, offered a glimpse of light tan undies.

She bent her head closer.

Those weren't undies…that was flesh. The part of Raven that never saw the sun. And considering the spot's position, the man didn't wear boxers. Maybe he wore those stretchy, low-hipped undies worn by studly Calvin Klein models.

She knew she should look away, veer her gaze back to the sun or maybe focus on a passing bird, but too late. She was riveted to how Raven-the-stretchy-underwear-boy straddled the leather seat, his molded hips nestled against the leather cushion. Her gaze traveled down the length of his muscled leg to the rough, black boot pressed firmly against the ground. It was as though he and the Harley had merged into a new-age millennium satyr—part motor, part man.

What kind of woman could possibly satisfy this mythical, mechanical, masculine beast? A groan escaped her lips.

"You okay?" Raven peered at her reflection in the mirror, his previously amused look now one of concern.

"Why?" she yelled defensively, trying not to think how loud her groan must have been for him to have heard it over the engine noise.

"You're pulling on my T-shirt."

She looked down. Her fingers were doing that cat-on-a-limb thing again, clutching the back of his T-shirt just as she'd clung to him in the diner last night. She never behaved like this, clutching and gripping without her mind being in control.

Her mutinous body was playing games with her brain.

Releasing his shirt, she swore her primal instincts would not get the better of her again. *Think work. Think deadline.*

"It's okay to hold on," he yelled over his shoulder. "Just didn't know why you were doing so before we started riding."

Because you're a hot mechanical-satyr stud whose sexy, stretchy undies should be bronzed and put on permanent display in the Smithsonian. But when he glanced behind him for an answer, she gave an innocent little shrug and folded her hands in her lap.

Raven put on a pair of sleek black sunglasses that wrapped around his face, adding a menacing edge to his mechanical-satyr look. She couldn't see his eyes through the dark lenses, which left her a bit disconcerted. After all, she was accustomed to checking out a person's eyes to monitor their reactions. Raven had just effectively blocked her out.

He passed something to her over his shoulder. "Put these on," he commanded.

Another pair of sunglasses. Big and silver-colored, with cut-out holes that ran the length of the plastic arms. She only wore Liz Claiborne—these looked like a convenience-store impulse item. If she put on these cheap, silver, holed things, she'd lose any remaining allure of upper-management dignity. She'd look as common as someone in the mailroom, for God's sake. Instantly miserable, she wished she'd remembered to bring her designer sunglasses when she left camp yesterday. Thanks to Belle's sprayed-on jeans and Raven's impulse-item sunglasses, she'd regressed from looking like a vice president to a member of the vice squad.

"I can't wear these," she said, dangling them over Raven's beefy shoulder. "They're too big and heavy." She left out the part about the vice squad.

Over the vibrating hum of the motor, Raven leaned back his head. "What?"

She cleared her throat, as though that would help her compete with the rumbling engine. "I can't wear these!" she yelled.

He cocked one eyebrow over those Darth Vadar sunglasses. "Why?"

"They're too...big!" She gestured around her head with her free hand, trying to convey her meaning.

"What wig?"

"Big! Big!" She held her hands apart, the way men did when showing off how big the fish was they'd caught.

Raven, obviously getting the fish imagery, nodded. "You haven't tried them on."

Wasn't that like a man to use logic when the real issue was about style, taste, and looking good. But rather than compete further with the engine roar, she put on the sunglasses. The arms, miraculously, slipped comfortably behind her ears. And they didn't feel too terribly heavy where they rested on the bridge of her nose. Maybe they were wearable, after all.

Craning her neck, she glanced in the rearview mirror and stifled a shriek.

She looked like a gun moll. No, worse. A tramp

moll. All she needed was a gaudy beauty mark on her top lip and blood-red lipstick and she could lead her own rebel motorcycle gang. *Bad Biker Babes on the Loose.* Or *Vixens for Vengeance.*

Oblivious to her mental horrors, Raven gave her a big thumbs-up. Probably because she looked like the kind of women he dated. Motorcycle gang gun-tramp-moll types who breathed shallowly thanks to their two-sizes-too-small jeans. Which was probably the reason why he didn't date women who smoked—with all that shallow breathing, they lacked the lung capacity to inhale properly.

"Now you can see," Raven yelled, "rather than squint for the next two hours."

Squint? Liney glanced up at the sun, which had a spectacular green tinge thanks to the lenses. He was right. She wasn't squinting. Maybe she looked like a vixen, but a vixen without crow's-feet, which put a positive slant on things.

"Thank you," she said loudly. All right. She'd put up with the temporary Motorcycle Gun-Tramp-Moll look because she had a plan for repairing her image before they hit camp. But she wouldn't mention it yet. First, she was tired of yelling. Second, she and Raven were doing fabulously well considering the recent kicking incident—it was best to preserve their peace for the time being.

Raven punched the accelerator. The engine growled. "Ready?"

She waited a beat. He hadn't said "Baby" so he must be talking to her. She opened her mouth to yell "Ready!" when she remembered. Biker babes had a cool, I've-seen-it-all-done-it-all attitude. If she looked like one, she might as well enjoy being one. Easing back against the backrest, she lifted her hand and flashed a thumbs-up, trying to ignore the chip in her nail polish.

The metal-and-chrome beast slowly circled, as though stalking its terrain like an animal before a hunt. Liney squeezed her thighs tightly around her leather cushion seat, fighting the urge to grip his T-shirt. But as the Harley lurched forward, she forgot the importance of being cool and lunged for Raven's waist.

She glanced anxiously in the rearview mirror. He didn't seem to notice—or care—that she was holding onto him for dear life. As they hit the smooth road and established their speed, Liney gradually released her panicked grip and leaned back.

The wind was refreshingly cool as it blasted past. She hadn't seen this many trees since she took that tour of Bel Air. And she didn't know when she'd last seen so many fields and farmhouses. There was something to leaving L.A.—one got to see more primitive lifestyles. Closing her eyes, she tried to identify the scents in the rush of warm air. Grass. Something sweet. Jasmine? And something else...

A man's musky aftershave. She inhaled deeply, catching an underlying soap scent—a remnant from Raven's morning shower. Surrounded by the roar of the engine and the blasts of invigorating air, she let her mind wander. Just as it probably took yards of cloth to cover Raven, it probably took a waterfall to bathe him. A waterfall of soapy foam that sluiced down ridges and over bulges of muscle...

She felt a tap on her leg. Jolted from the waterfall, Liney opened her eyes. Raven, peering at her in the rearview mirror, jabbed his thumb at the approaching

Blue Moon Diner to their right. He mimed tipping a cup to his lips.

He was asking if she wanted to stop for coffee. She didn't dare say the stuff was so thick and strong, she'd need electrolysis after drinking it. She tried to smile, but a pocket of wind made her top lip flap uncontrollably.

"No thanks," she yelled, realizing her words were eaten by the wind before they even reached Raven's ears. When their gazes again caught in the mirror, she shook her head "no" while holding down her top lip with her bottom teeth.

Although he looked somewhat confused, he nodded his understanding and they zoomed past the diner.

Liney settled back into the powerful surge of Macavity—what was that name about, anyway?—and the powerful presence of Raven. Maybe she didn't want the rest of the crew to see her as a Bad Biker Babe on the Loose, but for the next two hours, the vixen veep could indulge the fantasy.

FOR ALMOST TWO HOURS, Raven had listened to the whistling wind rather than the tapes he'd brought for this trip. But wearing the headphones would have been rude to Liney, the first passenger who'd ridden with him since Charlotte.

Charlotte. His insides twisted. Not so long ago, their love had competed with the best of 'em—Hepburn and Tracy, Bogie and Bacall, Gwyneth Paltrow and anybody. But after Char dumped him, Raven had felt more used and unwanted than one of her discarded Gucci outfits. Thanks to one of his tapes, "Cleaning Your Kharmic Plate," he'd finally grown to accept that their love affair had simply been another course in the feast of life.

Although that particular course gave him heartburn, he trusted the ache would eventually go away. After all, the soothing voice on the tape promised that if Raven went through the pain and experienced the grief, he'd eventually heal. Which meant he'd almost stopped beating himself up every time a memory of his former almost-wife traipsed unexpectedtly through his memories....

Like how, at first, she'd been thrilled to ride on his hog. Hell, he could hardly keep her off it. Or *him*. But after a few weeks, she started complaining that riding the Harley blew too much soot into her facialed face. And the bike's vibrations—which she'd once said primed her for sex—loosened the caps on two of her teeth.

At least Liney hadn't complained. So far.

As though his thoughts triggered a reaction, he felt a finger poking his shoulder.

He glanced in the mirror. Liney, her head tilted sideways, stared at his reflection. She looked odd, biting her top lip with her bottom teeth like that. Catching his gaze, she pointed frantically to the side of the road, obviously wanting him to stop.

He pulled over onto the shoulder. Dust swirled around the bike as it hit the soft dirt and cruised to a stop. He placed his foot on the ground as he killed the engine. In the following silence, broken only by a twittering bird sitting on a barbed wire fence, he asked, "Gotta hit the head?"

"I beg your pardon?"

"Do you need to use...the ladies' room?" He motioned toward a cottonwood tree about twenty feet away.

Liney followed his line of vision. Her rosebud lips formed a surprised "o" as she realized the "ladies' room" meant the cottonwood. "I don't need to... I need to freshen up before we arrive."

Freshen up? "We're in the middle of cowboy country, baby. Sandwiched between miles of sagebrush and blue sky. Who're you freshening up for—a wandering jackrabbit?"

Although she stiffened a little, a pink flush crawled up her neck. "I need to look my best," she said, although her veep tone sounded a little shaky. "First impressions are always based on how one is attired. Now if you would be so kind as to move, I'll descend from this...hog."

He flipped his wrist, checking the watch. "We don't have time for you to 'freshen up.'" He leveled her a no-nonsense look. "If you gotta go, use the cottonwood. Otherwise, we need to keep riding."

With a perturbed huff, she did that acrobatic, contortionist thing, culminating in a full-body slither off the passenger seat without once swinging or kicking any part of her...or him.

Standing on the dirt, she coughed a little. "It's so dusty," she said, waving her hand as though the motion might clear the air. "Couldn't you have parked on the asphalt?"

"Yeah, I could've stayed on the road—and gotten both of us—and Macavity—run over by the next semi barreling down the highway." He kicked down the bike stand and swung his leg over. Being with Liney was like being with Eva Gabor in that old *Green Acres* sitcom. He had to remember to breathe...and remind himself that in four days he'd have the money for his bike-and-book shop.

"Sorry," Liney murmured, busily retrieving her tan leather purse from his pouch. As he headed toward the cottonwood, she looked up. "Where are you going?"

"To the ladies' room." He headed across the uneven, grassy earth, *knowing* the look on her face behind him. Liney had probably never used the "ladies' room" outdoors—probably thought roughing it meant there were no little mints on the pillows. Despite his irritation, he caught himself smiling. *Maybe she wants to be the appropriately "attired" vice president when she sees her crew, but I've seen her dressed as a hot babe.* And surprise, surprise. The lady dressed down nicely.

Out of respect, he positioned himself out of her sight while he stood behind the tree. She'd probably never seen a man do his duty before. For that matter, considering how persnickety she could be, maybe she'd never seen a man's privates before.

Nah. She had to be in her mid-to-late twenties. And despite her prim and proper demeanor, she was too attractive to not have experienced lovemaking. Although he seriously doubted any of her corporate-type guys had made love to her properly, which had nothing to do with being proper.

After buttoning his jeans, Raven strolled back to the bike, enjoying the heat of the sun and the smell of earth and grass. As he approached, he saw Liney hunched over his rearview mirror, frowning fiercely while rubbing something on the side of her face. Closer, he had to bite the inside of his cheek to not laugh as he realized what she was wiping. Thanks to the dust and sun, the outline of her removed sunglasses was clearly visible around her eyes. Worse, the round cut-outs looked as though someone had painted light brown circles in a path from Liney's eyes to her ears.

"Look at me," she said, her voice rising shakily. She stopped rubbing and pointed to the sides of her face. "I don't have tan lines—I have tan *circles!*" Her chin wobbled. Her body quivered.

Before she internally combusted, Raven stepped closer and brushed gently at one of the circles.

It didn't come off. Those really were tanned spots.

He looked into her chocolate eyes, red-rimmed from threatening tears, and felt grateful his reaction was safely hidden behind his shades. Maybe he had wanted to laugh a moment ago, but now he felt downright sorry for her. She was genuinely distraught and he couldn't do a damn thing about it except be as kind as possible.

"And my hair," she said, her voice breaking. "It looks as though I stuck my finger in an outlet and electrocuted myself."

"It looks better than that," Raven said soothingly, frantically thinking what he might say to ease her anguish. Forget another movie reference—if he valued his life, he had to say something that would make her feel light and feminine. "It looks like…cotton candy."

"Right," she said, half speaking, half sobbing. "*Fried* cotton candy."

She had a point there.

Her shoulders heaved as she gulped breaths. "And…and I'm caked in dust, like some kind of Shake-and-Bake Biker Babe—"

"Now, now," he said, as though talking to a child. "It's not the end of the world—"

"No, just the end of my career! They already hate me…now I'll give them even more fodder for snickering and joking behind my back!'' She leaned close to the mirror. ''Look at those circles!'' She outlined a round tan spot with her index finger. ''I could star in one of those Star Trek shows without any special makeup effects!''

Her shoulders went from mild heaves to major shakes. Turning suddenly, she fell into his arms with a weighty sob. ''Take me back to the Blue Moon. I can't face the disgrace.''

This was the antithesis of the woman who was part drill, all veep. But growing up with three baby sisters, he knew how to caretake this situation. As she sniffled and cried on his chest, he rocked her gently, murmuring how he always loved cotton candy as a kid and that *Star Trek* was one of his favorite shows. She began bawling after his last statement, so he decided to just stick with the rocking and stop the talking until she gained some control over her emotions.

Which took a solid ten minutes.

Finally, when her sobs decreased to light crying, she pulled out of Raven's embrace and looked him in the eyes. ''I need to get my act together.''

Thanks to her crying bout, wet, smeared mascara encircled her eyes. With her fried hairdo and black eyes, she was starting to look a little scary.

She must have caught the look of horror on Raven's face, because she whispered, ''What's wrong?'' When he didn't answer, she looked down her body, then back up to his face. ''My zipper's still up, so what's wrong?''

''You need to…wash your face.''

This time when she looked in the mirror, she emitted a shriek. From the nearby cottonwood, birds flapped their escape into the air.

"I need help!" Liney exclaimed, looking at him. "I look like Winona Ryder in that *Beetlejuice* movie!"

Except Winona looked better. This day was going rapidly downhill. He'd survived being knocked out, but he was clueless how to deal with a woman having a *Beetlejuice* breakdown in the middle of the Wild West. Char had had other types of breakdowns, such as the one at Tiffany's when her false eyelash fell on her upper lip giving her a Hitler-in-drag look. Raven had saved the day by steering her toward the china section, where she'd plucked off the errant eyelash.

He looked around at the rolling grasslands and the cattle grazing in the distance. What was he going to do with Liney? Steer her into the steer section?

He'd talk her down with some common sense. After all, she was a high-and-mighty vice president. Someone with that kind of title and responsibility had to appreciate the benefit of rational thought.

He hoped.

"Nobody's going to care how you look," he said, brushing the black soot from around her eyes. "After all, we're in the middle of cow country." He gestured toward the distant cows just in case she'd never seen one before. "Everybody wears jeans out here. And everybody's hair looks fried. People in cow country, especially people who've been riding on a Harley through cow country, always look a bit more windblown." He stood back, rubbing his mascara'd hands against his T-shirt. Good thing he'd worn a black one today. "There. Goodbye Winona, hello Liney."

She ducked and looked into the mirror again. Rubbing at a stray smudge, she murmured, "Thanks." She dipped her head to better see her hair. "If I can get my hair under control and change my clothes, I'll be okay.''

Change her clothes? He didn't mind some roadside counseling and mascara removing, but enough was enough. ''We're already an hour-plus late. You ain't— aren't—changing your clothes.''

She flashed him a who's-gonna-stop-me look. ''It's not for you to say one way or the other. I'm changing—'' Liney stopped midsentence as Raven lunged for the pouch, grabbed her silk dress in one handful, and raised it high over his head.

''Put down my dress,'' she demanded, fisting her hands on her hips.

''No.''

''Put it down or I'll—''

''What? Call the Designer Police?''

''Call!'' She literally jumped in place. ''I forgot to call to say we'd be late. They've been set up since six a.m., waiting for the Rugged Man. Hold on, I need to check in, let them know...''

With some effort, Liney retrieved the cell phone from her back pocket. Raven was amazed she'd ridden all this way sitting on that thing. Maybe that's how the upper crust in L.A. lived...what's a little phone sticking in your behind as long as you can make a call whenever you want.

''Hello, Zoom?''

Zoom. Had to be one of her L.A. crew. Maybe the rest of them were named Snap, Crackle and Pop.

Liney began pacing, her Guccis kicking up a little dust every time she pivoted. ''We had a slightly late start, but we'll be there within—'' she caught Raven's eye ''twenty minutes?''

He nodded, although he had no idea if it was ten, twenty or forty minutes.

"Twenty minutes," she repeated affirmatively. "Are you set up?" She sucked on her bottom lip as she listened. "You have been for the last hour," she said, obviously repeating Zoom's words. "I apologize for our tardiness."

Raven felt a little bad holding up her dress when he heard the sadness in her voice. Anybody could see that she was an expert control freak, but he saw the crack in her armor. And through that opening, he knew there were other sides to Liney—the needy little girl, the untamed head-kicker, Winona Ryder's big sister...

"Please give my apologies to the others. We're on our way. Goodbye." She pressed a button, then looked into the distance for a moment, a look of defeat shadowing her features. When she caught Raven looking at her, she plastered an odd smile on her face. One of those smiles that curled the lips but left no twinkle in the eyes.

"You were right, Raven," she said, shoving the phone into her back pocket. "No time for me to change. Although I need to do something with my hair before everyone sees me. I'd kill for a cigarette, too, but I'm trying to be better. Could you hand me my purse?"

"Will you kill me if I don't?" he asked, lowering the dress.

This time her eyes twinkled when she smiled. "No. Just maim you a little."

"Thought you were trying to be better. At smoking, not maiming."

She grinned. He liked seeing her more relaxed. From a distance, she almost looked...angelic. "I won't smoke it," she promised, raising two fingers in a scout salute.

He did as told. She opened her purse, took the cigarette, fondled it lovingly, then tossed the purse back to Raven. The way she stroked and massaged that cylinder of tobacco, it was all Raven could do to act preoccupied with a hawk circling overhead. But when she snapped it crisply in two, he had to suppress his own primal shriek.

"Are you all right?" Liney headed toward him, letting the tobacco flutter away in the wind.

"Fine," he croaked. "You should have warned me what you do to those poor cigarettes."

"It's my way of not smoking," she answered, obviously missing his ulterior meaning. Forlornly, she patted her hair. "I suppose I could brush it out…but the Dragon Lady doesn't need to look scarier than she already does." She sighed heavily. "To look at me, who would know that in the six years since I've graduated from business school, I've escalated profits and renovated product styles at two multinational corporations." She emitted the longest-suffering sigh he'd ever heard. "If I walked past one of my former co-workers now, they'd probably hand me spare change."

He had no idea how to help a self-pitying corporate type suffering from wilderness-itis and unleashed bun madness. Then a memory flitted through Raven's mind. He pointed to the pouch.

"There should be a scarf in the bottom of my bag. Wrap it around your hair."

"Now you tell me!"

"I'd almost forgotten about it…"

His voice trailed off as he watched Liney industriously rummage for the scarf. Within moments, she triumphantly lifted the brightly colored silk object, which glinted and shone in the sunlight. "Yves St. Laurent," Liney said approvingly. "Your biker babes have good taste."

"I don't have 'biker babes,'" Raven mumbled under his breath. *But once upon a time, I had a babette.* Char had picked up the scarf the day they'd been arrested after the crazy Hollywood Boulevard showdown with Liz and her now-husband Russell. Because the police holding cells were filled to capacity, they'd allowed Raven and Char to wait together in a cell, where they'd first fallen in love.

After her lawyer had posted bail for both of them, she'd insisted she wanted to ride his Harley home...and on the way they'd stopped by some ritzy Beverly Hills store where she'd purchased this scarf. She'd even made Raven wind it around her hair, saying she wanted to always remember the day she became his Harley Babette.

Harley Babette. She was so in another stratosphere, she didn't even know it was "Babe" not "Babette."

"How do I put this on my head?" Liney was holding the scarf one way, then the other.

Raven fisted his hands. He didn't want to touch the scarf, or wind it around another woman's hair. But the way Liney draped the thing over her head, she looked like a nun on a bender. So much for the angelic look.

With a weary shake of his head, Raven stepped toward her, cursing himself for repeating history with that damn scarf. After today, he would burn the thing.

Taking the scarf, which fell in silky heaps in his big hands, he carefully refolded it. "Lean down," he ordered, surprised that Liney did as told. He carefully laid it over the top of her cotton candy, then reached behind her ears to tie a knot at the nape of her neck.

Even though he was close enough to count her eyelashes, he studiously avoided those chocolate-brown eyes. And he cursed the delectable vanilla scent that teased his senses. Holding his breath, he fumbled with the knot. Where his fingers accidentally brushed the back of her neck, he felt a rising of goose bumps. She was too warm to be cold...were those bumps a reaction to his touch?

Hundred and eight.

Dropping his hands, he turned and headed back to the bike. "Time to go," he said gruffly.

5

LINEY FELT WORSE than the time in eighth grade when she'd accidentally swallowed part of Robin Roberts' homework. Specifically, the bottom right corner of her math homework. In a moment of thirteen-year-old hormone frenzy, Liney had used the homework to shield her blushing face from Eddie Walton, pubescent stud of the universe. But when she'd peeked over the paper and had caught Eddie looking at her, she'd gotten so nervous that she'd chomped off two fractions. As Eddie had walked toward her, she'd chewed and swallowed, too embarrassed to spit out the paper. An angry Robin had ever-after called Liney "Eight-It" for chewing up one-eighth of her homework.

Today, "Eight-It" stood behind Gomer's red pickup truck, using it as a shield so she could observe her photo-shoot crew before walking into their midst. But instead of being flustered, as she'd been with Eddie, she was apprehensive. At least there was no chance of her chomping off one-eighth of the truck.

I'll take a few moments to gather my wits before I face them.

From the vehicle's vantage point, parked high on a ridge overlooking the shoot, she observed the "A Rugged Man Cooks" setting. They'd recreated a campfire site, which consisted of a pit filled with charred wood surrounded by several wooden stumps. On the periphery were a table, covered with props such as frying pans and utensils, a camera on a tripod, and several black cases containing photography equipment and supplies. Milling around the set were the members of her crew, each like a character from *The Wizard of Oz*.

Zoom, *Cooking Fantasies* elitest forty-something photographer, was meticulously adjusting a camera lens. To Liney, he was the Scarecrow—more stuffing than substance. His assistant Timothy, a nineteen-year-old photography student and Zoom-wannabe, stood nearby taking notes. He reminded Liney of the Tin Man—stilted, in need of oiling.

Cookie, the group's Dorothy, a pushing-thirty makeup artist, was busy primping in a hand-held mirror. Liney wished the flying monkeys would carry Cookie away; unfortunately, her skills were needed for this shoot.

Gomer, the crusty but lovable cowboy, sat on a far rock observing the three others with a look of bewilderment. Gomer was the lion. A shaggy, beloved addition who had the courage to join this motley crew.

Liney swallowed, hard. In this Oz fantasy, she was the Wicked Witch because, except for Gomer, they all hated her. Which she could handle with more maturity and panache if she didn't look like a Biker Babe Gone Bad. She absently touched the side of her face. *A Biker Babe Gone Bad with Tan Circles.*

"What's the prob?" Raven walked up behind her, his boots crunching on the rock-crusted dirt.

"Prob?"

"Problem."

Liney swiped at a drop of sweat that beaded where the scarf met her forehead. "Those people," she answered in an ominous monotone.

Standing next to her, Raven checked out the small gathering below. "You know them, right? Don't tell me we drove several hours in the middle of nowhere to the wrong photo shoot."

She tried to laugh, but it came out like a dry cackle. "This is the correct shoot."

"Then...why aren't you down there?"

She held out her hand, palm up. "I need a cigarette."

"You didn't answer my question."

"I promise not to smoke, just snap."

Raven laid his hand around hers and gave it a reassuring squeeze. "I think you need some human contact, not cigarette contact."

His comment stabbed her heart. She wanted to say something, anything, but didn't trust her voice to not reveal that he'd zeroed in on a painful truth. Darn this man, anyway. Tilting her world at the very moment she needed to gather her strength and prepare herself for battle.

As though sensing her inner turmoil, he tightened his grip. "Liney, are you...afraid?"

She jerked loose her hand and glared at him. "No!" A lizard, scurrying across the dirt, stopped and cocked its head at her. She shot it a warning look. "Don't you start with me, too." It sped away.

After a beat, Raven said, "Okay, I shouldn't have asked such a question. But we didn't come all this way to hide behind a pickup truck and intimidate lizards. Let's get to work."

"Can't."

"Why?"

"My legs." When he looked down at her jeans, she explained with a shrug, "I can't walk yet. The blood isn't fully circulating after that rigorous motorcycle ride.''

He cocked one black eyebrow. "Give me a real reason."

"Because...I'm afraid."

Neither spoke for a long, drawn-out minute. In the silence, a light wind blew past, rustling the dried leaves of a nearby bush.

Raven gently rubbed her shoulder, his fingers expertly kneading muscles she hadn't even known were sore until this moment. "You're tight," he said.

"Uptight," she murmured, more than a little ashamed at her childish excuse.

"That, too." He positioned himself behind her and placed both hands on her shoulders. Rubbing the tension in her upper back, he said in a low, husky voice, "Try surrendering."

"Surrendering?" she repeated. Her body was surrendering all right...to all the shoulder rubbing and stroking. To the *human contact* she so rarely allowed herself. Forcing energy into her voice, she continued, "You mean walk down there with my arms held high, carrying a white flag?" Before he could answer, she said, "Better yet, I'll carry the scarf with my hair unfurled. Then while I'm surrendering, I'll also scare them half to death. That should put me in a position of power."

"You're already in a position of power." Raven leaned closer, his musky aftershave penetrating her angst. "Surrendering isn't about giving up yourself," he whispered into her ear. "It's about giving up your attachment to how things ought to work. It doesn't diminish your power, it enhances it." He gave her shoulder a reassuring squeeze. "I memorized that from my

Hearty Man tape,'' he confessed. ''But it's good advice.''

Liney closed, then reopened, her eyes. ''All right,'' she said. ''I'm going down there. Hold these.'' She removed her sunglasses and handed them to him. ''I don't want to look like a gun moll. If they notice the tan circles, I'll just say you wouldn't let me carry my purse so I had to tape dimes to the sides of my face.''

He hooked the glasses through a belt loop. ''I didn't get the gun moll part, but the dimes were a joke, right?''

''Yes,'' she said grudgingly. Back in L.A. she'd taken a humor class to learn how to make light of difficult situations. Unfortunately, she'd fared even worse in that class than in the kick-boxing one. But even when she swore she'd never tell another flop joke, she always rallied. Before she knew it, she'd try another punch line, determined that one of these days she'd hear that sought-after laughter of approval.

She straightened and blew out a pent-up breath. ''Here I go...'' Walking away, she added over her shoulder, ''But I'm *not* surrendering.''

Raven watched Liney stride down the hill with that purposeful I-go-after-what-I-want walk he'd seen yesterday in the Blue Moon parking lot. She might be afraid, but like an actor with stage fright, Liney would nonetheless face her audience. He had no doubt she'd also give a dynamite performance. His mouth twitched with amusement. She could be a monumental pain in the rear, but he had a growing respect for the lady's tenacity.

He started down the hill behind her.

A high-pitched female voice greeted Liney's entrance. ''Well, it's about time!'' Attached to the voice was a slim, saucy body wearing a flower-print halter top and denim short-shorts. "We've been ready since the crack of dawn!"

"We were detained," Liney answered, a hint of anxiousness in her voice. She positioned herself at the edge of the faux campfire. On the other side stood a yuppieish middle-aged man, some young guy, and Ms. Short-Shorts. Which, thanks to their lack of material, should be renamed No-Shorts, Raven thought.

"We?" The woman's gaze swerved to Raven, who had walked up behind Liney. Short-short's terse features rearranged into suggestive interest.

"Listen up, everyone," Liney called out. "I have some important news."

Raven didn't have the heart to tell Liney she was standing on part of a sagebrush. Mainly because he didn't want to interrupt her take-command stance as the vice president of this stalled production. Plus, from the looks on the faces of the crew, she needed all the support she could get.

The middle-aged man, dressed in neatly pressed khaki pants and a Gap T-shirt, wore a beige-and-blue bandanna tied stylishly around his neck. His hair was slicked back into one of those thin, graying ponytails that Raven detested. Okay, he'd worn a tail himself for years, but that was different—he looked *good* wearing one. This dude looked like he was at the beginning of a serious middle-age crisis.

"No need to tell us to 'listen up,'" Ponytail responded, "for you, we're all ears." He sounded anything but amiable. In fact, his words dripped of sarcasm. If Raven wasn't trying to be the new Raven, and give Liney room to do her veep thing, he'd charge across this Hollywood campfire scene right now and have a little man-to-man with Pony-'tude.

Liney nodded, although Raven saw sweat glistening on her forehead. It was warm, but not that warm outside. He was beginning to realize that Liney Reed's cool and collected facade housed a bundle of nerves. "Thank you, Zoom," she said.

Liney cleared her throat. "I'd like to introduce our new Rugged Man, Raven Doyle." With a grand gesture, Liney swung back her arm and slammed smack into Raven's abdomen.

Snickers greeted him as Liney, red-faced, began touching Raven's stomach and apologizing profusely. "I'm so sorry," she murmured. "I didn't know you were standing right behind me. Did I hurt you?"

He was in good enough shape that he barely felt her solar plexus thunk. What concerned him, however, was the wild-eyed hysteria he detected in her eyes...and the stream of sweat that dripped down the side of her face. Liney was in bad shape.

"Great, Liney," chided Zoom, "you're damaging the star before the shoot even begins."

More laughter.

Ms. Short-Shorts, whose stringy brown hair dangled in a ponytail from the side of her head, was laughing so hard she had to hold her stomach. It wasn't *that* funny, Raven thought. Unless this group was enjoying the opportunity to laugh *at* Liney.

The sullen kid, probably about nineteen, also laughed, the sound more forced than genuine. When he turned away, Raven saw a rubber-banded stub of hair at the back of the kid's head. A germinating ponytail.

Raven felt as though he was attending some kind of unisex ponytail reunion.

Beyond the group, about ten feet from the campfire, Gomer was perched on a rock. Hunched over, his elbows on his knees, he watched the goings-on as though trying to figure if this is how L.A. folk always behaved.

Raven, realizing Liney was still semihysterically patting him down, gently caught her hands in his. They were small, and despite the weather, cold. "Go to your heart," he whispered.

Her watery chocolate eyes blinked. "Go where?"

"Go to your heart," he quickly repeated. "Quiet your mind."

Liney withdrew her hands. "This isn't the time to be quiet," she said, flashing him an are-you-crazy? look before turning back to the group. Plastering on a professional smile, she announced, "He obviously has a stomach of iron." After an awkward pause, she added, "Maybe they named the Iron Man after him." She looked around, but no one reacted. "Iron Man. That's the name of that race in Hawaii."

Silence.

After clearing her throat, Liney continued. "Anyway, Raven will be perfect as our Rugged Man. Any questions?"

"How'd you find another model so fast?" asked Timothy.

"He was in the right place at the right time," Liney answered.

"And where was that?" Zoom asked, although it sounded more like a taunt than a question.

"Just outside the Blue—" Liney flicked a drop of sweat off her chin. "Just outside Cheyenne."

"Are those *circles* on your face?" asked an incredulous Cookie, moving closer.

There was such a long pause, the passing buzz of an insect was almost ear-shattering.

"I'm...a big Star Trek fan," Liney answered awkwardly.

When silence again greeted her, Raven attempted a guffaw, which sounded more like a cough. These people were even getting to him.

With a small smile to Raven, Liney forged ahead. "So, let's give a big welcome to our new Rugged Man." A smattering of clapping followed. "Raven, this is our makeup artist, Cookie McCutcheon." Liney started to gesture broadly toward Cookie, then stopped. After a quick look behind her, Liney instead nodded toward the woman. "You'll be reporting to her first thing each morning."

Smiling, Cookie did a swively number with her hips. "Better make it extra early. A big guy like you, it's gonna take lots more time to put on body makeup."

Raven frowned. "Body makeup? I don't wear no body make—"

"And this is Zoom," Liney cut in. "He's *Cooking Fantasies'* staff photographer." Zoom barely looked up from the camera lens he was still fiddling with. "And Timothy, his assistant." Timothy, following Zoom's lead, remained preoccupied with his note taking.

Raven was starting to understand why Liney had "leg-trouble" behind the truck. Who in their right mind wanted to hang with this bunch?

"I'm mighty glad you're here," piped up a craggy voice. Gomer sauntered over from his rock and held out his hand. Raven picked up a memory-jogging scent...Old Spice cologne, the kind his granddad wore. "Welcome, son," said Gomer, vigorously shaking Raven's hand. "*E Pluribus Unum.* That's Latin for

From many, one. In other words, we're all here, working together as one.''

A cowboy spouting Latin? Even stranger was his comment that this group worked together. Maybe the Ponytailed Avengers did, but they had definitely closed ranks when it came to Liney. "That's how people should work," Raven agreed, raising his voice so it rumbled ominously. "As a team. As one." Anger heated his blood. Anger and…protectiveness. Just like he had for his kid sisters, he wanted to protect Liney from this kind of mistreatment.

"If you need anything," Gomer said, interrupting Raven's thoughts, "just ask." He pushed back his dusty Stetson, revealing a full head of thick, white hair. "I'm the gofer. Not the rodent variety, the go-get-it variety." He grinned at his joke, causing his weathered face to break into a sea of wrinkles.

"Speaking of which," Liney said, addressing Gomer, "after Cookie gets Raven's measurements, you need to go into town and pick up some new outfits for him. I don't think anything we had for Lord Byron will fit Raven."

Cookie, doing another hip-swivel thing, chimed in, "You kidding? This guy's way bigger." With a look at Raven, she hitched her head toward a tent about twenty feet away. "Come on over to my place so I can see just how big, Rave."

"It's Raven," he corrected, not budging from where he stood.

"Raven." Perching her hands on her short-short hips, Cookie gazed over at a gnarled tree where a crow perched on a top branch. "Isn't there a poem that goes 'Quote the Raven, two-three-four?'"

Raven closed his eyes, recalling the hours he'd spent

in Charlotte's family's library, reading everything he could get his hands on, including Poe. "Nevermore," Raven said, opening his eyes.

"Nevermore?" Cookie tilted her head to the side, causing her ponytail to point like a divining rod toward the ground.

"Not 'two-three-four.' *Nevermore.* Quoth the Raven, nevermore."

"Oh-h-h." Cookie straightened her head. "We had to recite that poem in fifth grade—never got why the bird counted. Didn't know I was saying the wrong words because they blended in with everybody else's." She mouthed "nevermore" to herself several times, bobbing her head as though to pound the word into memory. "Okay, got it! Now we can do measurements." Sashaying away, Cookie put so much oomph into her walk, Raven wasn't sure if that was her underneath her short-shorts or two beach balls bouncing madly off each other.

With a wary look at the exiting beach-ball exhibition, he said in an undertone to Liney, "I'd rather crawl, naked, across burning coals."

Liney did a confused double take. "I want you to look hot and sexy, but you don't have to go to extremes—"

"I mean," he said, exasperated, "I'm not going into that tent with Beach Ball."

Liney looked over at Cookie's jiggling, exiting form. "Her name's Cook—"

"I know!" He took a moment to center himself. "The point is," he said, keeping his voice as level as possible, "I don't want her to take my measurements."

"What's the prob?" Liney asked.

Now it was his turn to give a double take. "I think

she's interested in taking only *one* measurement, if you get my drift.''

Liney barely suppressed a grin. With a playful wag of her finger, she whispered, ''Sounds like you need to quiet your mind.''

Before a taken-aback Raven could respond, Gomer cut in. ''From many, one. That girl takes *E Pluribus Unum* a bit too literally.'' He chortled, clapping Raven on the back. ''Guess you're just too handsome for your own good, son. Y'know, out here, we build fences so nobody gets confused who owns what animals or land. Just build yourself an imaginary fence, and let that li'l gal know where it is.'' Gomer shifted his gaze to Liney. ''After I get them measurements from Cookie, I'll need to know what kinda outfits you're lookin' for.''

''It's going to be tough finding clothes to fit.'' Liney gave Raven a critical once-over. ''Maybe for one of the photos,'' she mused, ''we can wrap him in yards and yards of rough-hewn cloth....'' Raven swore her eyes glazed over as she stared at him, lost in thought.

''If we're going to use yards,'' Raven suggested, ''then we won't need the measurement stuff.'' When she started to disagree, he raised his voice, overriding hers. ''My measurements are off the map—most clothing stores wouldn't have the vaguest how to calculate a size from my numbers. It'd be a lot easier if I just tell Gomer the sizes I wear and save Cookie breaking her measurement tape.''

Gomer nodded. ''That might work. I'll need to head back to Cheyenne—doubt any of the other towns carry sizes big enough. Maybe I'll stop in Chugwater, see if King Karl bought any new duds lately...might be able to borrow somethin'.''

Blinking, Liney tuned back into the conversation. "King Karl?"

Gomer nodded. "Instead of calling him King Kong, they call him King Karl 'cause his name's Karl."

When Raven chuckled, Liney muttered something about everybody else's jokes getting laughs. Raising her voice, she said, "Maybe King Karl is willing to loan some of his clothes, but remember...we don't want Raven looking like a hick."

Gomer drew back. "Hick?"

Liney nodded as though it was perfectly obvious. "You know, hick. Hillbilly. Oddball."

Raven groaned inwardly. Maybe he wasn't the suavest guy who ever walked the planet, but Liney "The Drill" Reed was inserting one Gucci'd foot after another into her rosebud mouth. No doubt she believed she was simply discussing business, but referring to the Wyoming dress code as "hick," "hillbilly" and "oddball" was insulting to a Wyomingite.

"My Rugged Man must look sizzlingly sexy," she said, her eyes glistening as though she were running a fever. "Women will buy the magazine because of the cover model's Travolta-Willis-Clooney looks, not because of the recipes." She started pacing, her excitement building. "We need some more body-molding jeans, Gomer. Black if you can find a pair. A couple more muscle-clinging T-shirts, too. Avoid any silly jargon on them. You know, any 'Go Within or Go Without' stuff. If you can find a cowboy shirt big enough, great. No fringe, though. We'll unbutton it to reveal some of that..." She stopped pacing and stared at Raven's chest. Holding her hands in front of her, she wriggled her fingertips. "...some of that black, thick dig-your-fingers-in-carpeting chest hair," she said breathlessly.

Raven, stuck on the "Go Within or Go Without" being silly jargon, started to say something in his defense when Liney cut him off.

"He has awfully big feet," she continued to Gomer, her gaze stalled on Raven's boots, "but get his shoe size, too, and see if you can purchase another pair of boots. Leather. No fancy designs. Just something dark, rough looking." She grasped the old cowboy's shoulders and looked him in the eyes. "Remember, Gomer, think sexy. That's what we want."

Gomer's blue-gray eyes widened. "Haven't thought that way in years...."

"You can do it," Liney insisted. "After all, you were almost the Rugged Man's stand-in, remember?"

He stared back into her twinkling eyes with an almost helpless look. "Me? Your Rugged Man?"

"Yes, *you*. Except you said we'd have to put a gob of Vaseline on the lens." She leaned closer, almost pressing her forehead against his. "But I don't think that's true," she whispered, "because you, Gomer, are just naturally sexy."

"I am?" Like a watered plant, or in this case, a man watered with compliments, he seemed to grow a little taller. "I'm likin' this job better 'n' better."

Dropping her hands, Liney pivoted neatly on her Gucci pumps and turned to walk away. "I'll let Cookie know she won't be taking measurements—"

"No need to," cut in Cookie, who'd rejoined the group. Looking mildly miffed, she said, "When my model didn't show up, I came back to see what's happening." She leaned her weight against one hip and arched an eyebrow. Raven swore her ponytail looked a little puffed up, like its owner's attitude.

"Raven's giving his sizes to Gomer who'll be his personal shopper," Liney explained.

Taking his cue, Raven did as told. Gomer penciled the numbers on the back of an old business card he dug out of his shirt pocket.

"And, Zoom!" Liney snapped her fingers to get the photographer's attention. "I like what Raven's wearing right now, so proceed with the planned morning shoot until new attire arrives."

When Liney turned her head to give some added instructions to Gomer, Zoom said out of her earshot, "Yes-siree, Mizzy Dragon Lady." Timothy laughed, a sound more mean than mirthful.

Although Liney had wooed Gomer into submission, Raven saw she treated the others as though they were her puppets with her "do this, do that" style of command. She might mean well, but her sharp-tongued, take-charge attitude rubbed people the wrong way. His kid sister Moira had the same headstrong, I-know-what's-best-for-you approach to life. Few people outside the family knew that Moira's tough shell protected an insecure, vulnerable girl. Moira and Liney had a lot in common. Too bad they both thought they needed to hide their softer side. If they'd risk revealing it to others, he'd bet his Harley the two would learn they were lovable outside and in.

"All right, crew," Liney said exuberantly, clapping her hands. "I have everything under control. Zoom, set up for the first shoot. Cookie, put makeup on our model. Raven, go with Cookie. And Gomer, bon voyage." Obviously satisfied with the chain of events she'd just fired into action, Liney rolled back her shoulders and looked over her domain. As another drip of sweat broke loose from her hairline, she brushed at her brow. Her fingers caught underneath the scarf, which she accidentally pulled off in one sweeping motion.

As though it had been aching for release, her cotton-candy hair sprung to freedom, reminding Raven of those fifties black and-white footage of A-bomb tests.

For several long moments of eerie silence, everyone stared at Liney's mushrooming hair. If they'd all been wearing shades, Raven thought, they'd look like those A-bomb spectators who all wore special sunglasses.

Cookie finally broke the silence by bursting into laughter, followed by Zoom and son-of-Zoom. Gomer stared, openmouthed. Raven was tempted to plug his ears to muffle the impending train-stopping screech.

Liney, blinking rapidly, clutched the scarf so tightly, her knuckles turned white. Her chin quivered. Staring into space, she opened her mouth to speak. Raven lifted his index fingers, ready to insert them as earplugs. But she surprised him. In a shaky-voiced aside, she whispered, "If I'd worn my dress, I'd at least have looked halfway acceptable."

Then she turned and walked away, her head—and hair—held high.

Raven took a step to follow her, but stopped. If he'd learned anything from his sisters and other women, it was to let them have their space, where they could safely vent their hurt, before offering consolation. That had to hold doubly true for Liney Reed. With all that pent-up, nerve-bundled angst, the lady might vent her rage with a barrage of kicks...and he sure as hell didn't want to get in the way of one of those again.

Gomer, his hands in his pockets, stepped closer to Raven. As they watched Liney's stiff-legged exodus,

Gomer said, "Wonder where she's off to? There ain't nuthin' but sagebrush and grass out there."

It saddened Raven that Liney, with her purposeful I-know-where-I'm-going walk, hadn't a clue where she was headed. That had to be a first. "She needs to be alone."

Gomer made a thoughtful sound. "She makes life tougher than it oughta be. But her heart's in the right place."

"The lady has a heart, all right," Raven agreed. "Too bad she keeps it in an airtight compartment most of the time."

"With some people," Gomer said, squinting as Liney's slim form headed directly into the sunlight, "it takes a little prying to give their heart breathing room. But the effort's worth it. After all, why are we here?"

Why? For Raven, he was on a personal journey to create the new Raven. But for the first time, it hit him that maybe thinking it was only *his* journey narrowed the road. Maybe such life trips were like highways with multiple lanes...you not only helped yourself, but also helped others along the way.

Maybe helping others is also helping yourself.

If *that* were the case, however, helping Liney felt like he'd pulled off the highway in his asphalt-eating Harley to kick-start a slow-as-a-dinosaur diesel.

Gomer laid his hand on Raven's shoulder. "Whoever said it was easy?"

The words reverberated through Raven's mind. By the time he had the wherewithal to ask how the old cowboy knew what Raven had been thinking, Gomer was waving goodbye from his truck window before disappearing into a cloud of dust.

6

Swinging her arms and huffing breaths, Liney marched across the dusty, grassy ground. Not an easy task in her Gucci pumps, which were made for walking across carpeted boardrooms, not hiking in the wild Wyoming frontier. But the heels, at least, were short. And sensible, the way Liney used to be. She swiped a damp curl off her sweaty forehead. *If Mrs. Acheson could see me now, I'd get an A for speed walking in a straight line—an A-plus for doing it in leather heels.*

And an F-plus as a vice president, she thought glumly. *Maybe I can stress-test designer shoes as a second career.* But the irreverent idea didn't offer a gram of comfort. It only reinforced the fact that life was currently stress-testing her. Talk about a bad hair day. She was also having a bad tan day, a bad jean day...face it, she was having a bad bad day. Flaring her nostrils, Liney forged ahead, striding across the untamed Wyoming landscape to...

...to nowhere.

Angry tears stung her eyes as her pace slowed. She'd never headed nowhere. Not driven-to-success Caroline Reed, former college wunderkind and current corporate golden girl. Nowhere wasn't even in her vocabulary. Liney's direction in life had always been up, up, up!

Emotion welled within her as she slogged toward the sun, now a blurry glop of gold thanks to her tear-filled

vision. For the first time in her overambitious worka-
holic life, she wasn't going up up up. With this rocky
terrain, she wasn't even going level. She gulped back
a self-deprecating laugh. *At least I'm not headed down.*

Her toe caught on something. Pitching forward, she
flailed for balance. A bird shrieked—or was it her?—
as the world swirled past in a blur of blue, brown, and
green.

Whomp! Thump!

Her palms slammed against the earth, her body close
behind.

Stunned, she lay on the ground and stared at a gargantuan spiky bush that blocked the distant mountains.
After several moments, she realized it was really a
clump of grass only inches from her face. She licked
her lips and tasted dirt.

She had never gone down? At this moment, if she
got any more down, she'd be under the earth.

Shakily, she hoisted herself to a sitting position and
brushed soil and pebbles from her palms, which tingled
painfully from the crash. Her knee hurt. Her toe
throbbed. Her shoes were seriously scuffed. A self-
pitying tear trickled down her cheek as she studied her
filthy hands.

"I need a manicure," she said in a choked voice.
She looked up at a hawk weaving big lazy circles in
the sky. It seemed to know its purpose. Plus, it had a
better view than her three-corner window office back
in L.A. How come a creature—who didn't give a hoot
for designer labels or sleek sedans or corporate lad-
ders—got to have such an easy, stress-free existence?
With a great view, to boot.

I'm having a serious envy attack over a bird. "Forget the manicure," Liney whispered hoarsely, "I need a *life*."

She didn't want to cry, but it was so damn exhausting keeping it all together. Exhausting to play corporate bigwig...exhausting to oversee the photo shoot in the middle of the Wild West...

...*Exhausting to pretend that every muttered "Dragon Lady" didn't feel like a knife through her heart.*

She hitched her chin a notch. "Some big vice president you are," she chided herself, pretending she didn't hear the wobble in her voice. "Didn't you ever hear that sticks and stones can break your bones, but names will never hurt you?" However, deep down, she didn't buy the childhood ditty.

She suddenly picked up a stone and hurled it with all her strength. Although she threw it straight, it careened wildly off to the right. "Names hurt more than you!" she yelled as it landed with a dusty sputter and rolled to a stop.

Her words reverberated through the air, taunting her.

Names hurt.

Dragon Lady.

Those nasty utterances had taken their toll. Maybe no one could see the effect they'd had on her, the way one might see a broken arm or leg, but Liney could feel them. Words, like weapons, had torn through her, purpling into bruises on her soul. Another tear rolled down her cheek.

When she looked at her shadow and caught the raggedy silhouette of her troll-doll head of hair, the dam broke. With a tear-laden wail, she let her bottled-up emotions rip loose. She kicked and cursed, thrashed and wept. At one point she leaned back and pummeled the ground with the heels of her shoes, not giving a damn that they had cost her a week's salary. Her clothes were already caked in dirt, her hair was shot to hell, and she'd cried off all her makeup—what did she have to lose?

Finally, exhausted, she lay on her back and stared up at the vast blue sky and frothy white clouds. She breathed in the warm, sage-scented air and realized she felt calmer, more relaxed than she had after spending a week—and a bundle—at that exclusive spa in Southern California.

Even sex never felt this good.

She frowned at a passing cumulus cloud, which looked eerily like an unmade bed. "That's a sad commentary," she said to it. "A roll on the ground better than a roll in the hay?"

Sitting up, she quickly thought back, mentally listing her hay rolls. Jerome, the student. They'd been great lab partners in chemistry; unfortunately, the chemistry stopped there. Alan, the lawyer. His mother's urgent phone calls took the urgency out of sex. "Klunky," the corporate headhunter. His nickname said it all.

She toyed with adding a fourth, but decided her sixteen-year-old grope-a-thon with Reginald Irving behind the donut shop was, at best, a semiroll.

Donut shop. Semiroll. Liney threw back her troll-doll head and laughed. "Just my luck!" she explained to a nearby sagebrush. "I finally have a decent joke—and there's no one to hear!"

Dropping her gaze to her dusty jeans, she brushed at a clump of dirt that clung to her knee. "Troll-hair and a down-and-dirty Harley Vixen babe look. I look like Cinderella before the biker ball." Her favorite story had always been *Cinderella*. She indulged the long-ago fantasy of wearing an elegant silk gown and dancing with a handsome prince. A lizard scurried past. "You again." She crossed her arms. "I said prince, not pest."

After a weighty sigh, she murmured to herself, "You can't sit in the middle of nowhere, Liney, talking to lizards and fantasizing about being Cinderella." Grudgingly, she stood…and nearly jumped as a group of birds shot into the air like splatters of black paint against the aquamarine sky. They swerved and dipped giddily before regrouping to soar toward another destination. "Just like that hawk, those birds know exactly where they're going…which is how I felt until today."

Wincing, she patted the thick mess on her head. "I should have stayed in L.A. Had the crew call me with daily reports. But no-o-o-o, the Dragon Lady had to trot herself out here to oversee the shoot because she doesn't think anybody else can do a decent day of work unless she's micromanaging, her nose firmly embedded in everybody else's business."

Ouch. That little epiphany hurt.

"I never wanted to be a vice president," she confided to a nearby rock. "As a kid, I dreamed of running a fantasy shop, filled with fairy-tale books and toys." Crossing her arms, she looked at her shadow on the ground. "When did I give up the dream?" she asked it.

But the answer came from within her, not without. It bubbled upward, from someplace deep and silent, forming in her mind like the answer in an eight ball. She'd given up around her tenth birthday. The year that she let her childhood wither on the vine. The year she became three-fourths adult, one-fourth child.

That realization filled her with an aching sadness.

"No wonder no one likes me," she admitted. A faint scent, like jasmine, passed on a gust of air, but it didn't sweeten her self-analysis. "I'm a fantasy-store mutant masquerading aˢ a vice president. I don't like my job, I don't like me, and it shows in every interaction."

She almost succumbed to another bout of serious self-pity, but decided to forego it. She was tired of weeping. It was time for action.

"I'm going to call Dirk and quit," she announced to the bush, which had become her best pal in the last few minutes.

She reached into her back pocket and tugged. The hard object refused to budge. What had it done? Swelled in this heat? She yanked. Nothing. "Okay, you mutha—" With a string of curses, she gyrated, thrust, and twirled until the phone loosened and popped free.

She wiped the sweat from her brow. "I don't need my Jazzercise classes anymore," she muttered, "I can burn off more calories just retrieving my phone from these jeans...." She punched in the numbers for the Blue Moon Diner. "I'll tell Dirk I'm the wrong person in the job," she continued. Tapping her foot impatiently, which sounded like fump fump fump on the dusty ground, she listened to the ringing on the other end. "Raven wanted me to surrender? Well, baby, I'm surrendering."

A husky, sexy woman's voice answered. Had to be Dirk's bride, the woman with whom he was on an eternal date. Although Liney had only spoken to Belle once, that voice was memorable. "Belle? Liney Reed. Put Dirk on." Liney caught herself. "Please," she added, trying to sound pleasanter than she felt.

Liney watched the lizard zigzag across the dirt as she waited for Dirk to come to the phone. "Are you following me again?'' she said irritably. ''I told you earlier, I want a prince, not a pest—hello, Dirk! No, no, I was talking to a lizard....''

Great conversation opener, Liney. You sure know how to impress your boss, the CEO.

''What's up?'' she said, repeating his question. ''Well, I...I...*I quit.*'' Her lack of finesse surprised even herself, but then she'd never quit before. At anything.

She tilted her head, listening to Dirk's soothing, deep voice. He sounded a lot better than he did in L.A. Calmer. More...confident. How could that be? A tycoon who lived the life of luxury in L.A., sounding more confident and happy out here in nowhere bohunkville? But that had been Dirk's choice after marrying Belle. He'd wanted to relocate his office from L.A. to Cheyenne where he'd work long distance as CEO of Harriman Enterprises. And to think part of her master plan for locating the shoot in Wyoming had been so she could also convince Dirk to return to L.A. Well, that was no longer an issue because she was resigning. Now.

But she couldn't get one resigning word in edgewise because Dirk was complimenting her, telling her how qualified, how perfect she was for this job. Why did she want to quit?

''Because...'' of my fried hair, breath-inhibiting jeans, and new starring role as the Wicked Troll Witch on *Star Trek*. But when she started to offer a strong, reality-based answer, her voice betrayed her. Sounding as though she'd been sucking helium, she squeaked, ''Because I don't have what it takes.''

The words just slipped out. She hadn't even thought them through before opening her mouth. What was it with her body functions today, anyway? They were in mutiny against her intellect, overriding reason with shaking, thrashing, and throwing.

Get a grip. Restate your reason in a compelling, non-helium way. She opened her mouth to calmly explain why she was quitting, but her mutinous body overruled her mind again. Just as dreams and memories from years ago had previously been unleashed, so were the torrent of words that followed.

"I've been at Harriman Enterprises a month, yet I've created more enemies than I have in a lifetime. I created this special magazine project—*A Rugged Man Cooks*—but I've alienated my crew. I found the perfect model, yet in twenty-four hours, I've kicked and socked him...although I only knocked him out once." She drew in a ragged breath. "I fail at management. I don't know how to relate. I can't tell jokes. I've never had good sex and I still feel really, really bad about Robin Roberts' homework."

There. She'd hit on anything and everything. If he didn't fire her for gross mismanagement, he'd at least fire her for temporary insanity.

Or maybe it was permanent at this point.

But no. When her twirling thoughts refocused on Dirk's response, she heard him launching into yet another minispeech, this one about the necessity of plunging through chaos in order to find one's true self. And how Liney was probably a better vice president and person for what she was going through than all of his other vice presidents rolled into one. He ended up saying something about *this* being the life—she assumed "this" was "Wyoming" although she didn't want to interrupt and ask. After a grand pause, Dirk summarized by saying the simple life is richer than anything money can buy.

The simple life. Boy, could she relate. What Liney would give right now to be back in L.A., doing the simple things—driving her BMW, wearing a comfortable Donna Karan ensemble, and sipping a skinny double latte with just a touch of vanilla.

But she stiffened when Dirk said, "I don't accept your resignation."

"Why not?"

"Because you're the best person for this job."

"I look like hell."

He paused before answering. "I can't see you. Besides, looks have nothing to do with it."

"Looks are everything!"

Dirk chuckled. "That's a good one. Trust you to maintain a sense of humor. Now, finish the shoot, feel the reward, and afterwards, we'll talk about what you want to do next."

He chuckled? She wasn't even trying to make a joke! She toyed with giving the "donut shop" and "semiroll" a test run, but he was already saying goodbye in that warm you-can-do-it tone.

She mumbled "goodbye" and tapped the End button. Staring glumly at the phone, she wondered what had ever inspired her to call him in the first place. And had she really said she'd never had good sex? She squeezed shut her eyes, wishing she knew some magical words that would forever erase the past conversation from her memory cells.

She opened her eyes and tucked the phone back into her pants pocket. "Maybe you were babbling so fast, Dirk didn't catch the sex comment—" She stopped talking as her gaze caught something on the horizon.

In the distance, on a ridge, stood the biggest, tallest sagebrush she'd yet seen on this trip. Had to be at least, oh, ten times the size of any shrub around it.

Her insides knotted.

That was no megasagebrush. That was Raven.

SHE SEES ME. Or, Raven thought, Liney had seen a mountain lion or a bear because her body visibly stiffened. He swore her hair stiffened too, but decided the mushroomed mass had lifted on a passing gust of wind. He opened his mouth to call out, "You okay?" but stopped. He didn't want the crew, milling around the fake campfire down the hill behind him, to hear his yell and rush up to this ledge.

Because the last thing he wanted was Zoom, his sidekick and Cookie also witnessing Liney's little wilderness breakdown. And to think just yesterday, he'd pegged her as an uptight, proper veep. In the last few minutes she'd become the Tasmanian Devil's twin sister. Raven hadn't seen that much thrashing and writhing since Char forced herself into that spandex girdle.

But Liney's wilderness fit *way* outdid Char's retail one. If there were a thrashing and writhing Super Bowl, Liney would be the world champ.

In the distance, she stood stock-still, staring at him. He waved. A huge, sweeping I'm-up-here wave, which both of them knew damn well was really I'm-up-here-and-I-saw-you-go-berserk wave. Probably best to keep some distance right now...thirty or so yards seemed about right.

After a beat, she raised her hand shoulder-height and meekly waved back.

Sadness washed over him. He couldn't distinguish her features, and he was too far away to hear her rantings but he could guess the look on her face and what she was thinking. Those big chocolate eyes blinking rapidly as she realized her out-of-control antics had been observed. Those rosebud lips trembling as she vacillated between sniffling or stiff upper-lipping it. And although she might desperately want to hide—and sniffle—from a predicament, just as she'd hidden behind Gomer's truck, she inevitably squared her shoulders and her attitude and faced situations head-on.

Which meant at this very moment, she was stiff upper-lipping it.

"Bet you're wishing you had a cigarette right now, don't you?" he mumbled, squinting at her. "Yeah, I know, you wouldn't smoke it, but you'd snap it so hard, it'd sound like a bullwhip cracking." With a small smile, he gave his head a shake, imagining Liney venting herself on a defenseless cig. "Then after you were through snapping, Rosebud, I'd take you in my arms and cradle you."

A hot ache coursed through him as he imagined holding Liney, her slim form molded against his. At first she'd be hesitant, not wanting to let down her guard. She'd probably pull back a little just to show who's boss. But he'd hold onto her, murmur she could let go because he'd be strong for the two of them.

And the defiant, scared look in her eyes would soften as she'd slowly, slowly sink her weight against him. He closed his eyes and drew in a long, deep breath. She'd smell of vanilla...and when he leaned down to kiss her, she'd taste even sweeter....

He popped open his eyes. Kiss? When had this consoling fantasy taken an amorous turn?

One hundred and nine.

Get back on track, buddy. The lady might need some

human contact, but you're in no mental shape to get involved with any woman—especially *that* woman—right now.

He dragged his hand through his thick mane of hair. "I gotta get back to camp," he muttered. After all, not so many minutes ago, Cookie had warned him it was time for his body makeup. He'd come up here to scout for Liney because he was concerned for her safety. But now that she saw him, and knew her way back to camp, there was no need for him to play beacon or bodyguard or whatever the hell he thought he was doing up here on this hill....

A light wind blew the hair off his forehead. Warm breezes pushed against him, as though teasing him to go back to camp.

But he didn't want to leave.

Any woman who stomped off into the middle of the wilderness obviously didn't open up and talk to people about what was bugging her. He'd learned that life lesson from his sister Moira. Whenever she'd storm off in one of her black moods, he'd stick around and wait for her. Sure enough, within an hour or two a sheepish Moira would return, needing a sympathetic ear. And Raven would listen, cradle her, and offer his pillow-sized shoulder for her to cry on.

He might sometimes be clumsy or unknowledgeable about the finer things in life, but he was trying to be more careful and understanding when it came to people. It stuck like a crankpin in his belly when people treated him like a cretin. Just because he wore jeans and a battered leather jacket didn't mean his heart was also roughened. Which was one reason, if he were totally honest with himself, he'd fallen so hard for the Bel Air socialite Charlotte Maday. Part of him had felt

redeemed that a classy dame didn't judge him as an
animal, a Neanderthal.

But unfortunately, she had.

That was his painful secret, which he shared with
nobody. Like a misaligned sprocket and chain, that
ugly truth still ground away at his insides. He sometimes wondered if he'd ever get over how Char—at the
end of their relationship—called him a "beast."

Forget it. It's old history.

His head and gut were rocking and rolling from that
side trip into Char history. *Loiter up here a few more
minutes, get your act together.* Besides, if he waited
long enough, Liney would have someone to talk to....

Nah. Not Liney. In spite of his mood, he chuckled.
She might drill others with questions, but when the
tables were turned, she donned her suit of invisible
armor. His eyes raked over her slim form as she started
trudging purposefully toward him, that wild head of
hair held high. She never broke her stride even though
her long legs wobbled as they maneuvered across rock
and grass in those leather pumps.

What kind of crazy woman wore Beverly Hills shoes
in the middle of Wyoming? Emotions clashed within
him. Sometimes he wanted to scold her for being so
wilderness-challenged. Other times, he wanted to protect her from her nasty-hearted crew. The lady made
him insane. She irritated him! Frustrated him! Hell,
she'd even knocked him senseless!

But her vitality also captivated him.

Intrigued him.

Excited him.

He gritted his teeth against the blast of heat that
seared through him. *One hundred and ten.* He should
leave this gig. March back down this mountain, mount

Macavity, and barrel back down the highway away from Liney Reed....

"Rave-en!" Cookie's high-pitched shrill shattered the silence. "Get your rugged behind down here."

Another reason to leave—he was fed up being tagged "rugged" all the time. Maybe he should start answering "Rugged and ready!" whenever they called for him. Raven tossed a look over his shoulder. At the bottom of the rocky slope stood Cookie, her fists planted on her short-shorted hips. "I've been looking all over for you! It's time to do your body makeup and I don't have all day!" Her ponytail bounced with each emphatic motion of her head.

Being in the middle of Liney-the-Drill's and Cookie-the-Tail's attitudes made him feel as though he was starring in a bad B flick, *Mean Girl Sandwich*. But if he gave in to his angst and split this scene, he could kiss his bike-and-book shop goodbye.

With great restraint, he plastered on a broad smile and flashed Cookie a thumbs-up.

"I'll be in my tent!" she responded with her own thumb wave. "See you in five." She expanded her hand signal from a thumb to five splayed fingers, which made him wonder if she thought he might not understand what "five" meant. Then she turned sharply and headed toward camp, those beach balls bouncing off each other like two Sumo wrestlers.

Four days. Only four more days. He headed down the slope toward the land of wrestling beach balls and body makeup.

Minutes later, he strode into Cookie's taupe-colored tent. Through a rectangular mesh opening in the top, hazy sunlight filtered into the shadowed interior. To the left stood a portable clothes rack. In the center, two canvas-backed folding chairs. To the right, a card table, upon which Cookie was busily arranging different bottles and canisters. The room's organization and attention to detail surprised Raven. He'd expected the decorating sense of a harried teenager, but instead saw the organization of a woman who took her career seriously.

A thought froze in his brain. *You judged her the same way you hate people judging you.*

"I had to look all over for you," she said peevishly. "Zoom wants to start and we still have to get you ready."

Raven swore her ponytail twitched, as though seconding Cookie's words. "Sorry. Had to use the…men's room." He felt a ripple of guilt for lying, but thought it better if he avoided any discussion of Liney.

Cookie looked over her shoulder and frowned, an act that compressed her painted features into a series of colored lines. It reminded him of the Cubist painting that hung in Char's family's living room. "I thought we had those port-o-things over that hill," Cookie said, pointing toward the tent wall with her glittery purple fingernail.

"I'm an outdoors kinda guy," he mumbled, warily eyeing the containers of goo and glop that were going to be slathered on his body any moment. He rolled his shoulders to dislodge the tension that had decided to take up residence there.

Straightening, a silver canister in her hand, Cookie's blue eyes widened as she looked at Raven. "Oh my," she breathed. "He slithers!"

"I never sli—"

"Ohhh! And he rhumbas!" Cookie did that hip-swivel thing again. Raven wondered if she was one of those delusional types who had invisible people as friends. Except Cookie, instead of conversing with them, danced with them. "What is it?" she asked, still hip-swiveling.

He followed her line of vision to the multicolored iguana on his arm. "It's my tat."

"Thought it was your bicep."

He paused. "Tat is short for tattoo," he corrected, enunciating the word carefully. It was getting awfully hot in this tent.

"Why'd you get a dinosaur?"

"It's an iguana."

"Same diff." She held up the canister. "Okee, take off your shirt. Let's see what we have to work with."

"My T-shirt stays on," he said gruffly. "Liney told Zoom she liked what I'm wearing—and for him to proceed with the planned morning shoot until new clothes arrive." Plus, no way in hell was he playing Neanderthal Stud for this group. He was more than just a body...he was a man with a heart.

Cookie blinked her thick, mascara'd lashes at him. For the first time he noticed a tiny sparkling ladybug stick-on at the outside corner of her eye. His right eye twitched as he stared at the bug.

"Okee, but Zoom's planned morning shoot is a first-thing-in-the-morning buff shot. You know, as though you've just rolled out of bed and you're aching to fry up some ham and eggs." She licked her lips, although Raven didn't think she had breakfast items on her mind.

He smiled politely. Or tried to. After riding three long, hot, grueling days across country, he didn't have any leftover energy for a man-eating makeup artist.

"When I wake up in the morning," Raven said solemnly, "I don't ache for anything." Well, he used to, but women were a thing of his past. "And I put on my clothes before I cook. Especially before I cook ham and eggs, otherwise hot grease splatters all over my skin and burns me." He crossed his arms over his chest, an unsubtle blockade to any further T-shirt-removal discussions.

Cookie scrunched up her face. It took Raven a moment to realize she was thinking.

"Forget the ham and eggs part." She rolled her eyes toward the ceiling as though reading something up there. "It's first thing in the morning. You've just fallen out of bed, all brawny and sweaty and semi-naked, and you're stumbling around your kitchen checking out what's for breakfast before you cook. Or maybe you're all brawny and sweaty and seminaked and talking to your dog, you know, like 'What's up, pooch?' Or maybe you're all brawny and sweaty and—"

"Can we can the brawny list?" He held up both hands in a stopping motion. "I ain't—am not—baring my chest for any camera."

Tilting her head, Cookie eyed his tattoo. "You got another animal under that shirt? Is that what you don't want me to see?"

"It's only me underneath the T."

Dropping her hands, she sighed dramatically. "Don't you get it? That's what women want. They're not buying the magazine for its recipes…they're buying it for your *body!*" Her gaze slid all over him as though her eyeballs were greased.

"Speaking of bodies," a male voice interrupted, "Why isn't our Rugged Man made up and ready to shoot?" Zoom, foregoing any formalities, stepped inside. Looking from Cookie to Raven, Zoom shoved his blue-tinted sunglasses on top of his head. Like an obedient shadow, Timothy followed close behind. He also shoved his sunglasses on top of his head, but they stuck halfway up his forehead, giving him a bizarre four-eyed look.

"We need you naked from the waist up," Zoom said matter-of-factly, acting more like a movie director than a magazine photographer. "It's our first—"

"First thing in the morning shot," Raven finished for him. "But Liney never said I had to get naked."

"Shame," murmured Cookie.

Zoom looked bored. "It's not about you, it's about the shoot. And we're only talking seminaked. Besides, models aren't paid to write the script, they're paid to act it out. End of story."

Raven was outnumbered and out of sorts, but Zoom had said one word that hit home. *Paid. Don't blow your dream, buddy.* Raven pulled off his shirt and tossed it onto the other canvas folding chair. "Rugged and ready," he said between his teeth.

"Oh-h-h." Cookie staggered forward a step, then caught herself. "Stallone, move aside," she said breathlessly. "You're a beast!" Her eyes darted to his jeans, but she had the good sense to keep further thoughts to herself.

Raven gritted his teeth. He had too much pride to put the T-shirt back on after he'd willfully taken it off, but he refused to be called a beast. Rather than raise the issue in front of everyone, however, he'd find a moment alone with Cookie to tell her to watch her vocabulary.

"We're going to have to figure out what to do with

that dinosaur," Cookie murmured as she stared at his tattoo.

"Iguana," Raven corrected.

"What iguana?" Zoom crossed in front of Raven and looked at his arm. "Whoa!" he exclaimed, seeing the tattoo. "I missed this little number when we were outside—you must have been angled away from me." Zoom made a square with his thumbs and index fingers, then peered through it at Raven's arm. "It would take some work," he said, shifting the frame of his hands this way, then that, "but we can position him so it won't show...."

Timothy, who'd finally gotten his sunglasses to perch on top of his head, chimed in. "We could drape a saddle bag over his arm. Or an Indian blanket."

"Or maybe a corner of the tent," Raven offered. "Or better yet, we could park a corner of Gomer's pickup on my bicep."

Silence greeted his comment. He knew he sounded less than cooperative, but it needled him that these three talked about him as though he didn't exist. Especially when he stood in front of them, stripped to the waist. He no longer felt like Raven. He felt like a piece of meat.

"We'll deal with the tattoo later. I have another idea." Zoom looked at Cookie. "Let's shave his chest."

"You and what army?" Raven stepped toward Zoom, fighting the urge to grab him by his sparse ponytail and swing him into orbit. "Nobody's shaving me. End of story."

"Raven," said an exasperated Cookie, "just think how brawny and sweaty—" Seeing the scowl on his face, she stopped. "If you don't look good shaved, I'll simply glue some fake chest hair back on—"

"No!" Raven held up a warning forefinger when Cookie started to speak again. He cocked a menacing eyebrow at Cookie, Zoom, then Timothy. The boy had his mouth open so wide, two silver fillings glinted from his back molars.

Shaking off the molar image, Raven growled, "One razor comes near me and I walk."

Zoom, obviously seeing his authority threatened, puffed out his chest. Which might have looked imposing if he had a chest. "You're the model, I'm the photographer," he said in a voice that sounded like a bad Jack Nicholson impersonation. "Got it?"

"And I'm the vice president," said a cool female voice. "Got that?" Liney, dressed in a wrinkled blouse and skirt, complete with another pair of matching pumps, stepped into the tent. Her hair still had that fried-mushroom look, but she'd managed to tie most it back into a loose ponytail. Her face, freshly washed, was devoid of makeup except for a light frosting of pink on her lips. Raven thought she looked like a young girl pretending to be grown-up.

"If anybody has the right to pull rank," Liney said authoritatively, "I do." Her chocolate-brown eyes calmly surveyed the scene. "Now what's the problem here?"

7

"THEY WANT TO SHAVE ME," Raven said, his dark eyes flashing with defiance.

Zoom adjusted the light meter that hung on a strap across his chest. Avoiding eye contact with anyone, he said innocently, "It was only a suggestion and the model overreacted."

Raven snorted something under his breath about "the model."

Liney surveyed the room. Cookie was winding her index finger around her ponytail. Zoom was toying with his light meter. Timothy, whose ponytail wasn't long enough to twiddle and who didn't have a light meter, fumbled with the sunglasses perched on his head.

It was like being at a fumble-with-your-favorite-object gathering. Surprisingly, she didn't have the urge to snap a cigarette. "We want a masculine model," she said, looking each one of them in the eye, "not a skinned one. No shaving." She purposefully kept her face expressionless, mainly because it gave her the appearance of being coolly in control. "Anything else?"

Cookie scanned Liney's wrinkled clothes. "Looks as though you found your tent."

Found? On the way back into camp, Liney had stumbled upon a small tent at the base of the hill where Raven had stood. Peeking inside, she saw her lovely clothes tossed in a heap in the middle of the floor—a not-so-kind tipoff that it was her tent. Too tired to throw another tantrum, she'd gone inside and quickly shed her dusty jeans and sweatshirt, then shimmied into a blue crepe blouse and tan skirt she snatched off the top of the pile. They were seriously creased, but if her choice was between looking like a dirty biker babe or a crumpled corporate woman, the latter was the lesser evil.

"Yes, I found my tent," she said sweetly. "Thank you to whoever unpacked my clothes." Just to confound them further, she smiled. "But enough about me. Are there any other issues relating to this morning's shoot?"

The four of them just stared back at her. Except for Raven, they all looked guilty. He, on the other hand, looked relieved. And grateful. It was quite a contrast seeing this mammoth-sized man, who looked as though he could crush this entire group with a sweep of his fist, tenderly looking at her with unabashed indebtedness. Knowing she'd done something so wonderful for him embarrassed her. Unable to maintain eye contact, she dropped her gaze.

Big mistake. She stared at his naked, chiseled chest, which had more definitions than a dictionary. Dark swirls of hair fanned across his bulging pecs and pooled into a shadowy pocket of curls underneath the center of his sternum. Her fingers twitched involuntarily. She clenched them tightly into fists in case her body overrode her mind and forced her to dig into that cushion of thick, black hair and knead the hell out of it.

As she tried to remember how to breathe, her gaze dropped farther.

Ebony hair swept down his ridged belly in a teasing path toward the waistband of his low-slung jeans. And she wouldn't have gone that far, but the curls literally pointed south as they tapered to a V, like a big furry arrow saying "Hey, look down here!"

"Liney?" Zoom's face zoomed into her peripheral vision.

She meant to say "what?" but it came out a breathy "Whugh?"

"Liney, are you feeling all right?" Zoom asked, his gray-green eyes peering intently into hers.

His pungent-smelling cologne, acting like smelling salts, shook her from her hairy reverie. "I'm all night," she said haltingly. "Right," she said, catching herself. "I'm all *right*." She swallowed, hard. She was also thirsty, but if she opened her mouth again, she might say something idiotic like "I'm hairy." Or worse, "I'm horny."

She didn't dare look at Raven's chest anymore. She needed to focus on something drab, lackluster, unappealing. Her gaze landed on Cookie's ponytail. Perfect.

Maintaining ponytail-to-eye contact, Liney gestured limply over her shoulder toward the tent opening. "Let's go," she said, but only after carefully rehearsing the words several times in her mind before trusting her mouth to speak. She started to pivot ever so gracefully, but hadn't anticipated that leather soles against a nylon tent floor could be slicker than ice skates on ice. With an unladylike "whooo-eeee-aaa!" she swiveled in a full three-sixty turn and ended up facing everyone in the room again.

As waves of embarrassment heated her body and her face, she did her darndest to look unaffected. Maybe if she acted as though that wild spin was normal, they'd buy it.

Right. Just like maybe they'd buy I was Dorothy Hamill in a former life.

Liney felt a drop of sweat emerge from her hairline, but no way would she swipe at the sucker. In her current state of acute klutziness, she might accidentally sock herself in the eye.

"You sure you're all right?" Zoom asked slowly as though speaking to someone who might twirl out of control any moment.

"My shoes are new," Liney explained in a squeaky voice. "I haven't had the opportunity to…swivel-test them." After her fiercest I-defy-you-to-respond look, she turned and left, grateful her feet remembered how to do that one-foot-in-front-of-the-other bit as she strode away.

AN HOUR LATER, Raven squatted next to the campfire, the sun gleaming off his bronzed back as he pretended to use the spatula to cook something in the frying pan.

"I can still see the iguana," Zoom said, squinting into the viewfinder, "turn a bit more to your left. Not that far. Back a little. No, too much…" Pulling away from the camera, Zoom straightened and shoved back the rim of his straw Panama hat. He exhaled loudly before speaking. "Next time you pick up a model, Liney, could you please check he doesn't have tattoos the size of Manhattan?"

Liney, sitting in her canvas folding chair a few feet from the campfire, thought it best to simply listen to Zoom's latest outburst—it'd probably only further aggravate him if she offered any words of consolation or encouragement because so far, nothing seemed to be going right. The sweltering Wyoming heat was fraying everyone's nerves. The shoot, already a day behind schedule, had started late. Plus, Zoom's first camera had jammed or done something terribly un-cameralike, so he was in a snit from the get-go.

Mopping the perspiration from his face with his beige-and-blue bandanna, Zoom peered into the viewfinder. "Okay, more to the right...a little more. Yes!" He waved his bandanna in the air. "Fan-tas-tic! Now, hold that pose...."

Raven suddenly bolted upright and slapped at his arm with a resounding thwack.

Squeezing the bandanna into a ball, Zoom straightened slowly. "One of those biting flies again?" he asked, the words barely masking his irritability.

"Yes!" Raven barked, glowering at the photographer. "That goop Cookie put on me draws 'em like honey." He slapped his shoulder. "There's another one."

After stuffing the bandanna into his pants pocket, Zoom yanked off his sunglasses and rubbed his lids with his thumb and forefinger. "Cookie, darling, whatever the hell you put on the model, take it off."

"I was testing a new body makeup—"

"Yes, and it's testing my sanity," Zoom cut in. "I'd rather we swab his sweat and adjust the light reflectors than have a hundred photos of a fly-bitten, slap-crazed Rugged Man." Zoom slipped his sunglasses back on. "At this rate," he warned Liney, turning his blue-tinted gaze toward her, "these photos are going to look like 'A Tattooed Man Smacks' instead of 'A Rugged Man Cooks.'"

Cookie, who'd changed from a flower-printed halter top to a neon pink halter top to go with her signature short-shorts, bounded onto the set like one of the antelope they occasionally spied in the distance. Cookie's bounding was all the more impressive because she wore fuchsia-colored sandals with inch-high heels.

Cookie began studiously wiping Raven's chest and shoulders with a tangerine-colored washcloth. Liney shifted in her seat as Cookie painstakingly rubbed in slow, methodical circles around each molded pec.

Raven just stood there, like a bronzed god being given his due. At one point, he lifted his tree-sized arms over his head so Cookie could wipe along the vein-rippled, corded undersides.

When Liney realized she was running her tongue along her top lip with each motion of the rag, she clamped shut her mouth. Stealthily shifting her gaze from side to side, she checked that no one had noticed her literal slip of the tongue.

"Cookie, just wipe it off," Zoom called out, "don't buff him to a shine."

"Just one more little spot." Bending over, which caused her short-shorts to get even shorter, she stuck the tip of the washcloth into the dark pool of hair right below Raven's sternum. "There," she said, her voice more simmering than the heat. "I think I got the last little bit." Tossing the rag over her shoulder, she sashayed back to her chair.

Everyone watched her hip-swaying exit in silence. Liney figured Cookie could polish the side of a car just walking past it.

When Liney looked at Raven, she figured he was having similar car-polishing thoughts…minus the car. A red blush had crept over his chest and neck, giving his tan a ruddy glow. Her lips puckered with displeasure. Was he attracted to Cookie? Not that it mattered. No-o-o, not one little bit.

She angrily scuffed the heel of her shoe in the dirt as she watched Raven again take position near the faux campfire. He lowered himself to a squat, resting his weight on those mighty quads that strained at the jeans. When he leaned over the pan, his bare midriff compressed into ripples of muscle, and not one centimeter of excess baggage hung over the waistband. Liney felt a tingling in the pit of her own stomach as she stared at his tightly muscled middle. In an attempt to curtail her sudden panting, she sucked in her breath and held it, figuring if she passed out she'd blame the heat.

"Timothy!" Zoom pointed toward his young male assistant. "Get me the number two filter. Cookie!" He pointed at her with his other hand. "There's a big sweaty spot in the center of his back—"

Not waiting for further instructions, Cookie almost tripped in her zealousness to resume her buffing role. Positioning herself behind Raven's hunched form, she started stroking his sinewy back with her washcloth. As though she couldn't quite see where that "big sweaty spot" might be, she leaned close, brushing her breasts against him.

Liney burst out of her chair. Standing, she announced loudly, "Wipe with the cloth, not your halter top." As everyone looked at her, she smiled apologetically and sat back down. "I was concerned about the, uh, dry cleaning bill for our, uh, clothes." *Yeah, right.* She was concerned about Raven liking melons...on his back. And she thought she wasn't jealous? Right now she probably looked greener than the grass in Oz.

Cookie flashed Liney a perplexed look as she tossed

the washcloth back over her shoulder and exited the campfire scene, polishing invisible cars all the way.

"Start cooking, Mr. Rugged...." Zoom began clicking away. "All righty!" he said enthusiastically after a few minutes. "We got ourselves some great frying pan shots." After taking a few more photos, he stood, smiling with satisfaction. "Okay, let's try something different...something else that's first thing in the morning...something suggestive, sexy, buy-this-magazine instead of *Bon Appétit*...."

Despite the heat, Cookie leapt from her seat and began waving her hand as though asking the teacher for permission.

"Yes?" Zoom said, taking the leadership position.

Liney decided to take a back seat. She'd let Zoom have his moment of power even though she, as the vice president, was the person to decide which shots they should try next. But she backed off because, for one thing, Zoom was finally in a good mood. And second, a happy photographer meant happy pictures. She hoped.

And although she hated to admit it, she had a third reason. A happy photographer might hesitate to call her Dragon Lady the next time the urge hit.

Cookie swiveled her hips as she faced the group. "This is a cool idea!" she said enthusiastically, her ponytail quivering like its owner. "What about a shot while he's still sleeping. You know, before the first thing in the morning frying-pan stuff. He's dreaming of what he'll cook for breakfast as he's lying there, all brawny and sweaty and naked."

"Naked?" Raven unfolded to his full height. He turned to Liney. "Do you want me *naked?*"

Some hyperactive inner voice went amuck. *Yes,*

ohmyGod, yes please! Liney gripped the arms of her chair to steady herself. "No, yes, maybe, I don't know," she mumbled, her voice riding little puffs of breath. Sweaty splotches had formed wherever her blouse touched her skin. She hunched a little, hoping no one would notice.

Raven, blinking in bafflement at Liney, opened his mouth to say something when Cookie cut in.

"Rave, it'd be utterly fab! And you wouldn't be totally naked." Obviously excited by her idea—or something else—Cookie hopped in place as she spoke. "You'd be sleeping with a spatula or a muffin pan."

Or if you had it your way, Liney thought, *with a cookie sheet.*

"It's a fantastic idea," enthused Zoom, "but without the spatula or pan. We'll get a few shots of the Rugged Man sleeping, which will set the sexy mood of the story. The article could be captioned..." Zoom swept his hand through the air as though seeing the words written there. "The Rugged Man Dreams About a Hot Breakfast." He stared, smiling, at the imaginary caption, then clapped his hands. "Let's set it up!" As though realizing he had overstepped his role, he shot a look at Liney over the top of his blue lenses. "I mean, of course, if the vice president agrees."

This was Liney's opportunity to take his and Cookie's side, which meant the four of them might finally be a *team* instead of them against her. Although she'd vetoed their wanting to shave Raven, and for good reason, that didn't mean she vetoed anything that wasn't her idea. Besides, a partially naked shot around the campfire was in sync with what she'd envisioned for the "A Rugged Man Cooks" piece. Not only would it make for good photos, but Cookie would feel validated because it was her idea. Zoom would feel important because he championed the idea. And Timothy would feel vicariously important because Zoom felt important.

Yes, they'd be a team! Finally! It'd be a great shoot and she'd return to L.A. victorious. And redeemed.

She shifted her attention to Raven, who looked like a thunderstorm encased in human form. Although sunlight kissed his skin bronze and highlighted his hair with hints of gold, his eyes were two black holes where no light escaped. Despite the heat, a shiver rippled through her. The man didn't have to speak. His entire body said "no way in hell."

Oblivious to the showdown between Raven and Liney, Zoom issued commands. "Timothy, position the reflector over there." While motioning the exact location to his assistant, Zoom kept up a stream of conversation. "You know, Liney, I shouldn't have balked over including shots of the tattoo. Women will go nuts over the iguana. It adds to the Rugged Man's allure."

It hit her that this was the first time Zoom had showed any excitement over the shoot—or compromised his opinion, especially with her. And she would have responded, shared some of Zoom's newfound exuberance, but for the chilling fact that Raven continued to stare her down, not moving a muscle. Well, except for a neck muscle that twitched.

Liney's heart hammered as though she'd just run a marathon. It wasn't that she was afraid of Raven lashing out—she was afraid he'd walk out. And no model meant no shoot. If she wanted this project to be successful, she desperately needed his buy-in.

With an unsteady laugh, she said casually, "It's just

a few pictures...and you won't really be, well, you know..."

The only change in Raven's rock-solid expression was the caustic lifting of a brow. "No," he said in a steely tone, "I don't know what I won't really be."

Zoom, busily checking his light meter, called out to Raven, "You heard the boss lady. Get raw, Raw Man."

Angling his dark gaze to Zoom, Raven said in a hardened voice, "My name's Raven. And I'm not getting *raw*. End of story."

Liney stood, suppressing a surge of hysteria. She'd seen him plenty pissed before, but she'd never seen him give in to his rage. "Raven," she said, feeling as though she was facing a typhoon without any shelter, "would it help if Cookie and I left? Then it's just the men?"

He gave his head a toss as though shaking off the entire ridiculousness of the situation. Looking back, he pinned her with his fierce gaze. "But the end result is still thousands of women checking me out like I'm some piece of meat. I ain't—am not—getting raw!"

Liney, realizing this was best handled face-to-face rather than in front of the entire crew, stepped gingerly into the campfire set and planted herself squarely in front of Raven. Raising her gaze, she whispered, "You won't be *totally* raw. I mean naked. You'll have on your..." Without breaking their eye-lock, she gestured toward his crotch. "...your underwear." When he didn't respond, she added, "That is, if you're wearing any."

He leaned down until his scowling face was inches from her own, his eyes narrowed into two glistening slits. This close, Liney caught the scent of his musky aftershave mixed with the tang of sweat. "I'm wearing underwear," he said roughly, "But considering how snugly they fit, I might as well not be, if you get my drift."

She meant to say "Snugly?" but her throat was so tight, it came out "Gnughly?" Coughing slightly, she said, "I, uh, believe I get your drift." The air felt so thick and hot, she had difficulty drawing a breath. Panting slightly, she continued, "But you can...take off your jeans...underneath a blanket. That way...no one will see your..."

"What?"

"Underwear," she said quickly. "No one will see your underwear." Was it getting hotter out here? Forget her former sweaty splotches...her entire outfit now clung to her sweat-drenched body.

His scowl smoothed out a little. "And Cookie will want to rub that bug-loving glop on my legs...or somewhere else."

Liney tightened her fists. "I'll trip her first," she said, her voice dropping to a guttural fierceness. Meeting Raven's surprised look, she unclenched her hands and offered a weak smile. Had she really just had a primal outburst over Cookie? She couldn't possibly be that jealous over Ms. Ponytail—could she? Even if she was, Liney Reed was *always* in control of her emotions.

Or used to be...

Rolling back her shoulders, she stood taller—which had zero effect considering she stood next to Mount Everest. Infusing her voice with all the professionalism she could muster, she said evenly, "I'll speak to her about rubbing your back with melons."

He pressed his eyebrows together. "She rubbed my back with a washcloth."

"That, too." Liney nonchalantly brushed at a glop of sweat that hung on the tip of her chin. "So it's settled?"

"What?"

"You're..." She eased in a calming breath so she could say the rest without mangling her words. "...you're taking off your pants?"

He looked at her so long, she thought maybe another glop of sweat hung off her face somewhere. Finally, he said through clenched teeth, "Three and a half days." Staring sullenly into Liney's eyes, he began unbuttoning his fly, each opening button making a coarse popping sound.

"Don't you want a blanket?" Liney asked.

"No." Pop. Pop. "If thousands of woman will see me, what's two more?" When he tugged down his pants, she abruptly turned away, grateful she didn't spin into another three-sixty. With her back to him, she walked away stiff-kneed.

Cookie, standing behind Liney's chair, emitted a low whistle. "Oh-h-h, Liney, you're missing the show."

Liney stood stiffly, her back to the campfire set. "I prefer to give the man some respect."

"Yeah, me too. And lots of it. Oh!"

Liney jumped. "What?"

"You know my jumbo-sized curlers?"

Liney frowned. "What does that have to do with anything?"

"He's *mondo* jumbo," Cookie said, winking conspiratorially. "You can look now. He's under the blanket."

Liney slowly turned and sat before she dared to

glance at the campfire set. Raven, propped on one elbow, lay on a pad with a brightly colored Navajo blanket draped casually across his middle. The bottom edge of the blanket lay teasingly on a rock-hard curve of flank with a shadowed indentation you could sink your teeth into.

Liney pressed her lips together. After her unaware lip-licking a few minutes ago, she didn't trust her mouth to not start biting at the air.

Below the flank indentation were a pair of the longest legs she'd ever seen. Powerful, muscled, brown legs dusted with wisps of black hair. It was a crime to keep legs like that locked away in a pair of old jeans.

"Okay Raw Man, let's see some sex appeal," Zoom said, peering into the viewfinder. "All righty, that's good." Zoom waved at Timothy. "Move the reflector to the right. I'm getting glare. Good. Okay, let's skip the sleeping shots 'cause we have somethin' hot happening here. Look at me with one of those tousled early morning baby-I-want-you looks."

Raven cast an irate glance in the camera's direction. "You're kidding, right?"

"That's not quite the look I want," Zoom said, clicking away. "Baby I want you, not Baby I hate you. Pretend Pamela Anderson Lee is standing behind me." Timothy, who'd been standing behind Zoom, quickly jumped to the side.

"Want me to stand behind the camera?" Cookie offered, scampering from her seat. She began hopping in place as though ready to bound in any direction like a lost, sex-starved antelope. Watching the stringy ponytail flap up and down with each bounce, Liney wondered if, on a windy day, it ever flew perpendicular to Cookie's head.

"I don't need no Pamela Anderson Lee—or anyone else—to look at," Raven grumbled.

A small thrill shot through Liney as she experienced a glorious moment of female satisfaction. So Raven wasn't a sucker for sex-starved antelopes with strange hair-do's, after all. Even as she told herself she didn't care one way or the other, she bit her bottom lip to stop herself from grinning.

"Let's try the baby-I-want-you look again," Zoom suggested.

Raven breathed in deeply, which swelled his pecs to twice their size. After shaking the sweat from his face, he stared at the camera, a sullen scowl on his face.

"Okay," Zoom said, "we got some great pec action here, but that look in your eyes has gotta go, Raw Man."

"I know what will help," Cookie said, still standing, although she'd finally stopped bouncing. Her ponytail hung limply against the side of her face as though exhausted from the frenetic workout. "Rave, imagine yourself as an animal. Imagine yourself a *beast!*"

With a surge of motion like Neptune crashing from the sea, except in this case from underneath a blanket, Raven leapt to his feet and faced down the camera. "I'm not a beast!" His deep voice reverberated through the air. "And I'm sick and tired of being called 'Raw Man' and 'Rave' when my name's Raven. What gives you people the right to call others names?"

With a threatening growl, he stalked out of the set toward Liney. Reaching her, he halted, his fists on his hips. "You hired me to do a photo gig, and I need the money, but not at the cost of my self-esteem."

Liney's mind still reeled from Raven's angry question, "What gives you people the right to call others

names?''—something she wished she'd had the wherewithal to say days, no, weeks ago. And her body reeled
from his massive, powerful, naked presence towering
over her. It was all she could do to concentrate on a
glistening stream of sweat that coursed a path down his
molded pec before disappearing into a jungle of black,
curly hair.

"What do you have to say about this, Liney?"
Raven demanded, fire shooting from his eyes.

She wanted to say something. To be the appropriate,
in-control vice president and defuse this tense situation.
But when she opened her mouth, all that came out was
a raspy sound, like air leaking from a tire. Fighting the
dizzying waves of summer heat—or maybe it was
Raven's body heat—she stared, dumbfounded, at the
massive hunk of male that stood before her like a
bronzed god in all his glory.

A bronzed god in his snugly underwear.

"Liney?" Raven prompted. "What do you have to
say?"

Widening her eyes, she whispered hoarsely,
"Mondo jumbo?"

8

"MONDO WHAT?" Raven asked between clenched teeth.

Liney grazed her fingers across her sweat-dotted forehead. "Mondo...jumbo...hair roller?" Her skin flushed several shades of rose, finally settling on a vibrant hue reminiscent of his kid sister's shocking-pink prom dress. He swore Liney was panting, but she managed to do it through lips pursed so tightly that it looked as though she were practicing ventriloquism.

Then it hit him. She was acting strangely because he was wearing only skivvies. He'd been so caught up in his rush of anger, the last thing on his mind happened to be the only thing on his body—his underwear.

Well, tough.

Everybody said they wanted him naked, or not "totally raw" as they seemed fond of saying, so they'd just have to put up or shut up. Emboldened by his rationalization, Raven stood defiantly in front of a pink-faced Liney. "So, what do you have to say about this?" he demanded, returning to his original question.

"This?" She shifted and squirmed in her seat like a kid facing the dentist, which was ironic considering Liney behaved like a drill most of the time. "This what?" Her wide-eyed gaze swerved to some spot in the sky above his head as though a cloud suddenly demanded her attention.

"This habit of your crew calling me 'Raw Man,' 'Rave,' 'Beast.' Were those terms in that contract I signed?"

"No," she mumbled. "And I don't like names, either." Even though her gaze was still glued to some cloud, a sadness filled her eyes.

Of course. *Dragon Lady.* She painfully understood his angry reaction to being called names, so what he had to say next he'd direct to the others. Turning toward the rest of the group, he looked each one of them in the eye before speaking. "The problem with nicknames," he said in a booming voice, "is people start to believe that's what the person really is. So if you call me a beast, soon you'll start treating me like one." He almost growled for special effect, but figured it'd defeat his purpose if they all ran screaming off into the wilds of Wyoming, thinking a humanoid beast was on their trail.

It was so quiet, you could hear the gurgle of a nearby stream. Raven fixed a level stare at the photographer. "How would you feel if I called you 'Photo Man' or 'Zoo' instead of 'Zoom'?"

Surprisingly, Zoom—who always seemed to have a nasally Jack Nicholson retort—opted to scrutinize an anthill next to his right foot. Timothy stared at the same anthill, although he looked confused as to why it was of such interest.

Cookie, her eyes moistening, stumbled a few steps toward Raven. "I'm sorry I called you R-Rave," she said chokingly. As a tear rolled down her cheek, Raven noticed the glittery ladybug swimming with it.

He pointed at her face. "Your...bug..."

She halted and fisted her hands on her hips. "You don't have to call *me* names to get even," she said, her chin trembling. Her ponytail quivered as though in commiseration.

"No, your ladybug…it's being swept along with the flood…." He tapped his cheek, then pointed to hers again.

"Oh!" Swiping at the teary stream on her face, she salvaged the red glittery dot.

Raven had had his say. He'd spoken up about the one thing he thought he'd always keep secret. Maybe they'd learned something about labeling others—the labels they'd used for him, anyway. He wondered if Cookie, Zoom, and Timothy realized it applied to more than "Rave," "Raw Man," and "Beast."

The same rules applied to calling someone "Dragon Lady."

Raven looked down at the top of Liney's auburn hair, the previous mushrooming A-bomb whose power was now miraculously contained in a bushy ponytail. He didn't want to embarrass her in front of the others, but he had one last thing to say. Lowering his voice, he said, "You should have told me back at the Blue Moon that I was expected to play model *and* beefcake."

Blinking rapidly, she broke her stare away from the sky and stammered, "I-I'm sorry. I take full responsibility for what's happened. But in my defense, I had wanted to create a sensual piece because that's what women want—"

"How do you know what women want?" He hadn't meant to be abrupt, but this was similar to labeling people. It irked him when people lumped women—or men—into a group that liked this or that. Too often he'd been lumped in some "Harley-drivin' he-man" group, as though nothing occurred between the front and back of his brain.

"I know what women want because..." She clasped her hands together primly in her lap. "...because our marketing studies show a high level of sensuality appeals to our readership, which is eighty percent women."

She sounded as though she were reciting something off one of her low-fat gram menus. He gave his head a weary shake. "Have you ever thought that maybe, just maybe, some women might like a man for more than sex and sweat. That they might like a man for things like companionship and intellectual stimulation, too?"

Liney stared at him, her hands pressed together so tightly the knuckles turned white. Then she stood slowly. Her head was level with his pecs, at which she stared for a solid moment before raising her chocolate-brown eyes to his.

"I've already apologized," she said edgily, "but since you're pushing the issue, let me say unequivocally that I think men and women are equals. And this is from a woman who's had to compete neck to pec— I mean neck-and-neck—in a man's world. Do you know how many other vice presidents at my company are women?"

"How would I know?"

She curled her thumb and index finger into a circle. "Zero. Dirk, my boss, says he wants to change that, but right now I'm the only woman *veep*, as you like to call me. And, by the way, I never complained at *your* use of the nickname."

She drew in such a deep, indignant breath, her breasts strained against the sheer fabric of her blouse.

Until then, Raven hadn't realized she wasn't wearing a bra. When had she doffed it? He wished he knew what cloud she'd been staring at, because he desperately needed a diversion right now.

He opted to stare into her eyes, which flashed furiously at him.

"I've had to fight doubly hard for the same respect that's automatically handed to men," she continued, "so don't label me as some power-hungry woman who gets her jollies denigrating men."

Zoom and Timothy had shifted their attention from the anthill to Liney. Zoom seemed unaware that his ultra-cool blue-tinted sunglasses had slipped down his nose to rest atop his nostrils. Cookie, her mouth open, as well as her hand with the sparkling red dot, stared at Liney as though seeing her for the first time.

Raven had to admit—this formidable side of Liney was pretty damn awesome. If she ran for president, he'd vote for her. Hell, he'd be her campaign manager. This lady knew how to take control and woo an audience. Forget the audience—this lady had already wooed him. Maybe that was why thoughts of Char didn't creep up as often. In fact, Char had taken a back seat in his memory while Liney rode gunshot.

Liney, taking a breather, smiled with satisfaction as though she knew the dynamic impression she was making. With a roll of her shoulders she stepped past Raven, a teasing trail of vanilla following her. Taking center stage next to the campfire, she swept one arm through the air as though appealing to the masses, although this mass totaled four people. In a voice resonating with conviction, she summarized, "Not only do I revere and respect men, I have never, may I repeat *never,* treated them as sexual objects."

Raven, succumbing to a heartfelt sting of emotion, was ready to start applauding when a craggy male voice called out, "Howdy, Liney!"

Everyone swerved their gaze up the hill to where a smiling Gomer waved his Stetson in greeting. Seeing he had their attention, he plunked the hat back on his head. "I thought sexy, Liney, just like you told me to," he yelled, "and found some body-moldin', chest-clingin' clothes to make our Mr. Rugged look sizzlingly sexy!" Kicking dust up behind him, Gomer began lugging a battered suitcase down the hill toward them.

Raven slid a glance at Liney who stood stiffly, watching Gomer's entrance with an expressionless look on her face. Maybe, Raven decided, he wouldn't be her campaign manager after all. Like many politicians, there'd be too much explaining to do after her speeches.

Reaching them, Gomer dropped the suitcase on the ground with a dusty whomp. Swiping the back of his hand across his brow, he gave Raven a once-over. "Looks like I got back just in time, son. You plumb ran outta clothes to wear!"

Brushing his hands, Gomer turned his attention to an abnormally subdued Liney. "I dropped by Chugwater and, as luck'd have it, King Karl had just gotten back from the annual Wheatland pig-hollerin' contest. He was a li'l blue cuz he placed second—lost first place to Georgie Bodie who attracted a hundred sows with his mating grunt. But Karl cheered up right fast when I told him his clothes might be seen in a slick L.A. magazine."

Gomer snapped the latch and opened the suitcase. From within, he lifted a humongous pair of black jeans.

"One pair of black body-moldin' jeans, just like Liney requested for our sexy star." He tossed them to Raven, who caught them midair. "See how they fit, son. Seems our boss wants 'em tighter than a drunk cowboy on Saturday night."

Raven shot another glance at Liney's face, which was more pinched than an Italian starlet on Saturday night. Liney started to sputter something when Gomer interrupted.

"And this here, Liney..." Gomer held up a pink T-shirt upside down, "is one muscle-clinging T, just like you asked for—"

"Those instructions," Liney interrupted, "were simply euphemisms for 'rugged' and not meant to connote sexual denigration."

Gomer reared back and squinted at her. "Whoa! That's quite a mouthful of big words—no wonder you're a vice president!" He chuckled under his breath. "But you did say you wanted our Rugged Man to be 'sizzlingly sexy,' and with King Karl's body-huggin' clothes, that's just what you're gonna get."

Zoom muttered something to Timothy, who glanced at Liney and laughed. The same mean-spirited laugh Raven had heard that morning. So his earlier suspicion was correct. The Ponytailers might think twice when it came to nicknaming him again, but it appeared that courtesy didn't extend to Liney. Too bad she'd fired off that self-righteous speech right before Gomer started quoting her "sizzlingly sexy" clothes order.

Raven was torn between wanting to chastise Liney and comfort her. Mainly the latter when he saw her ashen face, which had taken on a look of mute appeal. He wondered how often anyone cared enough to reach out and discover why she hurt. Had he ever met anybody so important, yet so lonely? Maybe Raven had finally realized his journey was on a multilane highway, but he bet Liney still thought she was the only one on the road.

Gomer, oblivious to the screwy group dynamics, peered into the suitcase. "Got some more T-shirts in here. Sorry about the pink one, but ever since King Karl visited Miami, he's had a thing for that flamingo color. There's also a lime-green and a white one." In a somber aside, he added, "Karl saves those for church."

Tilting back his Stetson, Gomer said to Liney, "Sorry, Karl had no boots. He had a pair of mukluks and three pairs of bowlin' shoes, but I told him we'd pass on those 'cause they ain't sexy enough. Right, Liney?"

"Right," she murmured, avoiding eye contact with anyone. "I think that's enough discussion on clothes and shoes—"

"Holy Heifer!" Gomer interrupted, "almost forgot this li'l number." He yanked out a long, thin black object. "Thought this might be perfect for the Rugged Man."

"What...is...that?" Liney looked at it with uneasy puzzlement.

Gomer grinned so wide, a gold-capped molar flashed in the sunlight. "A whip! Karl uses it when he rounds up the calves."

"Our Rugged Man isn't rounding up any calves," Liney said quickly.

"But he's out here in the wilds, huntin' and cookin' his food, ain't he? He might need to round up somethin' to eat!" Gomer flicked the whip, which made a sharp cracking sound.

Liney wished for another sound. A sharp *snapping* sound, but she'd left her cigarettes back in her tent. The ground shook slightly as, from behind her, she heard a thump thump thumping.

She didn't need to look to know Cookie was hopping.

Whips. Pig calls. Hopping, sex-starved women. When had Liney's speech-making moment of glory turned into a three-ring circus?

Angling her chin higher, Liney said to Gomer, "No whip."

"You sure?" Raven asked sarcastically, pulling up Karl's black jeans over his hips. "I'd look sizzling sexy *whipping* up a meal with one of those, don't you think?"

Liney tried not to watch Raven dress, but considering he did it in front of the entire group, she'd have to be blind to avoid him. Gomer was a great personal shopper—those jeans fit Raven like black Saran Wrap.

After her recent humiliation, however, she made a mental note to never again, for the duration of her life and possibly longer, say the words "clinging" or "molding" unless she was referring to children or fungus. After years of climbing the corporate ladder to be a vice president, in the short span of one suitcase opening, she'd regressed to being a vice vixen. Oh, for the simpler life when all she worried about was being a gun-tramp-moll.

"You know," she said, wondering if the others heard her voice wobbling like Mary Tyler Moore's. "I never asked Gomer to get you a whip—"

"But you asked him to get me clothes that were, quote, body molding and muscle clinging." Raven flashed her a knowing look.

Realizing when *she* was whipped, she conceded with a nod...but her head kept bobbing in time to Cookie's hopping. Flinging down her arms, Liney blurted, "Cookie, stop it! I'm getting a headache with all that thump thump thumping!"

Silence.

A fly, which Liney swore was buzz buzz buzzing, flew in a zigzagging pattern around her head. She flailed at it, missing of course.

"Going to yell at the fly, too?" Zoom asked snippily, adjusting his bandanna around his neck.

"No," Cookie responded, "because Liney views all flies equally."

Cookie, Zoom, and Timothy laughed in unison. To Liney, sinking deeper into a bottomless, buzzing misery, their laughter sounded like some kind of a cappella group harmonizing a malicious chortle.

If only she could say something witty, amusing, or even slightly offbeat at this dismal moment, she might salvage a shred of her splintered self-esteem. In her bleak state, one tiny thought brought a ray of hope. Raven had put a stop to their antics with his honesty. Maybe she could, too.

She paced a few hesitant steps and swiveled to a neat stop. *Think sane. Think leader.* "You know," she began, "I meant it earlier when I said I treated men as equals."

"But you don't treat your co-workers as equals," Zoom said coldly.

She fisted her hands to stop herself from strangling him with his precious blue-and-beige bandanna. "Not true!" she snapped. "This entire episode got out of control because I accepted Cookie's idea that we do an almost-raw shot of Rawen—Raven." She blinked at

Raven. "Sorry." Turning back to Zoom, she continued, "And you were part of this with your—" She swept her hand through the air, inadvertently brushing the fly away. "'—The Rugged Man Dreams About a Hot Breakfast,'" she mimicked, attempting a Jack Nicholson impersonation, but sounding more like Yosemite Sam. With a derisive snort, she added, "Here's a better one!" She dramatized the sweeping hand motion again, missing any other flying insects. "The Downtrodden Vice President Dreams of a Better Job with a Better Crew."

Breathing huge gulps of warm air, she flicked a drop of sweat off her nose. She'd done it now. Jumped off the deep end. Think sane? Think leader?

Right now, she was barely either.

"Hey," Zoom retorted, although she noticed he was backing off slightly. "Cookie had a great idea, and I acted on it. Unlike you who…" His voice trailed off.

"Me what?" Hell, she was already on the edge, might as well take a flying leap over it. Or maybe, like Cookie, a flying hop. "I took a back seat and let her idea happen." Liney pointed at Zoom, who flinched as though a bolt of lightning might fly out of her index finger, "And I let you run the show. I did it for both of you, my respected co-workers, but everything backfired and now I'm viewed as…" *crazier than sex-crazed Cookie.*

And, Liney had to admit, deep down she kinda liked her new image. Forget those crowd-rousing, victorious speeches…this I'm-so-crazy-you-don't-know-what-I'll-do-next style was a lot more fun.

"You might say you did it for us, but *you're* the one who designed this shoot to be sexy!" Zoom retorted. Suddenly his rage turned inward as he looked glumly at his camera. "Speaking of which, we have to retake those shots because his body might be sexy, but the look on his face could make it snow on *Baywatch*."

"I ain't—am not—going down this road again," Raven barked, his black eyebrows lowering over his blacker eyes. He blew out a frustrated gust of air. "I'm tired of all this arguing. It's time for me to take a ride and chill."

In lieu of a cigarette, Liney snapped her fingers. "You're under contract! You can't leave in the middle of a shoot!"

Raven frowned at her hands before meeting her wide-eyed gaze. "And what're you going to do if I leave midshoot? Fire me? Hell, I'll save you the effort. I quit!" He turned and walked away.

"You can't quit," Liney yelled after him. "You'll owe *Cooking Fantasies* the modeling fee plus any legal fees we accrue fighting you in court."

He halted. Even from fifteen feet, Liney swore she saw that muscle tick spasmodically in his neck. Slowly, slowly, he turned, his massive body revolving like a distant, dark planet.

"What?" he asked, his deep voice rolling through the air.

"Legally," Liney said, trying desperately to sound professional again, "you will owe us your entire income plus any legal—"

"I heard all that," he growled, cutting her off. "I just didn't believe it." Their gazes melded in a steely confrontation. "I've never met such a hardheaded, opinionated, gotta-be-in-control woman before in my entire life," Raven spat. "And believe me, baby, that says a hell of a lot." Without a second look, he took a giant step and walked away.

He'd finally called her "baby" again, but hardly in the tone—or context—she preferred. Liney the Bad Baby teetered forward a few steps, debating whether to follow him. "I can't quit so you can't quit!" she whined, a gust of wind swallowing her words.

She didn't have the energy to yell anymore. Or the stamina to throw a fit. Or the desire to cry. Instead, she just watched her future, her career at Harriman Enterprises, storm away and mount his motorcycle. After a heart-vibrating roar, the machine and rider disappeared in a cloud of billowing dust.

"Wish I was on that bike," Cookie said, sticking the red glittery ladybug back onto her cheek. "Anywhere would be better than being here with…"

Liney's insides twisted as she heard the unsaid words. *Dragon Lady.*

As Cookie ambled away, Zoom spoke up. "Thanks, Liney, for trying to blame us for following your sexy guidelines for 'A Rugged Man Cooks.'"

Liney almost answered, "And thanks for the knife in my heart," because that's exactly how she felt right now. Betrayed. Wounded.

Zoom carefully removed the camera from the tripod as he continued talking. "I've worked at the magazine for fifteen years, and these last twenty-four hours have been the worst." He set the camera into one of the black equipment cases. Clicking it closed, Zoom said to his assistant, "C'mon, Timothy, let's grab a few brewskies and toast the shortest job we've ever endured."

Timothy dutifully followed Zoom toward their tent.

After a moment, Liney sighed heavily. "You're being awfully quiet, Gomer."

"There's been enough talkin' without me joinin' in.

If words were weather, this woulda been one heck of a hailstorm.''

Despite how she felt, Liney had to smile. ''Well, they're all gone now, so tell it to me straight...am I opinionated, headstrong and disrespectful to my co-workers?''

He retrieved a toothpick from his shirt pocket and stuck it between his lips. After a thoughtful pause, he said, ''Nope, you're not disrespectful.''

She didn't know whether to laugh or cry. ''Anything else?''

''Yep. Let's get out of this heat before we both fry into bacon crisps. My truck ain't the most glamorous spot, especially for a lady like you, but it's got shade and a cooler filled with sodas.''

He called me "lady" not "Dragon Lady." ''Sounds like Shangri-La,'' Liney whispered, following him back up the hill.

Minutes later, they sat in the front of Gomer's red pickup. The lumpy vinyl seat made small squeaking noises as they settled in. The inside had a faint musty smell, diluted by the warm breezes that filtered in through the opened windows. Gomer opened two sodas from the small cooler that sat on the floorboard on the passenger side.

Handing her one, Gomer watched two birds soar through the air. ''Awful shame you 'n' your crew don't get along better.''

Liney took a sip of the fizzy lemon-lime drink. ''I'm afraid you're the only one I get along with on this trip.''

Gomer took off his battered Stetson and put it on the seat between them. Dragging his hand through his thick mass of white hair, he said, ''You're not an outcast, Liney, like some Cinderella sittin' in the ashes. You're a lovely, caring lady who sometimes makes life tougher for herself than it oughta be."

Earlier she'd had a lighthearted fantasy about being Cinderella at the ball…and now Gomer had used the "darker" side of Cinderella as an example of her current troubles. It hit home. She felt as though she were sitting in the ashes, an outsider to her crew, her project. "How can you call me loving and caring when you've only seen my uptight, micromanaging, bad hair side?" she asked softly.

"You think that's all I've seen?" he asked with a wink. Turning serious, he said, "I've also seen your heart."

She rolled the cold soda can between her hands. "Kind of hard to see a Dragon Lady's heart, isn't it? Probably takes X-ray vision to see through those thick green scales.…"

"Don't know. Haven't met any Dragon Ladies, lately."

She felt her guard slipping away, something Liney Reed never allowed. But what did she have to lose? "Just this morning I thought I got along fine with everyone. I believed we were a team. Cookie felt validated, Zoom felt important, Timothy felt vicariously important…now it's them against me, again. How come I can't get along with my crew?"

Gomer stared out the window for a long moment, his blue-gray eyes clouding over. "With people," he finally said, "if you figure out their core, you know where to start. Cookie gets competitive with other women, especially when a man's around. Someday, when she learns to love another woman's friendship as much as she desires a man's attention, I bet that girl'll flourish.''

"That doesn't tell me how to get along with her.''

Gomer cast Liney a knowing look. "And as for Zoom,'' he continued, ignoring her comment, "I get the feeling you two are more alike than you might wanna admit. He, too, needs to accept others' strengths and ideas. And the boy Timothy…well, he just needs a good mentor. Zoom'll work out fine.''

"Zoom, a mentor?'' Liney scoffed.

"Mark my words. Zoom has it in 'im to be a man of action, not words.''

In the distance, they heard a faint drone. A cloud of dust swirled on the horizon, growing in volume as the drone amplified into a roar. Within moments, a black-and-chrome machine barreled toward them on the dirt road. In the midst of the exploding dust, sparkling chrome, and heart-stopping roar sat a man.

"Raven,'' Liney said, her voice catching. "He's come back.''

9

THROUGH THE WINDSHIELD of the old pickup, Gomer stared at the approaching motorcycle as it barreled down the dirt road toward them. "Raven has a heart as big as his body," he said thoughtfully. "He just needs to trust it...let it learn to love again...."

As Liney watched Raven advance, she recalled his entrance yesterday into the Blue Moon parking lot. Just as before, he appeared as a powerful, growling black-and-chrome creature in a storm of dust. As he rode closer, the growl intensified until it filled the world with a heart-stopping roar.

And in the midst of the chaos sat Raven, all man.

His black mane of hair whipped furiously in the wind. His arms, bronzed and brawny, gripped the raised handlebars. His colossal, muscular body leaned back comfortably as though he'd long ago tamed the savage machine. She wondered if that's how he tamed life, too—grabbing the toughest parts of it with both hands and riding it into submission. And if someone didn't like his style, she thought, tough. He'd move on. A big, bold, solitary creature carving his own path through life.

And yet he'd returned. To her? Her pulse skittered. *Ridiculous. He's returning for the job.* Yet her heart raced madly, her mind spinning wildly with romantic fantasies.

What had Gomer said? That Raven needed to let his heart learn to love again? Competing with the engine roar, she shouted, "How do you know he needs to learn to love again?"

But just as she spoke, Raven killed the engine, making Liney sound like a human megaphone. In the shockingly quiet aftermath, her face went hot with embarrassment. She'd had her share of speaking up in business meetings, but she'd never before shattered the sound barrier in the front seat of a pickup truck.

"You got a good set of lungs there," Gomer said with a raspy chuckle.

"Thanks." What else could she say? How are your eardrums?

"To answer your question, I know because I had that same dilemma once—do I close up my heart 'cause I'm afraid I'll get hurt, or do I trust it to love again?"

"And?"

Gomer's eyes glistened as though viewing a distant memory. "I let my heart have its way. Ended up marrying the love of my life." He put on his Stetson, angling the brim so Liney couldn't see his eyes. "She's gone now, bless her soul," he whispered, his voice breaking, "but she made me the man I am today."

Liney touched Gomer's gnarled, vein-covered hand. "She was lucky to have you, too."

Gomer gave Liney's hand a squeeze. "Thanks for that, honey." Clearing his throat, he opened his door and said over his shoulder, "Let's welcome the returning warrior."

As she stepped down from the truck, the bright Wyoming sun poured down its heat, enveloping Liney in its molten embrace. For the first time on this trip, she envied Cookie's short-shorts and halter tops. Slamming shut the passenger door, Liney swiped at the perspiration along her hairline while watching Gomer stroll down the dirt road toward Raven.

Liney took a step, then stopped. *I'll stay behind the truck for a minute.* Pretending to adjust her hopelessly wrinkled skirt and blouse, she observed the two men as they shook hands in greeting. Hopefully Raven had "chilled" on his ride, but she worried a part of him was still steamed over being made into a sex object. But then she heard Raven laugh, the sound deep and rolling. He definitely sounded more chilled than steamed. Taking a calming breath, she left the safety of the truck barricade and headed toward them.

Gomer, seeing her approach, waved her over. Raven stood loose-hipped in King Karl's black jeans, now creased and dusted with dirt. From a distance, she hadn't seen the logo on his white T-shirt, which he must have put on before his ride. But now that she was closer, she read the familiar words, Go Within or Go Without.

Will the shoot go on with or without Raven?

"Told Raven you'd show him where I stash the sodas," Gomer said, "Meanwhile, I'll go round up the rest of the crew. After all, I'm the gofer."

"Round up—?" She shot Raven a look. "You're with?"

Behind his dark wraparound sunglasses, one black eyebrow arched. "With?"

"You're staying?"

He nodded.

"Great," she said, attempting to be pleasantly cool even though her insides were whooping, "He's staying! The shoot will be completed!" She turned to Gomer. "Please tell the others to reconvene in an hour—that'll give everyone a chance to rest. And tell them I'll...I won't be part of the afternoon shoot." When Gomer cocked his head questioningly, she explained, "I think the crew needs a break from the Dragon Lady, but don't tell them that part." She self-consciously swept a stray hair off her face.

Gomer studied her for a moment. "The *lady* needs a rest, too, after all her hard work." After a friendly clap on Raven's back, Gomer sauntered down the hill, whistling with each step.

Liney stood awkwardly, feeling like one big sweaty, crumpled pile of silk and crepe. She didn't even want to think how her ponytail looked. "Care for a soda?" she finally asked, holding up her can as though Raven might not know what a soda was.

Raven grunted something that sounded like yes, so she turned and headed back to the truck. Behind her, she heard the crunch of his heavy steps on the pebble-strewn ground. Reaching the truck, she yanked open the passenger door. Its hinges squeaked miserably.

"His cooler is down here," she mumbled, glad to keep her back to Raven as she reached into the shadowed floor area for the white plastic container. After flipping open its lid, she stared at the cans cushioned in ice cubes. As she moved the drinks around, the ice crunched and sloshed. "Looks like there's lemon-lime, cream soda, cola...what's your pleasure?"

A familiar musky scent traced the air as Raven leaned over her to check the cooler's contents. As he reached for a drink, his arm pressed against the length of hers. Talk about *pleasure*. His arm felt substantial, hard. The sensation of his skin brushing against hers was nearly unbearable. Her stomach flip-flopped as sparks of electricity skittered wildly along her arm. If the front of her thighs had not been braced against the side of the seat, she'd have sunk to the ground like some swooning Victorian heroine.

And considering her nonexistent sex life, Victorian was the right era.

"What's this?" From behind the cooler, Raven lifted a bottle half filled with an amber liquid that glinted like honey in the sunlight. He gave a low, rumbling chuckle. "Whiskey. Good for Gomer. He unwinds just like a cowboy should." After carefully setting the bottle back where he found it, Raven helped himself to a soda. "You okay?"

Liney, still braced against the seat, whispered to the vinyl covering, "Yes. Why?"

"Well, either you see something extremely interesting in that old seat or you're crouching as though something's wrong."

She turned her face so she could see him. "I—I think I have heatstroke." She closed her eyes, mentally chastising herself for the dumbest thing she'd ever said in her life.

"Oh, baby, why didn't you tell me..." Before she could say "Victorian," Raven's strong arms scooped her up and held her tightly against his chest. "Hold onto me," he instructed, his voice gruffly tender.

The Good Baby did as told.

"Let's get you out of the sun." As he leaned into the truck cab and gingerly laid her on the front seat, she clutched her soda with one hand and dug her fingernails into the hem of her skirt with the other. She didn't want her skirt riding up for another impromptu underwear show. Through his sunglasses, she glimpsed his dark, glistening eyes.

"Where's your phone? I'll call a doctor."

"No!" She shook her head vehemently. It was one thing to miss one afternoon of the shoot—a noble offer on her part—but if she ended up in the hospital for observation, she'd miss the rest of it! How could they survive without her? "I'm okay. Really. Heatstroke's over. Now it's just warmstroke."

Raven began unbuttoning the top button of her blouse.

"What are you doing?" she asked sharply, debating if she should drop the soda or release her death grip on the skirt.

"I'm giving you some breathing room. It has to be over eighty degrees outside…and you're buttoned up tighter than an air-locked bag." He undid another button and pulled open her blouse a little. "There. Feel better?" Pushing the sunglasses on top of his head, he gazed at her, his black eyes radiating concern.

The way he loomed over her, all she could think about was how his presence was so dark, so potent, so strong.

So hot.

Maybe Raven had chilled, but she was definitely steamy.

She lifted the cold can of soda and pressed it to her forehead. It cooled her skin, but not her thoughts. "Maybe you shouldn't lean over me like that," she whispered shakily.

He looked puzzled for a moment, then pulled away. "You're right. Need to give you more breathing room."

She held her mouth stiffly so Raven wouldn't notice her panting. "Yes. Breathing…room," she squeaked.

He looked puzzled again. "Drink more liquid. You sound dehydrated."

Good idea. I'll hide my panting behind the can. Lying prone, she lifted her head slightly and raised the soda to her lips. Slurping loudly, she managed to drink a little of the cold, fizzy liquid...and pour the rest of it down her chin, her neck, and onto her blouse. She would have shrieked at the onslaught of cold, but her tightly pursed lips were still in panting denial.

"Let me help," Raven said quickly. Taking the drink from her, he set the can on the cracked dashboard. After looking around, he yanked the bottom of his T-shirt from the waistband of his jeans and pulled the white cotton shirt over his head.

"What are you doing?" Liney asked hoarsely, stunned by the panorama of pure brawn inches from her face.

Using his shirt, he dabbed the spilt soda from her face, her neck. "Gomer doesn't keep any rags lying around, so my T is the next best thing."

No, your exposed chest is. She was surprised the lemon-lime soda didn't start boiling where it pooled on her skin.

Wiping, he murmured, "I should have helped you...."

"You did. You're staying." The shoot would continue. Her project would be completed. She blinked back sudden tears. "Sorry," she said, her voice cracking. "I'm never this emotional and out of control." When Raven flashed her an is-that-so? look, she confessed, "Okay, maybe *occasionally,* but I never let people see that side of me...."

"The side I saw when you were thrashing about in the wilderness?"

Darn him anyway. "Yes. That side."

He was bent over, dutifully sponging along her collarbone. His hair brushed lightly against her cheek, teasing her mercilessly with its feathery touch. Her heart started pounding so furiously, she swore it caused her thin blouse to pulsate.

"I have three kid sisters," he said somberly, seemingly unaware of her pulsating clothes, "so I've learned to give a woman her space. But I stayed and watched you because I was worried...."

When he pulled back and looked at her with those liquid, jet-black eyes, she bit her inner cheek to suppress a moan.

He frowned. "You okay?"

Be normal. Be non-pulsating. "A lot of things hit me at once while I was out there," she said, looking over at the radio knob in an attempt to sober her libido. "I had a..." Minibreakdown? Thrash fest? "...overreaction that started with Dragon Lady and ended up with Cinderella."

"That's quite a combo," he said, amusement flickering in his eyes.

His easy smile relaxed her. Feeling close and safe with Raven, she willingly let her guard down as she explained, "In a sense, both are me. Dragon Lady, as you know, is what the crew calls me behind my back. And Cinderella was a big part of my dream world when I was a kid."

"I'm sorry they call you Dragon Lady."

"I know I can be pushy and controlling."

After a beat, Raven said, "My sister Moira is a lot like you. Would you mind a piece of advice—?"

Few people were this direct with her. Or this kind. Liney nodded.

"Don't treat people as though they're your puppets.

Show people respect and that's what you'll get in return."

She saw the concern in Raven's face—but more than that, she sensed his genuine care for her. "Advice taken. I'm going to try and be a better vice president before this shoot ends."

"And now about Cinderella," Raven said in a lighter tone. "You thought Prince Charming would whisk you away?"

She paused. "Now that you mention it, yes. I probably wanted to be whisked away because my dad was so unhappy after losing his job. Before that, I'd often read to him from my fairy-tale book—stories like *Sleeping Beauty, Thumbelina,* or *Cinderella,* my favorite. But after the downsizing, if I tried to read to him, my mom would shoo me away, saying not to bother Dad 'cause he didn't feel well." She fought a surge of sadness as an image of her dad, sitting in his bathrobe and watching TV, materialized in her mind.

"So...what happened to your dreams of being Cinderella?"

"Cinderella?" she repeated softly, refocusing on the conversation.

Raven was taken aback at the sweetness in Liney's eyes as she shifted her gaze to his. She looked so young, so relaxed...it was the childlike Liney he'd glimpsed before, the young girl who sometimes surfaced.

"You promise not to tell anyone about this conversation, right? After all, I have my corporate image to protect."

Maybe he'd seen the little girl, but the vice-president was still in control. "Mum's the word," he assured her.

"Although I gave up ever being Cinderella, for a

long time, I dreamed of one day running a fantasy shop." Liney's brown eyes glistened with excitement. "The store would be filled with fairy-tale books. And those miniature pewter dragons and wizards. And tiny crystal ships, ballerina dolls…" She smiled up at him. "And you? Any dreams?"

"Didn't really have dreams as a kid, but I have one now." He hesitated a moment, then continued, "I want to own a bike-and-book shop. A place where you can repair your cycle and your soul." He hadn't told anyone about this dream. Maybe Liney would think he was crazy for claiming such a place could repair souls, too.

But she didn't. Instead, she touched his arm and said reverently, "Whoever called you a beast should have their head examined."

"It was my former fiancée, Char…and believe me, the best shrinks in Beverly Hills have examined her head." He shrugged and took another sip from his soda.

"You're not a beast."

The determination on Liney's face moved him. "Since we're having this heart-to-heart, I'll admit that yes, I believed her. I told myself I shouldn't, but telling and feeling are two different things."

A sudden understanding lighted Liney's face. "That's why being the Rugged Man has been…"

"Difficult."

"I'm so sorry." She blinked rapidly. "And I'm sorry I made you feel like a sex object."

"I suppose most men would think they'd died and gone to heaven to be paid to feel that way…but for me, after Char's put-down, it hit home." He gave his head a shake. "I tried so damn hard to be a better man for her. I still want to be a better man. A civilized gentleman who understands the finer things in life—''

Liney gasped, cutting him off. "I have a great idea!"

"Should I be frightened?"

"I'm serious." She perched on one elbow. "Let's change the direction of this shoot. Something along the lines of 'From Rugged to Refined…'"

"'…a Newfound Gentleman Cooks'?" Raven finished.

Liney's eyes grew wider. "Excellent! And you know what else I'm thinking?"

"No, but I bet I'm going to find out—"

"If you'd like, after each day's shoot, we can take some time and talk about the 'finer' things in life. I'm not Ms. Manners by a long shot, but I love art and history and I've wooed many a business client over an expensive meal so I can talk about food and wine."

"Talking. I like that. Much better than Char hiring tutors."

"We'll start this evening," Liney said exuberantly, "after the shoot finishes. Pick me up at my tent when you're ready."

"Rugged and ready?"

Her eyes twinkled. "Or refined and ready."

He liked how her lips, pink and full, spread into a wide smile. He liked the lilt of her soft laugh and how it made his stomach do that funny clenching thing again. For the first time since he'd landed in Liney Reed's world, Raven was sorry he had only three and a half more days here.

"I want to ask the crew how they like this new idea before the afternoon shoot begins," Liney said, turning back to business. "It'll be my first step toward undoing the Dragon Lady image."

"Okay, let's go—"

She touched his arm. "But first, I have to know something."

"Even if Char begged, I'd never go back to her."

Liney looked at him as though he'd lost a few cylinders. "Good. I'm glad. But what I wanted to know is, why do you call your bike Macavity?"

He felt like a bigger idiot than the time he called crème brûlé "cream bowl." "Oh. 'Macavity,'" Raven quoted, "'he breaks the law of gravity.' It's from T.S. Eliot's *Old Possum's Book of Practical Cats.* I read it while entertaining myself in Charlotte's family's library...Macavity seemed a perfect name for my asphalt-eating, gravity-defying Harley."

And perfect for himself, he thought as they walked back to camp, because Raven felt as though his feet didn't touch the ground.

"KNOCK KNOCK," Liney said, standing outside Zoom's deep-teal tent. From the outside, it looked like a minipalace with mesh windows and an outside sitting area complete with chairs and tables. Zoom and Timothy shared the tent. It was agreed upon, beforehand, that the model would stay there as well.

"Knock knock," she said again, a little louder this time.

"Who's there?" called out Zoom.

"Orange."

There was a pause. "Orange who?"

"Orange you glad I'm not going to the shoot this afternoon?" It was wicked of her to tease like this, but she couldn't stop herself.

Zoom stuck his head through the front door of the tent. "Was that supposed to be funny?"

She shrugged. "A girl can always hope." So much for another crash-and-burn attempt at humor.

When Zoom continued to stare at her with an uptight air, she wondered if others saw her like that. All business, no pleasure. Maybe Gomer was right. Maybe Liney and Zoom had more in common than either of them wanted to admit. She cleared her throat. "May I come in? I wanted to discuss something with you."

After an awkward pause, Zoom shrugged dismissively and stepped back into the tent. Taking the shrug to be an invitation, she followed him inside.

The interior was a chaos of color, food, pictures. She'd never imagined Zoom with such a rich inner life, which made her a little envious. Her Brentwood condo looked like an ascetic's cell compared to Zoom's tent. Liney made a mental note to stay home more, decorate a little, discover the pleasurable things she wanted to surround herself with.

Although there was an impressive array of snacks on one table—crackers, cheeses, and fruit—Zoom offered her nothing. Instead, he retrieved a camera, pressed some switches, then brought it to her. "This is one of the morning shots," Zoom said matter-of-factly. "Thought you'd want to see how morose and miffed our Rugged Man looks."

She looked where Zoom indicated, at a small image displayed on top of the digital camera. Although the picture was only a few inches square, one could clearly see the sour look on Raven's face. But everything else, especially his body, looked great.

She looked up. Recalling Raven's advice to treat people with respect, she said, "I agree with you. He looks morose and tiffed."

"Miffed."

"Right. Miffed." Infusing her voice with enthusiasm, she continued, "But I've had an idea that will turn this shoot around." She purposefully stopped before launching into her usual this-is-how-it-is routine. Remembering Raven's words—*Don't treat people as though they're your puppets*—she said, "But before we put it into action, I'd like your opinion."

For a moment, Zoom appeared to pale. She wondered if the shock of her comment had siphoned blood from his face. "You'd like *my* opinion?"

"Yes, *your* opinion." She took a moment to let it sink in. "Zoom, I'm sorry I've been difficult at times. I know I have a tendency to…micromanage. That's one reason I'm not attending the shoot this afternoon. I want you to be in charge. Afterward, we can talk and discuss any issues you think need addressing."

His mouth literally dropped open.

She waited to see if it closed or if he wanted to say something, but when he did neither, she added, "The only thing I can say in my defense is that I wanted so much for this project to be successful, I lost sight of how I was treating the people involved." That pretty much summed it up. She offered a small, conciliatory smile.

"Zoom, baby!" Cookie strolled in and stopped abruptly upon seeing Liney. "Oh," she said, jutting out one hip. "Didn't know you had company."

"It's not company—it's Liney," Zoom answered, his mouth working again.

Liney turned to Cookie. "Just as I did with Zoom, I'd like to apologize to you, too, for my overzealousness in my vice-presidential duties."

"For micromanaging," Zoom interpreted.

"Micro—?" Staring blankly at a far wall, Cookie

bobbed her head to one side as though mentally searching for the word in her memory banks.

Liney spoke up. "I'm apologizing for being controlling. Opinionated. Telling bad jokes."

"Oh, right!" Cookie straightened so quickly, her ponytail quivered for several moments.

"So before this afternoon's shoot commences," Liney continued, "I'd like to suggest a direction change. Instead of 'A Rugged Man Cooks,' what about 'From Rugged to Refined—a Newfound Gentleman Cooks'?" Liney paced a few steps, but carefully pivoted so she didn't spin into another three-sixty. "This way, we can still use the scowling shots from this morning because he'll look happier as he grows more gentlemanly. And we'll appeal to all kinds of women as our Rugged-to-Refined Gentleman wears an assortment of clothes, from the Navajo blanket to a button-down Oxford shirt. Raven's already talking to Gomer about doing another shopping trip to Cheyenne because we're fairly certain King Karl won't have Oxford shirts."

Zoom frowned. Cookie looked perplexed. Finally, Zoom said, "Maybe some of the last shots can be in my tent…it definitely has a sophisticated ambiance."

Liney grinned. "Excellent idea!"

"I've done makeup for civilized types before," Cookie chimed in. "I did all the makeup for that Queen Elizabeth look-alike contest last year."

"Great," Liney said, hoping Raven didn't end up wearing a tiara. But she knew better than to cite her concerns right now. At the moment, they were acting like a team again. This unmicromanaging felt good. Before, if she'd been in Zoom's tent brainstorming ideas with him and Cookie, Liney would have snapped at least three cigarettes by now.

"I need to check my supplies before we start the afternoon shoot," Cookie said, heading toward the tent door.

"May I walk with you part way?" Liney asked.

Although Cookie looked surprised, at least the blood didn't drain from her face. "Uh, sure."

"Have fun this afternoon—I'm sure you'll do great," Liney said to Zoom as she exited with Cookie.

The sun burned brightly overhead as they walked together toward Cookie's tent. Other than the whistling trill from a chickadee that swooped from the branches of a nearby spruce, they walked in silence. Liney noticed that Cookie seemed demure, almost shy. It hit Liney that she had been so caught up in how *they* had treated her, she'd never fully realized that *she,* in turn, might intimidate Cookie.

But that was all going to change. Today was as good as any to be a new Liney. She sidestepped a clump of grass. "May I ask a favor?"

Cookie looked over. "Uh, sure, what?"

"I brought all the wrong clothes for this trip. I'm overdressed, uncomfortable, miserably hot. You, on the other hand, brought exactly the right outfits for this weather. Would you be so kind as to loan me some of your clothes? I'd gladly pay you. Or, if my request is too invasive, you can tell me 'no' and I'd understand."

Cookie stopped in her tracks. Turning her wide blue eyes on Liney, she dipped her head to the side as though seeing her for the first time. "You'd feel comfortable dressing like me?"

Liney nodded.

With a grin, Cookie slipped her arm through Liney's. As they continued walking, Cookie said, "You know, girlfriend, I have the cutest halter top that would look utterly fab on you...."

10

RAVEN WALKED TOWARD Liney's tent, a nagging sadness weighing him down like a steel weight in his gut. Tonight, Thursday night, was the last night he and Liney would share their post-shoot walking lesson. The last night he'd look into her chocolate-brown eyes, hear her soft laughter.

And the last time he'd see her in those killer shortshorts.

There should be a law against women with long, lean legs wearing denim short-shorts. That "sizzlingly sexy" image was permanently burned into his brain, standing in the way of every damn thought that flitted through his gray matter like a jackknifed diesel blocking a four-lane highway. If he were still counting, he'd be hitting a thousand by now.

But he'd stopped that number habit two days ago on the front seat of Gomer's pickup truck. While Raven had sopped soda off a heatstroked, flushed Liney—trying to remember if he was up to hundred and ten or eleven—he'd decided to hell with the number game. Time to revel in the moment.

But those moments were rapidly coming to an end. And although he repeatedly told himself it didn't matter, that life moved on, that soon he'd be busy with his bike-and-book shop, *it did matter*. Like in the movie version of *My Fair Lady* where Rex Harrison sang about the impish Audrey Hepburn, Raven had grown accustomed to Liney's face. And grown accustomed to her intelligence, her intensity, her growing sense of self...

And accustomed to those sexy short-shorts.

Who woulda thought that Liney Reed, Vice President of Mucky Muck, had more sex appeal than Cindy Crawford, Julia Roberts, and Hillary Clinton rolled into one. Okay, some guys might dispute the Hillary part, but Raven thought she was one cool lady. Put her on-stage to give a speech, and that lady *rocked.* Intelligence, looks, and spunk. He'd take that combo any day over some Baywatch Babe.

He reached Liney's small gray tent, nestled at the bottom of the hill. Because the tent barely had room for a cot, she'd spruced up the outside with a folding chair and a stump for a table. And even though she hadn't attended the last few photo shoots—part of her "unmicromanaging"—she said hangin' in the tent all day hadn't been lonely. She'd borrowed some Western novels from Gomer and occasionally entertained a visiting squirrel whom she'd nicknamed Bartholomew.

Because, she told Raven, the little animal deserved a lofty, regal nickname.

He wondered if she knew that nobody called her "Dragon Lady" anymore.

"You're here!" Liney stepped outside the front door of the tent, rubbing her hands. "Zoom just showed me the day's shots—great stuff!"

She leaned over to slather sunscreen on her legs and arms, a ritual she did every early evening before their walks. Fortunately, Liney wore sensible, skin-covering tennis shoes, which Cookie had also loaned her. As Liney's auburn hair—clean from bathing in a nearby stream—fell in loose, soft waves, she methodically spread the lotion in slow circles on her thighs.

Shifting his weight, Raven fought the urge to stare at every supple inch of her creamy, short-shorted, halter-topped body, but he wanted to be a gentleman. Although he'd have to be a blind gentleman to not notice how Liney's breasts, hard-pressed to stay put in Cookie's plunging halter top, mounded together like two scoops of vanilla ice cream.

And Raven was a sucker for anything vanilla.

Damn, he was going to miss her. But he couldn't go down that road. He needed to talk about something, anything else. "Zoom did some shots in his tent with me preparing canapés and chilling wine," Raven said nonchalantly, trying not to stare at how Liney smeared sunscreen across the top of her vanilla scoops. "Zoom, uh, doesn't mess around when he's on the road. He could be a traveling Club Med with all the wine and food he has stashed in there."

Looking up, Liney's rosebud lips spread into a soft smile. "He's a natural leader. I'm going to recommend he be promoted to Creative Director when we get back home."

Back home. "Let's start our walk," Raven said solemnly.

Last night they'd decided today's walk would be through camp and into the foothills. As they walked along a rocky path, Liney chattered about the Western novels she'd borrowed from Gomer. "Almost finished another Matt Braun. After reading a ton of self-help books, reading fiction is a treat—reminds me of the reading I did as a kid." She stepped over a small boulder. "I thought tonight we'd talk about books we've enjoyed. You said you read a lot at Charlotte's...."

"Yeah, spent more time in that library than I did in our bedroom."

Liney cast him a glance over her shoulder, but didn't say anything.

"Can't say I regretted it, though. Those books were my pals at a very lonely time in my life."

"How could she leave you alone like that?" she murmured. Raising her voice, she said, "Tell me about one of those stories...."

"One that sticks with me is a short story by Hawthorne about a man—a physician, I think—who despised a birthmark on his wife's face. It disgusted him, so she begged him to remove it because she knew that until he did, her life would turn lonelier and lonelier. When he removed it, he ended up killing her. Accidentally, of course."

"Sounds cheery," she said drolly. "Why does that particular story stick with you?"

"Because with Char, I felt like one big birthmark."

LINEY AND RAVEN had been walking, talking about books for thirty minutes. In the gathering dusk, they grew silent for a moment as they hiked up a steeper part of the trail. Breathing in deeply, Raven smelled the tang of sage intermingled with the scents of grass and earth. Above the rolling Laramie Mountain foothills, pink and orange clouds streaked the blue Wyoming sky.

"They say smog makes for magnificent L.A. sunsets, but I'd take a Wyoming sunset over L.A. anytime," Liney said, walking ahead of Raven. "I understand why Dirk stays here now. Silly of me to think I could convince him to return to L.A."

Raven's heart lurched. "Are you thinking of staying?'' Not that he knew where he'd end up...but if she remained in Wyoming...

She laughed under her breath. ''Oh, no. My home and work are in L.A.'' Halting in her tracks, she gasped.

He stopped. ''You okay?''

''A-ahead,'' she whispered hoarsely.

She remained frozen, except for her trembling hands that hung at her sides. Although she stood a good five feet ahead of him on the path, he could see over her head if he shifted slightly. Easing his head to the right, he spied over her shoulder to see what was so frightening.

What he saw made the hair on the back of his neck stand up.

Thirty or so feet ahead, in the center of the path, crouched a mountain lion emitting a blood-chilling growl, its savage eyes focused on Liney.

''Don't run,'' Raven said quietly.

The golden, muscular creature inched a broad paw forward. Its pointed ears flattened against its head.

Raven could hear Liney's labored breathing.

''Listen carefully,'' he said under his breath. ''No sudden moves. Don't turn around. Step back slowly, very slowly.''

Liney, staring down the animal, slid one foot slowly behind her. Her heel hit a rock.

The lion snarled. Its muscular haunches rippled as it took a step forward.

Liney froze.

''Don't stop,'' whispered Raven. He thought about grabbing her and shoving her behind him. He might be quick enough to put himself between her and the animal...and he might not. If he wasn't, and the animal attacked, could he save Liney? Raven couldn't take that chance.

"Keep moving back," Raven whispered. A drop of sweat coursed down the side of his face. The world turned surreal, as though his senses were cranked up too high. Colors hurt. Scents overwhelmed.

Liney, visibly shaking, slid one foot back, then the other. The animal cocked its head, shifting its gaze to Raven. The air seemed to vibrate with the lion's low, curdling growl.

"Keep going," Raven instructed, staring down the beast.

Liney edged ck another foot. She was only three feet away now. At this distance, Raven could thrust himself between her and the animal...

The lion crouched forward another step, as though acting out some kind of macabre dance with Liney.

"On the count of three," Raven said, keeping his voice steady, "raise your hands and scream."

"You're kidding," Liney said between clenched teeth.

"One. Two."

"It's moving—"

"Three!" With a blood-curdling yell, Raven took a giant leap, landing in front of Liney. At the same time, he swept his arms over his head—making himself appear over eight feet tall. Behind him, he heard Liney let out that ear-piercing train-screeching shriek.

The animal growled and backed up a few feet. Then, bunching its powerful muscles, it sprang through the air.

HUDDLED IN THE Navajo blanket, Liney sat in front of a roaring fire, shivering. Next to her was Cookie, her arms wrapped around Liney.

"You're so brave," Cookie said for the hundredth time.

"I don't know about that. I'm here thanks to Raven's quick thinking."

"He was a hero up there," Zoom said solemnly, standing on the other side of the fire. His tanned face was drawn, serious. "He knew what to do with that mountain lion." Timothy, standing beside him, nodded gravely.

Liney stared into the crackling flames, seeing in them the animal's broad, planed face and sparking eyes. It had stared at her, fearless, before setting its sights on Raven. "He's a hero, all right," she murmured, drawing the blanket tighter around her. "One of a kind."

"This should warm you up, honey." Gomer emerged from the darkness, lifting a bottle of amber liquid.

"I'll get a cup for her," said a deep familiar voice behind Gomer. Raven, big and dark like a piece of the night, emerged into the firelight.

Liney didn't think she'd ever seen anything as magnificent as Raven at this very moment. Although he was dressed in his usual jeans and a T-shirt, he exuded a magical larger-than-life aura. Like a mythical god who walked among the mortals, he towered over everyone. But the sincerity in his face—and his heart—made him human. Checking out his T-shirt, she smiled. So what if it was pink. How many men could wear that color and look more drop-dead masculine than ever?

As Raven retrieved a cup and poured some of the whiskey into it, Cookie said earnestly to Liney, "And to think, after what you went through, your hair still looks great.''

Liney smile tentatively. ''Guess I'm finally having a good hair day.''

Everyone laughed. A happy, communal laugh. Wryly, Liney thought if near tragedies brought out her sense of humor, she should have been funny from day one of this trip.

Raven crossed to her and handed over the cup. ''I should have remembered to bring a cigarette...you're probably needing to snap something.''

She reached out and touched his hand. ''I'll take human contact instead.''

The air around them seemed charged, electrified, as though signaling an impending storm.

''Take a sip or two,'' he said, giving her a look that made her heart reel. ''It'll ease that chill.''

What chill? As long as Raven stood nearby, her motor was in high gear. But because he stood there, watching her expectantly, she dutifully took a sip. The whiskey burned delightfully as it slid down her throat. ''Thanks,'' she said, meeting Raven's dark eyes.

He looked at her for a long moment. ''You're quite a woman, Liney.''

''I know.'' She liked how his eyes twinkled when he smiled. ''And you're quite a man.''

''Thanks to you.''

Remembering Gomer's words, and now hearing the same from Raven, Liney had to blink back the sudden emotion that swept through her. Her heart swelled with a feeling she had thought long dead. Did she...love Raven? Too stunned to follow that line of thinking, she shifted her gaze to the rest of the group.

They stared back at her with such caring looks, she

wondered if she should just stare up at the sky instead. But instead, she met each person's gaze, silently acknowledging their goodwill.

They'd become more than a team. After what they'd shared this week, they were like an extended family...a group of people who knew the very worst and the very best about each other—and, after a few gut-wrenching trials and errors, each chose to embrace the best.

"Thank you, everyone," Liney said, knowing intuitively that they'd understand.

Each person nodded or smiled.

Gomer took a step closer to the campfire. "I'd like to propose a toast," he said, raising his bottle. "To Cookie," he nodded his white head of hair toward her. "Who's flourished, as a makeup artist and person, on this trip." Gomer turned his attention to Zoom. "And to Zoom, our photographer, a man of action and vision who artistically directed the last few days of the shoot." As everyone applauded, Gomer smiled at Timothy, waiting until the clapping died down. "And to you, son, who learned about life on this trip. Use your lessons well."

Gomer took a step toward Raven. Placing his hand on Raven's shoulder, Gomer said solemnly, "To the man who saved the shoot and saved our Liney. A toast to Raven, who opened his heart to us." Gomer took a swig from the bottle.

Turning to Liney, Gomer gazed at her for a long moment. "You'all forgive me if I say that I saved the best for last, although I think we're all in agreement on that one." He hoisted his bottle. "To Liney, a special lady who accepts others' strengths and ideas. Thanks to her, we've all grown into better people."

Cookie started sniffling loudly. "Don't forget to add that she dresses better now, too."

After the laughter died down, Gomer smiled, his gaze slowly traveling around the group. "And the last toast is to us. *E Pluribus Unum.* We all worked together as one, my friends."

AN HOUR LATER, Liney and Raven stood outside her tent. With the blanket wrapped around her, she turned and looked at the dark hulk of Raven. Although his face was a shadowed oval, the moonlight glazed his black mass of hair with threads of silver.

"Thanks, again, for saving my life," she said.

"Anytime."

She giggled. "A funny thought just hit me."

"And that is—?"

"What if that mountain lion's name is Macavity, too?"

He blew out a gust of breath. "It's true he defied gravity—that was some powerful leap into the underbrush."

"Maybe he didn't like our singing."

Raven chuckled, a throaty, mirthful sound that warmed Liney's soul. "Singing. That's one civilized lesson we can skip."

Liney's insides caved in a little. "Our lessons are over," she said softly. "I'll—I'll miss you, Raven."

"I'll miss you, too."

She leaned forward to hug him, or meant to hug him, but it was as though they suddenly fell together like two magnets. The next thing she knew, she tossed off the Navajo blanket and wrapped her arms around his massive body, holding on with a ferocity she never knew she had. His body felt powerful, warm, hard against hers. She felt overwhelmed, out of control...all the things the old Liney fought against.

But the new Liney embraced. Hungrily.

He made a sound like a subterranean growl. It reminded her of when, a few days ago, he'd stood before her like a typhoon, a storm ready to erupt. Then she'd been afraid.

Not now.

She pressed harder against him, nuzzling her face into the crook of his neck. Impetuously, she nibbled the lobe of his ear, then drew it between her lips and suckled.

His growl intensified, like a tortured animal needing release. He pulled back, stared at her in silence for an intense moment, then claimed her with an open-mouthed kiss that consumed her. She hungrily met his kiss, plunging into the hot, wet storm.

Like a trigger to an explosive, passions detonated. Raven tunneled his fingers into her hair as his mouth branded its need against her lips. She felt greedy, starved for more. She wanted to devour and drink every inch of him. Cradling his head with her hands, she held his face to hers and moaned and kissed and licked with a bottled fervor finally released after too many years.

Throwing her head back so she could gasp a breath of air, she groaned out loud. She felt hot and needy. Euphoric and giddy. "I feel like I'm floating on air," she whispered, staring up at the stars that splattered across the vast, inky sky. She breathed, filling her lungs with the night's warm, fragrant breezes as Raven's hot mouth planted kisses on her chin and throat....

She kicked her feet a little. She *was* floating. He'd lifted her so high, her feet dangled midair.

A minor inconvenience.

Maybe she'd failed her kick-boxing class, but the

exercises had definitely strengthened her thighs. With a heave of her hips, Liney wrapped her legs around his middle. She flattened herself again him, fastening her legs and arms around him tighter than pins in a French twist. But it wasn't close enough. Instinctively, she thrust her pelvis against his and held it there, rubbing, pushing, wanting...

He threw back his head and let loose a primal roar.

Not needing much more encouragement, Liney reached down and tugged loose his T-shirt from the waistband of his jeans. A corner free, she pulled it up his magnificent torso, barely resisting the urge to bite and lick his exposed flesh. In the middle of her yanking and tugging, she heard Raven's deep voice talking.

"What are you doing?"

She stopped for a millisecond before returning to her all-consuming tearing, ripping, and wrenching. Between pants, she said, "Taking...off your...T-shirt." She muttered under her breath. "One damn piece is stuck—"

"Why?"

"Don't know. Probably caught on something." With a snarl, she tugged again.

"No, why are you removing my shirt?"

"Because...it's...on your...body." With an elongated rip, the shirt suddenly shot loose. The top half of Liney's body reared back, a swatch of shirt in her hand, while her thighs retained their death grip around Raven's waist.

He caught her as she fell backward, then gently pulled her toward him again. Her arms draped around his neck, he pressed his forehead against hers. "What do you want, Liney?" he asked, his voice quietly serious.

"Your shirt off."

"Why?"

"So we can have...sex?"

"Is that all I am?" he asked gently. "Sex?"

"No!" Pressing her face against the coarseness of his cheek, she whispered into his ear, "It's *you* I want. The closeness, the connection with you." She kissed his cheek, inhaling his musky scent. "I want to be with you, Raven, the man I've always dreamed about, fantasized about. The man I tucked back into a corner of my mind, along with all my other dreams, because...because I thought I'd never find you...."

He gently set her down on the ground. They stood, holding each other—the circle of their arms like a haven, a cocoon of warmth and safety.

"I never thought I'd find you, either," he murmured. "But I don't want sex."

It was like an elevator plunged twenty floors down the center of Liney's stomach. "You don't?" she croaked.

"No, I want to make love with you," he whispered huskily.

She wasn't sure if she'd heard correctly because he turned away from her, picked up the crumpled Navajo blanket, and shook it. He then arranged the blanket on the ground with great care, as though he were spreading out the finest silk.

Without a word, he took her hand and led her to the edge of the blanket. For a long moment, they stood close, simply holding hands. A cool night breeze skittered past, tracing the air with sage and jasmine. Layered within the swirl of the mixed fragrances was another smell. Musky. Masculine.

Raven.

She breathed in deeply, filling her lungs with his arousing, potent scent. "Raven," she murmured, the utterance sounding more like a moan than a name. Strong arms pulled her close and effortlessly lifted her. "Liney," he responded, his breath hot against her cheek.

He cradled her against his chest as though she were something fragile, precious. She'd never been held like this. Treated like this. Made to feel as though every cell of her being was something to be cherished. She dropped her head against the expanse of his warm, furry chest, listened to the thudding of his heartbeat, and was excruciatingly aware that this moment, this precious moment, was perhaps the very best moment of her life.

"Open your eyes," Raven said, his gravelly voice thick with arousal. He wanted to look into her eyes, see what she was feeling, know that she wanted this as much as he did.

Slowly, she opened her lids. In the sunlight her eyes were chocolate brown. In the moonlight, the brown deepened into pools of sable. Despite the night shadows, he swore he caught a simmering glow from deep within her gaze, as though her soul pulsed its desire to him. He sank to his knees, never breaking eye contact with her. "I want to undress you."

As he lay her down on the blanket, a small noise escaped her, like a mew.

He hesitated, wondering what that meant. No? But when she raised her tennis-shoe'd foot and wiggled it, inviting him to start there, he knew that mew meant "yes."

He carefully removed her shoes, one at a time. Crouched in front of her, he pressed the bottoms of both feet against his torso. As she rubbed her soles against his hairy chest, he caressed the length of her legs, relishing her small gasps of pleasure as he traced light patterns on her bare skin. Seemingly lost in the sensations, she stretched her arms seductively over her head and giggled sexily.

To be desired—to know a woman gleefully, exuberantly wanted him—filled him with a pleasure that bordered on painful. A hurt, he realized, from feeling rejected. But with Liney, that anguish turned inside out, becoming acceptance. Was there anything sexier, sweeter than being wholly accepted by the woman of your dreams?

"I want you," he whispered gruffly, the words like an ache in his throat. "I think I've wanted you from the first time we met."

"But you told me you didn't want sex when we met."

Her playful tease caught him by surprise. Then he chuckled, recalling their fateful meeting in the Blue Moon parking lot. "I thought you were—"

"A call girl." She laughed softly. "If you only knew..."

He waited, but she didn't finish. "Knew what?"

She plucked at the blanket, as though hesitating whether to continue. After a small sigh, she said, "It's a little embarrassing, but you've seen me thrashing and kicking in the middle of the wilderness, so what's one little confession?" She took his hand and meshed her fingers with his. "For a would-be call girl, I've only had three lovers. But I wouldn't call any of them...well...fulfilling."

"No crashing waves?"

"Barely a ripple."

He squeezed her hand. ''Then hold on, baby, 'cause we're gonna cause a tidal wave.''

He meant his response to be light, to maybe coax another giggle from her, but he only heard her breaths, coming in ragged pants. Hell, he didn't know if he could deliver the tidal wave, but he had never wanted more to please a woman. Pulling her legs down, he lay beside her and kissed the pulsing crevice above her collar bone. Her vanilla scent enveloped him as he trailed kisses up her neck to her cheek, then positioned his mouth over hers. After a few shared kisses, she surprised him by pressing her open lips to him, inviting him...

His tongue eased between her lips and explored the velvety warmth of her mouth. He wanted to take it slowly...to keep a rein on his hot need...but when she pressed the full length of her body against his and whimpered his name, fire tore through him.

Burying his hands in her hair, he plundered her mouth. She tasted hot and sweet and wet. He felt like a drunkard, intoxicated from drinking her scents, consuming her textures.

''Take me,'' she whispered hungrily. Draping one leg over his thigh, she pulled him closer.

That bit of encouragement pushed him over the edge. With a growl of need, he rolled onto his back, raising her to a sitting position on top of him. Reaching behind her neck, he untied her halter top and slowly peeled it down, unveiling her. The sight of her exposed breasts, gilded with moonglow, cranked up the flames.

''Oh, baby,'' he whispered, ''you're beautiful.'' He took a moment to simply look at her, revel in her womanly contours, before easing his hands behind her and unsnapping the back strap. He tossed the halter top to the side, then inched his hands up her small waist and cupped her breasts. They filled his hands, their peaks pressed in the curve of his palms. After circling the dark rings with his fingers, he gently massaged the hardening tips. She dropped back her head and gasped.

Still fondling one breast, he trailed his other hand down her midriff to the top of her shorts. Dipping a finger inside the waistband, he playfully fingered the warm crevice between fabric and skin.

"Let me take these off," she whispered urgently, scrambling to her feet.

"No," Raven said, standing with her. "Let me."

He felt her body trembling as he unsnapped the button on the shorts. Kissing and nuzzling her neck, he eased down the zipper. Then he sank to his knees in front of her and slowly pulled down her shorts.

Within moments, Liney stood naked in front of Raven. She'd never felt so exposed before. And not just physically...she felt exposed right down to her soul, as though the man saw all the way through her— through her skin, her games, her barriers. Yet, at the same time, she felt safer than she ever had before in her life. And she felt something else. A bonding with this man who knelt before her, different from what she'd ever experienced with a lover. It was as though this intimacy was a place she'd spent her life journeying toward.

She stepped out of her shorts, which Raven lay aside. As she tunneled her fingers through his hair, he remained on his knees, his gaze caressing her entire body.

"God, I want you, Liney." And then he embraced her, gathered her close, his face pressed against her middle. His breaths were hot and labored against her skin. "So beautiful," he murmured, kissing her waist, her stomach. The trail of his kisses burned against her skin, causing small fires to ignite and flame over her body.

His lips moved down and he kissed her in the apex between her legs. A smooth glide. A velvet stroke. His tongue, liquid and penetrating, propelled her to higher levels of ecstasy until her body quivered, on the edge, ready to explode. Barely suppressing a cry, she dug her fingers into his shoulders and arched her back. "Now, please."

He stood, one arm supporting her back. With his other hand, he undid his pants and stepped swiftly out of them. She caught the shards of moonlight rippling over his molded form. The shadowed indentations of muscle. And, as he turned to her, the darkened triangle of his manhood.

He was man and animal. Large, powerful, almost frightening in his bulk of muscle and strength. He was a beast—but also a magnificent human being. "You're perfect," she whispered, her words drowned by a rush of wind.

His broad, hot hands grasped her waist and lifted her. "Put your legs around me," he ordered in a guttural need that sent shivers of thrill zigzagging down her spine. She wrapped her legs around him. She felt crazy, out of control, needing this man as she'd never needed someone before. Flesh to flesh, heat to heat, she pushed her mound against his stomach while groaning his name.

"Raven. Please. Now."

He inhaled, the intake of breath fierce in its need. Even in the dark, she caught slits of lights between his hooded lids as he positioned her, then pressed his hips forward.

Hot tides swelled within her as he pushed into her slowly. She shifted her weight, opening herself to him fully.

"Yes, baby, yes" he murmured huskily. He rocked gently. She thrust back. Their passion consumed them as they enacted an erotic dance, the give-and-take motion building in intensity. They searched each other's eyes, seeing their mirrored need, losing themselves in their own private world.

It was as though some long dormant sexuality rose to engulf her, devour her. With a startled cry, she fell against him as her body convulsed with wave after wave of pleasure.

Raven thrust deep and roared.

Coo-coo-coo. Coo-coo-coo.

Raven lazily opened his eyes and watched a small brown dove perch on an overhanging branch. The bird again chirped its morning message before winging its way to another destination.

If his lips could form a shape, that's the sound he'd make, too, this fine morning. Coo-coo-oooooo... Memories of Liney, stretched naked in the moonlight, filtered through his mind. Her sweet face over his, those big brown eyes looking longingly into his. Their whispered words of desire as their bodies intertwined. He'd never felt so complete, so fulfilled.

His Hearty Man tape had talked about there being no such thing as coincidence.... Raven hadn't quite understood how that could be possible, but now he believed it with every cell of his being. Because finding Liney was no coincidence. She was meant to be.

"I love you, Liney."

Silence.

He should have said it earlier. Said it while they were making love. But it wasn't too late. He'd nudge her awake and, as his tape also counseled, he'd speak from his heart. He turned over.

No Liney.

Raven sat up, alone on the Navajo blanket. On the soft dirt, the blanket had felt like a feather bed. Their cover had been the warm summer breezes and each other's bodies.

He glanced toward the tent. She had to be inside, dressing. He grinned. Well, he'd put an end to that! Jumping up, he took two giant strides to the tent door and peeked inside. "Liney?"

Empty.

Not even a suitcase.

She was gone? Impossible. Her flight wasn't until this afternoon...unless she left earlier.

Stepping back outside, he glanced at the chair, the blanket, the stump. On top of the latter, something white fluttered underneath a rock. Crossing to it, he picked up the piece of paper and read the handwritten words.

Dear Raven,

I woke up early this morning and realized I've been no better than Char because I also tried to change you. I had no right. You're perfect as you are. Who was I to give you "civilized" lessons? When that mountain lion was ready to attack, you saved our lives because of your common sense and intelligence—if you'd used civilized means, we probably both would have died.

This trip has taught me to let go of who I think
I should be and trust a gentler Liney.

Last night means more to me than you'll ever
know.

                                                                    L.

Raven reread the letter several times. Didn't she get
it? He'd asked her to help him change because *he*
wanted to change—unlike Char, who demanded he
change because that's what *she* wanted. With Char,
he'd put his tail between his legs and left. No way in
hell was he doing that with Liney—he refused to let
her leave him without discussing this further, face-to-
face.

In his gut, he knew she was headed back to L.A.,
probably trying to catch an earlier flight out of Cheyenne. Made sense. She knew the last morning shoot
would run smoothly without her because she now
trusted Zoom and the rest of the crew.

Of course, Zoom might not be happy that the model
was splitting as well, but tough. If leaving to find Liney
cost Raven his paycheck, his dream of buying a book-
and-bike shop, then the dream would just have to be
put on hold.

Because right now, nothing else mattered but Liney.

He dressed quickly, debating whether to toss the
ripped T-shirt or go barechested. But when he thought
of that two-hour ride to Cheyenne, a ripped T was better than none at all. He threw it on.

On the way to his bike, he stopped by Zoom's tent.

"I'm leaving," Raven said, ready to explain further,
but Zoom cut him off.

"Gomer gave her a lift into Cheyenne several hours
ago," he said knowingly.

Raven dragged his hand through his hair. "I gotta

split, man. She's…'' But he couldn't finish. It was as though a knife ripped at his insides, severing his heart.

"Don't worry about the shoot—we have all the pictures we need." Spontaneously, Zoom hugged Raven in a man-to-man embrace. "Go to her."

TWO HOURS LATER, Raven strode into the Cheyenne airport. Fortunately, the building was small—it should be easy to find Liney…if she hadn't already left.

He passed through security and roamed through groups of people, scanning the area for her. He hadn't seen Gomer's red pickup outside, so she had to be alone.

He'd almost given up hope when he spotted a wrinkled dress moving through the crowd. He looked down. And a pair of scuffed Gucci shoes. Only one person in the world broke in designer clothes with more gusto than a cowgirl breaking in a bronco.

"Liney!" he yelled, his booming voice causing others to turn and look at him.

She turned, those big brown eyes widening. Those rosebud lips opened as though she wanted to speak, but she didn't say anything.

Speechless. A first for Liney Reed.

With two giant steps he reached her. Putting his hands on her slim shoulders, he stared into those blinking eyes. "Stay." At the moment, he couldn't form any other words around that single need. He wanted her. His life would be incomplete without her.

"My flight…" She pointed over her shoulder toward some doorway. "It's boarding. Now."

Raven shook his head. "Can the ticket. Drive back

to L.A. with me." He was vaguely aware that a small crowd was forming around them.

Her eyebrows shot up. "On your motorcycle?"

"You've done it before. And I still have Belle's jeans in the pouch. You can wear one of my T's." He smiled, remembering last night. "A nonripped one."

A rose hue crept over her cheeks. "I can't go with you," she whispered, casting a sidelong glance at the people who were obviously listening in. "You'd end up living in L.A. with another woman who tried to change you. What if you feel like a birthmark again? I'd be no better than Char."

"You're twenty, a hundred times the woman Char is!" He shook his head. "Comparisons don't matter, anyway, because there's no one else for me. Ever. You're it, baby."

She dipped her head and smiled.

Sensing his advantage, he continued, "Char called me a beast. But when I stared down that mountain lion, my strength was in being a beast, too...and I've realized that part of me isn't such a bad thing. I can embrace it instead of hating it." He lowered his voice to a teasing level. "Besides, as you yourself wrote, I'm perfect as I am."

She straightened, her smile vanishing. "But you need to finish the shoot—"

"Zoom said he has enough pictures."

"Your book-and-bike shop—"

"Never said it had to be in Wyoming. I kinda like L.A. Grew up there. All my friends are there. Besides, I need a business partner."

Liney flashed him a questioning look.

"Someone to help with the book part of the business, which I think needs a fantasy section...."

Her eyes moistened. "My dream come true," she whispered.

"Which you are, also, for me." As someone in the crowd sniffled, Raven pulled Liney closer, cuddling her slim form against his. "I need you in my life. Marry me, Liney."

"Marry—?"

An old woman jabbed him in the ribs. "For God's sake, tell 'er you love 'er."

He pulled back and looked Liney in the eyes, which shimmered with emotion. His voice broke with huskiness. "I love you, Liney. With all my heart."

"And I...I love you, Raven."

"Will you marry me?"

The crowd stilled.

"Will you always call me 'baby'?"

His heart took a perilous leap. She hadn't answered his question. "If that's what you want—"

"Yes," she whispered gleefully. "And yes to marriage, too."

A smattering of applause and laughter broke out.

Grabbing her bag with one hand, Raven slipped it over his shoulder before scooping her up. She nestled into the crook of his arms as though she'd always belonged there.

"You're my Cinderella," he stated, walking through the throng of people to the front doors. "And I'm your Prince Charming, although a little rugged around the edges."

She grinned mischievously. "I like you a little rugged and ready."

He pulled her tighter against him. ''Then that's what you're getting, baby.''

Carrying the woman he loved, Raven strode into the bright sunshine and headed toward their waiting carriage, Macavity.

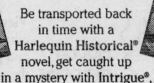

HEART OF THE WEST

Every Man Has His Price!

Lost Springs Ranch was famous for turning young mavericks into good men. So word that the ranch was in financial trouble sent a herd of loyal bachelors stampeding back to Wyoming to put themselves on the auction block!

July 1999	*Husband for Hire* Susan Wiggs	January 2000	*The Rancher and the Rich Girl* Heather MacAllister
August	*Courting Callie* Lynn Erickson	February	*Shane's Last Stand* Ruth Jean Dale
September	*Bachelor Father* Vicki Lewis Thompson	March	*A Baby by Chance* Cathy Gillen Thacker
October	*His Bodyguard* Muriel Jensen	April	*The Perfect Solution* Day Leclaire
November	*It Takes a Cowboy* Gina Wilkins	May	*Rent-a-Dad* Judy Christenberry
December	*Hitched by Christmas* Jule McBride	June	*Best Man in Wyoming* Margot Dalton

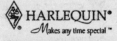

HARLEQUIN®
Makes any time special ™

Visit us at www.romance.net

PHHOWGEN

MONTANA MAVERICKS
Big Sky Brides

Legendary love comes to Whitehorn, Montana,
once more as beloved authors

Christine Rimmer, Jennifer Greene and Cheryl St.John

present three brand-new stories in this exciting anthology!

Meet the Brennan women:

SUZANNA, DIANA and ISABELLE

Strong-willed beauties who find unexpected
love in these irresistible marriage of
covnenience stories.

Don't miss
MONTANA MAVERICKS: BIG SKY BRIDES
On sale in February 2000,
only from Silhouette Books!

Available at your favorite retail outlet.

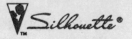

Silhouette®

Return to the charm of the Regency era with

GEORGETTE HEYER,

creator of the modern Regency genre.

Enjoy six romantic collector's editions with forewords
by some of today's bestselling romance authors,

**Nora Roberts, Mary Jo Putney,
Jo Beverley, Mary Balogh,
Theresa Medeiros and Kasey Michaels.**

Frederica
On sale February 2000
The Nonesuch
On sale March 2000
The Convenient Marriage
On sale April 2000
Cousin Kate
On sale May 2000
The Talisman Ring
On sale June 2000
The Corinthian
On sale July 2000

Available at your favorite retail outlet.

HARLEQUIN®
Makes any time special ™

Visit us at www.romance.net   PHGHGEN